Novels by William Michael Ried

Five Ferries (2018) "Full-hearted...Ried has created a believable and likable first-person narrator that speaks with a simple sincerity. An emotionally engaging travel novel that will prove difficult to put down." ~ ***Kirkus Reviews***

2019 American Fiction Award for Best New Fiction Finalist

Backstory (2021) "*Backstory* is a masterpiece, an intriguing read with a perfect blend of anger, resentment, love, hatred, excitement, and displeasure." ~ ***OnlineBookClub Review***

Winning Mystery in 2021 New York City Big Book Awards; Silver Medal Winner in Wishing Shelf Book Awards for Adult Fiction; Semifinalist in Kindle Book Award for Literary Fiction; 2022 Eric Hoffer Award Category Finalist

Pandion (2022) "*Pandion* is unreservedly recommended as a genre-bending mystery of puzzlement, betrayal and love. The result is an addictively compulsive page-turner from cover to cover." ~ ***Midwest Book Review***

2022 New York City Big Book Awards Distinguished Favorite Mystery; Red Ribbon Winner in 2022 Wishing Shelf Awards; 2023 Eric Hoffer Award Grand Prize Short List Honoree and Honorable Mention for Mystery/Crime

Wrong Hand Wright (2025) "Wrong Hand Right is a cleverly plotted crime thriller packed with twists, turns – and a little dry humour. Highly recommended!" ~ ***The Wishing Shelf Book Review***

TWO DEGREES

A Climate Change Novel

WILLIAM MICHAEL RIED

CKBooks Publishing

Publisher's Cataloging-in-Publication Data
Names: Ried, William Michael, author.
Title: Two degrees : a climate change novel / William Michael Ried.
Description: New Glarus, WI : CKBooks Publishing, 2023.
Identifiers: ISBN 978-1-949085-88-4 (paperback) | ISBN 978-1-949085-89-1 (ebook)
Subjects: LCSH: Climate change--Fiction. | Global warming--Fiction. | Environmentalism--Fiction. | Fossil fuels--Fiction. | Ecofiction. | BISAC: FICTION / Nature & the Environment.
Classification: LCC PS3618.I39228 T96 2023 (print) | LCC PS3618.I39228 (ebook) | DDC 813/.6--dc23.

LCCN: 2023921796

Cover design by Nanne
Flower image by Lorenzo Contessa

CKBooks Publishing
P.O. Box 214
New Glarus, WI 53574
CKBookspublishing.com

*And if railroads are not built, how shall we get to heaven
in season?*

Henry David Thoreau, *Walden*

*The darkest places in hell are reserved for those who
maintain their neutrality in times of moral crisis.*

Dante Alighieri, *The Divine Comedy*

We can and must win this battle for our lives.

COP27 Statement by UN Secretary-General
António Guterres

Prologue

Papers were spread over the conference table at Pearce, Jones & Hurwitz, where Daniel assessed the financial hit to the firm's clients if Congress didn't approve the Canada pipeline. Nell sipped coffee, glancing at the cell phone never far from her hand.

"Isn't your house on the Guadalupe River?" she said.

"Yeah," he replied absently, then stopped reading. "Why?"

"You should look at this." She handed over her phone.

"Texas Flooding" was the headline. He clicked into the story, but there was only a blurb about heavy rains and rising waters in the Hill Country. He rushed down the hall to his office.

"What can I do?" Nell called after him.

"Tell Alice to get hold of Howard Kane at Interior."

He hurried behind his desk and flipped on his screens. Fox had a breaking news story about flash floods across South Texas. A weather front had stalled over the mountains just miles from Daniel's home. There was video of houses breaking apart and people stranded on rooftops.

On another screen a CNN reporter in a rain slicker stood beside a swollen river. "As you can see behind me," he almost shouted over the intense wind, "the normally placid Guadalupe River has become a force to reckon with. Rainfall over the last twenty-four hours has shattered records here in the Texas Hill Country. The mountainside was denuded of trees from recent wildfires and couldn't absorb the water, so it forced coarse debris down swollen streams and rivers, destroying earthworks along the way."

Daniel tried his wife's cell phone again, and the landline, but neither call went through. A major drawback of working in DC while his family lived in Texas was the spotty cell service, but the landline was usually reliable.

"I have Mr. Kane," Alice called through the doorway.

"Howard," Daniel said desperately, "the Guadalupe's flooding, and I can't reach Bree. What's happening?"

"I won't lie, Dan; it looks bad. We're getting reports of serious damage and fatalities. I've got nothing specific...."

"It's my family!"

"I know, Dan, and I understand what you're going through, but I have to go. I'm headed to Denton to get a chopper to the flood zone."

"You've got to get me on that flight, Howard. Please!"

Daniel reached the tarmac while the FEMA cargo plane was loading. Once they were airborne, Howard filled him in. "The Weather Service has been monitoring the area since the Two Valleys Fire last month. The region suffered unusually high temperatures for more than three weeks. Then a nearly stationary convection along the Balcones Escarpment dumped continuous rainfall from San Antonio to Austin for thirty-six hours. By late yesterday afternoon, homes long the Guadalupe River from Kerrville to Seguin were washing off their foundations, and the Canyon Lake Dam is in danger of breaching."

"I'm too late!" Daniel groaned, wishing someone would slap his face like he deserved.

"We know nothing for sure," Howard said. "We'll get you there as fast as possible, and we'll see."

At Denton Daniel stuck by Howard to make sure he got a seat on the helicopter. In less than an hour, they neared the river. Daniel stared from the window at the devastation below. The landscape was so altered he hardly recognized the village of Tanswego. Where Main Street had crossed the stone bridge, water now rushed over broken shards. One of the German buildings, as old as the village, was just a tangle of stone. Everywhere displaced boulders, mangled cars and remnants of furniture, bedding and buildings littered the ground like detritus from some enormous shipwreck.

Once on the ground, Daniel was struck dumb. How could this be the sleepy village that was always so full of smiles?

"Sam! Sam Johnson!" he called out to a familiar face.

A big man in mud-caked overalls turned with no sign of recognition.

"It's me, Sam, Dan Lazaro."

A spark kindled in the man's eyes, but all he said was, "I don't...know...."

Daniel looked around for help with Sam but everyone was rushing one direction or another. He took the man by the elbow and sat him on a pile of broken concrete. Sam stared blankly and spoke as if recounting a dream. "We jammed a chair against the door, but something broke through, a tree or a boulder, and knocked me into the wall. Something stuck in my arm."

Daniel followed Sam's gaze to his forearm wrapped in a bloody towel. He again looked up for help as Sam kept talking. "Betsy screamed. It pulled her under. Then her voice was gone; everything was so loud. I grabbed hold—must have been part of the wall—but the water sucked me down. I couldn't breathe. But someone caught my arm. Was it you?"

"No, Sam. I just got here. Look, we'll get you to a doctor."

He waved over a Red Cross nurse. She squinted at Sam's face, nodded to Daniel and helped Sam to his feet.

He had to move on. Bree and Annabelle would have stayed safe at home. He had to get downriver to the house.

The FEMA credentials from Howard got him by the National Guard roadblock keeping people off the river road. He was soon alone, stepping over branches and through puddles. The Guadalupe River, in normal times close to forty feet across, had reached into the hills up both banks, tearing trees from the ground and scarring the hillsides with jagged channels.

Daniel came upon a large gap in the road. The only way past was uphill, through toppled trees. The air was sodden. He hung his suit jacket on a branch. He had already sweated through his white shirt. It was a relief, at least, that he had grabbed his hiking boots before rushing from his office.

He caught hold of a trunk to pull himself uphill but slipped and tore his forearm on a thornbush. Rising again he pushed on, fighting the muddy slope and heavy air, but more so the horror of what he might find. Sweat stung his eyes, making it hard to see, so he balanced against a tree while he knotted his necktie around his forehead.

Crossing a crevasse cut by the flood, he slipped and slid down, feet first, until he could grab a small tree. He held tight with both hands and tried to catch his breath but there just wasn't enough oxygen. This couldn't be the way to find Bree and Annabelle. Could he even reach River House?

He pushed to his feet and continued bushwhacking. After a bend in the river he was able to slide back to the road. This stretch was mostly intact, though strewn with branches and pockmarked with puddles. The still raging river lapped over the crumbled bank.

He reached what remained of the footbridge, which would have been the last way to cross the river before his house. He had walked that bridge so many times with Annabelle. His tiny daughter loved looking down with no fear of the height, which always made him proud. But he sometimes worried she was too trusting of the river she knew like a nanny who had overseen her whole life. Now, where a platform and wooden staircase had stood there was only cracked concrete footing with cables and boards tangled in the trees.

As he agonized over how to cross the river, a splintered telephone pole crashed into the bank, a kid's bicycle ensnared in wires dangling from the pole. It lodged against a sycamore at the river's edge, where the front half of a cat was wedged into a broken branch.

His stomach erupted. He stumbled to the side of the road and retched.

But he had to keep moving. He stood and wiped his mouth on his torn sleeve. What was wrong with him, getting sick about a cat when so many neighbors could be dead? He needed to keep a sense of proportion and push on.

But how to get across? There would be no way to drive across until the pontoon bridge was finished in the village. At the river's normal low for the season he could have waded or swam here, but now the seething current would sweep him away. His best hope might be to signal Bree from across the river, make sure she was safe and let her know he was there.

Around the last bend was a vantage point for the house where a friend had taken the photo they reprinted on Bree's thank-you cards. As he approached this spot, he had to keep his eyes on the uneven ground to avoid tripping. But when he looked up, what he saw tore his heart out. The bank beneath his beautiful house had crumbled into the river. Water had surged as high as the second floor even with the road behind and left only part of the foundation and a brick chimney. It looked like a ruin in the deep woods.

He fell to his knees, unable to catch his breath. The Guadalupe had given them such joy; how could it turn monstrous? The house they thought was solid was now just broken timbers and stones washing down to the flatlands.

But what did any of this matter? Where were his wife and child?

Near the remains of his house he saw something colorful, clothing or maybe trash stuck in a splintered pecan tree and marking the shocking height of the flood. The blue and orange colors of the patch stirred something inside him. He stepped as close as he could to the river's edge and squinted. It was the stuffed alligator his daughter never left behind.

Chapter One

A month before the Guadalupe River flooded, Daniel Lazaro was sitting in his office on K Street in Washington, DC when Branston Pearce barked through the intercom, "Where are we with the count?"

It made his jaw clench to hear that voice and picture the penetrating eyes under unruly gray eyebrows. Aiming for responsiveness short of obeisance, he replied, "We need two votes. Grant from Kentucky is holding out; he thinks he can play kingmaker. But he'll fold...unless he plans to retire after this term."

"Which leaves...?"

"Well, Langston could easily tie down Manfred's votes; he just has to use the highway bill."

"This is your deal, Daniel. Get it done."

He pushed back in his desk chair, looking past the framed photo on his desk of his wife and daughter to another on the wall of his visit last year to the White House. A quad monitor on another wall showed the news on Fox, Bloomberg, CNN and

C-SPAN. He watched C-SPAN to see things as they happened and Bloomberg for business news. The other channels spewed their propaganda from the two ends of the political spectrum. Sometimes all of it was relevant; sometimes none.

No network gave this vote the coverage it deserved, or maybe their producers thought viewers wouldn't understand its importance amid the constant noise about climate issues. It was votes like this that set policy and had real economic impact. And Pearce, Jones & Hurwitz was in the middle of the battle to protect industry, lobbying for the Oil Institute of America. The work paid extremely well, and he was good at it, good enough that Pearce had made him a partner two years before, although he was expected to develop his own business while still servicing Pearce's clients.

"Alice," he called out the door to his assistant, "could you please order some lunch, just a turkey sandwich?" Then he hit Haley Bourdain's number on speed dial.

"Still holding," she answered with no other greeting and no nonsense. Her voice was husky as if she smoked too much.

"We've got to push Manfred," Daniel pleaded.

"You know the senator won't play the highway card unless he has to."

"He *has* to. The Institute has no patience for brinkmanship. They want this vote closed...and you *know* it's good for Senator Langston."

"Yes, but methane isn't exactly in his wheelhouse."

"It's all the same in the end." He tried not to show his frustration. "We let the administration make us the methane police, and next they'll close off federal lands for drilling. Then it'll be too late to squeeze Manfred for anything."

She sighed impatiently. "Let me put it in terms you understand, Danny. Langston gives up his chit to pull in Manfred and your people do what, exactly, to show their appreciation?"

Daniel fumed. Requiring oil and gas plants to recapture

methane was unnecessarily burdensome. Ecologists cried that methane was a worse global warming culprit than carbon dioxide, but it was an inevitable byproduct of processing, like CO_2 from breathing. We need oil, so we live with methane. The cost of recapture exceeds the selling price, so gas escapes. When the market put a higher value on the gas—or on not releasing it into the atmosphere, if that ever happened—there would be an economic opportunity and no more issue. But requiring recapture now meant more wasteful regulations, inspections and expense, piling burdens on an industry already under strain from the teetering economy and volatile geopolitics.

So, defeating this bill was a no-brainer for the whole oil industry and thus for Texas. But Langston and his pit bull advisor knew the bill was critical to the Oil Institute and so were squeezing for some additional return. In this town everything had a price, and you always pressed your advantage. There was no standing on principle, no noble cause; it was always what's in it for me?

"Okay, listen," Daniel said, trying not to sound annoyed. "The Institute may be able to direct super PAC funds, as we've discussed...."

"As we've been discussing for far too long."

"I know. I know. I'm sure you can appreciate there are a lot of initiatives, with this administration hell-bent on stoking the green vote...."

"Fascinating," she said sarcastically, "but with Langston you have to talk turkey."

"All right. Okay, let me make some calls. I'll get back to you this morning."

"I'll be in the hearings. Text me a number; it's that simple. And you better get on this. The vote is tomorrow morning, and Langston takes off right after that for Texas."

Daniel hung up and buried his head in his hands. He hated to admit he couldn't close the deal on his own, but PJ&H could not risk losing this vote. He'd have to ask Pearce to go to the Oil

Institute. If they wanted to kill the methane bill, the price would be Langston's payoff, or what he would call "a generous donation to his campaign fund"—which at least had the silver-lining of drawing the leash tighter around the senator's neck, especially with the recordings PJ&H kept of telephone calls. There was no ethical bar in DC on attorneys recording their meetings or calls, absent fraud or dishonesty, and Pearce's archives arguably were meant only to record the facts. The other side of those conversations might not want those facts to get around, but this would never become an issue. If it ever did come up, the mere existence of those tapes would ensure no one rocked the boat.

Branston Pearce sat back to trim a fat cigar. He was proud of having brought Daniel to the point where he could engineer a vote like this on his own. It justified his judgment in plucking the young lawyer from obscurity, initially to exploit his family connection to a Texas representative but then finding he was a lobbying natural.

Pearce had been skeptical at first; Daniel's resume included time with a troubling save-some-obscure-owl organization. But he needed Daniel's connection in the short term, whether the kid worked out in the end or not.

His timing had been perfect. The young lawyer's wife had been about to give birth and their finances were clearly tight, judging by the shabby suit the kid wore and his address in a dubious Capitol Hill neighborhood. PJ&H offered him a way out of debt and into a comfortable life, and it was gratifying how quickly he learned to mouth the party line. He was good-looking and could talk a rat off a dung heap. On top of that he was smart, which distinguished him from most of the political junkies in this town.

Daniel had a bright future as long as he remembered who the big bear was in this firm. Pearce was the senior partner, which at Pearce, Jones & Hurwitz meant he dictated partner distributions.

His dozen partners accepted that he took what he wanted and passed around the crumbs he agreed to share. And since Pearce was his rabbi at the firm, the old bear's clout worked for Daniel as well.

When his secretary announced Mr. Lazaro was waiting, Pearce smirked and took his time lighting his cigar. It was always good to let a young buck cool his heels for a few minutes.

Pearce eventually buzzed his secretary to let Daniel in and then asked him in to lay out the situation. "We need two more votes to be sure," Daniel said. "Langston is chair of the Transportation Subcommittee and could trade for three votes Senator Manfred controls in return for Langston's support for some Indiana bridge to nowhere. But Langston is holding us up—I'm sure the idea came from his chief...what is she now, chief of staff?"

"Ms. Bourdain has defied categorization for almost two decades in DC and is chief of whatever the hell she wants. Right now, I think she heads Langston's campaign committee."

Pearce dismissed Daniel and called an old classmate at the Oil Institute, who arranged to wire funds into a PJ&H escrow account. The firm would transfer the money to an anonymous, unfettered organization set up to smear anyone running against Langston in the next election. The Oil Institute couldn't claim a deduction for the payment, since the PAC wasn't a charity, but Pearce's tax partner would find a way to credit it as a business expense. This payment was, after all, the rare business investment that translated dollar-for-dollar into results. He buzzed Daniel to tell Ms. Bourdain the fix was in.

Daniel was feeling satisfied with himself. He texted Haley that nine hundred thousand dollars would be deposited into the "By the People, For the People" political action committee once Langston got Manfred on board to defeat the methane bill. If the senator's priority had been to champion the desires of his constituents—to impede the transition away from oil and gas—the funds could legitimately have gone through the Oil Institute's Equitable Policy for Energy Foundation. But the senator made clear to Pearce—in another tape recording that would never get a hearing—that the money had to go solely to ensuring *his* reelection.

So, the senator got what he demanded, which should lock up the vote, and Daniel could be home Thursday night for a long weekend with his wife and daughter. He smiled; Annabelle was going to love the stuffed alligator—swag Nell brought back from a reception for a senator from Florida. The bright orange and blue University of Florida colors would make quite a contrast with the faded brown of her ratty old bear.

Jake knocked on his door to say he would finish the memo Daniel had assigned him by late in the evening.

"The one on land use...?" Daniel started to ask.

"The challenge by the Standing Rock Sioux...in South Dakota."

"What's the bottom line?"

"Their argument relies on tribal law and won't stand up in federal court."

"Excellent. I'm going to get in some laps at the pool, so don't kill yourself finishing it tonight. Tomorrow midday will be fine. And why don't you grab Nell and meet me about seven at the Stanchion?"

The Rusty Stanchion was the closest thing to a dive bar near the office. The main appeal of this dingy but comfortable hole in the wall was it didn't attract the inside-the-Beltway types who monopolized too much of Daniel's time. The bartenders knew he tipped well and always gave him a generous pour. The décor leaned heavily into local baseball, stretching all the way back to the Washington Olympics but focusing on the Senators under a 1950s banner: "Washington: first in war, first in peace, and last in the American League."

Daniel raised a glass. "To victory tomorrow," he toasted.

"Pearce must be pleased with you," Nell said after sipping her drink.

"Ah, the old goat is just pleased to win," Daniel laughed, "and make more money."

They toasted, and Daniel said, "And we have something else to celebrate."

Jake looked curious, Nell embarrassed.

"Yes," Daniel went on, "my sources tell me our own Nell Batterly will be named in Forbes' 30 Under 30 Awards for Law and Policy."

Jake turned to her. "No shit? That's dope! How did that happen?"

Nell grinned at Daniel. "Well, I admit I pushed for it, but it seems I had some help from on high."

Daniel shrugged his shoulders. "Who would have done that?"

It had taken Daniel considerable maneuvering to have these two associates assigned to work exclusively for him. Nell came out of Virginia Law School and worked harder than anyone he knew. She had a really sharp mind, but he sometimes worried that she worked *too* hard. It was as if she had no toggle switch to power-down. Her constant overdrive couldn't be healthy; he was afraid she'd burn out. And she was not bad looking, either. At her age and with her salary, she should be living it up, but she seemed to have no interest outside her career and politics. He suspected she spent her time off at home with her cat, reading the *Congressional Record*. In any event, the Forbes award would make her happy and give her something to brag about with her family. Her sister was in finance and her brother a surgeon, and Nell seemed to feel a driving need to compete with them.

Jake was also smart but got his work done without breaking a sweat, with self-assurance that might have come from his growing up in Manhattan as the child of a couple of big-firm lawyers. Daniel wouldn't raise his child in that liberal cauldron, but it was sure to make you grow up fast and attuned to what was going on around you. Jake had left for college at Middlebury, where he aced his courses and ran cross country, but returned for law school at NYU. He had the typical arrogance of a New Yorker, often putting down Washington as a "provincial town." But his irreverent frat-boy humor helped everyone through the long work nights.

What mattered most about Daniel's associates was their loyalty to him, even above Pearce or the firm. This grew out of how he treated them as a part of his team. He gave them responsibility for important matters, pushed to get them raises and choice offices and often took them out for drinks. In return they had his back, showing fealty rare in a world of political wonks.

"So what do you guys have on for the weekend?" he asked.

Nell shrugged. "I booked a tour at the Museum of Democracy; they have a new exhibit on the path to the presidency."

"Sounds like a blast," Jake said, rolling his eyes.

"Oh, and I guess *you'll* be hanging out with your…" she paused to make air quotes, "boys?"

"In fact," he said, grinning suggestively, "I'm going up to the City for a half-marathon and a date."

Everyone understood that, to Jake, "the City" could only mean New York, where his parents still lived and he spent many of his weekends. He bragged that he knew every crack and crevice in his hometown.

"Not the woman from Goldman again?" Nell said with a groan.

"Nah," Jake responded. "She turned out to be way too conservative."

"You mean in the bedroom, not her politics?" Daniel said, grinning.

Jake laughed so hard he spit out his beer. "Actually, she spent a little too much time quoting *Wall Street Journal* op-eds."

"You *talk* to women you date?" Nell said with dripping sarcasm.

Jake considered that. "You're right. Who needs to talk? In fact, I could even consider reaching across the aisle."

"I hear some of those socialists have extraordinary flexibility," Daniel said.

Daniel and Jake laughed.

Nell shook her head. "You two are disgusting."

Chapter Two

Mid-morning the next day Daniel and his associates joined Pearce in his conference room to watch the methane vote.

"We've got fifty-one," Jake said, brushing back his mop of brown hair. "But I bet we also get Bengrass from Arizona. A bottle of Scotch, anyone, on the over/under at fifty-two?"

Pearce looked unamused, so Daniel shot a warning look at Jake. Having a frat bro on his team sometimes presented challenges, but his associate knew how to behave when he had to.

Nell meanwhile sipped coffee and stared at the screen. Her killer instincts would not be diverted by Jake's ill-timed humor. Daniel caught himself staring at her legs wrapped in a maroon skirt that teased the limits of law office decorum. Not that that was a bad thing; it showed she was fearless, reminding Daniel of that statue of the little girl on Wall Street, and she did have the legs to pull it off.

He wondered again why Nell seemed to have no social life. He thought it must come from her parents. Raising their kids to be ambitious and successful was admirable, but Nell's folks came up short in teaching their daughter any sense of pride in her accomplishments or any kind of serenity. Still, Daniel sometimes wished he had her drive, which had pushed the whole team through late nights in the office.

He hoped being partnered with Jake would loosen Nell up a bit—while making him act a little more serious. But then, how could he complain? It was just personalities. He had the two smartest young lawyers in the office ready to go to war for him, and they made an effective team.

The vote dragged on, the drama playing out like a race between two snails who only seem to move when you weren't looking. Pearce sank within himself beneath his massive eyebrows. Jake tried to balance a pen upright on the tip of his finger. Nell continued to stare at the screen.

"Senator Manfred," the clerk finally read. They all looked up.

"Nay," Manfred responded.

The conference room erupted. Regulation & Control of Methane, SB-873, was going down to defeat.

Daniel shook Pearce's hand. Jake hugged Nell, lifting and twirling her, then he high-fived Daniel while she shook hands with Pearce. Staff poured into the room, which got noisy with chatter. Pearce's secretary wheeled in a cart of flutes and bottles of champagne.

Pearce toasted "our glorious victory," with a knowing look at Daniel. He knew his young partner usually flew home on Thursday nights, but this look told Daniel to plan on staying in town for the celebration.

Pearce made this intimation clear when he offered Daniel a ride to the restaurant. If he had to stay in town, he'd have preferred to go with Nell and Jake because Jake had mentioned having some blow. But it wouldn't do to turn down the boss's invitation. Realistically, Daniel should buy his own cocaine anyway—it wasn't the best idea to get drugs from his associate.

But Jake was his guy—and it was too easy to overdo it if he kept the stuff around all the time.

Most importantly, they won the vote! They'd be rolling in the success fee promised by the Oil Institute. And even after seven years at the firm, it was always a rush—not to mention diplomatic—to ride with the boss in his Rolls.

When Daniel went by Pearce's office, ready to leave for the party, the old man had planted himself in a leather chair and gestured Daniel toward the table crowded with crystal decanters. Daniel poured two bourbons and sat across from his boss.

Pearce lifted his glass. "You did it, my boy."

"I don't know what to say, Branston. You've been so helpful. It took your hand to see this one across the finish line." This was the truth, although it hurt to admit it.

"Rubbish. All I did was call an old friend. You did the heavy lifting."

It was gratifying to hear praise from Pearce, although it was always unclear what the old man really thought. But Daniel *had* done most of the work to manage this vote. Everyone on the ground—in Congress and at the firm—knew this was *his* victory. Things were looking up for his career, making him feel foolish he had ever hesitated about taking this job.

He had been in his third year of law school and working part-time, for not much money, in the House of Representatives. Like everyone on the Hill, he knew Pearce, Jones & Hurwitz was a big-time firm, which was reflected in exorbitant associate salaries.

He and Bree were sharing a house at the time in a sketchy neighborhood with three law students from Georgetown. It was not ideal for a newly married couple. Meals were, more or less, communal and privacy nonexistent. It was as if they were still undergrads. Then they learned Bree was pregnant.

They needed their own apartment, but there was little hope of pulling that off with their student loans to pay and the exorbitant rents in Washington. They talked about moving back to Texas after Daniel graduated, but that would mean giving up. Still, hiring a nanny so Bree could keep working would cost as much as she made teaching, and there were sure to be new expenses with the baby. Bree wanted to ask her parents for a loan, but that would have been even worse than giving up.

Bree's miscarriage late in her term removed the urgency about finances, but by then Daniel's career had taken off. The new job meant they could get their own place and easily pay off their debt.

Daniel was so grateful he was ready to do whatever Pearce asked. Still, he was surprised when the old man outlined his plans. It was shortly after Daniel started at the firm that Pearce called him into his office. It was unusual, as far as he could tell, for the senior partner to meet one-on-one with a new associate, but Pearce had personally offered him the job, so Daniel figured he must have done something to attract his attention.

"I hear from Wilkins," Pearce said, "that you've been doing excellent work on the public lands project."

This seemed a bit premature as he had only been on the job for a week. All he could think of to say was, "Thank you, sir. Mr. Wilkins has been really helpful showing me the way."

"That's good to hear. But now I'm thinking of moving you up."

"Up?"

"Yes. I've got an idea you might be just the lawyer we need for an important job. Urenergy, one of our major clients, is interested in uranium mining in Texas. But the anti-energy activists—largely from out of state, of course—are throwing up roadblocks. They cite junk science about air and water quality to complain about threats to wildlife, the typical rants about aquatic ecosystems and poisoned food chains. You with me?"

"Yes, sir."

The impact of mine runoff was all too familiar to Daniel,

given the accident that had cost his father his job and started the family's downward spiral. Thinking of that accident brought back his distress about watersheds being contaminated and his fury when the catastrophe was laid at his father's feet. For a time this had led him to flirt with an environmental group on campus, but then his father died and his mother quickly lost her grip on reality and cut him off. That was a desolate time, when he felt abandoned by the world. But salvation came in a pair of big blue eyes and long blonde hair, and he still wondered what Bree saw in him then. But she took hold and lifted him up and his only priority became building a life with her.

"Okay," Pearce said, "here's the issue. Our client has relied upon a law that's been in place since 1872 and gives miners access to public lands. The green lobby has allied with the radical left to try to overturn a hundred and fifty years of precedent and foist a raft of requirements on anyone seeking to mine, making them test and monitor and file reports till the cattle come home. And while this battle will be fought in the Texas Legislature, one congressman from Texas has a great deal of influence on the debate."

Daniel looked at Pearce, wide-eyed. This seemed like a roundabout way of handing out a work assignment...if that's what it was.

"I'm talking about Representative Jack Wolfson. I believe you have a family connection?"

This slap across the face explained why Pearce had brought him in. "Yes, sir. Representative Wolfson was a good friend of my father's. He got me my job in the House."

"Well, that could be very helpful. In fact, now that you are part of the energy team—which, of course, comes with a substantial raise—you will act as a go-between with the congressman. Call it a 'legislative liaison.' To start you will find an informal way to communicate how our interests align on preserving the status quo under Texas law. Do you understand?"

He understood entirely. Pearce wanted to use Daniel's one connection that survived the mine scandal and his father's suicide. It felt shady, but he concluded this must be how things worked in Washington. Of course, this also meant throwing in with the corporate types who had burned his father to cover their sins. But this was his seat at the table, and a chance to succeed at his first job: providing for his family. He wondered how "substantial" the raise would be.

"I'll give it my best, Mr. Pearce," he had said and hoped he could stick to it.

Later on, when he and Bree were enjoying their enhanced lifestyle, he had been grateful to his father for this boost to his career. Daniel's new job had rescued the family finances.

But when the doctors ordered bed rest during Bree's last two months of pregnancy, he had to put long hours in at the office just when she needed him most. Then she miscarried. And they were both devastated. Bree sank into depression, quit her job and spent too much time second-guessing how this could have been her fault. She also came to doubt she would ever be a mother. But Daniel helped her look toward the future, and eighteen months later Annabelle arrived, with bright eyes and the requisite numbers of fingers and toes.

Another five years and a lightning quick junior partnership later, Daniel was a champion of the right. He had no sympathy for the tax-and-spend big government supporters and over-regulation advocates. They were welcome to their say, but Daniel's side called the shots, even when a hostile administration came in. He led the team lobbying oil and gas issues for the Oil Institute of America, fighting to ensure the marketplace, rather than the government, would pick the winners and losers in the energy industry. Not coincidentally, this was where PJ&H made the big money.

"The Institute is very happy with this vote," Pearce said.

"They've expressed their appreciation with a generous success fee."

Daniel held his breath. This could be his payoff.

"You will find two hundred thousand in your account at the end of the month and can count on a similar transfer at year's end, an extra bonus for a job well done."

Daniel couldn't suppress a quiet chuckle. He clinked glasses with Pearce, wondering what the old bear had netted for himself.

The phone on the desk buzzed. "Sorry for the interruption, Mr. Pearce," a voice said, "but Mr. Lazaro's wife is on the line for him."

Daniel was annoyed at this interruption but took hold of himself and shrugged. This moment was as much for Bree as for him; he should share the news. He looked at Pearce in apology.

"Take the call, dammit," Pearce said. "I'll meet you out front at my car in, say, twenty minutes."

In his office Daniel pushed back in his chair and threw his feet up on the desk before picking up the receiver.

"Hey, Babe!" he almost shouted.

"Whoa," she responded. "What's going on there?"

"We won! Methane went down in flames. Our new deck is on the way."

He and Bree lived in a modern home they lovingly called "River House" because of its dramatic perch above the Guadalupe River, in the Hill Country of Texas. The existing deck was built around a big cypress tree ten feet above the languid water, but it had been damaged the year before in a "hundred-year" flood surge. They could have easily afforded to repair the deck, but they had learned frugality in their first years together and still tended to invest their money rather than spend it. Still, they needed to fix the deck, and this bonus was a clear sign they should go big, make it larger and grander. Sooner than expected they'd be sipping martinis perched above the flowing Guadalupe.

When she didn't respond, he said, "Is something wrong?"

"No, honey," she said, but sounded uneasy. "That's fantastic! I'm so happy for you."

He hesitated. "You should be happy for *us*, but you sound concerned."

"It's the news. The Two Valleys Fire has everyone on edge. I wanted to warn you about delays at the airport...because of smoke."

"Oh, shit. I was hoping for one summer without a fire that gets its own goddamned name."

The fire in the valleys was not much of a danger, although the smoke could be bothersome, and he'd have to reassure Bree. But the delay could also be a *good* thing. It freed him to join the office celebration and take a later flight home. "Listen," he said, "I'll see what I can find out about the fire. You remember Howard? He's at Interior now, working with the Forest Service, so he'll have the inside scoop. And rather than watching the delays and getting home late anyway, I'll just catch an early flight tomorrow. We'll still have the weekend."

"Oh, that's right," she said, suddenly chipper. "I should have thought. You all must be delirious about your victory. You should buy yourself a drink, captain."

He laughed. "I think I'll let the old man buy the drinks, and I'll get that early flight."

"Okay. You have fun. We'll see you tomorrow. Be sure to tell everyone I said congratulations."

Daniel checked his watch. "Listen, darlin, Pearce is waiting, so I have to go. Wish I could take you out dancing to celebrate instead."

Despite Bree's upbeat manner, which rarely flagged, he sensed disquiet. "Look," he said, "say the word and I'll commandeer a plane and beat my way home through the smoke."

She laughed. "You go get that drink. Annabelle and I will have a girls' night in and prepare a celebration lunch for you tomorrow."

He hung up and grabbed his briefcase but another call caught him. It was Haley Bourdain.

"So how does it feel, counselor?" she said, her voice more sultry than usual. Even over the phone he could feel her standing a little too close. She was not unattractive; on the contrary, she might be ten years older than Daniel but it was hard to miss her curvy figure and look of a man-eater.

"Great," he replied. "It feels really good. And we were dead in the water without you...."

"And the senator...."

"*And* the senator, of course. Speaking of whom, I assume we'll see you both tonight. You're stopping by the party, right?"

"Wouldn't miss it."

Haley hung up with a smirk. Working with PJ&H was a necessary burden of handling Senator Langston. The relationship was symbiotic. PJ&H pushed the big oil agenda, which benefitted the senator's supporters and provided jobs and tax revenue to pave roads and build schools. And beyond the obvious political advantage, domestic energy production also freed the country from the OPEC stranglehold that had paralyzed it as far back as President Carter. Blocking wasteful governmental regulation of drilling on federal lands was a win-win.

If PJ&H sometimes pushed broader energy initiatives, these also fell in line with the core interests of Texas. Efforts like slapping import quotas on Chinese solar panels and wind turbines, and opposing gas efficiency standards for automobiles really boosted the whole economy. Blocking government meddling in methane recapture was just the same; it allowed the free marketplace to value a production byproduct.

Capitalism had made the US the most powerful country in the world by getting the government *out* of the way of production, letting the marketplace determine what was produced and how it was sold. And PJ&H was a champion of this system, which was good for the senator's constituents, not to mention it had made Branston Pearce rich.

So, she "handled" PJ&H just like she had pressured and cajoled and seduced lawyers and consultants throughout her career in Washington, which had lasted longer than almost anyone, except the oldest senators and career bureaucrats. She might be looking back at forty-five but she could pass for ten years younger in the right light. Her vitality came from the drama of the work—which could be truly consequential—along with three sessions a week with her personal trainer. Still, it was a bloody shame she didn't have this kind of clout when she was twenty-five and could stop traffic in a tailored suit.

And as far as keeping life interesting, Pearce might be a misogynist who smelled of bourbon and foul cigars, but he was not stupid. He had recruited a handsome, young lackey with family ties, who turned out to be much more pleasant to deal with than his puppet-master. He also—surprisingly—proved to be quite good at the job. She had to ask herself what else Daniel might be good at.

Representative Jack Wolford wondered how his old friend's son was getting along at Pearce, Jones & Hurwitz. The firm was well known—if "infamous" was too strong a word—for its lobbying work. They leaned heavily into energy, which meant he had to deal with them in the course of his work on the Energy and Commerce Committee.

When Daniel had first taken the job, he came by for lunch and sheepishly told Jack he was assigned to be his "liaison" with industry, so they could work together "in the best interests of Texas business." If his constituents didn't favor those "best interests" as well, and if he hadn't been determined to help Daniel's career, Jack would have told Branston Pearce to go to hell. As it was, there was no use making enemies when their interests mostly *did* align.

He just steered clear of Pearce when he could to avoid breathing the swampy air that followed him into a room.

"Danny," Jack said when Daniel picked up the phone. "It's been a while."

"Congressman, it's good to hear from you."

"Yes, well, I wanted to congratulate you on the methane vote; that was y'all, wasn't it?

"It was, Uncle Jack. Thank you."

"You know, I assume it's not too hard to capture methane and make use of it."

"Yeah, I know."

"Which probably *would* be best all around."

"Right. But, as you know, Congressman, we each have to haul manure for someone."

"I hear you, Danny. It's sad but an unfortunate truth. But I wonder what happened to the kid who came to work for me, the one with the ideal of public service."

"He moved back to Texas; lives in a trailer park outside Houston."

Jack could not tell if it was the job or what had happened to his father that made Daniel a standard-bearer for the hard right. Jack mostly supported the conservative agenda himself, but it was still worrisome how Daniel embraced it with no hesitation. Still, Daniel's father had been his oldest friend and got the short end of things after the accident at his mine. And then his friend took his own life, and Jack felt compelled to step in and help get Daniel into law school and find him a job. Now, the young man was making something of himself, although in some circles being a lobbyist at PJ&H was considered no lofty goal.

Chapter Three

Daniel followed his boss into The Mace, Pearce's private club. A uniformed attendant opened the outer door to a hallway of dark wood and marble statuary. At an inner door, a tuxedoed host bowed slightly.

"So good to welcome you back, Mr. Pearce. Several of your party have been shown to the Jefferson Room."

Daniel and Pearce found a number of their lawyers, legal assistants and secretaries drinking in a large private room. Jake was regaling two pretty assistants with how he'd have won a bet on the vote if everyone hadn't been so anxious about the tally.

"Someone hand that man a Scotch," Daniel said, laughing as Jake looked up but continued without missing a beat.

Daniel waded into the crowd, accepting congratulations all around. He gave Nell a hug, then one of his female partners. Jake appeared at his elbow, not wanting to be left out, so Daniel hugged his tall, lanky frame as well, noticing his dilated pupils and passing a look to say he'd like to be invited next time to partake.

The celebration became raucous, with the young people downing tequila shots and dancing to music that grew louder with the bubble of conversation.

Daniel took his drink to an alcove, where he was joined by Pearce and Ed Jones, the firm's tax partner. After a silent toast and self-congratulatory smiles, the boss asked them both, "Have you followed what that Eco character has been up to?"

"He's at it again?" Daniel said with a pained expression.

"Is this the guy who blew up the pipeline?" Ed said.

"That's what our friends at the FBI think," Pearce said. "They see him as the 'intellectual architect' of Anthro, as if there's anything 'intellectual' about planting bombs."

"Well," Daniel interposed, "he also writes *Monkey Wrench*."

Ed looked at Daniel. "What's that?"

"A blog that publicizes protests and spreads environmental ravings. This guy actually seems to be the editor, although he's never been clearly photographed so he might be just some Robin Hood avatar."

Pearce added, "Stroking the public's unaccountable fascination with celebrity."

"Well," Daniel said, "if he does exist, he's got a real sense of theater, and ability to live off the grid."

Pearce scoffed, "That's one ideologue I'd love to see hoisted on his own petard."

"Petard?" Daniel laughed.

"He plants bombs," Pearce said without humor. "He should go up in a bomb."

Daniel grimaced, imagining pieces of a protester scattered over the sidewalk. "Well, I've seen the graffiti," he said, referring to the silhouette of two intertwined flowers that vandals painted on oil and gas facilities. He also had been impressed—though he'd never admit it out loud—by "Sleeping Dragon," where two activists stop logging trucks by handcuffing themselves together in a metal tube that sat inside a concrete-filled barrel buried under the road.

"Yes, our nut case knows publicity. The FBI thought they had him last week in North Dakota but he slipped the noose."

"Hard to catch him when you don't know what he looks like."

"There is one partial photo." Pearce held up his phone. "The director shared this with me, but they haven't made it public."

The grainy black-and-white photograph showed the partial profile of a man speaking with a slender woman, who was looking toward the camera. She had long dark hair and almond-shaped eyes.

Daniel laughed. "How do the revolutionaries get all the hot women?"

Pearce frowned.

"Well, so this is a lead, right?" Daniel said, wiping the smile from his face. "Have they identified the woman?"

"Dead end. They also don't know if she and Eco are together or if she helped him slip the trap or even participated in the bombing."

"Well, you've got to admire his ability to pull strings without getting tangled."

Pearce sipped his drink and then grumbled. "And another problem is these wildfires. Scientists—though, as always, what scientists? My scientists, your scientists, whose scientists?—are raising a stink about global warming causing destruction in the national parks."

"How many parks have active fires?"

"Just about all of them; more than four hundred is what I hear."

Daniel grimaced.

"It's bad press," Pearce said. Then he raised his substantial eyebrows. "Maybe we should send Langston for a weekend in a national park. Some publicity shots fishing or watching the sunset with his dog beneath a sky clear of smoke."

"Do they allow dogs in the parks?"

"They damned well will allow Senator Langston's dog."

"Does he even own one?"

"How the hell would I know? We'll rent one."

To escape the alcove, Daniel said he needed another drink. As he crossed the floor Nell pulled him to where others were dancing. He joined them, mostly jumping around with all his colleagues, not wanting to get too close to Nell, for all the trouble that could cause. But it felt good to release energy. Then, loosened by the drinks, Nell gave a look like she wanted another hug, so he moved on. She was going to have one nasty hangover.

Pearce rose and clinked his glass. "I want to say once more," he said in his rumbling public-speaking voice, "a big thank you to our team. We've shown we are the best. We did good work. We deserve this celebration...." He was interrupted by applause. "But once the hangovers fade, we have to get to work on a major new pipeline project. And keep in mind that, as our misguided administration prepares to head off to COP27 in Egypt, we also have much other work to do. Hopefully, with a non-event on that international stage, we can begin to make progress on the bigger prize of freeing our great country from the Paris Climate Accord. This, my friends and colleagues, will be a challenge to test our mettle. But for tonight, bottoms up!"

Pearce really knew how to take the air out of a room. At a visceral level, the Climate Accord was an honest attempt to address the human contribution to global warming but, like so many other liberal initiatives, it was naively directed and an economic disaster. As to COP27, the acronym for the twenty-seventh meeting of the "Committee of Parties"—a vapid name for the United Nations Annual Climate Summit—he was almost certain Saudi Arabia and the other oil-producing nations would kill any move against fossil fuels. He had to get more familiar with the real players at those conferences and see if he could land one of the oil countries as a client. But that—and the more immediate pipeline issue—was for another day. Where was Jake?

The music resumed. Chatter again grew boisterous. Added commotion at the door signaled the arrival of Senator Langston and his aide. Daniel closed in on them to thrust out his hand to the senator.

Haley watched Daniel swoop in as if he couldn't wait to greet Langston. "A great day for small government," the lawyer said with an electric smile.

"Yes, son, a great day," Langston replied, his eyes darting around the room in the politician's way of scanning for anyone of importance. Daniel grinned at Haley, who stood one step behind her boss. Daniel would go far in this town with that face and ability to lather obsequiously without a hint of sarcasm.

Langston spotted Pearce rumbling toward him and turned his back on Daniel and Haley. Daniel turned to her. "What are you drinking?"

"Nothing for me, thanks," she said, making her amused smile a bit roguish. "Someone around here has to keep her head."

"Senator!" Pearce intoned, reaching out his hand. "So glad you could join us."

"Ah, Branston," Langston replied, shaking with both hands, like a polished campaigner. "It's been too long. How's the golf game?"

"You know how it is, Bo. No time for games while we have serious work to do."

Langston laughed his good-old-boy guffaw and slapped Pearce's shoulder. "How well I know it. It's good we are helped along by such capable young people," he turned to Daniel, whose amused expression looked suddenly sincere, "like Mr. Lazaro here."

Daniel smiled. "Thank you, Senator, but you know we just do what we can...and *your* staff is the best in Congress." He turned to Haley with a bow of his head.

She responded with a look intended as both demure and confident. She appreciated the plug; it was quite unnecessary, given her hold over the senator, but it was endearing Daniel thought to do it.

"You needn't tell me," Langston said. "I often think Ms. Bourdain's talents are wasted running affairs of an old cowboy like me."

She joined in the laughter at this. "Old cowboy" was putting it kindly, but managing a politician as transparent and intellectually challenged as Bo Langston was much easier than working for someone with a backbone or an ethical compass.

Daniel sensed an undercurrent from Haley he didn't understand, and not for the first time. She was more experienced than he was and seemed always to be playing the angles. Pearce made it sound like she managed Langston so completely she was really the one in charge, and everything Daniel saw supported this. She also made a distinct physical impression, always dressed impeccably in a way that complemented her ample curves and sometimes left him fantasizing. And he had to admit she had been helpful to him. He had learned from her how to act like he knew more than he did and never to admit a mistake.

Daniel was pulled away by one of his partners to mediate an inebriated argument about the Electoral Count Act. This archaic law made his head spin at the best of times but with several bourbons under his belt it was hopeless, so he rattled off some double-talk and escaped to the bar.

Ordering another drink, he saw Jake signal from across the room so conspicuously it would have been comical if it weren't so meaningful. Daniel followed his associate through a door, down a hallway and through another door onto an empty fire stairwell. Jake sat on a step and started cutting lines of cocaine on a magazine.

"Now I remember why I hired you," Daniel said with his back against the door, in case someone tried to push it open.

"I thought it was my incisive legal mind," Jake said, pausing to look up with a grin. Sharing drugs with his subordinate was not a recommended human resources practice, but they had partied before Daniel became a partner, so what was the use of stopping now? Besides, Daniel had a real urge to get high.

Daniel squatted and snorted. He then rose and steadied himself on the banister while a surge of energy filled his body. Suddenly, he felt like dancing. This was a celebration!

After taking his turn, Jake looked up. "You know," he said, eyes now shining, "I was wondering: is methane good for anything? It's an element, right?"

"You developing a conscience?"

"Just wondered what we're celebrating."

"That's wrong thinking, young man. This is the time to rejoice, not think. Besides that, methane is not an element; it's a chemical *compound*. Don't you guys look at the science at all?"

"I just take orders, Boss."

"The Nuremburg defense?"

Jake looked confused.

"Never mind. Methane is part of natural gas and is used as a fuel. It's also a greenhouse gas, worse than carbon dioxide they say. It's emitted during oil and gas production."

"So why not capture it?"

"It's not economical."

"I get it. And our clients don't like being told what to do."

"Except by us," Daniel said and smirked. "No, our clients maximize shareholder returns. It's a free market. Regulating oil production is an assault on our economy and jobs."

Jake shrugged as if he was ready to forget about policy arguments and rejoin the party. Daniel watched him, wondering why a smart kid like him so readily accepted rationalizations Daniel spouted but sometimes doubted himself. But that, too, was a thought for another day.

Jake and Daniel rejoined the party. The air of celebration pulsed. Daniel made his way through the sporadic dancing and found his partner, Hack Jones, at the bar.

"You hear the latest from the anarchists?" Hack said loudly over the music.

"No," Daniel shouted, waving for the bartender to continue pouring into his glass. "I've been buried in the methane bill."

"Well, *Monkey Wrench* has a story about some ophthalmologist and his accountant girlfriend going on a spree in New Mexico cutting down highway billboards."

Daniel laughed. "What for?"

"Ah, you know, over-development, mucking up the environment...."

Daniel smirked. "Oh, of course. And so...?"

"It seems that as long as they were chopping down wooden billboards they eluded the sheriff, who was involved in *real* law enforcement like backing up ICE at the border. But when the developers erected steel supports, the doctor turned to using an acetylene torch, which attracted the attention of a passing motorist who swooped in for a citizen's arrest."

"The motorist had a shotgun, of course."

"This was New Mexico, amigo."

"So, were they convicted?"

"They haven't gone to trial yet. *Monkey Wrench* launched a GoFundMe campaign for their legal expenses."

"Hard to believe anyone would contribute to something like that."

"Maybe they just have a sense of humor."

They clinked glasses. As the conversation turned to baseball, Daniel's assistant tapped his arm. "There's a call from Howard

Kane," she said. "I told him you were busy, but he said you asked him to call."

It was annoying he could never get a moment's peace. But he *had* asked Howard to keep him apprised about the Two Valleys Fire, and he wouldn't call unless it was important. Daniel made his way to a house phone in the lobby.

"Hey, Howard. What's up?"

"Dan. Glad I found you. You didn't answer your cell."

"Yeah, I had it on do not disturb; it's loud in here. Is it about Two Valleys?"

"No, nothing new there. It has scorched most of the still-wooded mountainsides in the Upper Valley, but it's 80 percent contained."

"That's a relief."

"Yeah; there's no danger where you live, just maybe a few days of smoke. But we've got a bigger problem, a larger fire in West Texas jumped Highway 10 and trapped some firefighters."

"Fatalities?"

"Two so far."

"Damn. I can't remember when we had so many fires at once. Wouldn't happen if we'd get some rain."

"Well, rain or not, we've got more than our share now, and I thought you might want to know in case Bree's got family out west."

"Thanks, Howard. I owe you. Bree's folks live down by Lake Corpus Christi, but thanks for the heads-up. In the meantime, let me know if Two Valleys picks up again. I worry about Bree and Annabelle all on their own."

"Will do, Danno. You take care."

Talking with Howard had sobered him up. Bree didn't handle crises well. Even a bit of smoke in the air would make her anxious. But this conflagration could be a headache for a different reason. Senator Langston so often ridiculed climate change as contributing to an uptick in wildfires that this might pose a political problem for him. And even though the senator was no more qualified than Daniel's bartender to sit in Congress, the firm—and its clients—needed him to remain in office, particularly after paying so much to ensure his reelection.

Daniel went back to the party and pulled Haley aside. "We've got a situation."

She followed him out of the room. In the lobby he filled her in. She checked her phone and looked up at him. "The national news hasn't picked up on this yet."

"Which means...."

"Langston has a chance to be a hero."

Daniel nodded. Langston was no one's idea of a hero, but that wasn't the point. "It's a chance for him to show he cares about people without undercutting his position that global warming is a liberal fraud."

She smiled, her expression saying she admired his political acumen. Senator Langston had little concern for poor people caught up in wildfires, when they were probably all Democrats, but in politics appearance was everything. Here was a chance to reach out to independents and even some of his less delusional opponents without alienating his supporters. "The Senator needs to put out a statement," she concluded.

"And even get down there to shake hands with the first responders."

Haley's eyes lit up. "We could get ahead of this! We'll helicopter him to some burned-out ranch before the governor gets out of bed tomorrow! Bring some friendly press; put Langston in a hardhat; steer clear of climate talk and show how deeply he cares about *all* Texans."

Daniel was pleased he could pass this along. Haley's gratitude would make it easier to deal with the senator.

"And, you know what else?" she said.

He raised his eyebrows.

"I think—stay with me on this—you should come back to my

place right now. We'll line up the logistics and the press and put our heads together on a release. Without any distractions, that should be easy. Then maybe we can find some way to salvage this celebration."

"Pearce wouldn't like it if I left the party."

She grinned. "I think the gentleman doth protest too much. Business will always come first with Mr. Pearce. Just tell him what's up and that his young triggerman is on top of it."

She was right, of course, and he had to smile at her choice of words. He glanced at the breasts pushing against her suit jacket and the white blouse beneath with a sudden vision of "being on top of it." This night could be the culmination of more than just his homerun in Congress and a fat bonus; he had an overwhelming feeling he was about to be schooled by a seasoned pro.

Chapter Four

Bree Lazaro got off the call with her husband and bit her lip. They had won their vote, which would make Daniel happy. And despite the heat she looked forward to a great weekend. She just wished he could get home tonight. But he'd make it by lunchtime Friday. Anyway, PJ&H must be throwing a party. They put in so much effort; they needed to blow off steam, especially the young people who worked like dogs.

She had a good life. Their frugality—and his eventual success as a lawyer—paid off beyond their dreams. They had both grown up in Texas, but neither of them in a house as spectacular as this. It was totally modern, strikingly perched over the river and nestled in nature. Through the big kitchen window she watched the Guadalupe River flow by a hackberry tree. A canyon wren's descending chirp set her into a gentle rhythm, something that happened when she gazed hypnotically at the water.

She was reading Annabelle a book about local trees and flowers, which they would then try to find on adventure walks.

In spring the hillsides burst with bluebonnets and Indian paint-brush. In fall the banks of the river were painted with the rust-colored leaves of bald cypress trees. Upriver were stands of big-toothed maples and witch hazel, fern beds and lichen-covered limestone walls. In the Upper Valley they found a forest magical with ash juniper.

Daniel's bonus made them comfortable rebuilding the deck into something amazing. She reached for her new tablet to look for Adirondack chairs. Daniel's work in DC made all this possible; his time away was the price. He was the one who had to put up with a drab, cramped apartment during the week, and he never complained. She held up her end by making their home a refuge.

She decided to save the steaks defrosting on the counter for the next night. She would take Annabelle into the village for pizza. But first there was baking to do.

Jonah, their big dopey Bernese mountain dog, dozed. He may not be a herding dog, but he always kept track of his people. His position on the floor blocking most of the hallway meant Annabelle must be in her room.

Sure enough, her daughter was sitting on her rug, humming and "making art" with crayons and construction paper.

"Pardon me, miss artist," Bree said from the doorway.

Annabelle spun around to look up earnestly. "Is it time?"

"It sure is. If you'll get the bag of peaches in the pantry, we can start on a special cobbler for Papa."

"Oh boy!" Annabelle squealed and rushed past. It was funny and very cute. Annabelle wasn't much help cooking, but she filled the room with eagerness. Was there anything in the world as perfect as her beautiful six-year-old?

Next morning Bree was proud of herself for resisting a slice of the cobbler with her morning coffee. She got Annabelle dressed and piled her and Jonah into the car to head to the farmers' market. There would be summer squash and excellent corn, though she'd hold off on apples until Daniel was home and they could pick them at the orchard.

"Can we get a really big pumpkin?" Annabelle pleaded from the backseat.

Bree laughed. "It's a little early for pumpkins, sweetie, if we want them to last until Halloween."

"Oh...*please!*"

Bree looked in the mirror at her daughter. Her little pout was so delicious Bree wanted to eat it up. But she had to focus on driving. The road—the only way along this side of the river—was narrow and required both hands on the wheel and eyes straight ahead.

When they got out of the car, Bree threw on an over-large backpack—because she *always* filled it. To be like her mom, Annabelle also wore a backpack, hers with a glittery princess design. Jonah didn't need a leash, and it was much easier to let him wander than to hold on to him.

The market brought the village together. It filled Tanswego's small park along the river and one closed-off street. In open-sided tents farmers displayed fruits and vegetables that looked like bouquets of orange, red and green. Best of all, the radishes had come in. But the appearance of a pickup truck full of watermelons meant Annabelle would not let her leave without one. She considered telling her daughter they would buy a watermelon that fit in Annabelle's backpack.

The market—especially before the heat of the day—was the best place to catch up with neighbors, who were so spread along the river she rarely saw them. Her precocious daughter was a big favorite with the farmers, and she would inevitably find a school friend to play with and so give Bree a chance to gossip.

The talk that week was about a Greenpeace lawsuit to stop timber operations in the Upper Valley; hikers and campers—mostly from out of town—were trying to halt a new operation. She loved trees and wildlife, but it wasn't fair to interfere with peoples' livelihood when jobs were so scarce. Worse than that, some crazies had slashed tires on the logging trucks, and she heard outside agitators were hammering nails into the trees. Some poor logger with two kids and another on the way lost an eye when his chain saw broke on a nail. It was the same kind of thing Daniel had to deal with at work. He represented a developer building a resort in the Lower Valley, and it had been held up by protests. Just like with logging, it was beyond her how anyone could put saving a few trees over bringing in business and tax revenue.

On their way home they stopped at the community center in The Joshua Church on the hill above town. Pastor Vincent did so much for the community, and she tried to help whenever she could. She and Annabelle also attended church on Sundays. But Daniel would never come to services—his mother's religious fanaticism had soured him on organized religion. He did agree, though, that Annabelle should grow up as part of a spiritual community. He was also ready to help with church projects when he could, as long as he didn't have to sit through sermons.

"He'll come around of his own accord," the pastor told Bree with an inspirited smile when she apologized for Daniel's absence. She wondered at how graciously he accepted Daniel's recalcitrance and seemed genuinely to like him. So she put faith in the pastor's confidence. Daniel worked so hard these days; he deserved one morning in the week to sleep in.

They dropped off a bag of vegetables for the soup kitchen. Bree always had Annabelle help pick out the food, pay for it and deliver it, for her to learn that charity and service should be part of her life. Anyway, the people at the center were really nice, which made it a fun stop. Jonah loved to visit, too, because he always found scraps on the floor to devour—as if they never fed him at home.

Bree unloaded their donation and joked with two teenage volunteers. A deep voice from the kitchen called out, "Bree!

Annabelle!" and a large man emerged in a plaid shirt with an apron tied around his waist. "How are you two?"

Matt Reese was the father of Tyler, a classmate of Annabelle's. Tyler was sometimes Annabelle's "boyfriend" and sometimes not, depending on her daughter's mood. For that day the relationship seemed to be on, so the kids amused themselves playing with Jonah and the volunteers while Bree and Matt had coffee on a bench outside in the shade.

"We haven't seen you around," she said.

"Yeah, sorry, it's been really busy."

"What's up?"

"Well, did you hear about the sighting?"

"The what?"

"A Steller's sea eagle in the Lower Valley. It's incredible...." He stopped and smiled sheepishly. "I guess you're not fanatically into birds."

"No, I love birds, but what's a Steller's...?"

"It's a fabulous raptor, black with white shoulders and a bright orange beak. They estimate this one has a wingspan of eight feet."

"So it doesn't come from Texas?"

"Not even close. Probably flew across the Bering Strait from Siberia. You see, there's a thing called 'avian vagrancy,' where a bird veers way off course, beyond its normal habitat, and starts what can be an endless search for others of its kind. There are records of albatrosses living decades as vagabonds in the wrong hemisphere. Two years ago a bald eagle flew from North America to Japan.

"But, while avian vagrancy has existed through history, the warming planet is mucking up migratory patterns and making it more likely. And so yesterday they sighted a Steller's sea eagle from northeastern Asia. They're guessing it's the same one pho-tographed at Denali National Park last year; it's that rare. And it flew this far south and stopped here with all this smoke. This bird is lost and confused."

"Well," she said, "congratulations...I guess. Or is that for only for when you check a bird off on your personal life list?"

He grinned. "So you do know something about birding. But seriously, this vagrancy could be one more sign of how climate change is mucking everything up."

She smiled; he was so sincere.

He perked up. "Which gets back to what's been keeping me busy—besides watching birds. We've been fighting about land use in the valleys."

"Yeah, people were talking about that at the market."

"Right. Well, you know the Two Valleys Fire has taken out a swath of forest. In the Upper Valley it left a whole mountainside bare, and several other slopes had already been logged. That destabilizes everything and leaves loose soil ready to wash away, not to mention it destroys habitats for gray foxes and porcupines. And they're still at the logging, even with this fire not quite out. It's so damned frustrating people won't listen; they huddle together in their little houses, refusing to see the wolf at the door."

"But what can we do, really? Didn't the fire come from lightning?"

"So they say. But then they clearcut the other side of the river. And in the Lower Valley—forget about it—they throw up McMansions and guest lodges right up to the river and always want to build more. There's no way nature can fight the developers with all their lawyers and lobbyists."

Her smile was uneasy. She was sure Matt didn't know about Daniel's job; *he* rarely mentioned it to anyone in the village. And she avoided talking politics with Matt—as if she ever talked politics with anyone. It was her dumb mistake to ask why he was so busy.

"Well," she said, hoping to cut off the conversation, "it's great seeing you. Annabelle and I have to continue our errands, but we should get together. Let's arrange a playdate. Daniel will head back to Washington Monday morning, so any time after that."

"Sure thing," he said with the warm smile Bree always pictured when she imagined his face. He was a good man. Since his wife died years before, he had raised Tyler on his own—and he was a terrific kid, which said a lot about Matt.

There was nothing inappropriate about enjoying Matt's company. He was always nice, and the kids amused each other. If it felt sometimes like he was flirting, well, that was harmless and kind of fun. Anyway, it was Daniel's fault for being gone all the time.

"But hey," he said, as if the thought had just occurred to him, "we're in for a scorcher today, and Tyler made me promise we'd go to the swimming hole."

This was a favorite spot for families with young children because the backwater was deep enough for swimming—and it was out of earshot of the teenagers' hangout upriver.

Annabelle's eyes lit up, and she tugged at Bree's hand. "Can we, Momma? Please?"

"You have to!" Tyler said, appearing from nowhere to pile on.

Bree smiled resignedly at her daughter and at Matt. The kids were right; the temperature was already notching higher, and she didn't want to be shut up in air conditioning all day. "Okay," she said. "We'll go swim, but then we have to get home; we promised Papa a celebration lunch."

"What are you celebrating?" Matt asked.

She had put her foot in it again. "Oh, it's just something we do when Daniel's been away."

His expression was curious, but he let it drop. "Well, then," he said, "we'll see you both in an hour or so?"

By the time Bree and Annabelle returned home, it was really hot outside. Bree cranked up the air conditioning to make the house comfortable when Daniel arrived, which according to his text would be around one o'clock.

She unpacked the groceries and did some lunch preparation.

Annabelle appeared in the kitchen with her bathing suit on, more or less. It was adorable. "Well, I think we'd better reverse these straps," Bree said, adjusting the suit.

They drove up past the village to the makeshift parking area near the swimming hole. Fifty feet through the woods a wide section of the river was overhung with a canopy of old-growth cypress. Thick foliage provided shade from the relentless sunshine and turned the river green with its reflection. The swimming hole was especially placid as if, like everything else, the river was lulled into slow motion by the heat of the day.

"Here they are!" Matt shouted.

His son's face lit up. The half dozen other people lounging or swimming looked up with interest.

Bree was embarrassed to be the center of attention, even in this small group of neighbors, but she forgot her self-consciousness when she saw how happy the kids were to see each other after barely an hour apart. She sat on a towel before removing her T-shirt to reveal a one-piece bathing suit. She worked hard to stay in shape and knew she looked good but she wouldn't make a show of it. It was, nonetheless, hard to miss Matt's appreciative glance or to deny she'd have felt slighted without it. He looked pretty good in a bathing suit himself and kind of cute turning those broad shoulders away to pretend he was watching the kids.

She looked at him wistfully. What would it be like to have a big, warm body like Matt's to snuggle up to every night?

But what was she thinking? Daniel was her husband, and in her family people got married and *stayed* married. And how could she complain about her life? Daniel was a good man. He loved her and was helpful and thoughtful. He had stuck with her through her miscarriage and helped bring her back to life, and now he doted on Annabelle. And he was a respected and successful lawyer, in fact a very handsome, successful lawyer. She always felt proud to be with him when they went to one of the old dance halls near Tanswego. She was blessed a man like him loved her and supported their family. If she had to get by without him sometimes, that was a small sacrifice. Flirtations and minor regrets amounted to nothing weighed against the great things in her life.

The kids splashed at the water's edge. Bree kept a close watch over her daughter. If Daniel were there, he'd be giving her a swimming lesson, but Bree much preferred that she play on solid ground.

The children obliged and settled down on the bank to an indecipherable game involving sticks and stones. Jonah laid in the shade, worn out from the heat. Bree and Matt sat with their feet dangling in the water.

Matt looked over at Bree propped up on her elbows. He had only known the Lazaros a year, since the kids had class together, but thought from the start how lucky Daniel was. Matt was also fortunate, in a way, that Daniel worked in Washington and so was usually gone during the week. This allowed Matt to spend time with Bree and at least pretend they could be more than friends. She might not know much about birds or conservation, but she was really nice and so pretty he was sometimes at a loss trying to make casual conversation without staring.

Trying to think of something other than how she looked in a bathing suit, he said, "The river's running low."

"From the heat this summer?"

"And no rain. Streams are almost dry."

She coughed, probably from the smoke in the air but possibly also to signal she was tired of talking about the weather. He shifted gears. "You graduated from Texas, right?"

A surprised look came over her face. "That's right. My English degree was all I needed to become a best-selling author of children's books."

"You..." he started to say as his eyes brightened, but she interrupted.

"No, I never actually wrote a book. Or let's say I've written books in my head but never took it any further."

"Why?"

"Well, honestly, I never had the time. At first we needed the money, so I found work as a teacher, the early grades." She laughed. "I never got to write books for kids, but I sure *read* a lot of books to them."

He smiled to encourage her to continue.

"I'm happy right now to be a mom. I love our house, which takes a lot of work, and things are going really well. But as to how it happened, the short version is I met Daniel in college. In our junior year there was a mess when his father died. His mother got kind of wacko over some religious leader and cut Daniel off. Then we got married, but he had always wanted to go to law school. So, I taught while he went back to school. After he got his degree, I kept working because we could still barely meet expenses and pay off our loans. Then I got pregnant."

"So, this is what, like seven years ago?"

"More like nine. Then Daniel got a great new job, which helped our finances. But..." She paused, looking troubled. "We lost that baby. It was bad for a long time, but Daniel pulled me through it...and two years later Annabelle arrived, and she's been our whole life ever since."

Jonah trotted up and shook the water from his coat, sending them scattering. They came up laughing. The dog looked at them curiously and trotted back to the kids.

"Well," she said laughing, "I should say Annabelle and Jonah are our whole life."

"Well, you've obviously moved on from those lean times, given that fabulous house."

She smiled demurely. "Since Daniel moved to his new job, everything's been great."

"Wait!" he said urgently but quietly as he rose to his feet. "There," he said, pointing down the river. "In the tall cypress."

"What?"

"The Steller's eagle!"

A huge bird rose from the trees, hovered as if motionless and then swooped down with a deep barking cry. It splashed into the river and then rose and carried off a big fish.

Everyone had jumped up to look for the source of the sound. But Bree couldn't get Annabelle to turn around and look before the bird disappeared into the trees.

Chapter Five

Jonah's deep bark greeted Daniel when he opened the door to River House. Before he could even set down his suitcase, Annabelle was hugging his legs, and Bree planted a kiss on his cheek. He dropped his bag and lifted his daughter high in the air. She squealed, Jonah barked again and Bree stepped back, filling the room with her laughter.

Let down on her feet, Annabelle rushed to her room to get her latest painting. He took advantage of the lull to hug his wife, trying hard not to show the guilt he felt about Haley. For the entire flight home he had girded himself not to let this show, not to let his lapse infect his marriage. This was the first time he had been unfaithful, and it would be a one-time thing. The important thing was he was home now with his beautiful wife and daughter in their fabulous house; this was the payoff for everything the job took out of him. Besides, he hadn't meant to do it; it was part of his job to grease the wheels by keeping close to the senator's aide.

Although, if he was honest, spending the night with Haley had been exhilarating, at least until the sun came up on his guilt.

"You look exhausted," Bree said. "Did Branston make you stay up smoking those awful cigars?"

"You know how he can be." It was best to keep his responses as honest as possible. He had left the victory party early and taken a car to Haley's apartment. There she poured them each a stiff drink, and he got started on the press release for Senator Langston while she made calls to set up transportation and line up reporters. Then they had put their heads together to polish the press release.

The senator would call on all Texans to put aside their differences in the face of the tragic wildfire.

Langston wouldn't address the cause for the proliferation of wildfires. Anyone would expect the land to be susceptible to burning after the multiple heatwaves with temperatures as high as the Dust Bowl years of the 1930s.

It was hard to miss the damage caused by excessive heat when the yellow Indian grass all around Tanswego turned brown. But heatwaves and droughts were inexorable parts of nature. Logging and drilling were not at fault. People had to stop pointing fingers over what we couldn't control and focus on fighting fires.

After they finished the release, Haley had called the senator to read it to him. He was still at the party and too inebriated to take it in, but he trusted her to manage things. He also reluctantly agreed to the appearance in Texas she set up for the next morning.

She instructed a staffer to make sure their boss got home and caught the early flight to El Paso. Then she posted the press release on the senator's official website and sent it—with her signature personal notes—to her reporter contacts.

She worked like a machine, and soon finished her work, shut her laptop and told him to pour himself another drink while she changed out of work clothes. She returned dressed for another kind of activity altogether.

Had this been his cue to bolt for the door? Hadn't he realized this was insane?

He at least had to finish his drink and so took a hard swallow. She only sipped, watching him with an amused smile. She also kept staring into his eyes, as if she were reading his thoughts and saying it was useless to resist. He stopped thinking about his life, his marriage, how he'd feel if Annabelle's husband someday did this to her. It all faded while he lived in the moment, a moment that stretched nearly until dawn.

But Daniel needed to put the night with Haley out of his mind. He finished his shower focused on the positives: the win in the Senate, the bonus coming in, the new deck. In shorts and an old college tank top against the heat of the day, he came out to the kitchen and sat to a sumptuous lunch.

Annabelle giggled and barely touched her food. Bree only nibbled. But Daniel made up for them both, ravenously digging into his first meal in twenty-four hours. While he ate, Bree showed him screenshots of deck furniture, and they discussed whether to have an architect prepare blueprints for the deck or just have a contractor work from her rough sketch.

Finishing his coffee, Daniel took the sketch in hand and led Bree down the stairway to the deck. Half-way down he stopped and sniffed the air. "Howard said the Two Valleys Fire is pretty much contained, but it smells like we're in for a smokey weekend."

"I know," she said, obviously disappointed. "On the river this morning you could smell it in the air. Oh, and I meant to tell you: I saw a Steller's eagle!"

"A what? Wait, how do you know what kind of eagle it was?"

"Oh, Matt Reese was at the swimming hole—you know, Tyler's dad? Apparently, he's a bird nut."

Matt was the single father of Annabelle's classmate, big and fairly good-looking. Daniel had on occasion wondered whether this good-old-boy's friendliness had more to do with Daniel's wife than his daughter.

"Anyway," Bree said, as if to change the subject, "I was planning a picnic for this afternoon up at Enchanted Rock. You know Annabelle loves it up there."

He coughed, still thinking about Bree at the swimming hole with Matt but letting it go for now. "Well, I guess we could hibernate inside."

"Sounds like fun," she said sarcastically.

He looked over. Her pout was as cute as ever—it was easy to see where Annabelle got it. Sometimes it seemed Bree's biggest concern was whether they could go out and play. "Well, what then?"

"We could drive down to my parents' house," she said hopefully. "You know the folks would love it, and you like it there."

"Assuming they don't have smoke, too."

"I'll find out." She jumped up to look for her phone.

Bree was very close with her parents and brother. She often spoke with them on the phone and loved nothing better than getting the whole family together. Daniel had to admit he was envious, having no siblings of his own and being estranged from his mother. And visiting the in-laws wasn't bad. Her parents' house had a comfortable guest wing, her mother spent most of the day cooking or baking, and her father didn't blink when Daniel tore through his liquor cabinet. Living was easy outside the small town of Foswell, unless of course, Bree's brother Pete was home.

Pete enjoyed baiting Daniel about his job. "How can you work for those greedy bastards?" he said last Christmas as they shared a joint on the front porch.

"You don't get it, do you?" Daniel said, his discernment enfeebled by the weed or too much bourbon. "If lawyers only represented the good guys, there'd be no adversarial system and no justice."

"So you represent scumbags out to destroy the earth because, hey, somebody's got to do it? And, of course, they pay well, with all the money they make fucking up the world."

Daniel shook his head. "I earn my pay, and I take care of my family. You might try that."

That was harsh; Daniel knew he'd gone too far as soon as it came out of his mouth. Pete stiffened and left the porch.

Bree's brother had been divorced two years before by a sweet woman who believed she could get him to make something of himself. Instead, he drifted in and out of colleges, in and out of jobs and, of most concern, into the sway of one fringe group or another, most recently eco-nuts. Daniel had seen how blind devotion could debilitate a person when his mother joined her new church, and he worried at how Pete applauded anyone who spray-painted a fur coat or chained himself to a tractor. This was just bravado, though, as Pete wasn't about to put himself in danger or go to any great inconvenience. But his vitriolic rhetoric was still worrisome. Daniel hoped he wouldn't be talked into doing something stupid that would come back at Pete and devastate his parents and sister.

But what could you do for a guy so out of touch with reality? Daniel couldn't talk to Bree about it. "You're always attacking him," would be her reflexive response, along with, "He's had a rough time," and almost always, "He *is* my brother."

But he had to think about the larger issue. If Pete got involved with eco-terrorists, Daniel would have to alert Joe Coulder. Joe had been his classmate in college and was now at the FBI, so Pearce had assigned Daniel to handle day-to-day communications with the Bureau through him. Ever since the "Green Scare" in the mid-2000s, the firm had shared information with law enforcement about environmental activists. PJ&H had credibility with officials by pushing to classify radical groups like Earth Liberation Front as the nation's *leading* domestic terrorist threat and adding the destruction of ecologically harmful infrastructure and economic interests to the legal definition of "terrorism."

Joe had passed Daniel information to help win a fracking lawsuit in Arkansas but had made clear he was stepping over the line in sharing the information and expected Daniel to reciprocate if he learned anything the FBI could use. So, Daniel always looked for ways to pay Joe back.

It was ludicrous to think Pete had access to the people running one of these organizations, but Daniel still might learn something from him to pass along to Joe. He'd have to do this without involving Pete, of course. Bree would never forgive him if he put her brother on law enforcement's radar. Her parents also would find that hard to forget. It wouldn't matter that Pete had always been a screw up and was flirting with the far-left fringe; he was family, which would make Daniel the villain.

He would see Joe at their regular Wednesday poker game; Daniel could make up his mind then about what to pass along. And, realistically, Pete was a blowhard; his dalliance with the environmentalists likely would come to nothing. He'd tire of playing eco-warrior and move on to some other distraction, the same way he had lost interest in the broad social justice agenda the year before and his marriage before that.

The drive to Bree's parents' house took a couple of hours. It mostly went smoothly, Annabelle watching a video with earphones over her head, Jonah sleeping and Bree chattering about their neighbors and reading Daniel articles from a magazine. But then she read one bitter-sweet story of a long-distance affair, which left her pensive.

"What's the matter, Babe?" he said.

"It's just…sometimes I feel like I'm living half a life with you. When you're home everything's perfect. I sleep like a log and wake up eager for the day. I'm at peace, except in the back of my mind I'm counting the hours until you're gone again."

"You know I have to work out of DC," he said in exasperation. "We've talked about this; I don't want Annabelle growing up in the city, and you always wanted to move back home to Texas."

"I know. I'm being selfish. Don't pay any attention to me."

"Look," he said, "this new client, Surefit, has broken ground on a development in the Lower Valley, and that will mean more trips home for me, not to mention it will put me in position to call my own shots at the firm."

"I know," she said, doing a fair job of hiding her frown. "Is the county giving you a hard time about the project?"

"Far from it. They suggested expanding the resort footprint."

"But you'll still have to spend time here to see it through?"

"Yes, love," he said gently.

It was hard to ignore when Bree sulked behind a brave face. And, of course, it was not ideal for him to be away during most workweeks, but what choice did he have? The job was in Washington, and their home was in Texas.

She should be satisfied with the life he had given her, their beautiful daughter, their fantastic house, the freedom from money concerns. His mother certainly would have traded her life for Bree's. She had obsessed over status. When his father managed the gypsum mine, employing men from town, they topped the social order, but she still wasn't satisfied. She constantly pushed him to move them onto a higher stage, to San Antonio or even Dallas. Her ambition kept him from ever being truly content.

Then disaster struck when pollutants contaminated the groundwater and the EPA closed the mine. The suits in the corner offices made his father the scapegoat, even though he was the only one trying to come clean about the accident. Then the left-wing media painted him as an environmental monster, which wouldn't have mattered except their neighbors also blamed him for losing their jobs. The family became pariahs, taking hits from all sides.

Before that he had always attended church with his parents,

which was as much a community as a spiritual activity. But after the scandal broke, the congregation shunned them. During those dark days, his mother joined a new church and started putting it before everything, including her family. This left his father no one to turn to except Daniel, and for the first time he really opened up to his son. He told of his regret about not continuing his education, which would have given him options beyond running a mine. He wished he had studied law after majoring in engineering. A law degree would have prepared him to deal with the executives or to patent some of the innovations he came up with over the years.

His father's remorse stuck with Daniel; this is what drove him to apply to law school, even when he and Bree were just scraping by. Jack Wolford also helped out after the funeral. Uncle Jack had been his father's friend since they were kids, and he was the only person in town to stick by him. At the time of the suicide, Wolford was serving his second term in the House of Representatives. He pushed Daniel to follow his father's dream and wrote a recommendation that got him into Georgetown Law School. Then he hired Daniel as a legislative aide.

It was sad Daniel's good fortune had come too late for his father. Not that Daniel had been any help while his dad was still alive. He did nothing, really, to show him he was a good father with every reason to go on living. Like everyone else, Daniel had only thought about how it all affected *him*. So the gentle man who raised him, taught him to fish and shielded him from his mother's temper, was left alone to take his life—opting for an overdose of prescription drugs to avoid making a mess. He had done what he could for the community and the land, but where did it get him? There was a life lesson there, about taking care of your own, making sure you had a seat at the table, and leaving everyone else to look out for themselves.

Chapter Six

Peter Morrison had a job in an electronic vehicle factory near Austin. Blue collar work hadn't been the plan, but he never seemed to catch a break.

He had to give up on college after bad experiences at three different schools. Then a friend got him a job driving eighteen-wheelers. The quiet time on the road brought peace but also pain in his lower back, and it was hell on his social life. So he tried making it as a nature photographer. He managed to sell a few shots to magazines, and his parents fronted the money to open a gallery. But foot traffic was not what he'd hoped for. Then the greedy landlord raised the rent. In the end there was just too much bullshit to deal with instead of just taking pictures.

The one good thing coming from the gallery fiasco was meeting Sally. She loved his photos and convinced him to keep at it while finishing his degree. So he enrolled at his fourth college, they got married and spent a summer lost in love. But school again didn't work out. He finished his junior year, barely, but couldn't stand sitting through more classes; the professors were a pain in the ass, always acting like they knew everything. Instead, he found a job in residential construction.

He was happy working with his hands, but he couldn't avoid the look of disappointment in his wife's eyes. That was the beginning of the end for them. They floundered along for another two years and then she divorced him. They had no children or anything of value but a couple of cars, so the split was simple. But it made him so depressed he got into a fight with his foreman and lost his job. That got him blacklisted with other contractors. He was left with nowhere to go and had to move back home.

Those days were hard on his self-esteem. But two years ago he found work in the factory. The job was tiring and repetitive but it paid enough for him to move into his own place. No matter how comfortable his parents' house was, he felt like a loser living at home at twenty-seven years old.

Now on his own, he found it was a pleasure coming back to visit his parents. His family and childhood home were foundations that stood against the winds that had blown all his buildings away. He also liked seeing Bree, and his niece was a doll. Daniel was okay too, in short doses, though he was the type who'd wear a blazer and hard shoes to a barbecue.

The factory job was a turning point in another way, too. A guy on the assembly line named Carson became a friend. They started spending time together after work, and on weekends would hike in the woods. Carson was passionate about nature. He really knew about trees and birds. And then on a hike one afternoon they came upon a new logging site.

"Those timber companies are like cancer," Carson spat out. "We should spike the trees."

"What do you mean?"

"It's called 'monkeywrenching,' sabotaging bulldozers or lighting up tool sheds. You hammer in a big nail to fuck up their equipment when they cut down the tree. Or you can spike the tree higher up to screw with the sawmill."

"You'd really do that?"

Carson nodded. "Would do; have done." He looked hard into Pete's eyes. "Listen, dude, you can sit by and watch the world go to shit or you can stand up against the man."

"But what if you're caught?"

"You pay the price. It's past time to put on your big-boy pants and stop thinking only about yourself."

Pete had never met anyone willing to sacrifice himself to a cause. This was not like those prigs at college whose great contribution to the world was to stay up late and talk. Talk only got you so far. Carson was a man of action, which was what Pete wanted to be.

"I could help with that," Pete said tentatively.

Carson smiled warmly. "You know, I had a feeling you'd turn out to be one of the good guys. I think maybe you should come meet some friends of mine. You know Chuck Harris; he introduced me to these people. He even mentioned maybe inviting you along."

The next week Carson and Harris brought Pete to a "book club meeting" at a cottage outside town. "One thing, though," Carson said before they picked up Harris. "These people know Chuck as 'Ranger'; some of them use code names to make it harder for big brother to track them."

Pete felt like he was joining a secret society. And even though there appeared to be no hierarchy to the group or ceremony, they did start the meeting with everyone detailing the evasive routes they took to get there—which explained why Carson had driven in circles on the way. Then, over pizza and beer, they talked about environmental activism.

One man visiting from Dallas introduced himself as Assisi. He wore an old cowboy hat that looked like it had done some real work over long, dark hair just turning gray. He had a disarming smile and looked closely at each of them as if trying to etch their faces into his memory.

When Assisi had the attention of a few people, he began talking about the threat to local wildlife from logging.

"We all care about endangered species," Harris said, "but what about protecting people's jobs? My brother's a logger, and it's the only good job he's ever had."

Assisi looked sympathetic. "What's your name, mate?"

"Ranger."

"Well, Ranger, the *real* tragedy is that we live in a society where a man is forced to destroy old-growth trees just to feed his family. But there's a bigger picture; call it 'deep ecology.' Nature has an inherent value, beyond its utility to people. Nature *must* survive. We need to rip out all trace of human intervention in large swaths of land and let nature be. James Lovelock theorized that the planet is a single living organism he called 'Gaia,' which for eons righted itself after all manner of disruptions. But the appearance of humans, in just one million-year blip on the four and a half eons since Earth was formed, might destroy it all."

Most everyone in the house was listening to this conversation. The faces showed general sympathy, but Assisi seemed to sense doubt. "I just ask you to keep an open mind. Think about these issues, and for God's sake, keep watching. The worst you can do is become complacent, because big-money interests will suck the country dry."

"And we should blow up bulldozers," Ranger said.

Assisi turned to him. "Now, hold on. No one said anything about blowing things up. We might hope for mechanical failure in those big, belching instruments of destruction, but there is plenty we can do without violence. We're trying to preserve, not destroy."

Pete was intrigued, but intimidated. Did this guy travel around on his own, or was there an organization behind him? Anyway,

Assisi was obviously smart and acted like he expected them to listen to him. At the same time, he had a disarming way that made you trust him. Before Assisi left, he told them to look forward to another visit from a man who would open their eyes about the calamity nearly upon us. He sounded like John the Baptist preparing the way for the Messiah.

Three weeks later two guests from out of town joined the book club meeting. The man introduced himself as Eco and his partner as Verde. It seemed his reputation preceded him because no one even cracked a smile at how his name sounded made up to fit an environmental activist. Pete wondered if, like Assisi and Eco and even Ranger, he should adopt a made-up name.

Eco was probably thirty-five, tall and wiry with an easy smile. What most impressed Pete was how well he spoke. Then there was Eco's companion, a solemn beauty. She watched and never smiled, but her piercing green eyes mesmerized him.

Unlike the usual gathering, where people wandered through the house and conversations overlapped, everyone quietly paid attention to Eco, as if *he* were the leader of this group.

Eco looked around the room slowly, engaging each of his listeners before he said, "Welcome to the sixth mass extinction of biodiversity. Oh, and we should take a moment to mark that 2022 may tie the record for the fifth hottest year on record, *all eight* of which have occurred in this decade! So, what are we doing about it?"

The room fell silent.

"Sea levels are rising," he went on. "Glaciers are melting. Extreme weather is killing people. But though these changes bear the footprint of human-induced climate change, what are we doing to sound the alarm?"

Again there was no answer.

"Mainstream environmental organizations miss the point. They enable people to ease their conscience by making piddling donations, used to pay salaries and fund marketing machines to garner more donations. They post newsletters focused on making industrial capitalism more sustainable when they should be questioning capitalism itself. The radical green movement has to move past this impotence. The time for talk is past; what we desperately need now is direct action: civil disobedience, tree-sits, blockades, disabling tools of destruction."

"Blowing up bulldozers," Ranger volunteered once again.

Eco eyed him with interest and then turned back to the room. "But I've got some good news. The Hambach Forest occupation, which for ten years has involved hundreds of partisans fighting coal mining in an ancient German forest, has launched a public awareness effort called '*Waldspaziergang,*' or 'walk through the forest.' A nature guide leads hundreds of people on a visit each month to the occupation. This has brought needed attention to our brothers and sisters on the front lines. We salute our German comrades and are inspired by their success."

"Now, I haven't attended any of your meetings before, but I suspect you have spent some time debating tactics. I've taken part in these discussions all over the world. I'm sure some of you believe the best we can do is work through mainstream politics, vote out of office industry tools like Bo Langston and Governor Chism. Well, defeating a crooked puppet like Langston would certainly be a good thing—assuming he's not replaced by an equally corrupt apologist for the oil industry—but it's not enough. Look at commercial whaling. Calls to end this inhumane practice fall on deaf ears. What we need is more groups like Sea Shepherd, which took its boats into the fight to disrupt Japanese whaling—at least until the exploiters upgraded to military technology to mask their genocide.

"Face it, folks, if humanity doesn't pull it together to meet the Paris Accord goal of limiting global warming below two degrees Celsius over pre-industrial levels, the planet is doomed."

"How can just two degrees matter?" Ranger said, sounding like a stooge.

Eco looked at him condescendingly but said gently. "The last drop of five degrees Celsius in the Earth's temperature a hundred thousand years ago brought on an ice age. A two-degree rise in the oceans, the generally cooler two-thirds of the Earth's surface, means a four or five-degree rise over land, especially inland or up north. Five degrees Celsius is about nine degrees Fahrenheit—for those Americans who prefer to digest their apocalyptic scenarios in familiar terms. If we had an average mean temperature five to nine degrees above normal, we'd all be dead."

While Kristof took on his "Eco" persona to captivate people with stories and statistics, Mia assessed the audience for potential recruits. How convinced were they that action needed to be taken? How devoted to the cause were those who stepped forward? Were any of them too volatile to control?

But like everyone else, she listened to Kristof's presentation. This was the first she'd heard about the "nature tours" in Hambach Forest. The news was encouraging, although it brought back a dark time in another ancient European forest, her harsh initiation to the hazards of standing up for the planet.

She had been just sixteen. She idolized her brother Metica, who was four years older and a university student active in a campus environmental group. She had attended meetings at his school and helped paint protest posters to hang around the city. Then she gradually moved into more direct action. They snuck into parking lots to pour sand in tractor gas tanks and hiked through the forest destroying the tags marking ground to be logged. It was exciting to be doing something righteous that made Metica proud of her.

When the group decided to document illegal logging by filming a documentary in the Dealu Negru Forest, Mia jumped at the chance to be part of a serious struggle alongside her brother and learn about filmmaking at the same time. But someone alerted the logging company. Thugs in ski masks descended on the film crew, broke up their equipment and beat them with truncheons. Friends landed in jail when the police arrested *them* instead of the perpetrators. Metica went to the hospital and two days later died from his injuries. Her bottomless despair still lingered at the corner of her thoughts.

Mia came out of that attack dedicated to avenging her brother by taking up the mantle of his activism. Unlike him, however, she would not be quick to trust others who claimed to share her goals. Someone had betrayed their group, leading to the failure of their mission and Metica's death. She would not let that happen to her. Even now, thoroughly committed to Kristof, she knew the only person she could trust completely was herself.

Still, Anthro needed to spread information and recruit supporters, so these speaking appearances were necessary. She only hoped the security measures she had introduced—code names, diligence about GPS tracking, avoiding being photographed— would keep them safe.

At this meeting it was hard to miss Pete. He wore an eager look and a green T-shirt with a picture of a globe under the acronym "E.A.R.T.H." This kind of person—with his bad haircut and worn blue jeans—could be useful for tasks others avoided.

Another man named "Ranger" worked as a recruiter. But he seemed almost *too* eager to launch into direct action, and his use of an assumed name, even before joining Anthro's inner core, was suspicious.

Pete came away from this meeting convinced he finally had a calling: the Earth was in trouble, and people like him needed to join the fight. Talking with Carson at work the next week he learned Eco was, in fact, the leader of a group called Anthro, which coordinated acts of resistance. Carson couldn't say anything about plans for direct action, which made Pete suspect he wasn't really part of the group. But he turned Pete on to *Monkey Wrench*, an Anthro newsletter that publicized toxic corporate activities and promoted responsive actions. He read every back edition he could find on the internet.

Chapter
Seven

At the end of the previous summer his sister had told Pete about Daniel's work for the oil companies. She was proud of his success, while Pete was repulsed. And, after he heard Eco speak, he had to confront his brother-in-law. It was Christmas at his parents' house, and Daniel's response was to throw Pete's divorce in his face, as if *that* was comparable. Oil processed and sold by his clients was destroying the Earth, but Daniel still thought he was some kind of husband of the year. Was he thinking of his daughter's future when he helped huge companies rape the planet?

Through the winter and into the spring Pete had followed Anthro's activities through *Monkey Wrench* and continued to attend book club meetings. He yearned to get involved directly, but they didn't seem to trust him. Then he realized Daniel's connection to the oil industry could be his ticket in. His brother-in-law might have information he could pass along to Anthro.

When in June his mom said his sister was coming down for the weekend because of the smoke, Pete drove down to join them.

He would make it up with Daniel and steer clear of politics while pumping him for something to give Eco.

When Daniel parked in his in-laws' driveway, Pete greeted them with big smiles. He hugged Bree and twirled Annabelle in the air. He even pulled Daniel in for a manly hug.

"How was the trip?" he asked cheerfully. "Not too much traffic?"

Annabelle had run off to Grandma, followed by Bree, leaving Daniel alone with Pete. Daniel couldn't discern what was up with his brother-in-law. Why was he suddenly effusive instead of abrasive? He even insisted on carrying the two suitcases. But peace in the house was the most to hope for, so Daniel was fine with his brother-in-law playing porter. Time would tell whether he was also over his eco-warrior schtick, which would be best for everyone.

Daniel, Bree, Annabelle and Jonah spent the weekend. Bree's father, Ed, was a retired engineer who had become a gentleman farmer. He was generous and hospitable and had always been close with Bree. She called him "Papa," the same way Annabelle addressed Daniel. This was cute in his five-year-old but in Bree it reinforced how she still seemed like a little girl, which was both enchanting and surprising given the lean times they had navigated together. But he envied Bree's closeness with her parents, especially her father. She had been unusually insistent they name their baby for him if it had been a boy.

Julia, Bree's mom, was sweet, if a little kooky. She fawned over her children, and her lone grandchild could do no wrong. While she spent an inordinate amount of time in the kitchen, she was at best a middling cook and no one ever had the heart to tell her. More importantly, she was always warm and nurturing, and spread her love in a nonjudgmental way that made Daniel wonder how his life would have been different with a mother like that.

Still, Daniel felt uncomfortable opening up to her, and tried to keep their conversations to cooking and gardening...and talking about how extraordinary her granddaughter was.

When Bree was a toddler, her parents had built a standard ranch house outside Foswell. Since then they had tacked on a second story, an expanded kitchen and a spacious guest suite. This gave everyone plenty of space and allowed Daniel to sleep in while activities bustled elsewhere in the house. He also enjoyed fishing with Annabelle in a nearby stream while Jonah chased butterflies. They rarely caught anything, but that was just as well as Annabelle couldn't stand seeing a fish on a hook. She liked holding the pole, though, and talking to the fish to lure them to bite. Fishing with her was the perfect break from DC politics.

That afternoon Daniel and Annabelle walked to the stream, but they contented themselves with tossing sticks into the water and watching them race downstream. The way back to the house passed through a field crowded with purple and blue flowers.

"Why don't you pick some of those for Grandma?" he said.

Her eyes lit up, and she jumped to it.

Once she had gathered a bouquet, a thought raced across her face, and she shouted, "Momma, too!"

He laughed. She handed him the bouquet and bent down to pick more, careful to select perfect stems. She was growing up too fast, and he felt bad at having missed too much of it. Bree had done a great job raising this earnest little girl, but was leaving her to do so much on her own another way he was a bad husband?

There was no smoke in Foswell, but it was still hot, so on Sunday after church, Ed packed the gang into his pickup to go for a swim in Lake Corpus Christi. At earlier times Ed had taken Daniel out on the lake in a friend's boat. Catfish ran large in the lake and made a delicious meal. But this day was for relaxing with the family.

Daniel had been a competitive swimmer as a kid and still

enjoyed a workout when he could find a pool and the time. It was also important for his daughter to learn to swim.

"She's too young," Bree complained. She could hardly swim herself and stood nervously on the bank while Daniel paddled out into the lake with Annabelle clutching his back.

"It's for her own good," he said, stopping where he could still stand. He held his daughter out in front of him. "She lives over a river; what if she falls in?"

He put his hands beneath Annabelle. She began to splash about. He reminded her how to kick and stroke with her arms, which she seemed to enjoy. "Besides," he called out to Bree, "it's fun."

When Annabelle tired, Daniel delivered her to her mother's anxious arms and got in twenty minutes of hard swimming himself. Later, he walked the shoreline with Bree and Jonah and played in the sand with his daughter. Finally, he pushed an air mattress into the calm water and lay in the sunshine, where he would happily have stayed all afternoon if someone would just keep bringing him cold beers.

Pete maintained his new cheerful persona throughout the day, playing with Annabelle and kidding his sister. He even sought Daniel out to talk, although he didn't seem to know what he wanted to say. "Don't you love this wide-open nature?" he said as if to spark a response.

When Daniel just smiled and nodded, Pete took another tack. "Bree says your work is going well."

This got Daniel's attention; he didn't want to reprise their falling out the prior Christmas and so chose his words carefully. "Yeah, well, it keeps me busy and so far they haven't kicked me out."

Pete smirked. "You're modest. My sister says you pulled off some big win?"

"We've been doing well; it's true. But lawyer talk is boring. Tell me what's up with you. How's the job?"

"It pays the bills. But what I'm finding more interesting is the outdoors, you know, learning about the woods."

"Hunting?"

"Mostly hiking. I've got a friend who can identify almost any plant or tree. He's been teaching me. He's really in tune with nature."

Daniel hoped Pete was truly just enjoying the outdoors. But with Pete, you never knew; his motivation typically involved a woman or a hair-brained scheme or both. When a friend of his came down with Long COVID at the start of the pandemic, Pete had shifted from virulent anti-vaxxer to champion of efforts to fight the virus. He seemed to have no short-term memory, and whatever position he took at the moment became his passion.

"Do you camp?" Daniel said. "There are some great secluded spots near Austin."

"We mostly day hike close to the city. My buddy's more interested in finding where people are screwing things up than in just spending time outdoors."

"A nature lover who doesn't care for nature?" Daniel asked sarcastically.

"Just the opposite. He looks for threats to the land and...well, it's complicated. He's in a just fight, but I can't really explain."

This mentor-like friend of Pete's sounded like something other than a hiker. Pete's vague description of this guy, along with his abrupt shift from attacking Daniel's work to eagerly inquiring about the details, suggested he could be up to something risky.

Chapter Eight

Daniel barely had time to repack before the car came to take him to the airport. By lunchtime Monday he was back in the office and up to speed. Pearce had put him in charge of efforts to promote an oil pipeline connecting the shale fields in British Columbia with the Gulf of Mexico. He would have to deal with the usual suspects: Indians, eco-doomsayers and over-regulation advocates on one side and business imperatives on the other.

"The pipeline should be like any other large public works," Pearce said, "like subways or roads. The Canadians have no problem with this; the US government needs to follow their example and just condemn the land. Parochial interests about where your ancestors hunted or saving some obscure ferret cannot outweigh free market principles. How else do we fight countries with no qualms about optimizing *their* natural resources?"

Daniel was all in for this. In addition to the business case for building the pipeline, any opposition put a substantial number of construction jobs at risk, along with the threat of villainizing businesspeople and hindering technological advance.

He loved the buzz of the team digging into a new job: people rushing around, consulting and debating, drinking too much coffee, wolfing down delivery food. And he enjoyed recounting the day's small victories at the bar after work.

He still had to manage the relationship with Senator Bo Langston, which meant interfacing with Haley. But he was resolved not to screw up again. They had to work together, so they needed to maintain a professional relationship, and that was all. When they next spoke on the phone, he said, "I feel like I should apologize if I led you to think we could have some kind of personal relationship...."

Her guffaw interrupted him. "Sorry," she said, regaining control. "Don't apologize. We had a moment; we moved on. It's no more than a dim memory."

This should have been a relief, and it was, but it was also insulting she could hardly remember having sex with him. But Haley never actually forgot anything, certainly not their night together. He wondered how she *really* felt, but knew he shouldn't pursue it. It was best just to be back to a friendly working relationship—and they did work well together.

Wednesday the following week she called again. "I want to give you those papers," she said, "but I won't trust them to a messenger."

The documents detailed payments to Langston's super PAC—the kind of sensitive materials they never copied or sent electronically. It made most sense for PJ&H to keep them secure in its private offices because their whole arrangement would blow up if they became public. Daniel would lock them in Pearce's safe, along with recordings and photographs Haley and Langston knew nothing about, which all together was insurance against the senator or his cronies ever turning against the firm. Pearce was the *last* person to let someone throw him under the bus.

Mid-afternoon Pearce's assistant summoned Daniel to the boss's office. Daniel obeyed the command, bristling at this typical, pejorative treatment by his "partner."

"There's a shit show with your associate," Pearce said with a look of revulsion.

"Nell?"

"No, the tall kid, the one who tries to get by on his goofy smile."

"Jake Gambol. But what do you mean? By the way, he's smarter than he looks."

"Well, *this* wasn't smart. Helen Casper and another woman from HR found him smoking marijuana at three in the afternoon on the fire stairs."

"Oh, my God."

"Yeah, real smart. So anyway, you and Helen talk to him together. Have him sign a release. We'll give him six weeks' severance, and the story will be that he left to pursue other opportunities."

"No, wait!" Daniel said. "We can't fire the kid for one bonehead move that didn't hurt anyone. He's a good lawyer, and I need him. And if he came off the pipeline project, we'd have to get someone else up to speed; it just wouldn't work."

Pearce grumbled. "We cannot have a pothead interacting with clients. It's bad enough he does it on his own time but in the office? During business hours?"

"Okay, look," Daniel said, holding up both hands in a gesture of slowing down. "Let me handle this. I'll tell him how close he got to being fired, and get his promise to clean up his act. He really is a good kid. It would be a mistake to let him go. I'm sure he's beating himself up over this. And, by the way, I assume you know marijuana is legal in Washington now."

Pearce squinted, as if to see the solution in front of him. "Right, Daniel," he concluded. "He's your associate and your problem. You resolve this. And smooth this out with HR, while I return to the work that keeps this office running."

Jake had not been able to concentrate since he was busted. The ladies from HR went off fussing and obviously would go straight to Pearce, so it was just a matter of time. He didn't know if Pearce would fire him or would have Daniel do it. Either way, it couldn't end well.

It was embarrassing when those women had pushed open the stairway door. There was no reason for them to be on the fire stair. What were they even doing there? And he had pleaded that they keep it to themselves, but that bitch Helen wouldn't let it go.

When his phone buzzed, he almost jumped out of his seat. He made his way quickly to Daniel's office and, at the boss's ominous request, closed the door behind him.

"I guess you know," Daniel said, "why I have to talk to you."

He took a deep breath, girding himself to face his fate. "I screwed up," he blurted out. "I don't know what to say. I'm sorry."

"You don't need to say anything. As your employer I have to tell you this is a firing offense and certain people have demanded that result, but...." Jake squirmed as this sentence hung unfinished. "But PJ&H is giving you a second—a final chance."

Daylight! A reprieve! He let out an enormous sigh. "That's great, you have to..."

"But..." Daniel interrupted and paused. Jake's heart started pounding again. "As your friend and more-or-less mentor, I have to say you fucked up, and you put me in a bad position with Pearce. We should kick you out, but you're too damned valuable to the team, especially to me. Besides, we kind of like having you around. So in the future don't be such a dumb ass. Now, go your merry way, say no to drugs, stay out of Helen's way and consider yourself roundly admonished."

It was easy to see how this had played out. Helen wanted him gone, and Pearce could care less, but Daniel saved him. He started in for a hug, but Daniel's look told him a grateful smile was sufficient.

"And one more thing?" he said before leaving the office.

Daniel looked up, waiting.

"Any way we could avoid telling Nell about this?"

"Nell?"

"Yeah, please. I mean, she knows I smoke weed, of course, but she'll think I was stupid to do it in the office. I'll never hear the end of it."

Daniel rolled his eyes. "Okay," he said. "And, oh yeah, for future reference, they never send only one person to give you the ax."

"Got it, boss...and thanks."

Daniel showed up at the restaurant to meet Haley a few minutes early; he knew she would, by design, be exactly ten minutes late, but he could make use of a quiet few minutes. He took a table, ordered a drink and checked the news on his phone. There was a blurb on Google News about how dedicated the administration was to the Paris Climate Accord—to which the US had signed on and then off and now on again. Reversing this position once more would have to await a new administration, but like Pearce said at the methane party, a more immediate win would be no substantive pronouncement coming out of COP27. It was certainly too late to influence that, but there was no telling if Pearce might already be angling to get hired by the Saudis or the Russians to help keep the oil flowing. At any rate, the disparate interests of the conference participants doomed any plausible chance of action. Jake had organized an office pool on whether the final meeting statement would *even mention* fossil fuels.

He clicked on a headline about storms and saw that the Hill Country was in their path. "Old Jonah's not going to like this," he said out loud, picturing his big dog trying to squeeze under a bed to escape the thunder.

As if on cue Haley entered on a gust of wind, closing an umbrella and shaking rain from her hair. "It's ghastly out there," she said with a suggestive smile, convincing him he had been right; she remembered their night together.

The flush in her face and her hair coming loose made her look younger. He realized she must have been a knockout in her twenties.

"You okay, counselor?" she said, amused.

"Oh, sorry. Sure. What are you drinking?"

Daniel ordered her a chardonnay and another martini for himself. She settled in and slid a large envelope across the table, which he stashed in his briefcase. The delivery complete, they enjoyed their drinks while laughing about the latest flareup between the mainstream and radical wings of the House Democrats. "Given the demographics," she said with a satisfied smile, "we'd be in real trouble if they ever got out of their own way."

He raised his glass. "To the befuddlement of our enemies."

His phone buzzed, but he had done enough work for one day. He reached into his pocket to switch off the ringer, waving the other hand for the waiter to bring another round. His three martinis became four and then five and, before he knew it, they were back in Haley's apartment.

This wasn't smart. He had promised himself he'd keep their relationship professional. Messing around was not fair to Bree and was especially dangerous with a Machiavellian like Haley, who might be scheming in so many ways opaque to him.

But she was an attractive woman and knew it. She also brought a level of confidence and imagination to the bedroom that left him panting for more. It was not only exciting but easy to be with her. He didn't need to coddle. He didn't need to explain; she generally knew what was going on in DC better than he did. He could just live in the moment.

He woke the next morning alone in her bed, both tired and refreshed. She had left a note asking him to lock up when he left. But lying there gazing out the window, he was gripped by a new wave of guilt. What the hell was he doing? This wasn't what Bree deserved or what he wanted. It made no sense and couldn't end well in any scenario. He had to pull himself together, focus on work and his family.

He went to his apartment for a shower and fresh clothes. Getting dressed he remembered he had turned off the ringer on his phone, which he rarely did given how fast things could move in this town.

He was surprised to see two voicemails from Bree.

"Hi, sweetie," she said in the first one. "Just checking in. We're stuck in the house because of this awful thunderstorm. There are notices about road closures. Give me a call when you get this, okay?"

He gritted his teeth with bleary thoughts of the night before. He had meant to turn off calls from the office, not from home. A call from Bree might have been just what he needed to remind himself he was happily married.

In the second voicemail, Bree sounded anxious. "Danny, I really need you to call. The storm stalled in the mountains. The river's rising. Matt Reese has been saying rain in Two Valleys could cause flooding. I'm getting a little scared. Why aren't you answering your phone?"

He cursed. This felt like divine retribution. He knew getting involved with Haley would lead to a bad place, and here it was. Worse, he had agreed to have dinner with her again the following Thursday. What was he thinking?

But he also didn't like Bree quoting Matt Reese. What was going on between those two?

In the cab to work, he tried Bree's phone but the call didn't go through. When he arrived at the office, Pearce's assistant was waiting to escort him to see the boss, and then he immediately got engrossed in the pipeline finances—until Nell showed him the story about the Guadalupe flood.

Chapter Nine

Bree woke to the patter of raindrops on the roof. She liked sleeping on the top floor, where she could listen to the gentle patter; it brought back mornings before Annabelle was born, when she and Daniel would make love and drift back to sleep, indifferent to anything beyond their bed. Even the sound of thunder rolling out of the hills sweetened the feeling of contentment, of being safe in their beautiful haven.

But the intensity of the rain hammering the house this morning made her fidgety. And, after the deluge of the day before, the rain promised more long, soggy hours trapped in the house trying to keep the dog dry and her daughter entertained. She blotted this out by again picturing those rainy mornings with Daniel. Where had those days gone, the closeness of time flowing endlessly like the river outside their windows?

Daniel hadn't answered her calls the night before. He could have been on a business call or in a late meeting, but why hadn't he gotten back to her later...or at least this morning? Did she sound whiney in her voicemails? That would be regrettable but even more reason for him to call back.

She still lay in bed, eyes closed. She'd try him again. *He* should be the one to call *her*—after ignoring her messages—but she really needed to talk to him.

Before she picked up her phone, Jonah's paws sounded on the wooden stairs. He slept on the lower floor in Annabelle's room—Daniel said that was to protect the smallest member of the pack—but he would always find her or Daniel when nature called.

The bedroom door nudged open. The mattress tilted as Jonah hoisted his big front paws onto the bed. She reached over to his snout, and he licked her hand. Then she pulled the covers over her head until he made his whimpering sound, so cute coming from such a big hairy beast. But when she peaked out, his eager look made clear this was no time for jokes.

"Okay, big fella, but you're not going to like it." She reached out a hand to scratch behind his ears, sensing the rain had only increased since she woke up. "But when you gotta go..."

She hauled herself to the edge of the bed, found her slippers and shuffled down the hallway to the door. Jonah stepped eagerly onto the wooden porch and down two steps to the gravel driveway, but then stopped short. He turned with a perplexed look, rain trickling down his snout.

"I told you," she laughed. "I'm not coming out in that rain. You go do your business while I find your towel."

She went downstairs and through the open living room to the kitchen. Pausing, she heard only the sound of rain—nothing down the hallway from Annabelle's room—so she started the coffee maker and turned on the radio. The local news was part way through a report: "...forecast to continue until tomorrow afternoon, as a near stationary cold front stalls in the hills. Authorities warn a convection could develop in the Upper Valley, leading to heavy rains and flooding along the Guadalupe River and its tributaries. Officials are keeping a close eye on Canyon Dam and warning residents to evacuate low-lying areas."

She frowned. Two years ago a flood on the Guadalupe had taken out half the deck. The floorboards buckled and the railing and wooden chairs washed away. It wasn't like there had been any danger to their house, not like some of the older buildings down near New Braunfels, but they hadn't been able to use the deck for several weeks, and then it was only patched together. They planned to replace it once they had the cash.

That day had been frightening, reminiscent of historic Hill Country floods, but Daniel convinced her it was no big deal. Afterward he laughed about wanting to expand the deck, anyway.

She was never scared of anything when he was around; he had such a confident way about him. And now, with his bonus, they could rebuild the deck with all the features they wanted. They could make it into the centerpiece of the house, perched as it was so romantically over the river.

But the news kept repeating in her head. Thunderstorms. Flood alerts. Roads closed. Why did Daniel have to be away now?

Scratching from the door upstairs reminded her she had to find Jonah's towel. It was worth at least an effort to dry the hairy monster out on the porch. Otherwise he'd track water through the whole house. But as she walked back to the pantry, she heard her daughter call out, "Momma, is it raining again?"

"Yes, sweety," she said gently, turning into Annabelle's bedroom. Her daughter's little round face looked up from the bed with such eagerness Bree's heart almost melted. "Here it comes," Bree intoned as she leaned in for the morning hug that was the true start of her day.

"Don't you worry, princess," she said when she brushed the locks from her daughter's frowning face. "We'll find something fun to do. We'll have pancakes for breakfast and then maybe paint some pictures, and you can help Momma bake chocolate chip cookies."

"Yum!" Annabelle cried out, her eyes lighting up.

Then Bree remembered the dog. She straightened up. "But right now it's time for *you* to get up and find your robe and slippers while *I* dry off Jonah so he doesn't drag the river inside and float us all away."

Annabelle gave her a playfully defiant look, as if she intended to stay in bed. Bree reached down to tickle her. She squealed and dove under the covers.

What a perfect little person her daughter was, and how little it took to turn a pout too cute to be believed into a sparkling smile. But this rain would ruin what she had planned for the day. She had wanted to drive into the village to the pharmacy, pick up Daniel's suit from the dry cleaner and stop at the playground Annabelle loved up at The Joshua Church. But it would not be smart to drive at all in this weather.

So they'd have to turn to plan B. It would be fun to have Matt and Tyler over, but that was probably a bad idea. Spending time in public with this single father and his son was innocent, but having them to the house when Daniel was away could suggest an intimacy she should avoid; Tanswego was a small village; people would talk. Anyway, Matt would have the same trouble as her driving right now.

She took a towel out on the porch, where Jonah had pushed up against the house to get out of the rain. She did what she could to dry him, but the dog thought it was a game of tug of war, and she had to play along, on her knees grabbing one big leg at a time while he growled and slobbered. He managed to pull free at one point and demonstrated a quicker way to get dry by shaking violently, splattering her face.

"Just how I wanted to start my day," she said to the dog, "a spritz of dog-scented rainwater."

In the end they were both wet, but at least she had tried. Back inside she filled Jonah's food bowl and set out cereal and orange juice for Annabelle. The coffee was ready. As she poured a cup, the news reports bounced between postponed local events and dire weather reports. When Annabelle shuffled into the kitchen in her orange terry cloth bathrobe, clutching her stuffed alligator, Bree smiled, thinking her daughter's new best friend was an improvement over the mangy old bear Bree had to keep stitching together. Her daughter especially liked the blue and orange colors. She didn't care a bit when Daniel apologized that these were *not* the colors of real alligators; it was a present from her Papa, and that was all that mattered.

When Annabelle screwed up her face looking at the radio, as if she were paying attention, Bree switched to a pop music station. Her little girl did *not* need to be frightened sitting in her own house. Annabelle's eyes brightened at hearing a favorite song, and she started singing her own version of the lyrics.

Bree sighed. "Let's finish breakfast before we start a concert, okay?" she scolded unconvincingly.

Annabelle laughed, seeing through her mother's attempt to look stern and forcing Bree to laugh with her. Taking care of a six-year-old was a full-time job, but she had to admit it was fun.

After breakfast Annabelle returned to her room to get dressed. Bree tried calling Daniel again. But there was something wrong with the cell service. She turned to her laptop on the kitchen counter. The internet connection was down. She then tried the landline, which they never used because of all the spam calls, but got only a fast busy signal.

She began to hear loud sounds that sounded more like crashes than thunder. How could that noise be coming from the river? She really began to worry, and turned on the radio again. A Weather Service announcement said there was serious flooding along the Guadalupe. That meant River House!

Suddenly, there was an enormous roar outside. She pulled aside the curtain over the kitchen sink. The river, usually narrow enough to toss a stone across, was a torrent overrunning its banks! A jumble of branches and trash hurtled downstream, ripping up trees. The ragged frame of some kind of building surged by on the fuming foam, splintering the big cypress on the far side of the river. Boulders cascaded down the flood like corks. The deck was completely gone.

She rushed to Annabelle's room. Her daughter sat on the floor wrapped in a blanket, wailing with her hands over her ears. Bree scooped her up and turned back to the hallway.

"Gator!" Annabelle cried, squirming to reach her stuffed animal.

Bree held tight and ignored her daughter's cries, tiny in the din. She raced toward the stairs to get up to the front door. But Annabelle's blanket tripped her and she fell, slamming her shoulder into the staircase. Pain shot down her side. On her knees she clung to the railing and her daughter. She had to save Annabelle! She needed Daniel!

A crack sounded over the tumult. The floor started to give way. She grabbed the banister with one hand, holding Annabelle with the other arm. The floor behind her collapsed with a roar, opening the house to the raging river.

She struggled to her feet as the staircase jolted beneath her and started to sway. Then she crawled up, desperate to reach the driveway. They made it to the main floor, but the front door was jammed closed. The whole house started to bend downriver, beams splintering and blasting shards like shrapnel. Something pierced her thigh, adding a new spasm of pain.

With a crash the window beside the door shattered and the frame broke into pieces. She got Annabelle to her feet, and they sidled toward the broken-out window. Water was up to Annabelle's knees, so Bree picked her up. As she waded through debris-strewn water, something jammed against her leg. She stumbled. Annabelle screamed as they fell, but Bree held her tight around the waist.

Then the floor beneath them was gone. For a moment she felt weightless, then they crashed down.

Under turbulent water Bree flailed for something solid to grab, anything to save them. But the current rushed her through a chaos of wood and brick, and...she lost Annabelle!

In another moment she was sucked down and then siphoned upward. She gasped for breath, seeking any kind of hold. Her hand brushed a block of masonry and she latched on. She tried to clear her eyes to find her daughter.

But Annabelle was gone! Her daughter was lost, and Bree's world was going under.

She screamed "Annabelle!" as something punched into her back, and she pitched forward into the seething river.

Chapter Ten

When Daniel stood across the Guadalupe from the remains of River House, he feared his family must have perished.

There was a chance they were saved. They could have gotten out of the house, found their way to higher ground. Maybe they escaped before the roads closed down? The damned alligator in the tree didn't prove anything.

But he was just fooling himself. The flood came, and he wasn't there. And now what hope was there, really? His world became a swirling torrent of pain. Bree and Annabelle were pure, blameless souls. What perverse universe could call this tragedy down on them but leave him alive?

He turned away from the sight of his broken home. It didn't matter where he went next. Bree and Annabelle were gone... maybe...probably. He'd check in the village; surely someone would know for sure.

He turned back upriver. Blinking away tears, he saw images of his wife and daughter smiling, laughing, loving. He paid no attention to the washed-out road, his tattered clothes or his bleeding arm.

But as he approached a pool stretching over the road, a segment of the roadside collapsed, sending a wave of muddy water at him.

He jumped back, horror stricken, and retreated into the trees at the edge of the road. The water barely lapped at his shoes, but a muscle spasm shook his arm, and harsh light flashed behind his eyes. The pool filled his vision and swirled around him. He grabbed onto a tree trunk, squeezing his eyes closed.

In minutes—was it just minutes?—the dizziness cleared. His heart stopped pounding.

What happened? What was wrong with him? Sensing again where he was, he recognized the muddy pool as one he had waded through on his way downriver; why did it now fill him with terror? Was he hallucinating?

He was suddenly startled by the proximity of the river. It was a beast trying to swallow him! To escape he scrambled into the broken woods rising from the road's narrow shoulder.

Well up the incline, he stopped to catch his breath. His violent reaction to the river made no sense, but he'd have to sort that out later. For the moment, he was clear of it. He was panting and thirsty, but the thirst made him think of water, which pumped him with enough adrenaline to push him across the hillside creased with fissures and clogged with brambles.

He reached the village an hour later, exhausted and disoriented. The Guadalupe had rushed out of the hills to the east and picked up speed as it carried along telephone poles and sheds and boulders. Tanswego sat at a bend where the river fronted the village from two directions. At the height of the flood, the Guadalupe simply cut across this bend to sweep over the village.

The river had retreated from the village center but still flowed fast and full, lapping onto streets. Destruction was everywhere. The hardware store and bakery were leveled almost to their foundations. Several buildings across from them had entirely disappeared. One house was gone, yet the wooden gate to a garden still swung crazily on its hinges. Big trees downriver rose like solitary islands in places where the bank had collapsed and the river widened. A red car looked as if it had been squeezed by some colossal hand; the parts were there, compressed and mangled, but somehow the tires weren't flat. There was a stench in the air, and he realized the sewage system had been destroyed; pipes and septic tanks had been dragged off with the rest of the village.

Workers were assembling pontoons to replace the stone bridge that had connected the two parts of the village. A nurse hurried by with a box of water bottles. She handed one to Daniel. "The Boerne water treatment plant flooded," she said. "They're saying to boil water before using it."

He drank the whole bottle down and then took deep breaths to try to regain his composure. How could he find out about Bree and Annabelle? Where could he report their names?

He trudged through a commotion of workers and equipment up to The Joshua Church, which stood at the highest point of the village. Pastor Vincent liked to say this vantage point helped him watch over his flock, but it also minimized flood damage to the church. Bree and Annabelle attended Sunday services there, and it was a village meeting place. Now, its doors were propped open and rescue workers streamed in and out. Two women behind a table handed out sandwiches and coffee. He pushed up to the table where a young woman looked up.

"Where can I check names?" he tried to shout but his dry throat made it come out like a cough.

The woman waived to another volunteer, who took Daniel's arm and asked him to sit. He collapsed heavily in an empty pew.

"Give me the names, and I'll check what we have. I'll also get someone to look at that cut on your arm."

Daniel saw he was bleeding onto the pew. He reached to apply pressure with his other hand, but by then a nurse arrived. As she bandaged his arm, he began to feel light-headed. Radio reports poked through the ebb and flow of talking and sobbing. But it was just commentary from afar with no real information. He could see more looking out the window than listening to those reports.

In a lull he heard one newswoman say, "Survivors are blaming logging and the failure of reclamation efforts in the Upper Valley for the ferocity of flooding, but officials insist the cause was an historic rainfall no one could have predicted. A spokesperson for logging interests in the valley was quoted as saying people who built homes in low-lying areas and flood plains assumed the risk, but this official has since been replaced and this statement withdrawn. The president of Surefit Development, which against activist opposition has cleared land in the Lower Valley, has asked the community to join the company in keeping attention on efforts to locate and aid survivors and shore up remaining structures."

It made Daniel sick to hear his client's name and the narrative spin already in place before the bodies were even found. His wife and daughter were lost, and all his client cared about was deflecting blame.

But *they* were *him*! It was PJ&H and Pearce and the Oil Institute and every one of those sorry bastards who crafted reality to fit their agenda. If this flood had happened somewhere else, he'd have been the one scripting the sleight of hand. The insouciance was astounding...and nauseating. He felt physical pangs of guilt in his shoulders and down his arms.

"It's good to see you, Daniel," Pastor Vincent said gently, interrupting his thoughts and resting a hand on his shoulder. "I'm so glad you're safe. A volunteer asked me to tell you your wife and daughter are listed as missing, and someone will find you when there is more information."

Vincent paused as if to let Daniel digest this news. "That's got to be hard, but you mustn't give up hope. Is there anything at all we can do for you now? Have you eaten? You look like you could use a shower."

Daniel felt a release of tension at the minister's touch. "Thank you, Vincent. I guess now you're the only one who *can* help."

The pastor's face brimmed with sympathy. "I know your past hardened you against seeking solace in the church," he said, "but I have always sensed your spirituality, or sense of morality. I pray you will find some comfort in this."

Daniel was anything *but* moral. The pastor wouldn't have said he was if he knew the work Daniel did, how he had made the flood worse. "Thanks," Daniel said, nonetheless, attempting a sad, toothless smile.

The pastor moved on to a sobbing woman on the floor, hugging her knees. He stooped down to speak with her, waving for a volunteer to help get her to her feet. Vincent was addressing immediate physical needs of his neighbors, but what he provided most was his presence and his calm.

"Daniel!" came a shout from Matt Reese, the dad from Annabelle's school.

Daniel looked around, hoping to see comfort in a familiar face. But Matt's look was pained. "What about Bree?" he said anxiously. "And Annabelle?"

Daniel shook his head as tears welled up in his eyes.

"I think there's a board," Matt offered. "They're listing people who were airlifted or taken to hospitals, those who are missing and...."

"They're missing," Daniel said wretchedly.

Daniel wanted to hope but he knew his family was gone. He tried hard to think what he could do physically, knowing he otherwise would collapse at the thought of losing Bree, of his daughter never having the chance to grow and become her own person. Then a nagging thought poked through. Matt was the man who went swimming with Bree; he told her about some eagle. And now he was looking for her? Why was he so interested?

His grief turning to suspicion, he looked up but saw only concern in Matt's eyes. Then he broke into sobs, loathing himself for feeling petty jealousy when Bree was gone and his world lay in ruins. What right did he have to suspect his innocent wife when he was the only villain in this story?

Matt's heart went out to Daniel. Two days ago he had envied Daniel his beautiful wife and his fancy job in Washington. Now he pitied him. Matt had lost Bree as well, but to him she was just a friend and a fantasy; this guy had lost his whole life. Clearly, Matt could be most useful now by taking in hand this mud-soaked man with death in his eyes. He asked Daniel to wait while he found him dry clothes. Then he got him to change and convinced him to eat a sandwich while Matt spoke to volunteers and checked the lists.

When he returned to where he had left him, Daniel was on his feet, looking anxious.

"I want to join the rescue," he said.

"Great," Matt replied, thinking Daniel should be taking care of himself but wanting to do whatever the man asked. "They're digging all over the village. We'll go together."

Matt brought him to a truck where they were handing out work gloves and hardhats. A big man in a muddy flannel shirt directed them upriver, where workers were digging out houses.

Daniel and Matt each picked up a shovel, joined three others at a collapsed stone house and started to clear away rubble. Daniel focused on how his shovel hit the dirt and the strain in his back and arms. The pain from the cut on his arm, the oppressive heat and the mosquitoes buzzing his face were minor distractions. He thought only of moving the pile of brick and wood before him.

After he had dug around the sides of a big stone block, he called for help. Matt and two others joined him to move two large, stone blocks toward the front of the dilapidated building. One of the volunteers wearing a headlamp then climbed through the hole where the blocks had been removed, while the rest caught their breath.

"Thought I heard a sound," the man with the headlamp called out. "Everything's so damned loud I can't tell."

"It was a sound, all right," another rejoined. "A knocking on a pipe or something metal. It was right in there." He pointed into the basement of the collapsed building.

"Everyone quiet!" yelled the first voice.

Matt stepped toward the street to repeat this plea in a loud shout. All around the noise of nearby chopping and digging ceased. They could still hear distant voices and machinery, but it became still enough to hear tapping. Daniel looked at his fellow workers, desperation on their sweat-streamed faces, picks and shovels at the ready.

Someone stepped away from the crumbled structure and brought back an Emergency Management official with a large tactical flashlight. He leaned into the hole where the man with the headlamp had disappeared. "Here, take this," the official said and then stood back up.

The headlamp man came out from under the house and said he was sure someone was down there. The official then turned to the men around him. "You three help me lift this beam. The rest of you watch for any collapse and shout it out loud."

Daniel took up a position to the side of the beam. Four men moved it away from a pile of wood and concrete. The official climbed into the new proclivity with his flashlight.

They all paused, watching the official's legs protrude from the hole. Time grinded to a halt. Daniel met Matt's eyes. They were on the same side here, brothers in a struggle against the furor of nature.

They waited. Sounds from outside the building came as if from a far distance. Their grimy faces each registered the same expression of absorption in the moment, the whole disaster playing out in one crawl hole in one crumbled building. They needed—Daniel needed—some sign of hope.

Finally, the official backed out of the hole. He called into his radio, "We have a survivor at point D2. We need braces and a jack to lift beams. And send medical. We're going to pull someone out."

He illuminated a partial wall with his flashlight. "Some of you dig around the side of that wall. Just keep moving debris back, but don't push on anything until we get help."

Two more officials arrived wearing heavy gloves and helmets with headlights. They unfolded retractable metal supports to prop up the sides of the passageway. One of them, with a rope trailing from his belt, crawled through the opening. The second official kept a flashlight trained through the hole. Everyone else stood quiet.

In a few minutes they heard voices from the passageway, one a deep growl and another the pitiful moan of a woman or girl.

Moments ticked by. Daniel's back and shoulders ached. He put pressure on a new cut on his forearm to stop the bleeding.

They saw a light coming from the passageway. Then a head with long, mottled hair appeared. It was a woman. She looked delirious, but she was coughing, and her eyes blinked open. Daniel helped to lift her from the hole. Four men carried her to the street and laid her on a stretcher. A nurse checked her vital signs while someone strapped an oxygen mask over her mouth. The rest of the workers trudged out to the street as medical workers lifted the stretcher and carried it off.

In the stillness that followed, someone somewhere began to clap, slowly, and then others joined. Soon a chorus of applause washed over them from workers balanced on concrete slabs or perched atop earth movers. Daniel cried tears of relief as the applause rose and faded into the returning sounds of digging.

Chapter Eleven

Daniel dried his eyes and sat on a toppled refrigerator. His musical ringtone sounded almost mocking but reminded him there was still a world out there, away from this tragedy. He lifted the phone to his ear.

"Dan, it's Pete."

His brother-in-law's worried voice signaled where *this* conversation would go, and Daniel dreaded having to share the news.

"Are you okay?" Pete said. "I'm so glad I reached you; we're going out of our minds. Where are you? What about Bree and Annabelle?"

Daniel took a deep breath. "I was in DC and only got to Tanswego a few hours ago. They're listed as missing, but the house..." He choked for a moment before clearing his throat. "The house is gone, everything but the foundation."

After a moment Pete said, "But they're searching, right? I mean, there's hope? I'm coming to help."

"I...I don't know what you can do. They have TDEM and the National Guard and FEMA..."

"I need to do something." He paused. "And look, man, I'm so sorry."

"Yeah. Thanks."

Daniel turned off the ringer on his phone, picked up his shovel and went back to digging. It was better than thinking.

With the aid of National Guard searchlights, rescue work went on into the night. But Daniel ran out of strength as the sun went down. His hands were raw with blisters, his joints hurt and he needed to replace the bandages on his arms. But as soon as he sat on a pile of concrete, he was overwhelmed with an image of Annabelle propped up against Jonah on the living room floor, the two of them napping without a care in the world.

This was all his fault. He was the one who was unfaithful, who betrayed his wife and his daughter; how could he be left alive when they were gone?

He thought of the moment Annabelle was born. Friends had said how the birth of your first child changed your world forever. He had accepted this but never fully grasped the reality until it happened. The moment the nurse handed him his unbelievably tiny daughter—actually trusted him to hold her—it all came true. His life was not about only him anymore. He had long loved Bree as the mate who would take the journey through life with him, but this was different. Here was a part of him that would carry on, would be a grown person long after he was gone. He knew in an instant he'd lay down his life to keep this child safe, and the feeling took him by surprise. The circle of life claptrap he had always heard, the griping of his mother about what she had sacrificed for him, the concern in his father's face as he worried about Daniel even as he gave up his own life, all suddenly made sense.

And now his child was gone. More than from any death he

had ever known or could even imagine, a light had gone out in the world.

He eventually returned to the church. He realized he was hungry and ate some soup. Matt sat across from him eating but saying nothing.

Daniel contemplated Matt and looked into his own heart. What right did he have to suspect his wife of wavering affections when he was sleeping with a praying mantis who would devour him in the end? And what reason did he have to suspect her? She was always loving, attentive, a wonderful mother. So what if she met this guy at the swimming hole and he charmed her with stories about birds? Daniel should be grateful someone kept her company while he was away. And now...what did it matter? Bree was lost, lost to everyone who loved her. Any recriminations rested on Daniel alone.

"Thank you," he said grimly, looking up at Matt.

"For what?"

"For being here. Being a friend to Bree and Annabelle. Looking out for my family."

Daniel spent the night on a pew beneath a Red Cross blanket. In the morning he got a call from Representative Wolford.

"I've heard the news, Danny," the old man said. "Is your family safe?"

He tried to respond but his voice faltered. The devastation to the village and his life were total, and he didn't think he could feel any worse, yet trying to talk about it *did* make it worse. "The house is gone," he finally managed to say.

"Bree and Annabelle?"

"Missing."

"Oh, Danny, I'm so sorry. Is everything being done? I have contacts at Emergency Management."

"Thanks, Uncle Jack," Daniel said sadly. "All the state and federal people are here, but anything else you can do..."

"You know I will, my boy. Keep your hopes up. Call me with anything you need."

Daniel hung up and stared into the distance. He then mechanically laced up his boots.

"They said I'd find you here," came Pete's voice. Daniel looked up. His brother-in-law stood, somber and determined, in a hardhat and bright yellow vest with "Security" across the chest.

It didn't really matter that Pete was there, but Daniel was confused. "How did you get through the cordon around the village?"

Pete shrugged. "See this vest? A friend loaned it to me."

"You have a friend at Homeland Security?"

"Well, no, but someone with resources. She's here too, taking photos to make sure there's a clear record."

"A record? What do you mean?"

"Something like this happens, where climate change makes a disaster so much worse, and the people in power turn it into something that couldn't possibly have been their fault."

Pete apparently understood that a spin operation was already in full swing. But it was surprising his brother-in-law had become savvy enough to see this and know how to counteract it. "Who is this friend?"

"Just a woman I met, a photographer. She saw some of my nature shots and was really impressed. Anyway, she came along to take pictures of the flood, but I'm not sure where she's gotten to."

Daniel wondered what Pete was mixed up in now. This "friend" making a record of the flood sounded like an activist who was probably way out of his league. Still, they picked up shovels and together joined a work crew.

In another hour they broke through to a buried room and had to call for body bags. That was a somber moment, but he hoped at least it would bring someone the closure denied to him. And he was relieved the bodies were adults. He didn't think he could bear seeing kids in the wreckage.

At the request of some of the workers, everything paused in the morning for a memorial service. Pastor Vincent and his acolyte hiked down from The Joshua Church to the center of the digging. There was something poignant about the mud boots they wore beneath their clerical robes.

It was strange and moving to see two hundred begrimed rescue workers drop their tools when the wail of a siren signaled the start of the service. Perched on bulldozers or huddled in small groups, they bowed their heads—in the only moment during Daniel's time in the village that was truly silent—except for the ceaseless rush of the river still over its banks.

Pastor Vincent spoke through a bullhorn:

> *God is our refuge and our strength, a*
> *very present help in trouble. Therefore*
> *will not we fear, though the earth be*
> *removed, and though the mountains*
> *be carried into the midst of the sea,*
> *though the waters thereof roar and be*
> *troubled, though the mountains shake*
> *with the swelling....*

Some finality came for Daniel late in the afternoon. He was at a dig site while Matt and Pete were off somewhere else when a soldier with a clipboard approached.

"Mr. Lazaro?" the soldier said.

Daniel stopped working and nodded.

"I'm sorry to bring you this news, but a body washed up downriver that matches the description of your wife. The captain would appreciate it if you'd come up to the temporary morgue to identify the body."

Daniel dropped his shovel and stared.

"Mr. Lazaro?"

"Yes," Daniel said. "Right." He looked around for Pete but

didn't see him, and so he followed the soldier up the hill to where a Jeep waited on a cleared stretch of road. He got into the front seat and looked back over the village while the Jeep started up.

Before they passed into the tree cover, he caught sight of his brother-in-law on the rise behind the church. He was about to ask the driver to wait while he called out, but Pete turned and Daniel saw a woman with long, braided hair wearing another yellow security vest. A long-lens camera hung from her neck. It was just a moment before his view was blocked, but he was sure he'd seen that face before. Even in a camouflage hat against the sun, she was hard to miss. Was she the woman in that photo of Eco?

Chapter Twelve

"How long do you need to stay?" Pete asked Verde as she lifted the camera from around her neck.

They stood uphill from The Joshua Church in the one spot they could find out of sight of the carnage, though there was no way to escape the stench.

The day before Carson had asked Pete to join him and Harris surveilling a logging company. Pete said he needed to go to Tanswego to see about his sister, and the next morning he got a call out of the blue from Verde, asking if she could come along. That was more than okay with him. Even in the midst of tragedy, it was hard to ignore how attractive she was. If not for the circumstances and her being Eco's woman, he'd have been all over her. Even though that wasn't possible or even appropriate when his main concern was his sister and his niece, she was clearly in the higher echelons of Anthro, and he liked the idea of playing secret agent with her.

"I need a few more shots," Verde said, "and then I will be ready to leave when you are."

It was time for Pete to get back to his job, anyway. There wasn't much more he could do here, with the National Guard and the Red Cross and everything. He'd be able to report to tell his parents he'd seen Daniel. Putting aside that they had never really gotten along, and the crap Daniel did at his job, he had made Bree happy and now had lost everything; it was hard not to feel sorry for him.

Pete didn't see Daniel again or hear about Bree's body being found. It hurt too much to think about his sister, so as he drove he talked with Verde about climate issues. Actually, she went on and on about some report from the World Meteorological Organization while he mostly listened.

"It rained!" she said in exasperation. "Not *snowed*, but *rained* for the first time ever on one peak of the Greenland ice sheet. It spells doom for anyone living near a coast."

What she said was scary, for sure. But he couldn't concentrate enough to follow talk about the impending end of the world. He only cared about losing his sister and his niece, and trying to appreciate this crazy chance to drive with this woman beside him. He'd worry about the planet later.

He tried to get her to talk about herself, but she turned the conversation back to him. She asked about his sister and encouraged him to talk about happy family memories and to share how he felt about the tragedy. Her accent sounded East European, trilling R's and accenting odd parts of words, but her vocabulary was more sophisticated than his. She was most likely in her early thirties, and she and Eco were obviously partners, one way or another. Beyond that he couldn't tell much about her.

She asked uncomfortable questions about his time in college. She also was very interested in Daniel, which was annoying. Nonetheless, he told her what he knew about the work his brother-in-law did in Washington, although she seemed to know more about this than he did.

As they reached the Austin city limits, she asked him to drop her on a street corner.

"No way! I'll take you wherever you want to go."

Mia frowned at Pete. "You don't understand, do you?" she said. "This is war. If state troopers recognized me, I would not have had the luxury of riding back with you. Or possibly they would follow us now, in hopes to find Kristof."

"You mean Eco?"

She hissed. How could she have revealed Kristof's real name to this mouse? "Yes, Eco," she said, putting steel into her voice, "the man with standing invitation to local FBI office. Fortunately, the authorities do *not* know Eco's location, and this is because we maintain discipline, we follow *protocols*. You know what means protocol?"

She paused, hoping he realized that was a rhetorical question. "So, you will forget you have heard this other name. You must return to your home, park your car and act as if you have never met Eco or me. You went to Tanswego out of concern for your sister. You will truthfully say it was terrible, but you will say nothing about me. If someone saw a woman in your car, you will say I was hitchhiker, and you do not recall any detail about me. Remain most of all calm and alert."

"And you...?"

"I go to deliver the photographs."

After she stepped from the car, she leaned back in the window. He looked resentful to be parting there. She wished men did not always treat her like they wanted to sleep with her when circumstances required their full attention, even when she strived to be stern and unemotional. Kristof said she couldn't help looking sultry, and men loved it, but she didn't know how to look any other way. At any rate, Pete had been useful. They would keep him on call; there were ways he could help. But he was too childlike to be trusted with anything sensitive.

"Thank you for driving me," she said, trying to sound friendly. "We will be in touch."

Daniel arranged for Bree's body to be transported to Foswell, where her mother said she would take charge. After that he felt he could be of little help in the rescue efforts. Each passing hour made it less likely they'd find survivors, and this sapped his strength. He felt too battered to carry more bodies from the rubble.

When he left Tanswego behind, he hoped never to return. He drove to Foswell through countryside largely untouched by the storms.

The funeral service for Bree was at the small church the family attended. Everyone was united in holding out hope for Annabelle and so they focused the memorial on her mother.

The mood was solemn, as it must be for someone plucked from this world before her time. Afterward, they all gathered at the house.

Bree's father had grown smaller, as if he had lost part of himself. Her mother buzzed around greeting people and seeing to their needs. It was hard to say if this was a defense mechanism or she was losing her grip on reality.

For the first time Daniel saw Pete as the grownup in the room, comforting his dad and cajoling his mother to leave off the maniacal hostess routine. His brother-in-law seemed to have grown stronger through this tragedy. He didn't rant about global warming or Daniel's work; in fact, he didn't talk much at all, which itself made him seem more mature. He also showed a great deal of empathy, which made Daniel wonder whether he had long misjudged him.

Daniel took Pete aside and said, "Listen, I don't want your

parents bearing any of the costs of the funeral or transporting the body or anything else going on right now."

"Oh, they're good; they can handle it."

"You might think so but I'm not so sure. Anyway, that's not fair and not the point. Can you find a way to have the bills sent to me...without making a big deal out of it?"

"Sure, I can do that...and thanks."

"No need for thanks. This is my responsibility. They've lost a child, and I don't want them shouldering financial burdens on top of that. And if there's anything else I can do for them, you let me know. They'd never ask."

Daniel stayed within himself and didn't respond much to the neighbors' expressions of sympathy. He couldn't obscure the image of Bree's lifeless face in the morgue, a pale bluish tint to her skin and dark circles under her eyes. What had stuck with him most was that someone took the time to brush her golden hair—which looked so alive—but when he kissed her forehead, it felt like hard rubber.

The future he had always taken for granted had vanished. It disappeared in an instant or, more disturbingly, probably over long minutes or hours. His wife and daughter suffered all alone while he drank and screwed another woman. He was a shit; there was no other way to say it. He made money for the people who already had too much, and he paid the tab by losing his wife and daughter and home.

Surfeit clearcutting what was left of the forest may have been all that was needed to push the river beyond its hundred-year mark, maybe just enough to wash away the River House pilings. But was that fair? It was hard to know. Everything was so muddled. Daniel was a lawyer; he represented his clients with zeal, as the ethical rules required. And his clients weren't breaking the law; they were *making* laws that were sensible and took all the factors into account. Could excessive logging increase the risk of flash floods? Sure, but there would be risk in any event, and what was "excessive"? To get timber for building you have to cut down trees. Was weather more extreme as the world warmed? Yes, but the climate would shift regardless of what we did; we had to focus on how to adapt.

His rationalizations kept crashing into images of the broken River House foundation, the sign his daughter couldn't have survived. It was a relief they found Bree's body...but putting Bree to rest increased his frenzy to find Annabelle. And wearing down his hands digging out buildings wasn't the way. He was sure Bree had died trying to save their daughter, which meant Annabelle washed downriver as well. Such a small person could easily be lost in the debris or buried in the mud. Her body would never be found, and her unknown fate would haunt him forever.

Suddenly, he was anxious to return to Washington, where he could get back to work—the only thing he had left—and maybe find a way to pressure officials to redouble the search for bodies.

Chapter Thirteen

To find the safe house where she would meet Kristof, Mia first walked to the Credible Bookstore on Allen Street. The store was understated, with a modest display in the front windows and a sandwich sign outside promoting a "cozy mystery" signing.

She asked the young woman behind a counter piled high with books about first editions and was directed to the second floor. There, a distinguished but rather dusty man in his seventies stopped reading and looked over rimless spectacles, eyebrows raised. "Hmm?" he said.

"I understand you may have a first English edition of *The Labyrinth of the Spirits*."

"Ah, Carlos Ruiz Zafón." The man's eyes expressed surprise while his face remained placid. "I believe we might."

"Thank you. I have been looking all over."

"And pardon me, but we don't get much interest in Spanish writers from customers who are not themselves Spanish. Still, you are perhaps familiar with Madrid?"

"I often travel there, by way of Lisbon."

His eyes lit up. He looked to both sides and then dug into a drawer for a business card bearing the address of a café. He handed her the card.

She bowed her head and turned to go.

"You know," he said, causing her to pause. "Those of us who only help from backstage know what sacrifices you make. You are the true angels of our world."

She smiled uneasily, suspicious of heavenly pronouncements. Still, she had to trust protocol and this was her route to the safehouse. She nodded and moved on.

She continued up East Fifth Street, a backpack over one shoulder. Sunglasses and a Houston Astros baseball cap hid her face, so no one would remember her features. A loose jacket and cargo pants mostly covered her figure, to save her from unwanted attention. Her hair hung in a plain braid down her back.

Three blocks later a Texas Rangers pickup truck was parked at the curb. Two men in dark suits leaned in, talking with the driver. Agents of law enforcement in the US were easier to spot and less threatening than those in Romania, but they could be just as intrusive and had access to advanced technology. So, it was always best to play two moves ahead. Instead of proceeding directly to the safe house, she detoured left. She hoped the authorities didn't have a clear photo of her, but they were anxious to find people associated with Eco, and Mia was closer to him than anyone else.

When she had first arrived from Romania, she was in terrible shape, physically and emotionally.

The public outcry after the attack on the filmmakers had forced authorities to make a show of arresting several attackers, but no charges were filed against the logging company that sent them. After that she was so harassed by supporters of the logging company and the police that she left the country for London. Later, she visited a friend in San Antonio, where she met Kristof at a protest against strip mining. His easy smile and intense eyes intrigued her. And soon she was swept up in his genius and devotion to environmental justice. He won her trust and quickly her love. Before her tourist visa expired, they were married—to each other and to the cause.

At the address on the card she found a quiet coffee shop with no sign outside. Bicycles were chained to a fence. Three metal tables stood empty by the sidewalk. She lingered outside, pretending to check her phone, until the last customer on line took his coffee to a bench and opened his laptop. Then she entered and stepped up to the counter.

"I'm just visiting," she said, "and wondered if you serve horchata latte."

The woman behind the counter nodded. "So, you're from Madrid?"

"By way of Lisbon."

The barista looked at her other customers, who were paying no attention. She then quietly slid a key ring across the counter and gestured to her left. "I'm sorry, but we've run out of rice milk. Can I offer you something else?"

"No, thank you very much. I have my heart set on a horchata."

Mia turned, scanned the inattentive faces and left the café. She walked a short way down the empty sidewalk and ducked through an opening in a hedge to the side of the building.

Kristof heard the coded knock on the safehouse door and a key turning in the lock. He stayed out of sight until he saw Mia and then hurried to embrace her. They kissed and held each other tight as he buried his face in her hair. "If I could only carry that scent with me always," he said.

She gave him a playful shove. "Then you would not need me."

He kept his hands on her slender shoulders. "I shall always need you, my love."

Seven years earlier Kristof had worked for the Wilderness

Society but bristled at its compromises with corporations doing the harm. He quit and, with the money he had saved, traveled abroad, where he witnessed extreme weather disasters on three continents.

The traveling gave him time to think. Established environmental groups focused on centralization of authority and bureaucracy more than saving wilderness or stopping the burning of fossil fuels. Their professionalism bred compromise, and they failed to prioritize responding to the crisis at hand. Most of the more radical environmental groups had imploded two decades earlier over philosophical debates about how humans fit in with nature and the constant pressure of law enforcement to turn them against each other. But the threat now was more urgent than just pollution or logging old-growth trees; the very survival of the planet was in peril. There had to be a way to sound the alarm without falling into the trap of ecocentric environmentalism, some action that would trigger a chain reaction response. Sadly, it seemed the riskier the action, the more the alarm would resonate, and this radicalized and demonized the messengers, forcing them underground.

When he returned to the US, he borrowed a friend's cabin in Montana and buried himself in the history of anti-industrial activism, starting with radical labor groups like the Wobblies and the anti-industrialist Luddites in England. He subscribed to *The Journal of Ecological Resistance* put out by the radical group Earth First! He read Edward Abbey's *The Monkey Wrench Gang* three times, annotating methods for disrupting the engines of environmental destruction. He studied the Earth Liberation Front, from its victory in protecting the old-growth forest at Warner Creek to its decimation by the Justice Department infiltration.

But he was troubled by the internal conflicts that led to the demise of the radical ecology movement. There had to be a course between permissiveness and cynicism in judging people apart from nature. The climate crisis was a common enemy threatening both humanity *and* the planet it had occupied for such a miniscule fragment of its existence.

The next year he was in New Mexico for a protest march against coal mining when he met Mia. She embraced him at once as a comrade, and to him she was a true heroine, a haggard beauty battle-hardened from experiences in Eastern Europe and devoted to saving the planet. He knew immediately they had to be together and thanked fate for bringing her into his life.

The year after they were married, they took a camping trip with Kristof's two closest friends in the Pinacate Desert of Northern Mexico, where Earth First! had originated in 1980. The four ended the trip by creating a movement that would advocate the goals of the mainstream environmental organizations but reject their reliance on passive means. They would take on the world in order to save it.

They designed the group with little hierarchy, but they and a core group of helpers would coordinate actions by independent local cells. This would demonstrate their egalitarian worldview while also helping evade infiltration by the government and industry. It would be the job of the core group—who Mia convinced must each adopt a code name for security—to coordinate local efforts.

To create a common culture and promote consistent goals, Kristof edited a newsletter—cleverly illustrated in part by Mia and titled *Monkey Wrench* after the Abbey novel. Kristof had wanted to call it *Two Degrees Celsius,* to reflect the Paris Accord goal of limiting global warming, but Zeke convinced him *Monkey Wrench* would better engage readers as both playful as well as a call for direct action. Tech volunteers posted the newsletter anonymously on blogs and websites, where it got wide attention. Because Kristof edited the newsletter and was linked in the public mind with the bombing of an oil pipeline in 2017, he found himself the group's de facto leader. This meant nothing within the inner circle, but it did hang a target on his back. Anthro thus began planting false

"Eco-sightings" to make the authorities either chase after ghosts or else stop crediting tips to his whereabouts. Nonetheless, his notoriety meant he had to be mindful of security in planning visits to cells and protests.

"So what have you brought us?" he asked when they were seated in the modest kitchen, drinking coffee out of mismatched mugs.

She handed him the camera, and he scrolled through her photographs of the flood.

"These are really good," he said with an admiring smile. "If the eco-terrorist thing doesn't work out, you could have a future in news photography."

She laughed for the first time in days, but then her face turned serious. "It is tragic," she said. "It looks like Tanswego was a lovely village, but nestled against a river draining the Two Valleys, it had no chance. The river washed away almost everything. It looks like a bomb exploded."

Kristof focused on one shot of a little girl crying in her mother's arms, a building collapsed into the river in the background. "This is the one," he said. "This puts a face on the flood."

"So, we will post the photograph on social?"

"Exactly. That one photo might get the public's attention in a way all the scientific proof in the world cannot and serve as the kind of clickbait to attract the news outlets. We can use other shots to give color to Doctor Cahill's report."

"Has he finished?"

"Nearly, and while you'd think our tree-hugger friends could handle publicizing it, they have no sense of theater. They'd just put it out with some talking head to get lost in the noise."

"Well, we could benefit from some good press. By the way, how did your meetings go in Corpus Christi?"

"I think we made progress."

"Did Zeke join you?"

"We didn't need his fire and brimstone this time. It's not hard to motivate people who get hammered by nearly every hurricane in the Gulf, but they aren't quite ready to take to the streets. I kept it academic, showing them the rising sea levels since 2013, giving them a grounding in ocean acidification. To be fair, the city is comparatively forward in disaster management planning. But these people are watching their shoreline recede each year while the developers keep over-building. The time will come soon enough to send Zeke to rally them to the barricades."

Zeke Franklin was the third of the Anthro founders. He was code-named "Guy" for the sharp features and goatee that made him look like the Guy Fawkes masks worn at protest marches. He was a hothead, always pushing for more action, and Mia loved his passion. Zeke was the one who led the raid in the Hill Country the year before to slash tires on a fleet of logging trucks. That disturbance had slowed the deforestation, but logging soon resumed. He looked like a prophet now that everyone could see chaining junipers in the Upper Valley with huge bulldozers had contributed to the Guadalupe flood.

"Oh," she said, suddenly remembering, "about my driver...."

He looked up. "Was he much help?"

"Well, he drove me to Tanswego and could describe what was no longer there." She took the camera back and showed him a photo of Pete. He looked to be in his early thirties and fit in a flannel shirt appropriate to the wooded background. "The narrow eyes make him look like a brown bear," she said, "the volatile, not the cuddly kind. He is eager to join the effort."

"Well, he looks like a regular guy from Texas, which is a good thing. Will we be able to use him?"

She shrugged. "I am uncertain if he believes in what we are doing or perhaps is just looking for *something* to believe in."

"Or looking to get lucky," Kristof smirked. Men were always flocking around Mia, which admittedly helped in recruiting and convincing recalcitrant civilians to lend a hand, but it muddied the waters in assessing motivations.

She smiled knowingly. "Is this jealousy I sense, Mister Tyndall?"

He grinned, lifted her from her chair and carried her toward the bedroom.

She said seductively, "So, the Earth can wait?"

He laughed. "Just need to make it move a bit."

Late in the afternoon, they sat in the kitchen viewing the photos again. The signal knock announced the arrival of a friend. Stefan soon stepped into the room.

Mia had always liked Stefan, once she got over her initial suspicion of anyone claiming to be dedicated to saving the planet. He had grown up in Germany but found his way to the United States as a college student and then became a legal resident through marriage to an American. Like Mia, he had lost both his parents when he was young and so treated Anthro like his family. Unlike her, his marriage had been strictly for convenience, though he maintained a close friendship with his putative wife.

Stefan was the fourth of the friends on that camping trip to the Mexican desert. She was not sure who gave him the code-name "Assisi" but it referred to Saint Francis of Assisi, which had a credible nature connotation. He was a voice of restraint against Zeke's radical schemes. She sometimes shared Zeke's impatience with peaceful protest, but she was always fearful he would convince Kristof to dynamite a dam or sabotage another pipeline, which she was coming to think was too dangerous—for themselves and innocent bystanders. So, Stefan's influence on the side of non-violence helped keep Anthro in balance.

Stefan was a kind man. Like Zeke, he had known Kristof long before she met him, and this connection allowed her to admit him into the small circle of people she trusted. He did speaking tours on college campuses and helped edit *Monkey Wrench*. He also famously had produced a bit of guerilla theater where volunteers dressed in hazmat suits stood vigil outside parks in the National Coal Heritage Area of West Virginia to highlight the harm of burning fossil fuels. That got a lot of attention, but the press spun it as comical, which undermined its impact. In civilian life Stefan ran a small contracting business in Dallas, and under his legal name ran an eco-group separate from Anthro, a public platform to advocate reform by peaceful means. He had driven to Austin to take them north.

He hugged Kristof and exchanged kisses on both cheeks with Mia. He then backed off with a snide expression. "You two have been hard at work, I see."

While Kristof laughed, Mia threw a pillow at him, unable to hide her contented smile—and she realized with embarrassment her hair had come undone, and Kristof's shirt was misbuttoned. But this was Stefan, who knew them and whose affection for them both was unshakable.

Kristof made a fresh pot of coffee, and the three sat at the kitchen table. She showed Stefan the photos. He shook his head as he scrolled through the images. "These are good," he said, "though depressing as hell. Can you load them onto the encrypted site?" He turned to Kristof. "I assume you want to offer these to Doctor Cahill to use in his report?"

"Exactly," Kristof said. "He should pick the shots he wants."

"And you two need to get to the Dallas Airport?"

"Right."

"Headed to South Dakota?"

Kristof smirked. "Well, we've never seen Mount Rushmore."

"Right." Stefan grinned. "Oh, Charlie planted some 'Eco-sightings' in Vermont, so hopefully the evil eye will focus far from your path."

They shared tight-lipped smiles until Mia said, "With Stefan here we should talk about Peter Morrison."

Stefan looked at her questioningly.

"He is a man who wishes to join the battle. He is rather

childish, but his brother-in-law is a lawyer and lobbyist for the oil industry."

"No shit?"

Mia nodded. "This lawyer is involved deeply, we believe. He works for a firm involved in climate legislation—from the dark side, of course."

Kristof added, "Their fingerprints were all over the methane vote."

"Oh, God," Stefan replied.

"Precisely," Mia went on, "but there is more. This man's wife and young daughter were swept away in the flood of the Guadalupe River. Very sad, really. They had a house on the river near the Two Valleys Fire, where...."

"Where Zeke slashed those tires," Kristof interrupted.

"Do you think this guy Peter gets it?" Stefan asked.

"It is too soon to tell, although his sister and niece died in the flood, so he has good reason to question the sanity of climate policy. I pushed him to seek rapprochement with his brother-in-law; they have not always gotten along. We do not know what might come of his help, but Peter seems enthusiastic."

"And infatuated," Kristof commented.

Stefan looked at him quizzically and then smiled affectionately, turning to Mia. "Well, aren't we all?"

Chapter Fourteen

Daniel returned to Washington but not to work. He left a voicemail for Brandon Pearce that he would be taking some personal time, which he split between hounding authorities about the search for bodies and tormenting himself for his failures as a husband and father. He tried hard not to drink until after lunch but swilled enough to be comatose each day before the sun set.

In a few lucid moments, he called Bree's parents. They spoke about anything *but* the flood and their daughter and grandchild. The conversations left him drained more than comforted because Julia's pain through her brave words reminded him the catastrophe was his fault. But each time he spoke with them felt like a baby step toward atonement.

He tried to distract himself from thinking about Bree and Annabelle by dealing with the insurance claim on River House, which was a total loss. But he found that handling Bree's will took him to a dark place, so he asked his trusts and estates partner to see to this, and particularly to expedite her small bequest to her brother.

Watching the horrific news about Hurricane Ian didn't help. Florida's governor called the Category-5 storm a "500-year flooding event," but Daniel guessed it would not be half a millennium before this happened again.

He tried to focus on his own health, and after two weeks of fitful attempts, he finally overcame his revulsion of water enough to rinse off in the shower. If he wore earplugs and kept his eyes closed tight he only occasionally threw up on the floor. This allowed him, more or less, to clean himself up before going into the office.

He could handle only so much time scrolling through old pictures and videos, and there was a limit to how many tears he could shed each day. To distract himself, he tried focusing on a list of mundane tasks. It also helped that his phone still rang and memos still landed on his desk. Calls had to be returned. Nell and Jake needed direction; they were his people and he had to be fair to them. But the grind of ongoing projects left him numb. Wasn't everything he did for the clients more packaging of lies and engineering procedural maneuvers to stifle meaningful discussion of what would be best for the world?

With everyone at work—and even Haley—offering condolences, it was impossible to really forget Annabelle and Bree had been ripped from his life. The only thing that numbed the pain was drinking. Even then aching images continued to pulse in the background—and the despair returned each morning with a splitting headache.

In late October his team had to gear up for the regular quarterly meeting with Kent Coggin, the Oil Institute's executive director, on the competitive threat from alternative power sources. Nell would present on wind and Jake on solar. Daniel would add little more than gravitas.

As they prepared to head to the meeting, darkening skies made him queasy. Nell stuck her head into his office. "Ready to go, boss?"

"It looks like rain," he said uneasily.

"So?" She looked at him closely, and he feared she might guess what was troubling him. He only wished he understood this himself. Was it the word "rain" or the thought of getting wet? His heartbeat quickened. He felt light-headed and put two hands on his desk to steady himself.

Nell took hold of his arm. "Are you okay?" she said urgently. "Do you need something?"

"No," he stammered. He was catching his breath as his pulse slowed. "I just felt a little dizzy."

She held his arm until he was stable. "We need to get going," she said, looking at her watch. "I'll call the car."

Daniel made it to the meeting with the aid of an umbrella and a car service, but he felt nauseous until they were safely inside the lobby. There he took a moment to collect himself while Nell kept a close eye on him, and Jake announced their arrival. It was a good thing he had these two backing him up; they knew the material better than he did, and he could rely on them not to tell anyone about his dizzy spells.

An assistant showed them to a conference room and offered coffee and water. "But, Mr. Lazaro," she said, "the director would appreciate a moment before the meeting."

Coggin's corner office was predictably lavished with dark wood and leather-padded chairs, a tableau of oil industry opulence. Coggin was a large man with slicked-back hair who wore wire-rimmed glasses and a dour expression. His expensive three-piece suit was a throwback to an age before the truly powerful dressed any way they wanted.

Coggin rose, shook Daniel's hand and said, "I wanted to say how sorry I was to hear about your loss, and how impressed and thankful we all are at how you are back in the saddle so soon.

Also, the board was quite happy with how you handled the deal with Bo Langston. It was money well spent, and we were glad you led our team. We've got our eye on you, Dan. You've got a bright future working with the Institute."

"Thank you, Kent," Daniel said. This was exactly what he had long sought, a route to power independent of Pearce. Why did he feel ambivalent?

Coggin led Daniel back to a conference room with a broad view of the Washington Monument. Two underlings poured coffee, took notes and hung on their boss's every word.

Daniel's associates presented the reports, which put him in a supervisory role and thus closer in stature to Coggin. His only contribution was to make introductions and small talk with an air of authority.

Nell led off. "The wind power industry, although heavily subsidized, delivers only chaotically intermittent electricity. The magnets in turbine generators are made from rare earth minerals mined almost exclusively in China, the processing of which has fouled the land with giant toxic lakes. On top of that, the rate of energy generation divided by area is up to a hundred times lower than estimates. And this ignores the hazards to wildlife and the problem of disposing of worn-out wind-turbine blades."

She was good. Daniel sat back comfortably, pleased to see the director's satisfied grin. Coggin paid close attention to the graphs Nell projected on the screen, though at times he seemed more focused on Nell herself.

As much as they all needed to kiss up to Coggin, *that* was going too far. Pearce wouldn't hesitate to pimp their young associate to the director, but Daniel wouldn't permit it. Loyalty had to run both ways; he'd stand up against anyone, even Kent Coggin, to protect his team. Other than Bree's parents and her brother, there wasn't anyone else still deserving his loyalty.

Nell avoided getting lost in technical details or Coggin's inappropriate stare, and then Daniel introduced Jake, who delivered a similarly polished presentation on solar energy. He covered shrinking landfill capacity as consumers replaced solar panels with newer models, and the intermittent nature of sunshine in many locations. "But then," he added with theatrical flair, "in March the Democrats handed us a gift: a stake through the heart of the solar industry. Following a complaint by a small California manufacturer—drafted by PJ&H—the administration investigated Cambodia, Malaysia, Thailand and Vietnam for circumventing rules blocking China from dumping solar panels in the US market. They meant to pressure the Chinese for repressing their Uyghur minority in Xinjiang, but the effect was to choke off the supply of Chinese panels, which had accounted for 80 percent of the supply in the US. It crippled the industry."

At Jake's conclusion Daniel rose. "None of this good news undercuts the future of renewables. Continuing our current reliance on fossil fuels will bequeath a damaged if not dying planet to future generations. We all know that. But we believe it will take decades for wind and solar—or some as yet unknown source—to supply any substantial part of our energy needs."

"So it's business as usual," the director said, all smiles. He rose from his seat to shake each of their hands. "This is excellent news, Daniel. You've got a top-notch team here. We're grateful you took the time to give us this update."

Daniel was relieved the skies had cleared before they left the Oil Institute. He directed their driver to drop him at home. "You guys were great," he said. "Go get a celebratory drink on me. I'm knocking off for the day."

At home Daniel "knocked off" a bottle of bourbon. But this was no celebration; it was another cursed attempt to blank out thoughts of his wife and daughter.

Two days later Pearce returned from a trip and asked Daniel to join him for breakfast at The Mace. Daniel much preferred to ease into his day with coffee and the newspapers at his desk.

The prospect of eating with Pearce that early in the morning gave him indigestion.

He hadn't seen Pearce since his return and knew the boss would express sympathy—*as if* he harbored normal human emotions—but mostly would be doing a face-to-face assessment. Daniel would have to convince him his personal tragedy wouldn't affect his ability to do the job. He only wished this were true. Instead, he felt unsteady both in his ardor to advocate for fossil fuels and his physical stamina to get through the day. He wanted to just stay in bed.

That morning he had almost fallen over with dizziness when he turned on the shower. Even with his ears plugged and his eyes closed, the sound of splashing brought on a feeling of vertigo. He had to steady himself on the sink until his head cleared, and then decided to skip the shower.

He didn't need a psychiatrist to understand this. The thing was water, from the drowning nightmares he was having since the flood to tap water in a glass. Water in any form triggered the panic he first felt on the road by the Guadalupe.

It made no sense. A month ago he was lounging in Lake Corpus Christi. Now he couldn't even think about a lake or even a pool. But he had no time to dwell on irrational anxieties. He had to hurry to meet Pearce.

"Good to have you back, Daniel," Pearce said when he reached the table. "We are all truly sorry for your loss."

"Thank you, Branston. And thanks for the flowers; they meant a lot to Bree's parents."

"Oh, it was nothing, my boy."

It *was* next to nothing. Bree's parents probably hadn't even noticed the firm's bouquet among all the others, and that level of recognition probably fit how little thought Pearce put into whatever his secretary sent on behalf of the firm.

A waiter poured coffee and took their orders while Pearce

gestured at his phone lying on the table. "Have you seen the news about our man at the World Bank?"

Daniel shook his head, afraid he had missed something in the news.

"The ingrate got his appointment with the understanding he would stick to the party line that climate change is a hoax, but some damned German journalist pushed him at a public forum to admit that was a lie. Before TV cameras! To save his job—or from some wrong-headed notion of duty—this weasel threw it back in the face of the man who appointed him. It's getting to where you don't know who to trust anymore."

"Maybe the mistake was putting faith in a diplomat rather than a politician."

"You think ambassadors aren't politicians? How do you imagine they become ambassadors?"

Daniel sipped his coffee, thinking about the nebulous terms "duty" and "trust." Pearce held the honor-among-thieves view they all shared: it was your duty to stick by the people who put you in power and trusted you to press the party line regardless of "facts" thrown up by the opposition.

Pearce was relieved to hear Daniel's report on his meeting with Kent Coggin. He had grown fond of his protégé and was reassured his junior partner was still effectively delegating work to his associates and handling what he liked to call "the care and feeding of clients."

But there was more important ground to cover. "The pipeline fight has ramped up," he said. "Hack Jones has been standing in for you to direct the effort, but we need to start laying the groundwork for a vote early next term. Our client expects *you* to be the steady hand at the helm."

He paused for a response. A month ago Daniel would have jumped to affirm his loyalty. Now he just nodded, which was disquieting.

Pearce decided it was time for some tough love. "One other thing," he said, "and this is not a pleasant subject...."

Daniel looked apprehensive but said nothing. Pearce continued. "The publicity on the Guadalupe flood has impacted the firm because of our representation of Surefit Properties, *your* client."

Daniel looked taken aback. "But there was no way to foresee that."

"Possibly not," Pearce replied, "but the fact remains we are in bed with the villain here. Our clients won't condemn us for advocating for logging and development—which is all to the good—but they can and do object to bad press."

"I don't know what I could have done differently."

"It may not be fair but this is *your* problem to fix. Also, I'm afraid the second contingent payment of your bonus from last month has been deferred."

"But there was nothing 'contingent' about that bonus; it was for the methane vote."

"It's all connected, isn't it?"

Pearce looked closely at Daniel. The young man had suffered a personal loss, there was no doubt, and Pearce was as sorry for him as anyone, but the firm needed him to be on his game instead of giving them a black eye for involvement in the Texas flooding. Pearce had to show the clients he took this PR hit seriously and had exacted some kind of retribution. Besides, a little added financial incentive was all Daniel needed to get back up to speed. He had, after all, received half of the generous share of the success fee Pearce allotted to him and would no doubt earn back the rest in time.

Still, he had to account for the other contingency, that Daniel would *not* be able to handle the work. He considered who he had to back Daniel up, or take over if need be. Nell Batterly had a good head on her shoulders and hellfire behind her eyes, but she was young. That Gambol character was, too, and could be a loose cannon. Daniel said he was smart and worked hard, but could they count on his discretion? There was too much at stake to let baby lawyers run things, especially fools who smoked pot in office stairwells. If the pipeline vote failed with Daniel in the lead, Kent Coggin would question Pearce's judgment for putting him in charge, which could threaten future billings of the firm.

"What I need to know," he resumed, "is that you are fit and capable of leading this effort. It will be bare knuckles this time. The Institute needs a fighter in there."

"Sure," Daniel said. "Of course. You know me, Branston. I've never backed down from a fight."

Pearce peered at him, trying to see beyond the resolute expression Daniel managed. He concluded Daniel was his only real alternative for the moment; he knew the players—as well as where all the bodies were buried—so it would remain his job to lose. The best way to get past his Texas mishap would be for Daniel to bring in the pipeline vote.

To cover every contingency, though, Pearce would keep Hack Jones on the matter. He also needed to deepen his acquaintance with Daniel's two associates to determine if they could pick up the slack.

Daniel was enraged Pearce was withholding his bonus at the same time as feigning sympathy for the disaster that had smitten his world apart. He said the second payout was "deferred," but that simply meant it was no longer coming. It was not that Daniel really needed the money, but it wasn't fair. He had done exactly what he was supposed to do. He signed up a client that shared the interests widely represented by the firm and paid its legal bills on time. How could he know there would be a hundred-year flood and Surefit's development would point the finger at PJ&H?

Still, the subtle shift in Pearce's expression at the end of the meeting told Daniel he had won a reprieve, so he swallowed his rage and kept his mouth shut. He'd just have to pull it together, get to work and not be consumed with finding his daughter. Burying himself in the project would, in any event, be the best way to appease Pearce and move on with his life—at least until he came up with an alternative. The rest of his bonus? That was firmly in the old bastard's pocket.

He reached absently for his water, but looking into the glass made him dizzy. He quickly put it down, spilling on the table. To cover the abruptness of this move, he blurted out, "I'm all in, Branston. You've got nothing to worry about."

Daniel rode to work with Pearce, shut his office door and sat stiffly at his desk. Then he rose to pour a bourbon from the bottle on his credenza. But looking at the glass in the light from the window made him queasy. He put the glass down again.

He couldn't function like this, unable to stand even the sight of bourbon, and if Pearce found out, he'd be looking for another job. The old man had no patience for weakness.

PJ&H also had no room for decency. After pushing Daniel to develop his own clients, Pearce blamed him for signing up Surefit, which did the same kind of development PJ&H facilitated for other clients. The flood was just a business contingency no one could have foreseen. It was true the firm's reputation had taken a hit, but that was when Daniel's partners should have rallied around him. Instead, Pearce blamed the PR debacle on Daniel alone, and the rest of the partners rallied together to hang him out for public scorn. The parallel to what happened to his father was inescapable.

Daniel could recover from this setback, but he wouldn't ever trust his partners again, or even really think of them again as "partners." He longed for the kind of relationships he had in school, where the motivations were freedom and release and often enough idealism. Those bonds transcended time. The people he knew now, in contrast, had no faith in anything; all sense of allegiance rested on immediate self-interest. His only lifeline to empathy and compassion was his two young associates, and he could only hope they stuck by him out of more than self-interest.

Chapter
Fifteen

In November everyone's attention turned to the off-year election. The Republicans were sure to follow the usual pattern of the opposition party taking back the House and Senate. PJ&H had acted in some of the races, but Pearce and his partners followed the vote mostly as a spectator sport. It would help, policy-wise, for the Republicans to take control of Congress but, as the boss always said, the firm was more essential to clients dealing with an overbearing administration.

But the Republicans took only the House, not the Senate. The industry pressure would thus focus on the budget to keep the president in check. Pearce said they might work on a strategy to undermine the administration by refusing to increase the debt ceiling, which the Dems in their usual bumbling way had failed to do when they still controlled the House, despite dire warnings from their Treasury Secretary.

Daniel put his effort into showing up at work and not spending all his time badgering officials about the search for his daughter. When he did turn to work, he tried not to think too hard about the interests he was advocating. For the first time in his career he was paying attention to the actual social costs that meant nothing to his clients. How could it make sense to roll back clean water regulations or permit mining in fragile ecosystems? Should the government really have no role in calibrating gas mileage in new vehicles?

November and early December passed in a blur. Daniel kept clear of water in all its forms—beyond just enough washing to avoid being offensive. He put in time in the office to look like he was productive, although this was only possible by giving Nell and Jake ever bigger roles. He typically started drinking at lunch to ease the afternoon doldrums, when he too often dwelled on what he had lost. His soul felt cold, dark and empty.

The holidays were always slow at PJ&H, with Congress in recess. Daniel stayed in the city, jogging some and watching sports and often falling asleep on the sofa with a cocktail glass in this hand. Day after day waking up in this position, sick to his stomach, without even the prospect of going to the office to fill his empty day, convinced him, finally, that he needed help. But finding medical help would be a problem. He couldn't ask for a referral at work because it would get back to Pearce.

Then he thought of Glen Farrell. He was a college friend, although they had never been close and Daniel hadn't seen him in years. But he knew Glen was working in the psychiatric department at GW Hospital, which should qualify him to at least point Daniel in the right direction.

"Dan Lazaro," Glen said emphatically when he answered his office phone. "This is a surprise."

"I know, Glen. It's crazy how we all lose touch, what with work and families and all."

"I hear you're at PJ&H. Running with the big boys, huh?"

Daniel laughed. "I'm just a poor attorney trying to make

my way in the world. But you: a for-real psychiatrist; that's impressive."

"Well, I am, but I haven't quite finished my residency. So, Dan, not to cut this short but I've got a patient coming in. What can I do for you?"

"I have a personal problem right up your alley. It's something I need to keep quiet. I wondered if I might take you out for drinks to see what you think."

They met at a student pub where Daniel was fairly sure no one would recognize him. When his friend arrived, Daniel saw he had put on weight and lost some hair, but this made him look more like a shrink and reinforced Daniel's decision to turn to him.

Daniel accepted Glen's condolences, which felt sincere and what normal, caring people expressed after such a tragedy. But Daniel hurried through this, as well as talk about mutual friends, so he could turn the conversation to Glen's work.

Glen explained he specialized in forensic psychiatry, which concerned mental disorders in criminal offenders. "I spend a lot of time in prison," he joked.

"Well, I haven't been convicted of anything yet," Daniel responded, trying to keep the conversation light, "and I don't know if what's happening to me is even a psychiatric issue, but it's wrecking my life."

"I'm all ears."

"It's water. After thirty-four years, I suddenly can't stand water."

"You mean large bodies, like an ocean or lake?"

"I mean in any form. I get dizzy trying to take a shower and might have an attack from picking up a glass of tap water."

Glen looked closely at Daniel, but he didn't speak.

"It's messing up my life," Daniel went on. "The other day I almost passed out in a light drizzle. So far I've been able to keep it quiet, but if my boss finds out or a client notices, I'm sunk. In my business vulnerability just won't play."

Glen pondered this. "When did you first notice this condition?"

Daniel explained about the flood. "And after I saw the house was gone and my family lost, I tried to retrace my steps to the village, but at this big puddle a wave came at me like a tsunami, and I almost lost my mind. Ever since I've been a freaking basket case."

Glen nodded thoughtfully. "I'm really sorry about your family and everything. But you should know people develop phobias to many things. It could be spiders or enclosed spaces or heights, and practically anything might trigger the symptoms you describe. It sounds like you're suffering from aquaphobia, essentially a fear of water."

"But how does that make sense? How can someone be afraid of what we all need to live?"

"You suffered a trauma. In one moment you lost your family and your home, and it was all due to water. You know your fear is irrational, but it's nonetheless debilitating. You really should see a specialist."

"What about you? Can we deal with it now?"

"I'm not the right doctor for this, and you need help in a clinical setting."

"But there's a cure?"

Glen sighed. "As I said, I am no specialist, but there are a variety of treatments for phobias. You may eventually get over this. It's for your doctor and you together to come up with the best treatment."

"But I can't go to some psych ward. If they find out at work, they'll picture me in a straitjacket and sideline me. Then I won't be able to keep directing resources to finding my daughter."

"That sounds quite unenlightened for a workplace in the twenty-twenties."

"Nobody ever accused my firm of being enlightened."

Glen rubbed his chin, looking concerned, as Daniel downed his bourbon and waved for a refill. Glen said, "Look, Dan. You've suffered an unspeakable tragedy. It only makes sense your unconscious is running amok. I know a guy, a good doctor over at St. Elizabeth's named Haverly. Let me give you his number."

Daniel looked at Glen's business card with the number scribbled on the back, doubtful he would follow up. He needed a cure, not some doctor poking around his childhood trauma.

Glen seemed to sense his hesitation and spoke haltingly. "I'll leave the diagnosis to your doctor, but as a friend I can tell you aquaphobia is likely just a symptom, which may stay with you in some form or might disappear in an instant. But there is a phenomenon called 'comorbidity,' which essentially means any other disorder could make you more susceptible."

"What are you saying?"

"You've knocked back four bourbons in forty minutes. It could be alcohol is your real problem."

"Thanks a lot, *Doctor*," Daniel said caustically, his face suddenly flushed. "I ask for help with the water rushing through my brain and you tell me to cut out the one thing that brings me peace."

"Dan, you've got to see how that sounds."

"Oh, screw how it sounds." Daniel rose abruptly, almost knocking over his chair. "Thanks for your time," he said angrily, throwing a fifty-dollar bill on top of Glen's business card and storming out.

A cab took Daniel home. He bumped his way into his apartment, dropped his briefcase and suit jacket on the floor, poured a tumbler of bourbon and slouched down on the sofa. How could Glen think his water phobia came from drinking? It showed what a racket these psychiatrists had. They didn't have any answers; they just charged a fortune to tell you a lot of nonsense about hating your mother or not getting enough sex.

He was feeling sleepy but dreaded nodding off and returning to his nightmares. He wished he had some coke to wake himself up. But he had no problem with drugs or alcohol. He just liked them and had more than a good reason to medicate any way he could to face the image of his daughter washing down the river.

After draining his glass, he stumbled back to the liquor cabinet. The bourbon was almost empty. He lifted the bottle to his mouth to drink the few remaining drops, and then let out a guttural scream as he threw the bottle across the room. It shattered against a doorjamb. He leaned into the wall and sank to the floor, sobbing.

Daniel woke on the floor of the living room, still in his soiled clothes. He sat up and rubbed the back of his neck, stiff from sleeping awkwardly. The dent in the wall made him recall, suddenly though groggily, throwing the bottle.

What was wrong with him? This had to be rock bottom. His wife was dead. His daughter was lost. Water filled his nightmares and the terror followed him when he was awake. So now what?

He struggled to his feet and stumbled to the toilet to throw up.

The sound of flushing made him fall back heavily on the floor and almost black out. He had to stay conscious, slow his breathing. His shirt stuck to his back, soaked through with sweat.

He needed to get hold of himself. Drinking was a poor release; it changed nothing once he sobered up. Torment always came back hard and unsparing. It was no answer to this, what Glen called "aquaphobia." His hands shook. The room spun around him. He couldn't function like this. No one could live this way.

He had to clean up, pull himself together and get into work. At least he needed to be in the office, where he could keep up appearances and push the search for Annabelle.

He lost himself in the memory of an early Sunday morning when his daughter had just turned two. He had promised to let

Bree sleep in and, despite a thick head from too much wine at dinner, he lay on the bed in his daughter's room looking for a way to keep her amused without actually waking up. In a stroke of genius, he got out her box of berets and hung his head over the edge of the bed. He then dozed off to one of Annabelle's formless tunes while she went to work on him. When he finally rose and saw his finished coiffure, he knew he had to leave the berets in place until Bree got up. He could still hear his wife's delighted laughter later that morning filling River House.

But there was no joy this morning. His mouth tasted like chalk and his head split. He took a Tylenol bottle from the medicine cabinet, tipped three tablets into his hand and turned on the faucet to fill a glass. But the sight and sound of water forced him back onto his knees in dry heaves.

When his stomach settled, he was still on the bathroom floor. He had dropped the tablets but lacked the strength to look for them or stand up to get more, so he just sat, consumed by the pounding in his head.

After the dizziness passed, he found the Tylenol bottle and shook out three more pills. Steadying himself against the sink, he swallowed one at a time. The last one stuck in his throat. He reached for the faucet but held back, remembering how the gush of water had crashed over him like a wave. He coughed the tablet back into his hand and staggered out to the living room.

Liquor would wash down the pill. He could stand Scotch because it was medicine, not another disquieting form of water. A shot helped him swallow the last pill. Then he poured a second shot and raised it to his lips, pausing to inhale the cherished aroma.

In the back of his mind he heard Glen saying, "Alcohol could be your real problem." But that was insane. It was water that turned his stomach, not liquor!

As he raised the glass he saw the rising sun. He paused, again noticing the damage to the wall and broken glass on the floor. What was he saying? Drinking at dawn was *not* a problem? His trouble was water? The salvation from addiction and madness was to drink himself to death? That would almost be comical if it weren't so deluded.

He sat wearily on the sofa. There were only two ways this could go. He could give in, use ever-greater volumes of alcohol and drugs to keep up appearances and hold onto his job until he returned to some kind of normal. What "normal" would be he didn't know, but anyway he looked at it, this could not be the answer.

The other choice, the one he knew deep down he needed to make, was to get his life together. The water thing would sort itself out, he was sure of it, if he could just give up alcohol. He had long known his liquor consumption was out of hand, even before the flood. Bree tried to act like she didn't notice, but of course she did. People at work didn't care, as long as he got the job done. Half of them had the same problem. But he had known, really, that his health was suffering.

He went back to the liquor cabinet, stepping over broken glass. In a rush he grabbed as many bottles as he could and carried them to the kitchen, dropping a fifth of gin on the carpet. He poured one bottle after another down the sink, turning his head to avoid seeing the flowing liquids. In two more trips, all his liquor was down the sink.

He dug in the hall closet for a cardboard box, dumped gloves and winter hats on the floor and filled it with empty bottles. At the garbage chute down the hall he didn't drop the bottles in for fear of the racket it would make. This was going to be hard enough without calling undue attention to himself—as if his neighbors would have to guess who left a box of empty liquor bottles by the chute.

He returned to the bathroom to mop up the mess. Then he cooked eggs and forced himself to eat. With coffee and solid food in his stomach, he was able to clean up enough to get dressed. He was determined to hold off any nausea and focus on work. This would *not* be the first sick day he had ever taken at this job.

Before he left the apartment, he texted Glen: "You're right. Sorry. Give me that number again?"

Chapter Sixteen

"Honestly, there's no mystery to a fourteen-year drought hardening the soil."

It was late December, and Daniel was looking for answers. Did the development he pushed through for Surefit contribute to the Guadalupe flood? He felt guilty for other reasons—betraying his marriage, not being there for his family—but the thought of making the flood worse haunted him. He needed to hear the truth, which would never come from a politician or someone paid by industry. Howard was the only scientist he trusted to give him the facts free of politics.

"Fires and clearcutting eliminated vegetation in the Upper Valley," Kane said over the phone, "and development in the Lower Valley altered natural runoff patterns. Then throw on top of that the heatwave this summer—there were two a year in the '60s; now it's six. So, when a slow-moving weather system pulls warm, moist air from the Gulf and butts up against the hills...well, you saw what happens."

"But this is a natural cycle, right?" Daniel pleaded, staring out his office window. "Like El Niño and that other cycle in the Atlantic? There have always been floods and forest fires."

"Yes, nature clears itself out periodically, and we have identified climate cycles, some repeating every eighty years or more. And you must know the Texas Hill Country has long been called 'Flash Flood Alley.' Just look at the 1935 flood that washed out the Llano River Bridge, or 2002 when water over the Canyon Lake Spillway carved that huge gorge."

"Sure, but now we've got early warning systems."

"Yes, communities have adopted flash flood plans for warning, evacuation and mitigation. But the planet getting warmer makes everything worse. A heated ocean puts more moisture into the air. Increased rainfall on terrain denuded by forest fires and over-building turns into mud floods, which bulk up with sediment and debris.

"But how would it help, really, to rein in development? We'd still have wildfires, the air would still get hotter and in the end we'd all roast."

"Well, building on unstable slopes causes landslides and sighting houses up against forests puts them in the path of wildfires. But we should make like the frog in a pot who ignores the water getting hotter until he's good and cooked? Or, in this case, we figure the world won't go up in smoke for fifty years, so why change things now?"

"Right. Screw our descendants."

"Of course. Screw the descendants!"

Daniel gazed down. "We're all scoundrels."

"Uh-huh," Kane said. "The worst kind."

During his time off over the holidays, the phrase "screw our descendants" kept ringing in Daniel's ears. Doctor Haverly was away, like everyone else. So, while Daniel waited for an appointment in January, he kept going over the day of the flood.

There must have been some way to anticipate the river would take Bree and Annabelle. There was that call from Howard during the methane party. He was concerned enough about the fires to track Daniel down. Bree had said Matt Reese talked about the danger of clear-cutting near a burned-out mountainside. Why hadn't he put that all together and done something about it? He could have moved Bree and Annabelle out of Tanswego to her parents' house or anywhere away from the river—if he had only paid attention. But even after the reports of heavy rains in the hills, he did nothing, or worse than nothing; he joked about Jonah hiding from the thunder. That reminded him he hadn't given even a thought to his faithful old dog, who surely went into the river along with his wife and daughter. He had always been a good dog, from when he was a puppy with enormous paws sitting in Daniel's lap to when he got big enough for Annabelle to ride, but he was never much of a swimmer. Daniel had no doubt Jonah went into the river trying to save his family; his old friend could have taught him something about loyalty.

To distract himself he started following the news about Winter Storm Elliot, a "bomb cyclone" that hit from Colorado to Miami and made venturing outside an ordeal. What the National Oceanic and Atmospheric Association called an "historic arctic outbreak" buried Buffalo in fifty-six inches of snow over five days and caused temperatures in Denver to drop seventy degrees in eighteen hours.

But Daniel was growing skeptical of using hyperbolic terms like "historic" or "hundred-year storm" to describe extreme weather events that were no longer outliers. Using new terms like "weather whiplash" and "atmospheric river," showed environmentalists' increased savvy from the early days, when they relied on the stolid and imprecise term "global warming." While they had failed to affect any change in the world's response to the planet's downward spiral, they had at least learned something about marketing.

In the confines of his weather-locked apartment and tormented mind, it became a toss-up whether to torment himself about his still-missing daughter or the doomed fate of the planet. Either obsession tortured him. He had to fight hourly with the notion he could blot out both thoughts with a quart of bourbon.

The new term was in session, and Daniel's team was working with an economist from the Oil Institute on the pipeline bill about to be debated by the Commerce Committee. Pearce was concerned Senator Langston was not stepping up as promised to champion this bill.

"You have to convince him a pipeline for Canadian shale oil will be good for Texas rather than competition," Pearce said. "This is where you show everyone the old Dan Lazaro is back."

Daniel tried to look energized as he agreed to press the matter. He was sure Haley understood the big picture and this would be an easy sell—assuming she didn't get it into her head to squeeze more cash out of the Oil Institute. He called her assistant to set up a lunch for two days later, certain he could put the plan across in person but not wanting to meet her after hours. Sleeping with her again would *not* help him get his life back together.

In the afternoon he met with Nell and Jake along with a new junior associate to make certain everyone was on the same page. He was feeling reassured until Jake volunteered, "Have you seen Eco's piece on the flood?"

He sighed. "Honestly, I've been trying to avoid that subject."

"Oh, right, of course. I just thought you'd want to see how the greens are spinning it."

Daniel could *not* move forward by ignoring the past. He needed to keep up with the news, real *or* manufactured. "Let me see," he said, reaching for the laptop.

Jake brought up the latest edition of *Monkey Wrench* and handed over his computer. "I have to admit, that guy has a way with words."

As Daniel read the article, Nell added, "I can't understand the public fascination with that anarchist. Blowing up a pipeline makes him a hero? I wonder if he even really exists."

The headline read: "Human-induced Climate Change Upped Body Count in Hill Country Flood." Eco's name was not mentioned, although it was clearly his polished demagoguery. The article linked to and quoted extensively from a report by a Professor Cahill. What jumped out to Daniel, though, were the photographs. These were not stock news photos; they were poignant, ground-level images of suffering and destruction. The pictures were so evocative he had to swallow hard, envisioning his poor wife's body crushed by the river surge.

"Yeah, I see Eco's hand in this," he said after recovering himself.

"How does he manage to pull all the strings and yet we don't even know what he looks like?" Jake said. "He's a supervillain, like the Joker."

"You mean in how he taunts us?"

"That's right, Batman, and how he probably hides behind some secret identity."

Daniel smirked at Jake, wondering if he ever could have been that young. But then he pictured the woman, the one with the camera he saw talking with Pete up behind The Joshua Church. She must have taken those shots. And she could also be the woman in the photo with Eco. What was it about her face?

"What is it?" Nell said, apparently sensing he had figured something out.

"What?" he said, his attention snapping back. "Nothing; it's just you're right, Jake. This is Eco's work."

Daniel felt a growing need to understand this environmental messiah. Maybe this would show him a way out of his philosophical and moral morass. The way to do this—the only way he could think of—was to go through Pete to find that woman.

Chapter Seventeen

Daniel declined Jake's suggestion that they meet for drinks after work. At home he put on old jeans and a college sweatshirt and decided the clean the apartment. He didn't want even the people from his cleaning service to see it in its trashed condition.

The physical work did him good. When he finished he ordered delivery from his favorite Mexican restaurant and settled in to watch a familiar movie. He succeeded mostly in fighting off the cravings for liquor, thankful there was no alcohol in the apartment to tempt him.

He was nervous about his appointment with the psychiatrist. He had always seen weakness in anyone seeking therapy. How far gone did you have to be to need someone else to straighten out your mind? He now knew the answer to that question, or a couple of answers, at least. When you couldn't brush your teeth without feeling faint, or when you hated how you smelled because you couldn't take a real shower, it was time to ask for help.

When the hero of the movie found a boat and put out to sea,

Daniel lunged for the remote to shut it off, a rumbling in his chest threatening to bring up his dinner. How had he forgotten about that scene? His guilt was not going to let up, even in the security of his apartment. Remorse knew no bounds of time or place. He had to be more careful.

The day of his appointment finally arrived. He was nervous but also impatient to find out if medical science could resolve his trauma.

He walked to Doctor Haverly's office on M Street, keeping a close eye out for anyone he knew. When he ducked through the doorway, he scolded himself for imagining someone was watching. What he was doing was no one else's business. He had suffered a trauma; so what if he needed to talk to someone about it? Still, he added paranoia to his phobia for water and lurking alcoholism on the list of the maladies ruling his life.

The doctor looked younger than he had expected. No goatee or pince-nez, he had thick dark hair and wore a well-tailored suit. His calming manner immediately put Daniel at ease.

"It may come as a surprise to you," Doctor Haverly said, "but nearly 3 percent of the population have an irrational fear of water in some form or another. There is something called thalassophobia—a fear of large bodies of water—and ablutophobia—a fear of bathing. Some people fear being sprayed or splashed. Others even stop brushing their teeth."

Daniel was reassured to hear he was not alone.

"We treat some patients with exposure therapy," the doctor went on, "which involves psychotherapy and learning to breathe and relax during exposure. Others respond well to medications. But, to start, tell me about your issue. When did you first notice a fear of water?"

Daniel recounted the flood and his hike down the Guadalupe to find his house and family washed away.

"Well," the doctor said, "this sounds like a major factor, possibly the cause or perhaps a trigger for something more deep-rooted."

"I don't understand. I mean, I get how losing my family would mess with my head, but why do you think my fear might come from something else?"

"The mind is a curious thing, Mr. Lazaro. Our conscious mind sometimes masks what is really troubling our subconscious."

"Well, Glen Farrell—the doctor who referred me—suggested drinking could be the root of my problem. And I've turned that around. I'm determined to cut out alcohol and drugs to clear this up, but it hasn't helped."

"You must understand, Mr. Lazaro, that there are dangers to jumping to conclusions when we are exploring disorders of the mind."

"I get that, Doctor, but I am useless as I am, and I can't go on like this. My daughter is still missing, and my job is a mess. Can't you just give me your first impression? We can always revisit this later."

Doctor Haverly squinted as though pondering this. "This is not the preferred manner of treating an issue like yours, but I understand what you say and certainly do not want to exacerbate your condition." He paused, and Daniel looked at him with all the hope and sincerity he could muster.

"Well," the doctor went on, "Drinking to excess certainly is no good for anyone, and it could be a contributing factor, but I'm inclined to see this as one more symptom of the problem, or perhaps an indication of an addictive personality that could be susceptible to aquaphobia."

"Then this is some kind of response to the flood, like my brain can't process losing my wife and daughter?"

The doctor rubbed his chin, peering as if he were looking inside him. "The immediate trauma was clearly a trigger. Water did the damage and so water is a threat, but there may be more to it."

"Well," Daniel said haltingly, "there is more."

Doctor Haverly raised his eyebrows, gesturing to go on.

"I feel responsible."

"How could you be responsible for a natural occurrence?"

"I wasn't there to protect them. Bree was home taking care of my daughter while I was far away, living a separate life."

"You were here for your work?"

"Yes, but that was partly my choice. I mean, I went home for weekends, spent the holidays and vacations with the family, but I'd be lying to say I didn't sometimes stretch out my time in the city."

"Was that the case the day of the flood?"

He breathed in deeply. He had not expected the conversation to go this way. Was his guilt just about working in DC? What choice did he have? He had to provide for his family, which he did by giving them a wonderful home in a bucolic setting. He wasn't the first man to work far from home to make a life for his family.

The doctor had been sitting quietly but now spoke. "I sense there is something you would like to get off your chest."

He was not going to tell the doctor about Haley. That had been a mistake, obviously, and yes, it made him feel guilty, but if that was the cause of his aquaphobia, then he had the answer and didn't need to talk about it.

"It is clear, Mr. Lazaro, something more is troubling you. I have conducted more of these sessions than I could count, and I can see when a patient is holding back something important. I can tell you, this will not help; it will merely delay the healing process. I am your doctor, sworn to confidentiality. I am here for you but can only help if you open up to me."

They sat in silence. Seconds thundered by on some enormous clock in Daniel's head. Finally, he blurted out: "There was another woman. I mean, that's not why I wasn't there the day of the flood, but I was with her that day. It was a mistake I regret every day. But there's no escaping that I cheated on my wife."

"Well," the doctor said, as if they had reached a conclusion, "you are not the first spouse to have strayed, and your feeling of guilt seems like one more contributing factor to your reaction to water. I think we should explore this further. Our time is up for today, but I strongly recommend you come back. We have made substantial progress for one session, but there is more to do to understand your reaction and consider how I might help."

"That's it?" Daniel said urgently. "This isn't going to cure me?"

"Perhaps this has helped, but only time will tell. It is my professional opinion you would benefit from at least a few more visits. Please see my receptionist to set up an appointment next week. In the meanwhile, I urge you to stand by your resolve to refrain from drinking or using any drugs not prescribed for you. I suggest you also try to ease into using water as necessary, for bathing, etcetera. We'll talk again next week."

Daniel went to work, hopeful his visit to Doctor Haverly would have a positive effect. It was some relief to have spoken about it to someone, including about the affair. But the thought of water still made him uneasy, and he would proceed slowly in exploring whether he was any better.

He was having trouble concentrating on the pipeline project and so decided to spend the afternoon catching up on recent events. There was some news about COP27, the upcoming United Nations climate meeting in Egypt. Checking the meeting schedules, he laughed at the irony of the UN planning its 2024 "Conference of Parties" in Dubai. Leave it to the eco-idiots to hold a conference on climate change in a city built in the desert with oil and gas money. The UAE probably bid for this conference not to be outdone by Qatar's snagging the World Cup in 2022. And, whether in Egypt or Dubai, no movement on energy policies was likely beyond grandiose statements and commitments *about the future.* Unless and until the participants at one of those conferences agreed upon action *now*, his clients need have no concern about their business.

Still, he had to keep up to date on developments. "Alice," he called through his open door, "could you find and print me a copy of a climate report issued in the last few days by a Professor Cahill?"

"Right away," she responded. "But you have a call from Haley Bourdain."

He suddenly recalled he had agreed to meet Haley for lunch the next day.

"We'll have to put off our date," she told him, granting him a reprieve. "I've got to fly to Chicago to twist some arms and then on to Europe to pave the way for a congressional junket in May."

"Really? Well, I'm glad it's not my arm you'll be twisting and I hope you get some time off to see the sights."

She paused. He worried she might have sensed relief in his voice. "Yes, I will visit a supporter of the senator's at a villa in the south of France. But it's all work, one way or another. We'll catch up when we're both back," she said.

"We?"

"I'm afraid my schedule means you'll want to be taking a trip alone to bring the pipeline bill to the senator."

Much as Daniel wanted to avoid Haley, he would have preferred that to enduring a face-to-face with Langston. "Well, you know I am the senator's biggest fan, and I'm happy to walk the draft over to his office."

"Yes, well, I'm afraid the senator is in Texas with appearances set up into next week, so...."

"I have to meet him in Texas," he said resignedly.

"The best place to catch him will be Tanswego. I'm sure you know they're holding a memorial to commemorate six months since the flood. It will give you a chance to reconnect."

His breathing stopped for a moment. Haley was one cool

operator, but this was callous, even for her. Going back to that hell hole was the last thing he wanted to do.

At his apartment that night Daniel was about to settle down in front of the television with a microwaved chicken pot pie when his phone rang.

"Danny, it's Pete.""Pete," he said awkwardly, taken by surprise.

"Oh, sorry, dude. Didn't mean to freak you out. Just wanted to check in, make sure you're okay."

"That's nice of you, man. Thanks. And yeah, I'm good, trying to keep busy. *You* know. How are you...and the parents?"

"Ah, the folks are gloomy. We're all still sad; I don't have to tell you."

"Yeah..." Daniel said and trailed off. Neither spoke for a long moment, until Pete broke the silence. "So I take it there's no news about Annabelle?"

"No, but I promise you it's not for lack of trying. I've been all over the feds and the state officials. Trust me, everything humanly possible..."

"I get it, Dan. I shouldn't have even asked. But..." Again he paused.

"What is it, Pete?"

"Well, I've also got an unrelated problem. I know this isn't your field, but I wondered if you could..."

"I'm listening. What is it?"

"It's just...you see I shared an apartment with this guy who split town, and then, well, the landlord was hassling me, and the place was a shithole, anyway, so I moved out. Well, so now the landlord is coming after me. I got a summons to appear in court. He's suing for past rent—not just *my* half but *all* of it—plus damages for broken furniture and holes in the wall. It's crap, but I'm afraid his lawyers will eat me alive."

Daniel rested his head in his hands massaging his temples. This was no time to be dealing with some slumlord.

"Dan? Are you still there?"

"Yeah. Just thinking." His brother-in-law could avoid always getting into trouble simply by not associating with disreputable people—like this roommate, apparently—and acting irresponsibly by walking out on a lease. Like his sister, he had no concept of how the world worked. But that reminded him how Bree would always move heaven and earth to help her brother. Maybe he owed it to her to straighten out this mess.

"Whose name is on the lease?"

"We both signed."

Daniel took a deep breath. "Well, that won't matter if we can't find your roommate. Listen, I'm going to ask my real estate partner to talk with you. When's the court date?"

Daniel thought so long about that conversation his dinner got cold. Pete had never liked him but he had loved his sister to a fault. In fact, other than Bree they had nothing in common. But in Tanswego Daniel started to sense his brother-in-law genuinely cared for him. And now this sad guy was reaching out for help, which was easy enough to provide. It was moments like this, when trouble reordered the universe, that showed people petty differences didn't matter and brought them together.

After making a call to his real estate partner, Daniel's thoughts returned to Eco. His feeling had grown that talking to this man would help get his mind straight. Daniel had to find a way to contact him. Could he ask Pete to help? Was that Eco's partner behind The Joshua Church with his brother-in-law? Would Pete be able to introduce them?

Chapter Eighteen

Late Thursday afternoon Branston Pearce summoned Daniel to his office to discuss the pipeline project. Daniel was still seething about this insensitive bastard clawing back his bonus, but he had to hide his resentment.

Pearce poured two glasses of Scotch, handed one to Daniel and motioned him to take one of the leather chairs across from his desk.

Pearce sipped and then spoke. "Higgins at the Institute says they've vetted the bill draft. They have only minor comments. You should be able to share it with Langston tomorrow. Do you anticipate any resistance there?"

"No," Daniel replied, setting his glass on the desk and trying to ignore it. "I've laid it out for the senator's chief of staff. She says he'll be on board, once he sees the actual wording. He also wants to know who else will be sponsoring and..."

"And what?"

"Well, it sounds petty, but this *is* Langston. He insists his name be listed before the senator from Pennsylvania. Apparently, there's bad blood over a highway project."

"Whatever. I'm sure you can make peace."

Daniel nodded. "Looks like he just wants his big, old cowboy boots licked again." He was thinking how much the senator had in common with Pearce, although his boss was smarter and more manipulative—and he never wore cowboy boots.

"He has no idea who's really in charge," Pearce said.

"No, but we still have to play the game. He'll be speaking at a memorial at the flood site tomorrow. I'll fly down to make sure the bill moves."

"While you revive your close working relationship with Ms. Bourdain?" Pearce said, deadpan.

Daniel affected a smile. "Oh, Haley and I are all right. But she's got a meeting in Chicago, so I'll have to use my charm directly on the old turkey buzzard."

Daniel didn't want to return to Tanswego. Barring news of his daughter, which he had given up on ever hearing, he had intended never to return to Kendall County. There was hardly anyone still in the village he wanted to see again. All his happy memories of the place had washed away with the wreckage of his life. It would not be smart, in any event, to get near the river in the company of Senator Langston. He'd lose all credibility if the senator saw him collapse.

After a flight and a drive, Daniel found the senator sitting in a limousine parked above the village. They quickly went over the language of the bill. Langston was inattentive, as usual, only making sure his name was listed above his rival senator.

"Dan," Langston said in his patrician drawl as he exited the car and handed the draft to his aide. "We'll give this a thorough look-over and get back with you next week. Thank you for making the trip. I know this tragedy affected you even more than the rest of us, and I hope you'll take comfort from the ceremony. We've brought down a bishop from Dallas to preside, and local folks will be reading off the names of those who were lost, which I know touches you personally."

"Thank you for thinking of me, Senator, but I really need to get back."

Langston shrugged and moved off with his entourage. Daniel was thankful for that. The senator was a tool, without an original thought in his head or a glimmer of actual compassion. Whatever eulogy Haley had written for him would do Daniel no good.

Requiring Daniel to make the trip from Washington was how the senator reminded Pearce PJ&H was beholden to him. How would the good old boy react if the firm ever released the materials Pearce kept in the safe?

Any further thought of Langston faded when Daniel spotted Pastor Vincent leaving The Joshua Church. He had never really thanked the minister for helping him that first day, when he desperately needed a shoulder to cry on. He called out.

"Daniel!" the pastor said with genuine joy. "It's good to see you. We didn't expect you to make the trip."

"Not by choice, I'm afraid. More a courtesy call on our senator."

"I see," Vincent said in his knowing but nonjudgmental way. "So, how are you adjusting?"

"Ah, you know, Vincent. The world turns upside down, but we have to move on."

The pastor responded with a sad smile and a hand on Daniel's shoulder. Then he perked up to say, "Will you participate in the reading of names?"

"No. For me grieving is private, and you know my daughter is still missing. The only important thing now is to keep up the search. But what about you? What's this about a celebrity bishop from Dallas?"

"Ah, yes," Vincent said with a tolerant look, "Baptist Bishop Tanksbury has graciously made the trip down to lead the prayers."

Daniel tried to read the pastor's reaction to being upstaged in his own village. But it was no surprise Langston would recruit a preacher aligned with his party who knew how to play to a TV audience. Religion was just part of the spin of an event that would surely make regional if not national news. "I guess the senator needed a little star power," he said sarcastically.

"Well, let's not be unkind, Daniel. We are a simple community of believers. Ceremonies are better handled by our Baptist brothers and sisters, and Bishop Tanksbury is an eminent minister."

"Amen to that," Daniel said. "Although I must say, Vincent, your reading at the dig site that first day moved me like no ceremony I've ever attended."

As Vincent moved down the hill, Daniel had a sudden thought and walked up to the church. He had wondered how he could contribute to rebuilding the village, but his professional experience made him skeptical of organizations that solicited donations after natural disasters. Pastor Vincent, he now realized, provided the solution. He wrote out a check for a substantial amount to the Joshua Church and put it in the poor box. He only regretted he didn't have the cash with him so he could make this donation anonymously. He then stepped back into the sunshine and gazed sadly at the ruined village once more before departing, but was surprised to see Pete walking up the hill.

"I didn't expect to meet you here," Daniel said, shaking his hand.

"Yeah, it's a surprise to me too. I wouldn't have bothered except the folks wanted someone from the family to attend. But hey, I want to thank you for helping with my landlord thing."

Daniel nodded, thinking again about Pete's apartment problem for the first time since he had referred it to his partner. "So was it resolved?"

"Yeah. After I took the lawyer through the apartment, she threatened the landlord with all kinds of violations. I ended up paying my half of the rent, but they credited my security deposit. The lawyer didn't even charge me. She said it was on the house."

"Well, I'm glad that worked out. Landlords tend to squeeze tenants who don't know their rights."

Pete nodded appreciatively, as a speaker started to address the crowd. "So," he said, "I take it you're not going to the ceremony."

Daniel shook his head. "I had to come down to finish some business, not to commiserate with bleeding hearts and politicians."

"I hear you, brother. Fool politicians and greedy developers: they're good at the sympathy routine after the fact, but they continue to bring the shitstorms down on us all."

Daniel was surprised at how the tragedy—and possibly his wake-up call of dealing with an irate landlord—had matured his brother-in-law. Or maybe with Pete's sister gone, he realized he needed to step up. He seemed less wayward, as if he had found focus.

Daniel fumbled for how to bring up the subject of Pete's companion in Tanswego. Finally, he just said, "When we met here last time, you said you drove over with a woman?"

"Yeah. She wanted to photograph the village."

"But she was *not* with Homeland Security."

Pete laughed. "Oh, no, man. I just gave her a ride, and she had those vests to get us into the village."

"I'm pretty sure I saw you two up behind the church. She's thin, with long brown hair?"

"That's her. Her name's Verde, which I think means 'green' in Romanian."

"No kidding? She's Romanian?"

"Not sure. She's got this steamy accent, but she doesn't share much about herself."

He contemplated the "Verde" name, which could be made up or maybe it was common in her country, but more important was whether she was in the photo with Eco. He needed to meet her to figure this out, although now he was unsure what he would do if he got the chance. "Is she still in the area?" he asked, trying to sound casual.

Pete smiled as if with some secret knowledge. "Actually, I think she might still be in Austin. Maybe you'd like to meet her?"

Daniel felt a spark of excitement, his first real emotion since the flood besides guilt and grief. But Pete offering to arrange this meeting was unexpected...and a little suspicious. It was hard to imagine his brother-in-law involved with Anthro, but if he was, could this be some kind of setup? It couldn't possibly be Pete plotting against him, but then Daniel had for one thoughtless moment considered offering up his brother-in-law to Joe Coulder.

In any case, it made sense to meet this woman if he could. It might be his only way to reach Eco, which felt necessary to get over his phobia. And then Joe Coulder also was desperate to find Eco, and maybe Daniel could deliver him up without implicating Pete. Still, these aims clearly conflicted. What did he really want?

"Yeah," Daniel said, swallowing hard. "Can you make it happen?"

Daniel drove back to Austin with Pete. At a gas station, his brother-in-law stepped aside to make a call and returned looking pleased with himself.

"All arranged," he said, pulling back into light traffic.

Again, Daniel was impressed with this new version of Pete. He asked, "So where are we going to meet this woman?"

"Just outside of town. But there's a couple of things you should know."

Daniel turned to him, expectantly.

Pete glanced over and spoke quietly, as if to avoid being overheard. "Verde works with people concerned about climate change."

"Well, we're all concerned, especially after the flood."

"Right, but Verde is high up in a group that's *doing* something about it. And the thing is, she needs to avoid the kind of people you sometimes work for...."

"And the FBI."

Pete coughed. He apparently hadn't expected Daniel to make that connection.

"Let's just say she wants to avoid publicity. But she's willing to meet you *if* you give me your word this will stay private." He looked meaningfully at Daniel.

Daniel nodded agreement, though he worried that, by giving his word, he was committing to protecting fugitives and very clearly not cooperating with Joe Coulder. "You said a couple of things?"

"Oh, yeah." Pete laughed. "She's badass. I've never yet seen her smile, except maybe once with this other guy in the group. I mean, she'll meet you, but it will be strictly business. Don't expect her to be all friendly and shit."

Daniel spent the rest of the drive in internal dialogue. On one hand he felt compelled to meet Verde. She could be the key to finding this Eco guy everyone was so obsessed about. But what would she think of him? She must know who he was or she would never have agreed to meet. But then she'd know he pushed through the methane vote and helped facilitate the development that contributed to the Guadalupe flood. So what did she want, and why would she trust him? He wasn't sure himself what he was doing.

His guilt for helping Surefit, on top of his disgust at how Pearce treated him about the methane bonus, left him rudderless, exposed to mental currents he couldn't control. What if this woman was not some eco-banshee out to tear down the system? What if the activists were right about the planet's death spiral and had some sort of answer? And even besides this, his image of this woman—from that blurry photo to his brief glimpse in Tanswego—loomed large in his mind.

In any event, he had just promised to keep the meeting confidential. Was that a vow he could keep?

Chapter Nineteen

Daniel scanned the woods as Pete pulled into a dirt parking area at a trailhead outside Austin. There were no other cars.

Pete sent a text and watched his phone. "Okay, we're on," he said, nervously.

When they got out of the car, Pete's eyes moved past Daniel's shoulder. Daniel turned and saw her, ten feet away, a woman in a black tank top and cargo pants, dark hair in tied a long ponytail.

"Dan...this is Verde," Pete said, with an expression hard to unravel. In place of his usual dopey demeanor, he seemed intimidated.

She *was* the woman in the photograph! How had she appeared out of nowhere?

She extended a slender hand. "It is a pleasure, Counselor," she said, pronouncing her I's like long E's and enunciating each syllable. "We have much to discuss."

She glanced at Pete and said, "Take care of Mr. Lazaro's phone."

Daniel looked up in surprise but then understood this was a reasonable security measure and handed over his cell phone.

"You'll use a prepaid phone next time," she said, "if there *is* next time—to avoid tracking of your location or tapping into your line. For today we will simply remove your SIM card and battery and you can reassemble your phone after you leave."

What did she mean "next time"? Daniel intended this meeting as simply a way to get information and try to meet Eco. He hadn't thought through what came next and certainly did not intend to make this a regular thing...or did he?

Reaching into her shoulder bag, she added, "We also need to scan."

He sighed and held his hands over his head while she ran a wand up and down his sides.

"That is done," she said. "You understand we need to take precautions to ensure our conversation is kept in confidence."

If she knew how PJ&H recorded supposedly private conversations, she would have felt no need to apologize. But her caution surprised him, after all the stories he had heard about weed-smoking, granola-eating activists. In a way it reassured him he was dealing with an organization capable of holding a clandestine meeting.

"You will stay with car," she said to Pete. "Attorney Lazaro and I must have some private discussion."

Pete had started after them but stopped, looking from one to the other. Verde had wanted to meet Daniel, and he made it happen. Wasn't that enough to show his loyalty? Shouldn't he be part of the conversation? Or was he just an errand boy or a lookout?

"Shouldn't I come with?" he said, thinking too late how needy that sounded.

Verde shot him a look, which shut him up. She was gorgeous, but man, she could put on a face that said not to mess with her.

He'd seen this kind of initiation in movies, where the new guy had to prove himself to gain access to the inner circle. There were bound to be dues to pay before he made it to the inside of Anthro. Still, Verde could be nicer. She shouldn't just tell him to stay as if he were a dog.

"I'll keep watch," he said, as they walked away. "I'll beep once if a private citizen happens by, twice if it's police or rangers."

Verde seemed to ignore him as she led Daniel up a trail. His brother-in-law looked back curiously before following her into the woods, which made Pete a little embarrassed.

Mia gave little thought to Pete. He had served his purpose, but she wouldn't trust him with much more, not until he had proven his competence. Even then, he seemed useful only for simple tasks.

She also had serious misgivings about Daniel, but Kristof was excited by the possibility of securing a contact inside the oil industry. That prize was worth the risk of a meeting and the time away from other work. So, she led Daniel up the trail for privacy. And besides the security considerations, it was right this conversation should take place surrounded by the nature he worked callously to destroy.

She picked her way along the rough path, unconcerned about branches she let slap him in the face. This man stood for everything she despised. He and his kind left death and destruction in the wake of their greed. They used every artifice of deception and corruption to keep burning oil, and the price was paid by every person living by a stream or on the coast or near a forest, in fact every person who breathed air. If Kristof had not pleaded with her to meet him, she would never have wasted her time.

Out of sight of the trailhead, she stepped easily across a small stream, hopping from one large rock to another. But she heard Daniel stumble, and turned to see him shrink back with a look of terror.

"What is the matter?" she said, puzzled and impatient.

"It's nothing," he stammered. "Can we just talk here, I mean, on this side of the water?"

This was odd. What was wrong with this pitiful man? "It is not slippery," she said condescendingly. She knew he worked in Washington—and perhaps he had been raised in the city—but could that explain being too timid to cross a puny stream?

Still he held back.

She said, "Just step on the stones."

"I know, but it's just..."

She stepped back across the stream to peer at his face. He was sweating and looked as if he might be sick. His pallid face lessened her suspicion he might be putting on an act. Still, she had a bad feeling about this meeting and quickly went over in her mind her escape route. But then she could see there was no threat from him; he looked helpless.

"Are you ill?" she said, giving him one chance to continue the conversation.

"I am...I guess. It's only since the flood. I can't..." he paused and wiped his forehead. It was clear he was embarrassed.

"It's water," he said. "Well, you saw what happens. My doctor calls it aquaphobia, but all I know is water makes me nauseous."

This was difficult to believe. But a phobia about water might explain the sweating and spectral pallor. This weakness could even prove a positive thing, if his family's death affected him severely enough to make him switch sides in the battle for the planet. She did not trust him or like him, but maybe there was a conscience buried somewhere in his cursed soul.

She turned away from the stream and led him back down the trail to a log where she suggested he sit and catch his breath. He sat quietly with eyes closed while she looked around to make sure they were alone.

When he opened his eyes again, she resumed. "We know who you are."

"We?"

"Your FBI colleagues know us as Anthro. We have struggled for years to prevent incidents like the flood that has killed your wife and daughter...."

He gave a start. She realized she had been too abrupt. It was critical to handle a potential recruit carefully. Still, she needed to determine his usefulness without wasting time. She tried empathy. "Yes, like I said, we know who you are. I am truly sorry—I should have said at first—for your loss. This tragedy should happen to no one."

"Well," he said resignedly, trying *not* to talk about his own troubles so he could maintain his composure, "nobody controls nature."

It was exasperating to hear this kind of rationalization, but she had made the trip and so would once more try talking reason to the unhearing. "It is true, we cannot tame climate," she said, "but we *can* stop making things worse. We can address wilderness degradation, pollution, extinction and overpopulation. We can manage our forests and curb development of wetlands. We can stop pumping greenhouse gasses into the atmosphere. Where I grew up, those in power leveled the forests and defiled the land... and killed people I loved who tried to stop them. And now the planet warms faster than anyone could foresee, and yet people like your clients have no sense of this, no conscience about the health of their planet. They would leave the rest of the world, and generations to come, to live with the consequences of their greed. But we—the thinking people of the world—can still make a difference."

"I hear you," he said, and after a pause continued. "I've been soul-searching these last few weeks. And you see how the flood has made me a cripple. I have come to hate representing the people who fight what's staring us in the face."

This volte-face was a little too neat for her to believe. This man for years fought for big oil. He was instrumental in passing destructive legislation. Was the river killing his wife and child enough for him suddenly to grow a conscience? "What do you mean?" she said abruptly.

"I don't know. I'm feeling like I can't be part of it anymore. Anyway, with my wife and daughter gone, there is nothing left for me in that world."

She contemplated this. Daniel's words would not convince her of his sudden epiphany, if not for something in his eyes and in how his voice faltered. And he did not seem cunning enough to concoct a water phobia. But she still didn't trust him. She had to make sure before bringing him to Kristof. This man intertwined with the oil industry. Yet this was precisely why he might prove useful. She needed to test him.

"Have you considered doing something to make up for the past?"

"I have...I mean, I would. I just don't know how."

"Perhaps there is some way you could help our cause," she said.

"Tell me. What?"

"First—I hope you understand—we need to know you are in earnest. I am sure you know your FBI has a history of paying agents to entrap activists."

Daniel shook his head. "Yeah, I know about some of those efforts, like with Earth Liberation Front in the '80s."

"Yes, and many others; you can see a list of more recent informers on *Monkey Wrench*. We are *not* paranoid."

"It's not paranoia if they're really out to get you, right?" he said and for some reason grinned.

Unsure if that was a joke, she affected a smile without humor. "Exactly. And so you must see your sudden turnabout raises suspicions."

"I..." he said but paused, thinking this through in real time. This woman was severe and demanding, but he still wanted to help. "We—most of the people I work with—honestly knew all along we were doing what you say: putting greed ahead of the general good. But I'm not sure what will make you trust me."

"I know, and I appreciate your caution." Should he tell her he hated the work *and* the people he worked for? But this seemed petty when she was focused on survival of the planet.

She continued. "Perhaps you will bring us something to demonstrate your sympathies? Some information we do not already know?"

He was alarmed. He didn't want her to end the meeting, but it sounded like she wanted him to spy on his clients. How could he do this? How could he heal himself by disregarding his professional responsibility? "Well," he said, "as an attorney I've got an ethical duty not to reveal confidences of my clients."

"I see," she said, looking almost disgusted. "So we are clear, your duty as attorney outweighs your obligations of conscience?"

"It's not as simple as that."

"Then let us please explore this to help me understand. Is it not true an attorney in America has no obligation to keep secret the information if a client is about to commit a crime?"

"That's correct."

"And you agree your clients perpetrate mass, ongoing crimes against country and entire world?"

"In a general sense...yes."

"And yet it is ethics that prohibit you from revealing information to forestall these crimes?"

He rubbed his hand over his face to stall for time. How did she know about legal ethics? She put in simple terms the dilemma that made his head spin. Would a court or the bar association agree, or was he putting his law license on the line? He wasn't troubled by turning on Pearce; it would be sweet to stick it to that greedy bastard. But could he violate the law and breach his legal ethics while still doing the right thing?

He pictured Annabelle traipsing through the house in her orange bathrobe, humming and dragging her stuffed alligator behind her. Before the flood he had a whole life: his wife adored him; his daughter filled the world with curiosity and wonder; their home externalized their dreams. But it all went to shit, and he and his bloody professional responsibility were to blame. He spent years helping foul the air and strip the hillsides. Even worse, when the earth reared up to demand retribution, he failed in his first duty: to protect the innocents who relied on him.

So, now he had an opportunity. Could he turn his life around without throwing it away? What was his life worth, anyway, without the sound of those little feet and Bree's laughter and even Jonah's deep but harmless bark?

Chapter Twenty

Daniel's coffee had sat on his desk for an hour. It tasted like this day was shaping up: cold and bitter. But meeting Verde on Friday had opened a doorway. The emotions piling up inside him—grief, anger, guilt—had for so long been pushing him to do something, take some action; maybe she was showing the way.

The night before he had dreamed he was standing on the high diving board at the pool in his hometown. He must have been a teenager. He walked to the edge and peered at the water, impossibly far below, which made him stumble back and fall, but he caught hold of the board from below. His arms ached as he hung and strained to scream—and scream was all he wanted to do. He woke up with a cramp in his arm.

He had scheduled his third visit with Doctor Haverly, so he had someone to share his dream with. But he could see for himself his fear of water permeated not only his waking hours but his subconscious mind as well.

He sat through meetings as needed and gave half-hearted

instructions but mostly kept to his office. He couldn't concentrate on work; every step he took for his clients felt like another nail in his cross. So he turned to broader climate issues. He needed to wring the truth out of the noise—from both sides—and confirm his next step was right. He wouldn't jump to conclusions contrary to every position he had advocated at PJ&H just because his personal tragedy was wrapped in climate issues. He needed to know the facts.

He called Nell and Jake into his office.

"What have you two got on now?" he asked.

They looked at each other in surprise. Nell said, "The pipeline project, like you told us. Jake is dealing with the Dakota litigation, and I'm coordinating with Canadian industry."

"Well, there's something I want you to look into at the same time."

They both looked interested but perplexed.

Daniel took a deep breath. "We need to know more."

"About...?" Nell said.

"About what's actually happening to the planet and what can be done about it."

Both associates looked startled. "But that's not our job," Nell said.

"Yeah," Jake added. "Who's going to pay for pure research—especially when our clients might not like what we find out?"

Daniel nodded his head. "Exactly. But we're going to do it because we need to know. *I* need to know."

The associates again looked at each other and then back at Daniel, waiting.

"Okay, first," Daniel said, "the scientific literature—I mean from scientists *not* on the energy industry payroll—says the Earth is warming. You can see this on the news. Glaciers are melting and the sea rose twice as fast in 2014 as in 2002."

"So what's to research?" Jake said.

"That part won't take much. Since there is no honest dispute, just pull together a summary of the statistics. No hyperbole but no obfuscation."

"Simple enough," Nell said.

"A wrinkle I want to cover," Daniel added, "is how much of this warming can be explained by natural phenomena: El Niño and the like, the oscillations that occur in the Atlantic and the Pacific in varying cycles. Let's find out how far back the data goes. And while we're at it, figure in volcanoes; they spew ash into the air that actually cools the planet. But how many active volcanoes are there, and what's the net effect? Focus on the eruptions since Ponitubo in '91, when we first had modern instruments to record the data."

Jake held up his hand. "Can we use legal assistants on this?"

"Look," Daniel said abruptly, "this won't take much time. I'd prefer you do your own legwork and not let this get around the office, unless you can break off specific tasks that don't reveal the nature of the project."

At this Jake cocked his head and rubbed a hand across his face, while Nell looked concerned. "Is there something sketchy about this?" she said.

"Listen," Daniel shot back, losing patience, "a cooling La Niña made 2021 only the fifth warmest year on record, but each of the seven hottest years have occurred since 2015. I'm guessing this year will be as bad. And with all that heat, wildfires are bigger and droughts longer. We need to get a grip on this."

The young attorneys both sat back with serious faces.

"Now, that part will be simple, like I said, but what's next may be murkier—and I don't want you delegating *any* of this. I want to know what part human activity has in the warming."

He could sense his associates tensing; they obviously realized this project was not sanctioned by Pearce.

"All indications," Daniel went on, "are that humans are accelerating rather than slowing the warming. The concentration of carbon dioxide, methane and nitrous oxide in our atmosphere hits new heights each year, thanks to things like super-yachts and private jets. The world's forty-two wealthiest people own as much as the poorest three-and-a-half billion but account for more damage to our ecology."

"So...we're looking for soft spots in the scientific literature," Jake said, "for ways to undermine the green lobby?"

Nell's eyes brightened as she looked at Daniel for confirmation.

"How we'll use the information doesn't matter now; we first need to know what science tells us."

Daniel's view of the world was transitioning, but he couldn't expect his associates suddenly to change sides too—not when it was clearly against their career interests. But he wanted them to see for themselves the part PJ&H played in this mess, aligned with demons like Kent Coggin and Bo Langston against the people giving their lives to save the world.

"Look," he said, "I've read enough to know humans are making things worse, speeding up the warming. A two-degree Celsius rise in global mean temperature will profoundly disrupt our climate. Next will come fiercer storms, higher seas, animal and plant extinctions, people dying from heat, food shortages and mass migrations; the list goes on. But I want clear scientific evidence of the threat, unbiased by politics."

That wiped the smiles from their faces. Jake looked pensive, as if for the first time he suspected something beyond politics and marketing deserved his attention. Nell's expression was harder to gauge. She seemed to wonder less about objectivity than about Daniel's state of mind. But they were smart; the research would lead them to see what was now clear to him, that they were on the wrong side of history.

It was plain to see Daniel was not himself, but this hardly surprised Nell. Even though she spent most of her time competing with her brother and sister, she couldn't imagine dealing with the loss of your whole family. He had been such a good mentor; she wished there was some way to ease his pain. A walk in the crisp winter air would be good for him. He needed to clear his head and stop mouthing the opposition's talking points like he meant it before this got back to Pearce or the clients.

Maybe it was time for one of their impromptu dinners at Daniel's apartment, where they cooked together and drank too much and they got Daniel to tell the really good stories from the back rooms of Congress. Those were some of her favorite nights ever, and made her feel like a real Washington insider.

But maybe she was worrying too much. The boss would be fine. He just needed time to heal. She and Jake would do the research he asked for while still concentrating on the real work. In the end the firm's practice depended on Daniel, his experience, his contacts and his talent at putting it all across. It was very much in her interest to keep Daniel pitching and the lucrative practice bringing in the big bucks. She had from the start tried to absorb everything she could from him; maybe it was just time to pick up the pace of this learning. She hoped he would pull it together and maybe even end up running PJ&H. But if he crashed and burned, someone would need to step up.

Joe Coulder texted. He assumed Daniel would not make the weekly poker game, since he hadn't come to a game in months, but he wanted to speak with him. That evening they met in a secluded tavern booth.

Joe ordered a beer. Daniel grimaced, fighting how much he wanted a drink. Coulder wouldn't know about his giving up alcohol; this could be a one-time exception.

"A cold one for you too?" Coulder asked.

Daniel grimaced and shook his head, the swirl of rushing water washing away his physical craving. He hit his hands down on the table to stop the spinning.

Coulder half-rose, but Daniel motioned him back down. The concerned waitress also backed off.

"Sorry," Daniel said, catching his breath. "It's a medical thing. It's nothing, just...I'm fine. I won't have anything, but you go ahead."

Coulder watched him with a sympathetic smile. "You know I'm really sorry about Bree and Annabelle. You guys had such a perfect life."

His sympathy seemed genuine and brought Daniel some comfort, but there was no use wasting time. "So why the meeting?" Daniel said.

Coulder sipped his beer. "It's about your former brother-in-law...."

"Pete?"

"Yes, Peter Albert Morrison, your wife's brother. How well do you know him?"

"Like you said, he was my brother-in-law, or still is; I'm not sure how that works."

"I mean how close is your relationship? Have you spent a lot of time with him?"

"Time? What do you mean? What's this about?"

"I'll tell you, Danny, because of our friendship...and I think you'll want to know. We have information linking Morrison to Anthro."

"What? You're crazy."

"It may sound crazy, but you know the resources we've put into taking down that anarchist guru and his organization. We have to follow every lead."

"But Pete?"

"He's been linked to a woman we think is close to Eco."

"I don't believe it. You don't know this guy."

"You're right, I don't. But we do know another little fish in the group, an unhappy man we've been grooming. He told us Morrison drove somewhere accompanied by a woman who could be a connection to Eco. He was seen heading west from Austin with this woman but apparently returned without her."

Daniel tried to make his face express detached interest. If Coulder had connected Pete to Anthro, it was only one uncomfortable step to implicating Daniel as well.

As far as he knew, the only picture law enforcement had of Verde was the one he'd seen on Pearce's phone. That wasn't much to go on. Besides, Daniel met her in the woods, miles from anyone. No one could prove his connection with her. Still, who knew what Pete would disclose if they squeezed him?

Coulder asked, "When was the last time you saw Morrison, or talked to him?"

So, this was a trap. Good old Joe, his college pal, wasn't there to give him a friendly heads-up. The director sent him to catch Daniel in a lie, make him incriminate himself so he'd *have* to turn on Bree's family to help the FBI. He needed to answer carefully.

"I saw him in Tanswego," he said, as if searching his memory. "We were both looking for word about Bree, and stayed to dig bodies out of collapsed houses."

"Was he there alone?"

"Yeah, there was no one with him...no one *I* saw."

"Well, we have a report from a man named Chuck Harris, who apparently is known in the organization as 'Ranger.' He reported that Morrison left Austin with a woman who was spotted at the flood site taking photographs."

"Why does that matter? There must have been lots of news photographers there."

"Ranger reports that this woman is called 'Verde' and came to Austin last fall with Eco. And she—like Morrison—wore a Homeland Security vest in Tanswego, but no one at Homeland can identify her. Then Anthro used photos we attribute to her in a report blaming the flood on human-induced climate change."

Daniel sighed. "I saw the photos in Cahill's report, though I haven't had time to read it. It's voluminous."

Coulder stopped short, as if this surprised him. "Then you saw enough to recognize the scenes in those photos?"

"I could tell it was the village—or what used to be—but I didn't know who took the pictures. How do *you* know?"

"I'll tell you, Dan, but just between us. We identified a watermark on several of the photographs that apparently identifies the photographer."

"What does it say?"

"It doesn't *say* anything; it's a silhouette design, two flowers, very simple. Now, it's just a matter of finding where else it's used; we have an army of analysts on that, so it won't take long. But, as to your brother-in-law's traveling companion, we had code-named her 'Squeeze' because she apparently was romantically linked to Eco, but like I said, Ranger tells us she is known generally as Verde."

Daniel coughed to hide his discomfort. The FBI's initial misogynist code name for Verde suggested they underestimated her. He asked, "This is the woman in that photograph?"

"So, Pearce showed you? Yes, we think she is. Unfortunately, the photo isn't clear enough to identify the woman, and it's the only shot we have. No one on the ground in Tanswego thought to photograph the Homeland photographer."

"Well, I wish I could help."

"That's why I'm here, Dan, to ask your help."

Big surprise there. "What can I do?"

"First, we need to be sure you've told us everything you know and..." He paused and looked at Daniel fixedly. "And you've said you don't know anything about Verde or Pete's involvement with Anthro. So we would appreciate—*your country* would appreciate—if you would try to *initiate* contact. These people are bitter misanthropes, or at best naïve idealists, but either way they're a clear danger to public order. We want you to go through your brother-in-law to try to set up a meeting with that woman. Maybe she'll lead us to Eco. If not, finding Verde would still be a big help; we could follow her and maybe flush out all the rats at once."

Daniel seethed. Coulder was playing him and lumping Pete

in with the suspects and collateral victims, who counted for nothing in the FBI's well-ordered world. "I'll do what I can, Joe," he said with all the sincerity he could muster, "though I hate to think Bree's brother is really caught up in this. The guy is not the sharpest pencil in the box, but I'm sure he's harmless."

On his way home, Daniel left a voicemail for Doctor Haverly. He got a return call, moving up his appointment to the next morning. This would be Daniel's third visit to the doctor's office, and it was past time for the doctor to come up with some answers.

"So what can you tell me about your condition since our last meeting?" Doctor Haverly asked after Daniel settled in.

Daniel told him about his near attack in the bar with Coulder and his recent nightmares. He didn't mention his reaction to the stream where he met Verde because he didn't want anyone to connect him with his meeting in the woods.

"What about the other manifestations? The drinking?"

"No alcohol or drugs since we met, and I have to say it's killing me."

"Good," Haverly said and nodded. "I don't mean it's good you are in pain, of course, but it is excellent you have stuck to your resolve. The aquaphobia is a mental condition, and the first step is for you to *want* to be cured. You are taking difficult steps that show this."

"But cleaning up my life has made no difference," Daniel whined. "I have headaches from giving up alcohol but still lose control when I see water or hear it or sometimes even just think about it."

"Patience, Mr. Lazaro. As I have told you, there is no immediate relief, no one-cure-fits-all."

"You've got to do something, Doctor. I can't go on just talking about this."

"Okay, Mr. Lazaro. We could begin exposure therapy, using imagery to trigger your symptoms. We would work on breathing and relaxation techniques to employ before and during an exposure and talk you through your reactions. This could help you gradually learn to manage your response."

"I have no more time for 'gradual,' Doctor. I'm under tremendous pressure right now. I can't be held back by this ridiculous condition."

"Well, Mr. Lazaro, first you must appreciate there is nothing 'ridiculous' about your phobia. It is real and debilitating, and we must treat it with the same seriousness as any medical condition."

Daniel sighed. "I understand. Please go on."

"There are other treatment options. We could try cognitive behavioral therapy, which would help you learn to change how you respond to triggers. Noted practitioners use this in conjunction with exposure therapy or hypnotherapy. The latter, as you would imagine, adds an exploration of the underlying cause for your condition. We have already discussed your propensity to addictive behavior and your feelings of guilt at not being there for your family, but I suspect there may be a deeper cause. It will take hard work to uncover this. Finally, I could prescribe medication—antidepressants or sleep aids—to relieve your symptoms while we get at the underlying cause."

"I'll do anything, Doctor. I just need to clear this up *quickly*."

"Again, Mr. Lazaro, we need time to explore the root of your problem. So let us dig into this. Tell me about your family...I mean your mother and father, your siblings."

"None, I'm afraid."

"Oh, I'm sorry. So you never had siblings and your parents are both deceased?"

"Right, except my mother isn't *literally* dead, as far as I know."

"I see. How long has your father been gone?"

"Look," Daniel said heatedly. "Long story short: my father was scapegoated for a mining accident and killed himself. He was a good man, and I miss him. My mother badgered him into suicide and became a religious fanatic and a recluse who didn't even want to know me. She ignored the invitation to my wedding. She never once saw my daughter. But none of that is why I throw up when I see a glass of water."

Haverly shook his head patiently. "You must understand, Mr. Lazaro, the mind is a complex and mysterious organ. Your experiences growing up might resurface to cause you trouble, or they might not. You can see, however, how the little you have told me—and even the tone in which you shared this information—suggests avenues for exploration. We know your experience with the flood triggered your aquaphobia, but we need to find the cause so we can try to cure it. Aquaphobia can linger in some form for years or the rest of your life—or it might disappear as quickly as it began. But, our time will be best spent looking for the root cause of your distress, what contributed to your alcohol abuse and why the flood and your personal tragedy led to your fear of water."

Daniel didn't sleep much that night. He was haunted by images of the waves forcing Tanswego to its knees.

Lying awake he thought over every time he had reacted to water since that day by the Guadalupe, but he could see no consistency between cause and effect. One thing suddenly became clear to him, though: his aquaphobia was *not* brought on by liquor or his affair with Haley. It also was not because he wasn't there for Bree and Annabelle. Those things were his fault and his failures, and he deserved worse than he got for them. But the bottom-line cause of this mental whiplash...was guilt for causing the flood and a nation of floods and droughts and sweltering air.

The Oil Institute, the law firm, the crooked legislators: they were all evil actors in this. But Daniel was one of them, just as bad, just as culpable. The death of his family might not have happened without the work of the minions, the slaves to greed and power like him. But many others had died—and would die—because of his clients and others like them. The blood was on his hands. Cheating and neglect were personal failings that impacted only *his* family. But he was a villain on a grander scale when he fought to let companies heat the air and clearcut forests.

He could hear his idealistic younger self's derisive laughter that it took him so long to see this. When had he lost his way? Where had he lost those ideals? Even before the flood, he had suffered a different and even more significant loss of his way: his sense of what was right and wrong. This all had to change.

Chapter Twenty-One

Daniel sat in his office trying to review a memo but really wishing he had some way to contact Verde. This was getting way over his head. If he was questioned, should he deny knowledge of Pete's politics or say he had his suspicions about his brother-in-law? Should he admit meeting Verde outside Austin?

He could not only lose his job but also go to jail. But he'd made the decision; there was no going back. He wanted in on Anthro's plan, whatever that turned out to be. When all hell broke loose, he'd just have to deal with it. Why didn't Verde just give him a phone number?

The next step depended on what the FBI knew, but then a call came in from Pete.

"Hey, dude, how are things?" he said.

"Back at the grind," Daniel replied without enthusiasm, "taking one day at a time."

"Okay, well I don't want to bother you at work, but that

friend of mine, the woman you said you'd like to see again? She's in Washington and asked if you want to meet up."

Daniel's daze cleared. Suddenly, meeting with Verde was all he wanted to do. This could be the gateway to doing something righteous. No more wallowing in guilt for another day and another week and another month. She was right; he could not ethically help his clients commit crimes; he saw that now. He needed to join with her and Anthro and find a way to make a difference. Then it occurred to him...there was something he could give them to show his loyalty.

"Danny?" Pete said.

He realized he'd been lost in his thoughts. "Yeah," he said, "that's great. Where and when?"

"She said to call; let me give you the number. Oh yeah, and she said not to use your own phone. Get a burner."

He was moving into a world of espionage. Burner phones? Nonetheless, he stopped at a store on the way home and purchased a phone with sixty minutes of time, thinking this would be plenty given the lengths of his chatty conversations with Verde.

A woman answered, "Charles Industries. May I offer assistance?"

There was no mistaking how she enunciated each syllable too precisely to be a native English speaker and the accent when she said "assistance."

"Verde, it's Daniel."

"Yes, it is me. Go on."

"Good, uh..." he said, unsure if he was supposed to say it over the phone. "I have something for you."

"Which is...?"

"You want me to just say it?"

"That is how this must work."

"Okay, then. You've got a mole working for the FBI."

She paused. "How do you know this? Who is it?"

"A guy named Harris who calls himself 'Ranger.' He lives

somewhere near Austin, Texas. He told the FBI my brother-in-law is connected to Anthro and said he drove Verde to Tanswego."

In a moment he added, "They don't have good pictures, of you or Eco."

He grinned, proud of himself. She said nothing.

"Are you still there?" he said. "Did you hear what I said?"

"Message received. We will get back to you."

The line clicked off. He looked at the phone, as if it would tell him more. There was obviously a need for security, but that woman needed to adjust her bedside manner.

Two days later Daniel was meeting with Jake and Nell when the burner in his pocket buzzed. He took it out, saying, "You guys have to excuse me. I need to take this."

Nell screwed up her face and looked at Jake. He shrugged and they left.

"Daniel?" Verde said, with her now familiar economy of words.

"Yes, it's me."

"Noon at Vietnam Memorial."

"I'll be there."

"And do not come direct, in case you might be followed."

"Got it. I'll keep my eyes open."

She hung up without another word. He felt a surge of excitement. Things were starting to happen.

Daniel checked the clock. There was barely time to make it to the Mall. He told Alice he was going to a meeting and hurried from the office. He was energized.

He left at eleven, wondering how best to cover his tracks. He took the Metro three stops away from the Mall and then cabbed back to the Lincoln Memorial. Then he walked up the north side of the reflecting pool, giving it as wide a berth as he could and telling himself it was *not* full of water. When he could see no one watching, he ducked over the hill.

He had visited Vietnam memorials in Chicago and New York, and even a traveling monument in Tyler, Texas. But this black granite wall stirred him like no other monument. Sunken into the ground, almost hidden by trees, it was so much more compelling than statues and columns. Back in law school he would find peace here on quiet days when tourists were scarce. It felt sadly apt to join this battle for the planet at a monument to heroism in a flawed and doomed cause.

He stood where he could take in the whole wall and pretended to look at his phone while scanning for anything out of place. Precisely at noon Verde materialized beside him. Her hair was pinned beneath an Irish cap, but there was no mistaking her face.

"It is good you are punctual," she said. "And we are encouraged you have decided to join us."

He smiled uneasily, realizing that was precisely what he was doing.

She glanced around and seemed satisfied. Then she turned to him. "Let us take a ride."

She led him across the lawn to the street, where a shiny aqua Vespa was parked between two cars. She handed him one helmet and strapped on the other. He hesitated.

"You must try to look natural. Imagine we are making a French New Wave film and you are my lover."

He almost choked on how casually she said this. French New Wave? Pretend he's her lover? Who talked like that?

After they were seated, she turned her head slightly to say, "Wrap your arms around me so you will not fall."

He needed no encouragement.

The nausea he expected from crossing the Potomac was lost in the sensation of holding her. Was this somehow unfaithful to his wife? The guilt over his affair with Haley left him feeling any attraction to a woman betrayed Bree all over again. But this was different, and the feel of another person up against him was so comforting after all these months of pushing people away. Wouldn't it be amazing if riding a Vespa with Verde was the antidote to his phobia?

They drove northwest on the GW Parkway, riding the speed limit in the right lane. At Rivercrest they exited, crossed over and stopped beside the entrance ramp for heading back toward the city.

"Is something wrong with the scooter?" he asked.

"Tradecraft," she said, focusing on the bridge. "We observe who might follow us."

After two minutes she wordlessly headed south. In minutes more they exited in Arlington, and Verde wound through mostly quiet blocks to park behind a low row of stores.

She stowed the helmets on the scooter and gestured for Daniel to follow. Around the front of the buildings they passed a hardware store and a closed restaurant before entering a bar.

It was a typical old-man's bar, but empty at this time of day. The man behind the large wooden bar nodded to Verde and then focused a bit aggressively on Daniel.

"You will leave your phone," she said.

"Of course." He passed his phone to the bartender, who also ran a wand over his sides. He was getting used to this routine.

A row of empty booths stretched along the wall opposite the bar. Verde led him to the last one, set off from the room by a carved wooden panel. A man half-rose from his seat and extended his hand. "Nice to meet you," he said. "I believe you know me as Eco."

Eco was tall and thin. A woolen hat covered his close-cropped, dark hair. He wore sunglasses despite the low light.

"Daniel," he responded.

"Thank you, Verde," Eco said, and she left, not even glancing back.

But Eco, sitting with his fingers tee-peed, smiled genuinely. "Don't mind Verde," he said. "I think she likes you."

"How can you tell?"

"Well, I guess you have to know her. But on a more serious subject, I—or I should say all of us—extend our profound sympathy to you as a husband and father. We know about your tragedy, a small part of our global crisis that is, of course, all-important to you. Law enforcement tries to cast us as unfeeling, but that is exactly untrue and points to why we'll win in the end. Our movement is based on love, for each other *and* for the Earth itself, which is why we cannot help but prevail in the end over the forces of greed and destruction. As such, we acutely feel—I personally feel—your pain. There is no way ever to make up for your loss."

"Thank you," Daniel said, fighting back a tear.

"So," Eco went on, "Verde tells me you might sign on for the forlorn hope."

"That's what I'm thinking," Daniel said, smiling at the term, which reminded him of the Napoleonic wars.

The waitress appeared and asked Daniel what he wanted.

"Thank you," he said. "I don't need anything."

"Water, then?" Eco said.

"No," Daniel said too vehemently. "No water, please."

Eco looked curious but went on, "First of all, the social media handle 'Anthro' is of course short for the Anthropocene geological era, when humans are the dominant influence on climate and the environment. It expresses how we are less a group than an ideology whose time has come. We, the human population of the earth, have perverted the balance...."

"Balance?" Daniel interrupted, surprised he had spoken out loud.

"Balance, yes." Eco took a deep breath. "From the ancient Greeks to the indigenous Americans, people close to nature have always recognized that balance is essential to the health of any organism. Like the humoralists said of the human body: health is stasis between hot and cold, wet and dry. It's the same for the planet."

"You've lost me. What's humorous?"

"Not humorists, *humoralists*. They believed health came from a balance in the bodily liquids called humors."

Daniel was skeptical. "What has hot and cold to do with…" He trailed off as he met Eco's gaze and frowned.

Eco's smile acknowledged Daniel's epiphany. It was a little unnerving how he saw this as quickly as Daniel perceived it himself.

"So," Eco went on, "the humoralist would say natural disaster follows when the planet is too hot or cold, too wet or dry: when the balance is upset."

"Did these people have a cure for global warming?"

"Not in so simple a way. The doctors in medieval Salerno prescribed plants to address imbalances in the body, but specific plants did not cure specific maladies. Rather, the patient would sip tea extracted from plants whose 'nature' moved the body back toward balance, 'dry' plants for a man suffering from phlegm in the lungs, 'wet' plants for a woman with parched skin."

"I guess," Daniel said, doubtfully. "But what does it have to do with the planet?"

Eco smiled. "It's the same as the Eastern concept of yinyang, that all things from the annual cycle of summer and winter to sexual coupling between male and female, are governed by opposing, yet independent forces."

It was hard to say if Eco was smarter than him or if his years as an activist had just equipped him to slide from one analogy to another. Either way, Daniel wanted to get to the point. "What has ancient philosophy got to do with…?"

"Well, perhaps this is not the time to dwell on philosophy. Suffice it to say, the balance of our planet is as precarious as that in the human body. A healthy person's temperature ranges from say ninety-seven to ninety-nine degrees. Now, think of what happens when that temperature rises by, say, two degrees...and then by three or four—and we're talking Fahrenheit. It takes only a rise of a few degrees to bring on vomiting and hallucinations and finally death. We must stop our planet from enduring this kind of overheating—of just 'a few' degrees—which could put us back in the Paleocene-Eocene Thermal Maximum of 56 million years ago. That's why we pursue this struggle. It is unlike any work you've done before. We don't get grades or diplomas; we don't make money; there will be no public acclaim. We simply struggle in the shadows to bring the planet into balance."

"I'm here," Daniel said. "What do you need from me?"

Eco took a deep breath. "Okay, here's where we're at. I like you and feel comfortable that you're sincere. But we have security protocols, and some of my colleagues are not as trusting as I am. We acknowledge—more than that, we appreciate—your information about Ranger, but we need more. And here's my idea. There is currently a fight over locating wind turbines in the ocean off Massachusetts. A private group called the Energy Security Foundation is boycotting companies investing in the project. We want to know who runs this foundation and establish what we suspect is its funding by the fossil fuel industry."

"I'm not familiar with the name, but these groups trade information and tactics. I can dig into it."

"Exactly the answer I hoped for." Eco looked past Daniel and nodded. Daniel sensed and then saw that Verde had silently appeared by their table.

Eco said, "I apologize for cutting this short, but unfortunately I must turn to other things. I hope we find an opportunity soon to delve more deeply into cosmology over a bottle of wine. For now, Verde will get you back to the Metro and arrange how to reach out when you have something for us."

"Thanks," Daniel said, feeling he had passed a test.

"One thing, though," Eco said somberly. "We are on a death watch; there is no time to waste."

Verde gave Daniel a ride to the Metro. She said to mail what he found to a post office box in Arlington. Then she surprised him by saying, without a hint of condescension, "We look forward to welcoming you to the struggle."

Back in his office Daniel examined his newfound spirit. He felt energized, not only from meeting Eco and taking scooter rides with Verde, but from joining a just and needed struggle, in finding a sense of purpose.

He kept alert for suspicious glances or comments but no one paid particular attention to his arrival.

In a brief pipeline meeting with Nell that afternoon, he asked how she was doing on the climate research.

"Well in hand," she said, "and we can't wait to see how you'll use it."

"With time," Daniel said with a smile he hoped was disarming.

Nell brightened and looked relieved. "It's like I told Jake: just wait for the Daniel plot twist."

He shook his head, smiling genuinely at how he enjoyed working with these young lawyers but also feeling a twinge of guilt that they had no idea where all this was heading.

As she rose to leave, he asked with measured nonchalance, "By the way, what do you know about the Energy Security Foundation?"

She paused in the doorway, bit her lip and shook her head. "Nothing. Are they good guys or bad guys?"

"Oh, never mind. I just ran across the name and wondered who handled their legal work."

"Always thinking, right, boss?" She looked happier than she had in days.

Chapter
Twenty-Two

Daniel sat in his apartment trying to forget about his personal troubles and the planetary crisis by focusing on a novel he had started and abandoned twice before. It was three days since he mailed off what he had found about the Energy Security Foundation: a list of its directors, the date and location of their next meeting and a credible theory about the billionaire providing the funding.

The post office was a safe way to send his information, but he hated the delay. Now that he was determined to work with Anthro, he was anxious to get to it.

Thankfully, the call came the next morning, and this time Verde brought Daniel back to a parking lot behind a factory building in Arlington. She got off the scooter and stood with her back to the wall, gesturing to do the same. Everything looked deserted.

For two full minutes they didn't speak; they just listened and watched. Then she knocked on a door in what sounded like a prearranged code. A large man appeared and filled the doorway. He wore a bandana over his big, square head and a menacing look on his face.

"Verde," he said brightly, breaking into a smile. "Is this the package?"

"Step aside, you large oaf," she said as she pushed her scooter through the doorway, edging him aside.

After securing the door behind them, the big man gestured for Daniel to open his jacket. Daniel looked at Verde and frowned playfully.

"Protocol," she said, straight-faced. "And of course he will hold your phone for you."

"It's the burner phone. I left mine in the office."

"Just the same, we will take it apart. Call it an abundance of caution. We will be teaching you how to reassemble these things."

Daniel smiled to himself, thinking he could have used a reassembly lesson after their meeting in Austin.

Verde led him to a second-floor lunchroom with windows overlooking a parking lot out front. She removed her jacket and gestured him to a chair. He took the seat, trying not to stare at the fine lines of her long, lean figure. But she caught him staring and shook her head with a look that made him feel foolish.

Eco came through a rear door. He wore no hat or sunglasses this time, and Daniel was taken with his piercing blue eyes.

Eco smiled tenderly at Verde and took Daniel's outstretched hand in both of his. "Good to see you again, Counselor Lazaro," he said with a quiet smile.

"Please, call me Daniel."

"Yes, well, we'll have to think of some other name for you."

"So, 'Eco'...?" Daniel started to say.

"Someone came up with that after too many beers, I'm afraid. It's short for 'eco-warrior,' although one mainstream ecologist called me 'Eco-fascist' for prioritizing animals over people. I understand that, in their talent for imaginative phrasing, the FBI prefers 'Ecological Terrorist.' "

Daniel nodded. "I've heard the official version."

"Yes, well, the names are made up, but they grow on you and add a level of obfuscation for big brother. They also show our sense of humor. We have a Guy Fawkes, for example, in homage to the man who tried to blow up the House of Lords in the sixteenth century. Still, there is nothing frivolous about security or being forced to hide behind fictional names."

Eco turned and exclaimed, "Ah, and here is the historical personage himself."

A man with a theatrical, pencil-thin mustache approached. "Daniel Lazaro," Eco said, "meet Guy Fawkes."

"Call me Guy," the man said, extending his hand but then quickly excusing himself to join two young people working at a laptop.

Mia watched Guy's cameo appearance and then Daniel's interaction with Kristof. It was no surprise their recruit was taken with her husband—most people were—and this augured well for convincing him to help Anthro. Kristof also would be able to gauge his loyalties without discounting Daniel's apparent attraction to her. Would he take up the cause? Did he recognize the dire situation and believe in what they must do?

She had more pressing work to do—would prefer to do—than chauffeuring around a precious lawyer while he developed a conscience. The pipeline bill was the priority; she could be working contacts in the western cells. But Kristof insisted she babysit Daniel because, through him, they might be able to strike at the heart of evil. Since she had lured him in—*whatever* his motivation—Kristof believed she would be best at cementing the relationship.

Soon Eco led Daniel and Verde through a locked door and down a long hallway. Daniel looked around for a window to orient himself. At one turn he said, "Have we…?"

"Passed into another building?" Verde interjected, as if this would be obvious to anyone paying attention.

"Yes," Eco said, casting an admonishing look at Verde. "These old warehouses are connected in ways hidden from the street. You must learn to notice changes in your surroundings. Also, as I mentioned, you will need a new name. How about 'Ansel,' for the nature photographer Ansel Adams?"

"Or 'Al' for 'Al Gore'?"

"I like it," Eco said. "Not enough of a politician, maybe, but his election would certainly have set the country—and the world— on a saner climate path. From now on you're Al Gore."

They went up a staircase to a large, comfortable room where people huddled together over laptops. A bearded man in an old cowboy hat rose and extended his hand.

"Good to meet you Mr. Lazaro," he said with a slight German accent.

"We have christened him Al Gore," Eco interjected.

"Al, then," the man said. "Call me Assisi. I serve as the home-room monitor around here, making sure everyone behaves."

Verde rolled her eyes and went to pour a cup of tea. Eco chuckled quietly to himself while he led Daniel to a table. Assisi bowed his head as if to leave.

"Can you sit with us for a minute?" Eco said.

"Not right now," Assisi replied. "We're working with California on the aftermath of the flooding from their atmospheric rivers. Who ever heard of that term before climate change, right?"

Eco nodded and turned back to Daniel. "Sometimes it feels like we're running in place, trying to make people think about the cause of all this extreme weather instead of just the billions they have to pay for the damage."

Eco remained standing while Verde and Daniel took seats. As he spoke, Eco moved behind Verde's chair. Unpinning and loosening her long hair, he began to braid it. She closed her eyes with a slight smile of contentment. He wondered at the way they expressed such profound affection for each other without saying a word.

"So," Eco said, his fingers still moving dexterously, "Anthro's main goal is to make people understand the actions of human-kind—which may be profitable in the short term—put our collective thumb on the scale to make the planet heat faster."

"Working with Congress has taught me all about short-term goals outweighing long-term risks."

Eco's smile took on a tinge of condescension. "And you know firsthand that climate-based disasters are now the norm. Still, the general populace fails to grasp that the final notice has been nailed to the planet's door and foreclosure proceedings have begun."

Daniel smiled at Eco's knack for turning a phrase but pushed back. "But, like you say, natural causes will warm the planet regardless of what we do."

"Ah, but we could give our world its best chance and also ease the suffering of those innocents bearing the brunt of the catastrophe."

"Which is all..."

"Which may be all we can do for our Earth, given how close we find ourselves to the precipice. What *you* can do, though, is maintain your position in your firm; don't let on how your sympathies have changed. We need you on the inside, where you will be most useful. On the personal side, it also might be a good time to look for real estate up north in the mountains."

"And not on a river," Daniel concluded sadly.

Eco responded with a sympathetic look.

Daniel stayed into the evening. They moved back to the lunch-room to share a communal dinner. The food was vegan and not especially satiating, except for the best fresh-baked bread he had ever tasted. The mood at the table was intimate. Through words or a look, each person in turn welcomed Daniel. He had sat through hundreds of work dinners in his career but none had given him such a feeling he was just where he was meant to be.

With the meal through, Daniel rose to help clean up, but Assisi held him back with a hand on his forearm. "This evening you are a guest," he said with a friendly smile. "Next time you can join in the chores, like everyone else."

In fact, he saw that both Eco and Verde were clearing the table.

"You know, your reaction to water...." Assisi said, leaning in confidentially and pronouncing the last word "vater."

How had Assisi noticed his phobia when he hadn't had an attack? Daniel girded himself to be exposed to everyone or for a pep talk about not giving in to weakness. Instead, Assisi kept his voice so low no one overheard. "It's easy to understand," he said, "after your encounter with the river. If I can help—or you need to talk—please lean on me."

As everyone returned to work. Kristof invited Daniel to join him on "the terrace." They walked up the fire stairs to a tar and gravel rooftop punctuated with vents and laced with wires strung between poles. He watched Daniel take a full turn, surveying the surrounding dark structures.

"We have a river view," Kristof laughed, pointing through a narrow opening between two buildings.

Daniel shivered momentarily and avoided looking where Kristof pointed. That seemed odd until Kristof recalled what Mia had said about Daniel's fear of water. Losing everything to the flood had really messed with the poor guy's mind. He wondered if it was fair to draft him into service in this condition. But the struggle was as much his as anyone's, maybe more so given his loss. In any case, the situation was too dire to be put off while they each dealt with personal issues.

"So, Al," he said. "We've given you a peek inside our band of merciless brigands, and I think you grasp the seriousness of the situation we face and our dedication to do all we can to turn things around."

"I'm ready to use my access however you think best."

Kristof was starting to like this guy, a man who saw the harm he had done and seemed sincere in wanting to even his balance sheet. It would take more before he would totally trust Daniel, but he was ready to see what this convert could do. "Here's the thing," he said. "Verde and I will be leaving in the morning; we have some work to do out west."

"The pipeline?"

Kristof paused and smiled. "Yes, as a matter of fact. We will meet with some First Nations brothers and sisters who need our help. Crucial dates are fast upon us and..."

"The vote in the Senate next week?"

Again he smiled. This relationship could prove more useful than he had hoped. "Yes, there is the vote in Congress, and the House of Commons in Canada is considering a complementary bill. We hope to make a little noise to tilt the debate. How do you feel about that?"

"When you say 'noise'...?"

"I mean we may accelerate the depreciation of some construction equipment, maybe burn a few holes in pipeline valves, to forestall irreparable harm before the two governments come to their senses."

"I won't be part of hurting anyone," Daniel said, thinking of all the people he had already hurt through his work.

"We are all in agreement there, although you will find us of two minds. We are naturally inclined to peaceful methods, civil disobedience in the model of the civil rights movement or its predecessor under Ghandi. But in the end the battle *must* be won. We each must be part of the solution or part of the problem. As Greta Thunberg recently told the World Economic Forum: 'Our house is on fire, and we have reached a time when we must speak out.'"

Chapter Twenty-Three

It was disappointing Verde didn't drive him home on her scooter. The only time she wasn't bristly was when he sat behind her on the Vespa. And while he recognized how pitiable it was, he didn't even care how she treated him when she let him wrap his arms around her.

It was easy to see why she was devoted to Eco and that this feeling was mutual. They were so clearly partners in body, soul and purpose, and made an imposing couple, almost too perfect to be real. But at the same time they were more real than anyone Daniel had ever known. And, while they were each heroic and complete in themselves, together they were so wholly a team. Daniel had never witnessed a relationship like that.

In his marriage he and Bree had each played a role, he building their dream house at the river's edge while she made it a home. He decided how they would thrive in the world while she softened the way. She didn't question the means he used to support the family. He could not imagine her objecting to his work because it belied some public good. Her focus was firmly on the family. He gave her what she needed, and she made him comfortable and cared for their daughter.

But maybe this was just *his* version of the story, and he had forgotten Bree was a real person with her own story. She gave up a teaching career and never pursued her dream of writing books so she could devote her energy to Daniel and Annabelle and making River House a haven. Perhaps she could have been more of an equal partner if he hadn't been so absorbed in his own career.

But Eco and Verde had a different kind of tie. In Eco's terms, there was balance. While he was the philosopher and front man, phrasing the struggle in noble terms, Daniel sensed that she was the engine who got things done.

In any event, the drive home with Assisi was pleasant. Without the distraction of riding behind Verde, however, Daniel had to keep his eyes closed tight while they crossed the Potomac.

Assisi didn't mention his phobia. He had made clear he perceived Daniel's problem and offered his help but seemingly would leave it to Daniel to resume that conversation. He instead talked about the loveliness of the spring about to burst forth and how as a child in Germany he had love hiking when flowers covered the mountainsides. He worked this around to describing the heart of environmentalism as a call for humility, restraint and a sense of connectedness with the natural world.

When Daniel had recovered from the river crossing, he asked about Assisi's name.

"It is from St. Francis Giovanni di Pietro di Bernardone. You know, the friar with birds and bunnies gathered around?"

"And that makes sense because...?"

"Well, back in the seventies Pope Paul II named Francis the patron saint of ecologists."

"So you're a Catholic?"

"Lapsed. But the name has less to do with organized religion than Francis's preaching that all creatures on Earth—people and animals—are equal under God."

Assisi dropped him off two blocks from his apartment. Standing on the curb and leaning into the window, Daniel said, "If you don't mind my asking, what is it with Verde? Everyone else at Anthro has been so nice, but even though Verde is the one who brought me in, she clearly doesn't like me."

"Ah, there's a complicated story there, which I'll leave for her to share. Suffice it to say she has given everything to the movement. She has suffered more than any of us from betrayal, and this hardened her. Actually, her caution has forced needed prudence on us all. We were pretty slipshod in the beginning, as you might imagine."

"So, she doesn't trust *anybody*?"

"Well, there's Eco, of course. And Guy and I have known her a long time. You just have to give her time. She'll test you until she's sure, but then there's no limit to her devotion. It took a while for her to accept me as a comrade, but I have no doubt now she'd lay down her life for me."

Daniel was all in on helping uncover the corrupt interests pushing the Canadian pipeline, and agreed to maintain his PJ&H position as the Oil Institute's lead pit-bull. It felt dishonest to deceive Jake and Nell, who were only following his lead, but they were young; they wouldn't be held accountable for corruption at the top. As to Branston Pearce, Daniel looked forward to undercutting that greedy son of a bitch. The man's loyalty was exclusively to himself and his offshore bank accounts.

Sitting in his apartment, he watched the evening light fade. He kept thinking about the step he had taken. He had passed the point of being able to put his head down and do his job, stay at PJ&H or write his own ticket at another firm. He could not escape his guilt while he kept doing the devil's work, stow away his superhero cloak and root for Anthro from afar. What he did was wrong then and was still wrong. He might well be walking away from his prior life, but what life was left, really? He had no wife, no daughter, no job he could stand—he really had nothing left to lose. Even if he had to die for the cause, it would make his life count for something in the end.

How to handle Haley Bourdain was a concern. Their relationship had been turbulent from the start, so she should not be overly surprised at ups and downs. But in several phone conversations while she was traveling, she had insinuated that she had a claim on him. And, unlike his colleagues at PJ&H, she had the instincts of a predator and would not be easily fooled.

Before he had decided how to deal with her, Haley called his office. "I'm back, finally," she said in a tone suggesting he had been pining for her.

"How was the trip?" he said, buying a moment to think.

"Typical. Had to prod the junior senator from Illinois on the appropriation bill. Then I went to Europe for advance work on the senator's visit in May and spent time in France with a major contributor. But that's all done, and we have a reservation at eight at La Ganté."

Keeping Haley happy was part of his job, and it wouldn't be cheating anymore to be with her. But he got a bad taste in his mouth about continuing the wrong he had done Bree. She deserved better, even after she was gone. Besides that, Daniel no longer had any physical desire for Haley. Was this guilt? She was as attractive as ever and clearly available, at least when it was convenient for her. But seeing Verde with Eco had given him a glimpse of what a relationship could be—which painfully showed the limits of his bond with Bree—whom he did love—but also revealed the vacuousness of his affair with Haley. They had no prospect of a serious relationship; at best they were wasting each other's time, and at worst falling into something desperate and destructive.

"I'm really under it here," he said. "It's going to be a late night."

"We'll skip dinner. You'll come to my place later."

"No, Haley. Really. I can't make it tonight."

She paused. "What is this, Daniel, a brush off?"

"No. Listen, my wife died, I'm not sleeping, and I'm getting pushed from all sides, including having to kowtow to Langston."

"Senator Langston is what he is. You know it's more important to attend to *my* needs...and I am feeling very much in need at the moment."

"I just can't tonight, Haley. Maybe next week."

"Is there someone else?" she demanded. "Have you forgotten your poor wife and shacked up with some new woman?"

He seethed at her daring to mention Bree. He wanted to tell her to go to hell but had to keep his head. "It's not that. Look, I just can't do it."

After a silence her voice became steely. "You may look back on this conversation as a serious misstep."

"I guess I'll have to live with that."

Nell Batterly prided herself on not letting anything get past her, and she sensed what was wrong with Daniel was more than lingering sadness over losing his wife and daughter. He still directed her and Jake, but he didn't follow up like before the flood; he let them take meetings he formerly would have insisted on handling; his mind seemed to wander. She wondered if he should be in therapy about the flood, although that might tarnish his image as "the closer." Or maybe he just wasn't eating or sleeping enough; he did look pretty pale.

Daniel hadn't invited Jake and her to the pub for a while, so she took the initiative. "We're going to the Korean barbecue for lunch," she said at the end of a meeting. "Do you want to come along, get out of the office for a while?"

"I'm not hungry," he said, "but thanks."

"Well, barbecue was Jake's idea. We could get a sandwich and a beer at the Stanchion if you want."

"No. In fact, I'm drying out for a while. You two go ahead."

Over *bulgogi* on a linoleum table twenty minutes later, she said to Jake, "What's up with Daniel? You must have noticed how strangely he's been acting."

"Give the guy a break," he said. "Think of what he's been through."

"Yeah, obviously. Still, did he tell you he's on the wagon?"

Jake gulped down a mouthful. "No shit?"

She nodded.

"That's serious," he said. "I wonder if he's okay."

"And if he'll be able to run this project. If this goes south, it's not only *his* ass on the line."

"Always the compassionate one, aren't you?"

"Hey," she scoffed, "I love Daniel—you know that—and he's a great boss, but these are our careers, not to mention I need this job to pay the rent."

"Which reminds me! What's the date?"

"You didn't forget your rent again?" she said, laughing at how absent-minded Jake could be but never sure if he was kidding.

Heading into the afternoon, Daniel caught himself thinking it was Friday, so he should be getting ready to fly home to Texas. It was strange how the mind worked. He could go through whole sleepless nights thinking about Bree and Annabelle and wishing he could go back and do it all over, but in another moment he could forget anything bad had ever happened to them.

Friday afternoon now meant no more than staying late at work to limit his time alone in his apartment without drinking. He walked home—to kill some time—and got some sleep that night, thankfully. In the morning he cursed not being able to swim laps at his athletic club; even the thought of a swimming pool made him nauseous. Instead, he pulled on his running shoes for the first time in a year.

The distraction worked, to some extent. Fast rock music through his ear buds blocked out everything but the sidewalk in front of him. On the Mall he ran toward the Capitol but doubled back to avoid the reflecting pool and circled around the Washington Monument. He concentrated on the rhythm of his steps, and for an hour sweated out some of his tension.

After he got home and toweled off—wishing he could take a hot shower—he made a sandwich and sat to watch a basketball game. But there was no relief there, either, as his Dallas Mavericks looked terrible. He flipped off the set and pulled Professor Cahill's report from his briefcase. It was time to settle in with a glass of bourbon and read.

But then he remembered there was no liquor. He brewed tea instead, hoping this would be some kind of substitute. It wasn't.

Nonetheless, he dug into the report. This ecologist was clearly at the top of his field. He had degrees from major universities, the list of his published articles ran three pages, and he had testified several times before Congress. His report presented voluminous data made engaging by personal stories and photographs—Daniel was sure they were Verde's. But, while the anecdotes and graphics would draw in readers, the meat of the report was even more impressive. In contrast with the dumbed-down tripe the Oil Institute put out, the report was logical and believable, and cited its sources like legitimate scientific writing. Industry researchers could probably poke holes in some of these references, and Daniel was particularly good at exploiting minor discrepancies in this kind of work, but Cahill's reasoning was convincing.

In 2010 Hurricane Sandy sent a thirteen-foot wave against lower Manhattan. In 2017 Hurricane Irma hit Florida as the strongest storm on record. In Greenland an ice sheet the size of Mexico was melting. Cahill's preface to all these statistics queried: "Are these events precursors of what is to come?"

Daniel wondered if you could call these things "precursors" when extreme weather was already happening. He thought particularly about the unprecedented rain in California coming on top of a drought and the surge of tornados in the Midwest and South.

Cahill concluded we could no longer stop the planet from warming, but we could slow this down. Not only could we cut emissions, but we also could paint rooftops white, develop more reflective crops, disperse hydrogen sulfide haze to shade sunlight. But instead of working to address this crisis, we were dispersing more greenhouse gasses every year and doing next to nothing to prepare for the inevitable. It reminded Daniel of Howard Kane's comment about the frog calmly swimming in the water gradually boiling him.

As convincing as Daniel found the report on an intellectual level, it was how Cahill used the Guadalupe flood as a ground-level case study that hit him like a gut punch. In his afterword the professor sounded yet another alarm. Apparently, the area around the oil fields of the Permian Basin north of Pecos was for the first time experiencing earthquakes, which Cahill said were caused when wastewater from fracking lubricates the plates clamped together along natural fault lines. Both Oklahoma and New Mexico had addressed this danger by limiting fracking, but the attitude of the West Texas oil industry was it was worth having the ground shake every couple of months to keep a good paycheck coming in.

Chapter Twenty-Four

Daniel pretended to work but mostly tried to figure out how to contact Eco since the number he had for Verde was disconnected. But that afternoon he got a call from Bree's mother, Julia Morrison.

"Hi, Mom," he said, feeling a moment's pang at using that name. Bree's mother felt much closer to him than his own mother ever had. His real mother hadn't even called after the flood.

"Daniel, I'm so sorry to bother you at the office."

"Oh, it's no bother. How are you all?"

"Well, you know, we're very sad. It's hard not to think about Bree and little Annabelle. But we also worry about you being all alone. Well, and you know today would have been Bree's birthday, and we got together to remember."

"Of course, Mom. I wish I could have joined you."

"I know you do, Daniel. And Peter encouraged me to call to let you know we're thinking about you and make sure you know you'll always be an important part of our family."

He was shocked at having forgotten Bree's birthday and

felt badly about not calling her parents more often. Events had tumbled one upon the other so rapidly lately, he had lost all sense of time. "That's sweet of you, Mom, and you should feel free to call whenever you want. I apologize for being out of touch."

She didn't seem to have much else to say, except that her son wanted to say hello.

"Hey, brother," came Pete's voice.

"Pete, I'm glad you're with your folks today. Thanks for getting your mom to call."

"Yeah, it seems to have done her some good. Couldn't get Dad on—you know how he is about the phone—but he feels the same."

"I'm sure he does."

"And there's something else: a message about some property you were interested in. Have you got a pen to take down a number?"

This was it. Eco was reaching out. As he wrote down the number, he could imagine his idealistic young self smiling. This was the corporate whore as, what, an environmental commando? Everything was different now. There would be no more simply calling out to Alice to get someone on the line or casually shooting off a text message. Instead, he'd be hiding and concealing and trying to dance one step ahead of the surveillance. It was scary but thrilling.

He dialed the new number.

"Hello," Verde's voice came across, steady and serious, and quickened his pulse.

"Yes," he stammered, "I was told to call this number about a property in Arlington?"

"Would you be available to view it today?"

"This afternoon works for me."

"Well, then, perhaps we should meet at the same place, at say half past twelve?

"I'll be there."

Daniel told his assistant he'd be at meetings all afternoon, but as he was preparing to leave, Jake and Nell knocked on his door.

"We need to talk about the Dakota case," Jake said, plopping down in a guest chair.

"What's up?"

Jake looked distressingly at Nell, then turned to Daniel. "I messed up...."

"*We* messed up," Nell said.

"No," Jake insisted, "this is on me. It's that letter you sent the court. You're admitted just for the case, but local rules don't allow anyone not generally admitted in the state to sign court filings."

"And the other side made a stink," Nell added.

"Those rat bastards," Daniel said, thinking he had no time for this nonsense. "So just do the letter over and get local counsel to sign it."

"Yeah, it's an easy fix but..." Jake said.

"Pearce found out," Daniel guessed.

Jake nodded sadly. "His friend in Dakota told him."

"That's all we need," Daniel said. "Look, it's no big deal. You fix it with local counsel, and I'll deal with Pearce. Anything else?"

"Jake thinks we should say we're going to move for summary judgment this week," Nell said, "but why should we tip our hand until local counsel has the motion ready? Isn't it better to hit them with it on Friday afternoon without warning?"

Daniel had to smile at her penchant for hardball litigation, never missing a chance to make things harder on the other side. "Let me see the brief," he said and settled in to read.

"This second version is good," he said after a few minutes, handing it back to Nell, "and I think you're right about waiting—especially given what assholes these guys were about that letter, but add to the press release we are *considering* a motion in light of the undisputed facts."

Nell shot a look of satisfaction at Jake, who rolled his eyes. "Okay," she said, "we'll get this out today." Then she paused, looking at Daniel's desk. "You know, I meant to ask last time: what's up with the new phone?"

"Oh, just a cheapo," he said, bothered that he had let them see it. "I might use it on runs so I don't lose my real phone again."

She looked doubtful, but left without any more questions.

Via a new Metro-and-taxi route, Daniel approached the Vietnam Memorial from the street side to avoid the reflecting pool. He kept his eyes open for anything out of place, but there was only the usual stream of tourists, with a couple of gray-haired men in fatigue jackets leaning in close to the granite wall.

Verde called and picked him up on Lincoln Memorial Circle. This time they crossed the bridge and turned south. After navigating a maze of access roads at Reagan Airport, Verde pulled up behind a storefront in Old Town Alexandria.

As Verde got off the scooter, she said, "We moved as soon as we confirmed your information about Ranger. He was low-level recruit who didn't know much, but we suspected he might be able to lead the authorities to our Arlington location."

"But the FBI knows about Pete, now. What does that mean for me?"

"We will keep your brother-in-law at a distance. This is why his mother made the call to contact you. Perhaps we may be able to use the government surveillance of Peter to our advantage— while they don't suspect we know they are watching. You, for better or for worse, are a different case. Your industry access is too valuable to ignore."

He smiled at what sounded like a compliment, but realized his mistake when she simply turned away, apparently unimpressed.

For a high-powered lawyer, Mia found Daniel to be undisciplined. Even in this serious business, with police and jail threatening, he looked at her with the eyes of a puppy who wants his belly scratched. How could he be effective when he was so distracted?

She brought him into the new offices, where Kristof was going over a *Monkey Wrench* post with a young volunteer.

"So," Kristof said when he looked up, "our man on the inside." He gestured Daniel to an empty corner of the room and reached to shake hands as they walked. "We have to thank you for your help with security. It only takes one crack to let in unwanted light."

Daniel nodded, pleased.

"And the information on Energy Security Foundation was helpful. We passed it to a cell in Boston that will make use of it."

"So," Daniel replied, "what's next?"

Mia shared a subtle look with Kristof. This recruit might work out. But was there some more effective way to test his loyalty?

"Okay, first off," Kristof said, "we are going to put you through a little Tradecraft 101, an introduction to recognizing a tail and becoming invisible. It might seem excessive but following protocol saves us from needless mistakes. For that, I will leave you in Verde's capable hands."

Kristof's warning look reminded her she had promised to be gracious with Daniel. So she tried to be more pleasant as she led him to another room to introduce their "costume department," a woman named Bess who designed theatrical costumes by day. She sat with an opened makeup case and a rack of wigs. "Bess handles all things theatrical, from sewing props to creating disguises," Mia said. "She will show you ways to alter your appearance."

Later she led him through another room, this one buzzing with activity. Outside the room she quizzed him on what he just saw walking from one location to another. His recall was dismal. His success as a lawyer apparently rested on his engaging smile and ability to speak rather than intelligence.

"You will need to do better," she said. "The success of the operation could depend on this."

He seemed to try hard after that, and when they passed through a third room, his observation skills improved markedly.

She concluded his soft life had deadened him to what went on around him, just as it had muffled any sense of justice in the work he did. With time he might turn both around. She only hoped they were not revealing too much before they were sure of him.

Next, she introduced Daniel to their tech guru, a young woman who explained how to take a cell phone off the grid—and how to take a phone apart and reassemble it. Mia grinned inwardly, recalling how she had Pete dismantle his phone outside Austin, wondering how long it took him to put it back together.

Finally, she showed him how to deliver or receive a package without drawing attention. "These days," she said, "almost everything is digital, but every online transfer may be susceptible to tracing or interception. Also, there are times when physical delivery is necessary for original documents or something that cannot be reproduced."

Through the afternoon Daniel proved a quick learner, and she began to think she may have misjudged him. But he grasped the details of covert action so quickly that she grew concerned his experience as a lobbyist may have made him good at lying to them.

Over coffee in the afternoon, Stefan joined them with a happy smile. "Some good news," he said. "Our two friends in Utah were acquitted."

"Are they with Anthro?" Daniel asked.

"A cell out west."

"What was the charge?"

"Burglary and theft. They snuck into a Major Foods slaughterhouse to document sick and underweight pigs. They found two piglets covered in lesions who were destined for the landfill, so they took them and nursed them back to health. The company had no idea until months later, when we provided the rescue video to a friend at *The Times*. Next thing you know, FBI shock troops swooped in with warrants for the pigs."

"Sounds like an efficient use of law enforcement resources," Daniel said.

Stefan snickered. "You know it. A dozen agents with SUVs and drone coverage nabbed five hardened terrorists and recovered two piglets worth forty dollars each. Three of our people took plea deals and didn't serve time, but two went to trial. Then, yesterday, the jury let them off, finding they didn't intend to steal, but only to document conditions and rescue animals if necessary. The piglets actually had no value to Major Foods."

"To these people animals are only meat to sell," Mia said, shaking her head in disgust.

"But," Stefan added, "the third reason for the acquittal is the most hopeful. They bought our claim that a non-guilty verdict would encourage conglomerates to improve their treatment of animals and might help get a fair hearing for the next animal cruelty complaint."

"That could be helpful," Mia said. "Will you cover this for the newsletter?"

"I've got one of our more literary volunteers on it this morning. It's the kind of feel-good story the kids like to work on, where we're angels instead of devil anarchists."

"You folks have a wide range of interests," Daniel said.

"True," Stefan said, "but it's all related to what's destroying the planet."

"Piglets to pipelines," Daniel said, thinking this was the kind of catchy line Eco might have said.

"And everything in between. For instance, one group in Europe—not affiliated but of like mind—has gained notoriety by messing up displays of famous artworks."

"What is 'messing up'?"

"Well, the paintings are protected by glass—so the art isn't damaged—but they *do* make a mess. Last year Just Stop Oil smeared cake on the *Mona Lisa* in the Louvre and splashed tomato soup on a Van Gogh in the National Gallery in London."

"Were they caught?"

"They glued their hands to the walls to make sure they were caught, to make the message clear."

"Which was?"

Stefan smiled patronizingly. "It is a sad commentary, Al, when a society is more outraged by soup spilled on the glass over a painting than about its government investing in fossil fuels."

Daniel contemplated this. "It seems like a publicity stunt. And don't those actions alienate art lovers, who might be sympathetic?"

"Possibly, but more than all the lobbying and petitions and marches, this tactic gets people talking about the issue. Van Gogh himself said it isn't the language of painters one ought to listen to but the language of nature. Nature is crying out in its death throes while the obscenely wealthy pay millions of dollars for paintings of nature."

She watched Daniel closely as he took in what Stefan said. He looked receptive and serious, but something still troubled her.

Daniel's day at the Anthro site was his best since the flood. He was putting his energy into a cause that was right and urgent. And he had found a community of people working together, not in competition but in true cooperation, all contributing the best of themselves to a common purpose.

True to his adopted name, Assisi had the aura of a friar saint, as if at any moment songbirds might perch on his shoulder. Eco had the charisma of a born leader. And Verde came across as driven and confident. The whole crew, including the young people manning the phones and writing blog posts, were a team. The effort felt so zealous and imperative, and yet these people also found joy and humor in the struggle.

Chapter Twenty-Five

Pearce called Daniel into his office the next week to watch the pipeline vote. Given Daniel's decision to undermine his boss's world, he almost enjoyed playing the role of Pearce's drudge in this burlesque, although now he wished the bill could somehow be defeated.

"I want your assurance," the old man said. "No surprises today. Tell me we've got this locked up."

"Yes, sir," Daniel responded. "Langston held up his end, which gives us three or four votes extra."

Pearce nodded. Reaching for a cigar, he reminded Daniel of a fat, wallowing pig—not at all like those cute piglets rescued from the slaughterhouse. In a perfect world, Anthro would finally win the day and land Pearce in the mud where he belonged.

"You look ill at ease," Pearce said. "Not ready to count your chickens?"

It was almost too funny how Pearce extended Daniel's barnyard metaphor, but he tried to look thoughtful and cautious.

"That's right, Branston. Can't lose focus before they're hatched. You taught me that."

Pearce could count on Daniel being beholden to him. The young lawyer was good at his job, even if his present lack of enthusiasm was underwhelming. He might just be working too hard—on the methane vote and the pipeline—so soon after suffering his personal loss. Hell, life was full of tragedies; the winners were the ones who picked themselves up and got back to business.

He puffed long on his cigar, blowing the smoke over his shoulder before looking closely at his protégé. "After we pop the champagne," he said, "and the Institute shows its appreciation, you'll take a vacation. Book a cruise, sit on a beach, whatever. We need you in top form when we take on bigger projects."

"Is something in the works?"

"You know the old bear. Always something in the works. In fact, you and I might be taking a trip to the Middle East in January."

"That's amazing, and I appreciate the suggestion, but the last thing I need is time off to dwell on things."

Dwelling on things was exactly what Pearce wanted his young partner to do, things like how to build the practice and undermine the opposition. "Well," he said, "I say you need a break, so you *need* a break."

Daniel shrugged. "Okay. I'll take some time, maybe next week."

"That's the spirit. Who knows? A week in the sun might inspire you to come up with a plan to get the US out of the Climate Accord again."

"Win back the presidency," Daniel said matter-of-factly.

"Well, that would make it too easy. We earn no largesse from our clients without overcoming obstacles—the more insurmountable, the greater the reward. The clients must believe succeeding in politics in this town is like running a wild river; they need an able pilot at the tiller who can avoid the holes and thread the sieves."

"I didn't know you were a whitewater rafter."

Pearce scoffed, "As if I had the time—or the inclination. The only way I want to be on the water is on a large yacht with a drink in my hand. But one of our sponsors at the Institute is a fanatic. His son competes at whatever high level there is for that."

"I see. Well, as to the pipeline bill, our client knows it was PJ&H that got it across."

Pearce laughed and added, mostly to himself. "Can't solve a bet-the-company problem without us, just the way we like it."

Daniel's smile looked insincere. Was he still pouting about that methane bonus? Did Pearce go too far in slapping him down about the Two Rivers debacle? He made a mental note to set up breakfast meetings with Daniel's associates: the feisty young woman and the pothead who smiled too much. Daniel had pulled off the pipeline vote but his attitude had turned sour. If his forced vacation had to be extended, his assistants would have to step up. And if Daniel could no longer do the job, they'd have even bigger roles. In fact, they'd be useful in gauging if their boss was on his game. It was important for everyone at PJ&H to understand they worked for Pearce, and the end result mattered more than personal issues.

Daniel walked back down the hallway to his office. Why was Pearce sending him on vacation? It was unlike the man to empathize. Did he just want Daniel out of the way? Why? Had he sensed Daniel was no longer committed to their sordid business? He had to redouble his efforts to demonstrate he was a team player and keep his new climate consciousness under wraps. Maybe there was some easy win he could pull off, something to reassure Pearce without hurting the cause?

"Everything okay, Mr. Lazaro?" his assistant said, looking up as he passed her desk.

"What?" he said and realized he must look like he was in a daze. "Yes, Alice, thanks. I was just lost in thought for a moment there."

He had to keep up appearances, to smile and take whatever Pearce dished out. Still, the old bastard's overbearing manner threw salt in the wound left by the withheld bonus and all the other minor insults. And this forced vacation was unwelcome. He had come to terms about losing Bree, but time off now would just be days to obsess about finding Annabelle—while fighting the urge to drink. If he could spend the time aiding the search or even getting over his phobia, he'd take off even in defiance of Pearce. But those things wouldn't happen. Annabelle was lost to the river. His guilt for placing her there and leaving her to face the deluge alone would remain, as would his fear of water.

But what if he could use time off to work with Anthro? Since the vacation was Pearce's idea—or his order—Daniel would be free to come and go without accounting for his time. He could give whole days or more to Anthro with perfect cover. If Eco needed him to access something in the office, that would also be simple. Pearce wouldn't be surprised if he came in at random hours—if anyone even told him. He'd like the fact that Daniel couldn't stay away; it would remind him of himself.

He closed his door and spun his chair toward the window. He had joined the battle for the defenseless and penniless planet, and would never be welcomed back by the people with the money who had so generously compensated him for seven years. But he still struggled with why he had done the devil's work. Over his years at PJ&H, he had rationalized that every citizen and every company had rights, regardless of how they made their money or what positions they advocated, and they were entitled to legal representation. Big oil as a client was like a mobster everyone knew was guilty but who still was entitled to a lawyer.

But no mobster ever did the level of damage inflicted by corporate greed and government paralysis. Even large-scale villains that killed thousands, like tobacco companies and drug makers, never threatened the entire planet.

Chapter Twenty-Six

The mood at Anthro was somber. Just as Daniel had predicted, the news was that a senator from Kansas threw his support behind the pipeline bill, which would assure three more votes for passage.

Kristof sat with his head in his hands at a long table in Alexandria. How would this setback affect the movement?

Zeke joined him and paced the end of the room, eyes darting like a caged animal. "I don't get it," he blurted out. "Senator Dodge has no dog in this fight; why did he use up chits for this?"

"It's politics," Kristof said. "You can be sure he got some payoff in return."

Zeke breathed heavily, as if he might hyperventilate. "Just shows you," he growled, "it's no use working through the system. The environmental breakdown escalates with social inequality, and there's no end but civilizational collapse. Protest marches do nothing. Appealing to congressmen has no effect unless you've got the money to buy their support. The drive for endless economic growth dooms any chance at building an inclusive future. We've got to find a way to start making a difference."

"I hear you, brother. But let's take a breath here and wait for the vote."

Kristof longed for a world where people would listen to the scientists and see the maelstrom ahead. But their lethargy or willful ignorance gave people like Zeke, who pushed for more action, all the ammunition they needed. And dramatic action might be the only viable way forward.

Mia came into the room and wrapped her arms around him, filling him with the intoxicating scent from the long, soft hair falling across his cheek. In moments like this, he could almost believe there was hope.

Then they saw the vote on C-Span. The Pipeline Authorization Act passed. There was little hope the president would veto the bill, so it would become law.

Kristof cursed. Zeke kicked a radiator, shaking the room. As she walked out, Mia looked at Zeke as if he were a misbehaved child.

What would happen next? What did this do to Anthro's effectiveness? They had put maximum effort into defeating this bill, working with opposition groups in three states and two countries, posting data on fossil fuels, appealing to preserve indigenous sites. None of it got the attention of the sleepwalkers lulled by big oil propaganda. How did people not understand this was *their* future at stake, theirs and all their descendants?

He wished their efforts were enough, that you could convince people through reason and dialogue. But this vote killed his delusion. They had to face the fact that passive means had failed; Anthro had to find another way to sound the global alarm.

Mia thought about bringing Kristof a cup of tea but decided to leave him alone. Everyone in the office had known in the end their efforts on the pipeline bill would fail, but he was still taking it hard. He knew people would be discouraged and some would drop out of the movement while others would push to do something more radical. Zeke would want to go back to hobbling tractors and downing power poles, and Kristof seemed almost ready to join him. But at least Mia could count on Kristof letting her know before he did anything reckless.

The four founders soon gathered on the roof to talk about how to move forward. When Mia and Kristof came through the door, Zeke was already haranguing Stefan. "What about the fires in the parks? It's Armageddon! And that's just the wilderness system and national parks, piddling islands of habitat in coast-to-coast human development. We need more than help controlling wildfires; we have to reweave the natural fabric of North America."

"But we can't say our movement is based on love if we hurt people."

Zeke winced, looking aside at Kristof. "Look, I don't want to hurt anyone, but we're at war. We have to be heard."

"But where do we draw the line?" Stefan said. "Is it okay to spike a tree and take off a logger's arm? Can we send kids into action where they could be hurt? I mean, look, we all have the same goals, but the public sees some of this as terrorism."

"It's not terrorism or vandalism," Zeke replied. "It's resistance, worship of the Earth. It's spiritual."

"Well," Stefan said, "one man's spiritual is another man's...I don't know what. I'm just saying I won't take part in violence. I can't in good conscience go beyond passive resistance...active *protest* and advocacy, but *passive* resistance."

Zeke and Stefan continued to argue, while Mia and Kristof stood by. There was nothing new in this debate. Stefan was right; violent action alienated the population that paid no heed to the havoc ahead, and Anthro had to reach these people without threatening them. But Zeke also had a point: passive action did not get attention or lead to meaningful change. She had realized that long ago in Romania, where she felt justified pouring sand into gas tanks and spiking trees. She regretted that those measures might have injured workers, but it was their choice to take jobs doing much worse damage.

Zeke enumerated environmental efforts through the years, none of which had moved the meter on public perception. "Smearing a painting with tomato soup might get picked up as a human-interest story, but blowing up a pipeline gets real attention."

Two things kept her from voicing agreement with Zeke. First, somehow in this wide, doomed world she had managed to find her soulmate, a man who loved her with complete honesty and caring. Since her brother died, she had given herself wholly to his cause of saving the planet, seeing no room for another purpose in life. But then she met Kristof, and they came together, and she found hope she might find some kind of peace even while continuing the struggle.

There was also the second reason, something inside her she had not yet told even Kristof. She needed to give it time before she would share the news, just to be sure, but the life taking form inside her brought with it a growing reverence for *all* life.

The argument raged for an hour, rehashing the same basic disagreement that had festered within Anthro since its start in the Mexican desert.

Kristof largely stayed out of the debate, but he listened closely, as usual, and she could see that, like her, he internalized both sides of the dispute.

"Well, partner," Zeke finally said to Stefan, "it looks like our trails may part here."

"No," Mia blurted out. "That cannot always be your answer. We have disagreements, but we work through them. We are all on the same path; we need to find a way to be effective together."

"Right," Zeke said, shaking his head. "As if Greenpeace and the Environmental Defense Fund shared that path. Hard to forget or forgive how the Sierra Club offered a reward for turning us in after we blew the pipeline in Iowa. Anyway, there's no more time."

"Okay," Kristof interrupted. "How about this...."

Everyone turned to him, Stefan and Zeke doubtfully but Mia hopeful her husband could heal the rift.

"We pull one more action," Kristof said. "Not violent," looking aside at Stefan, "but not timid."

Zeke shook his head and turned away in a gesture of impatience.

"We hit the Stone Canyon Bridge," Kristof said. "Not 'hit it' like blowing it up, but hit it in a way to shake people and disrupt operations."

"You're not making sense," Zeke said.

"No, listen," Kristof went on. "Remember what Earth First! did at Glen Canyon? That huge banner freaked everyone out?"

Glen Canyon loomed large in all their minds. Activists had hung a banner looking like a crack in the dam. By bringing everything to a standstill, it brought attention to how damming the Colorado River to create Lake Powell had flooded majestic canyons and reduced the mighty river to a trickle.

"Well," Kristof went on, "we hit the Stone Canyon Bridge that connects clearcutting in the Monongahela Forest with the mills. We cut that artery and the operation has to stop. It will be sure to get national attention—and give supporters a way to look past the pipeline defeat."

Zeke smirked. "More smoke and mirrors," he said. "Better to take the bridge down. *That* would stop logging. Hey, the feds call us terrorists just for tree-sitting."

"That may be," Kristof replied, "but risking hurting people— our own *and* bystanders—plays into that image." He looked each of them in the eye, in his way of making you want to agree with him. "Can we please just try it? Pull this action all together, like we've done from the start?"

"I'm for it," Stefan said.

"I am, as well," Mia added.

Zeke abruptly turned to leave, obviously dissatisfied and angry.

Kristof called after him. "I'll take that as a yes, Zeke. We'll start planning."

Daniel had proven he could be trusted by exposing Ranger and providing information about the Energy Security Foundation. Now he had obtained details about trucking schedules out of the Monongahela Forest and made clear he wanted to be there when they put his information to use.

"Knowing the schedules was crucial to our planning," Mia had argued.

"But he's got no operational chops," Zeke had responded.

"Without Daniel we would have had to monitor shipments for weeks to confirm trucking schedules," Mia had replied.

"Let's not argue about this," Kristof had said. "Daniel has proven his worth, and his information allowed us to put together a plan for the bridge. If we deny him the chance to participate—at least in a support role—we risk undermining his eagerness and our access to his information. Besides, while I personally trust him, keeping him close will also be best, in case he has not been forthright with us."

All finally agreed Daniel had earned his seat in the car. He would just be a lookout, anyway, which required no tactical training.

Mia was okay with this. While the baby coming made her want to spend all the quiet time she could with Kristof, she would have found it hard not to tell him about her pregnancy over a long drive together, and her family history taught her it would be bad luck to tell anyone at this early stage, when things could go wrong. Anyway, bringing it up now would place their personal happiness before the cause, which would show weakness at a time they needed unity of purpose. Kristof might even have insisted she stay out of the action, which she would not abide. They could not carry on the struggle if they all looked first to their own safety and comfort. Besides, this action would involve little risk; the worst they would face was arrest for defacing the bridge. She would tell Kristof about the baby in a quiet moment as they celebrated their success.

Most important was that she and Kristof were in accord. Anthro's loose organization sometimes resulted in confusion about operations, so she always insisted they review every detail of a plan privately before they started. Whatever else happened, the two of them would have clear agreement about what to expect and where to turn if something went wrong.

So, Kristof would drive with Zeke and the artist they recruited to help paint the bridge. They would leave early in the afternoon to pick up materials, while she would drive with Daniel in the evening.

She and Daniel would take the Camry and meet the men at a staging area near the bridge, where they would already have unloaded the big Volvo SUV. Then she and Daniel would drive the cars back to the rendezvous point, three miles away on the road but less than half a mile by a trail through the woods. They would leave the Volvo there and drive the Camry out both approaches— from the mountains and from the valley—so they could post signs in each direction that the bridge was closed for repair. This would make certain the men would not be interrupted as they lowered themselves off the span to affix the banners. The third member of their team, Bess assured them, would paint the bridge so it looked like it was collapsing. Then they would pick up the men at the staging area, drive to the rendezvous point and separate to drive home by different routes. If there was any hiccup—a policeman showing up or a suspicious-looking tourist—they would meet at the rendezvous point. Stefan would stand by the telephone in Virginia, ready to assist, and two safe houses were set up ten miles from the site.

The plan was simple. It made sense. And the splash it would make on social media would be effective. She loved the adrenaline rush at this stage of an action, the feeling she was about to strike out against the monster she had fought on two continents. And to be fighting this righteous crusade alongside the love of her life was more than she deserved, more than she ever would have dared hope for when she was dodging company enforcers in the Romanian forest.

Kristof suggested she treat the time driving with Daniel as a challenge to her perception. What motivated him, what was this phobia about, and what was he looking for in the end?

She decided to just make the best of driving with Daniel. He wasn't so bad, really. She had begun to think she had been too hard on him. He came from such a different world than she did, and she found his stories about US politics unfamiliar and informative, being generous she might even say entertaining. She had a higher tolerance for risk than he did, given their backgrounds, but his heart appeared to be in the right place. His personal tragedy had instilled in him ardor for the cause that, with his unique position inside the oil cartel, made him a propitious colleague. And while she had poured her share of sand into gas tanks and pulled up more survey stakes than she could remember, she found herself leaning toward Stefan's view that they must not risk hurting people. Kristof told her Daniel also was unwilling to hurt anyone; if he found acceptance in the inner group, he might tip the balance toward non-violent means. He could at least help temper Zeke's sway over Kristof to take foolish chances.

Chapter
Twenty-Seven

Daniel was excited to be taking an active role in something real.

As a first step, he followed Pearce's "suggestion" and told everyone he'd be out of the office for a few days. But as he was dressing to leave, a call came through from Representative Arnold Wilkins of Delaware. Daniel had been trying to schedule a meeting with this congressman for weeks because he hovered on the edge of working with them on the Climate Accord. This was Pearce's pet project, and could be crucial not only to the Oil Institute but also as a lure to landing the Saudis as a client. If Daniel missed the chance to meet and there was blowback, Pearce would have his head.

He had to rely on his team. He asked his assistant to set up a meeting with Nell and Jake on his way to Alexandria. It would be much faster to do this by phone or a Zoom call, but he wasn't even sure what he would say. How much could he tell them without endangering the mission? At the same time, was it fair to keep them in the dark? He needed to do this in person, however it worked out.

They were both there when he arrived. He wore outdoor clothes—it would be cold in the forest. Besides, he was on vacation and should look like it.

"Quite the mountain man," Nell observed, looking him up and down. "Flannel suits you."

"Yeah," Jake agreed. "I had a shirt like that in college; wonder what happened to it?"

Daniel smiled, trying to minimize any suspicion about this odd meeting. But there was no way to obscure what he had to ask of them. With his door closed, he began. "Have you guys finished that climate research?"

The associates looked at each other, and Nell spoke. "We're pretty much there—though this still seems like a distraction."

"We've got it covered," Jake interjected. "Just need to put together our two parts. Should be final late tomorrow."

Daniel had poured over Dr. Cahill's report and expected his associates' research to add little, beyond affirmation of the science from an adversarial perspective. But the time was well spent if it opened the eyes of two bright young lawyers. Still, he needed to ease into the topic. "Have you ever stopped to think—I mean really think—about what it is we do here?"

Nell and Jake cast confused looks at each other, and Jake screwed up his face. "Like, should we really be helping drown Bambi in oil?"

Nell looked at him in exasperation and turned to Daniel. Her expression urged him to set their colleague straight. Instead, Daniel shrugged. "You're on the right track, but for now leave it at this...."

Nell looked dumbfounded and Jake curious. "You know," Daniel went on, "about my house and my family, and you now also know burning oil and cutting trees made that flood worse; who knows, maybe just enough to sweep away my life."

"Oh, dude," Jake said almost unconsciously, "I hadn't thought about that."

"That's not fair *or* accurate," Nell insisted.

"Well, I've come to believe it. But where we go from there... who knows?"

"So," Nell said, choosing each word carefully, "you...are now doing what?"

Daniel sighed, sensing he was not getting through. "What I'm doing is looking toward the future...for us all." He was thinking of this "all" as humankind but suspected his associates would assume he meant just the three people in the room.

"I know!" Nell said with a look of excitement. "You're forming your own firm. This research is for the pitch about how well we know the opposition."

"No," Daniel said. "It's not where we do it or who divides up the fees. I'm talking about the work, the positions we advocate, the legislation we push."

Their expressions were blank, and Daniel feared he should not have introduced this subject when he had no time to convince them, and on the eve of his first meaningful mission with Anthro. He tried to backtrack. "The only important thing right now is I need your help. I've got to be out of the office. You two have to take a meeting tomorrow with Representative Wilkins."

"He finally agreed?" Nell said. "But wait. You want *us* to meet him? Pearce will have a duck!"

"He will if Wilkins squawks. But you two know the facts and the spiel. You can let this guy run and start to reel him in. Get him on board with the Institute's thinking. I know you can."

"But he wants to meet with *you*!" Nell pleaded. "It's taken weeks to set this up."

"Look," Daniel said, "I know I'm being obtuse but trust me. Just take this meeting and stick to the script."

Jake threw up his hands, looking confused.

"But I thought you were taking a vacation," Nell said. "Where are you really going?"

"To spend some time in the woods," Daniel said. "When I get back you'll come up to the apartment, I'll cook dinner and we'll talk. For now, cover for me and make the congressman happy. Tell him I'll take him to the best restaurant in town next week."

Jake was confused. Daniel's recital of radical green talking points had him reeling. But the more he thought about it, the more it actually made some sense. On a recent night out with a college friend who worked for one of their Democratic opponents, more than a few drinks led them into the policy weeds and Jake found it hard to defend his clients' positions on climate science. That conversation—and what he had learned through the climate research—left him critical of the work he was doing. He allayed his ruffled conscience with the knowledge PJ&H paid better than any legislative job, but that rationale suddenly felt selfish and thin.

He also couldn't forget his recent treatment by PJ&H. It was true he had messed up on that letter to the judge in North Dakota, which angered Pearce, but it didn't hurt the case and Pearce didn't need to curse him out in front of Daniel and Nell—and bring up again his smoking weed in the office. He was ready to polish his resume and look for a job back home in New York. And now this dose of morality from Daniel hit him like a cold shower; maybe starting salary was not the most important aspect of his next job?

Daniel cleared out his inbox and answered some calls. Then he took a circuitous route to Alexandria via the Metro and Uber. He found Anthro's space quiet. Most of the young people had gotten an early start on the weekend. Those who remained were focused on the action ahead.

Verde sat down with him to go over the map.

"I thought you were driving," he said.

"That is the plan, but one never can be certain. We all must know each role in case there is a need to improvise. The Prussian general van Clausewitz talked about 'fog of war'; do you know it?"

"I know the phrase but not the general. Once the battle starts, all plans go to hell."

"Eco would say the uncertainty in situational awareness experienced by participants in military operations, but you know how *he* is."

He smiled but immediately sensed she wasn't kidding. More importantly, the plan sounded good. He was sure they could get in, do their worst and get out. They had contingencies built in if a cop happened by or whatever. Anyway, the worst-case scenario was what? Well, he could be arrested for conspiracy to destroy public property, lose his job, be disbarred for revealing client confidences and live in disgrace. But shit, his whole career had been a disgrace.

"Did you bring extra shoes?" she asked.

"Right here," he said, holding up an old pair of sneakers.

"And you left your phone behind?"

"Yes, boss."

"Good. So you will wear those shoes during the operation, and afterwards we will burn them, so the treads cannot be traced to you."

Verde made him change his blue-plaid jacket for a black fleece, dark green coat and black woolen cap. While Eco and Guy were dressed in dark climbing gear, Daniel and Verde needed to pose as tourists; if they were stopped, the police would have no reason to search the car and find the illegal police scanner. They also snapped blue filters on the flashlights so the beams would blend in with light from the half-moon.

The separate driving felt like overkill, particularly on their way *to* the job, but he supposed they needed two cars to move all the equipment. He had an uncomfortable feeling he might be getting in over his head.

As they turned west onto Route 66, Daniel wondered why Eco hadn't introduced him to the third man on the bridge team. "So, who is this new guy?" he asked Verde.

"Ludd is a painter of theatrical sets. Bess knows him and recruited him, and Guy ran him through the background check. Bess assures us he could paint Stone Canyon Bridge to disappear entirely if he had sufficient time."

"But tonight...?"

"He will have only an hour and will be hanging from ropes, so he will just fill in around the banners Bess made."

Daniel smirked. He would have identified Ludd as more military than regional theater, but there apparently was no limit to the types of people helping Anthro. "What good will the banners do, really?"

"Make a point, at the bridge and on social media. It will empower local resistance to clearcutting and send the message that there are consequences to destroying nature, and that there are people—good people—dedicated to saving our forests."

"I guess," Daniel said, gazing out the window. Then he turned back to her. "But I can see Guy's point, as well, that it will take more than performance art to wake people up."

"Well, there is a divide in the movement. Think of your Martin Luther King advocating civil disobedience while Malcolm X pushed for armed resistance."

"So you fall on the non-violent side?"

She looked over as if she saw right through him. "As do most of us."

Farther down the road he handed her a cup of coffee from a thermos, and said, "So, what about Pete? You obviously knew he was my wife's brother, but how did you connect with him?"

"He attended a meeting in Texas about development on waterways and this sort of thing. Eco and I stopped there last year as we passed through."

"He seems quite taken with Eco...and you."

She turned a dull look at him. "Our supporters help for a number of reasons. Peter—if you do not mind my saying so—was not the most intellectual attendee at that meeting, but he outdid his comrades in sincerity and eagerness. He wanted to accomplish something."

"So, you used him to get to me?"

"That sounds like more of a cold calculation than what transpired. We vetted him to use him as a driver, and your name came up, and then the connection to the flood. We had to follow up the possibility your experience might open you to approach and give us a way inside the oil cartel."

He smiled to himself. It seemed he owed a debt to his brother-in-law for this entrée to his new life.

"It is clear," she added, "that Peter holds you in high esteem and agreed to act as go-between to help you past your personal tragedy."

It touched Daniel that his brother-in-law would admire him—when they had so often been at odds. He grew quiet until they turned south on Route 81, when he asked, "So what do you and Eco do when you're not making bridges disappear?"

She turned to him with a tight smile on her fleshy lips. "We sometimes take road trips to knock over billboards or liberate laboratory animals...."

"No, seriously. You must lay low sometimes?"

She smiled, genuinely this time. "We take time when we can. There is a lovely house in Pocono Mountains owned by supporters, friends really." Her expression became wistful as she turned back to the road. "We have spent peaceful weeks there, planning and spending time in the natural world we struggle to preserve."

"I'd like to see that place sometime," he said, realizing with a pang of guilt that he meant he'd like to see it with her, or if not Verde someone very much like her. But then, was there anyone else like her? No matter how often he reminded himself how strong her relationship was with Eco and that he wouldn't do anything to disrupt it, he couldn't shake the fantasy of being with her himself.

Kristof and Zeke had finished unloading the Volvo in the staging area, careful to follow Ludd's instructions about handling volatile materials. Meanwhile, Ludd mixed iron oxide and pulverized aluminum in canisters, and combined barium peroxide with magnesium powder to produce the igniting mixture.

It was fortunate Zeke had been able to find an ex-Marine with expertise in explosives. For a job like this they couldn't rely on the old mixture of glycerin soap, diesel and gasoline, what the ELF had called "vegan Jell-O." That would only start a fire, and Kristof wouldn't be comfortable improvising something to explode.

As to deceiving Mia and Stefan about the action, well, that couldn't be helped. This was the first time he had lied to Mia about anything significant, and he felt guilty for it, but this time it was necessary. The alternative would have been to push the debate and end up with a schism in the organization they needed to pull this off. When the bridge went down, clearcutting in the Monongahela Forest would stop and everyone would be happy without anyone being hurt. As long as they each handled their responsibilities, the whole thing would come off without a hitch.

Once the canisters were ready, they waited for the sparse evening traffic to die down to move them close to the bridge. It wouldn't do for Mia to see the equipment at the staging area when she came to pick up the Volvo. They then had plenty of time to clean out any trace of explosives from the car and set up the camera downriver to stream the collapse back to Alexandria. He wished he could be there when Stefan saw the roadway fall into the canyon. It was going to blow his mind.

When everything was ready, they sat in the Volvo munching beef jerky and candy bars while they waited for Mia and Daniel.

"Let's go over the steps again," Ludd said, "so there are no mistakes. First, we send out the folks with the road signs, who will then take up a lookout position to watch the valley road. Then, we drop over the side and drill holes in the supports. We set the cannisters over the holes, light the thermite and let it flow. If everything works like it should, the thermite burns right through the steel."

"Did you say 'if'?" Kristof said.

"Well, whether there's enough thermite is a question—although we brought all the supplies we could pull together. We'll have to see. I can guarantee at least lots of noise and white heat."

"And you know exactly where to drill the holes?"

"Roger that. I've studied the bridge schematics. We'll hopefully collapse the near end, which may bring the rest down as well."

"Okay, but we can't forget to first tell the lookouts to meet at the rendezvous instead of picking us up," Kristof said.

Hearing the first blasts Mia would know they weren't there to hang banners. That would make her fighting mad. He was glad she'd be on lookout duty rather than with him, and he didn't look forward to facing her after the action. The one thing she wouldn't tolerate was his lying to her. He only hoped success would mollify her anger.

In fact, Kristof realized her suspicions would be aroused when he radioed to skip the staging area pickup and go straight to the rendezvous. Only her long experience and steel nerves would keep her at her post after that.

Chapter
Twenty-Eight

Mia pulled into the staging area at two in the morning, right on schedule. A half-moon cast little light over a few parking spaces by a trailhead. The Volvo was hard to see parked up against the trees, but it lit up when the men got out to meet them. Kristof flashed a smile that reassured her everything was going smoothly.

"The bridge is just past these trees?" she asked.

"About eighty yards down the road."

"Can we go see it?"

"No time for sightseeing," Zeke interrupted. "We're on a clock here."

That was needlessly harsh, but that was Zeke; he really did sometimes act like a commando going into battle. But his fervor was a driving force behind Anthro since its inception on that camping trip in Mexico, and they needed that kind of passion.

"The Camp Fire in California destroyed Paradise!" Zeke shouted to the desert on that trip.

The others had passed a flask of whiskey while they watched

Zeke rave. Their trip to the desert was supposed to be a break from the constant news of the world going to hell. But Zeke couldn't leave it behind and so they found themselves arguing about fossil fuels and extreme weather and what recourse they had.

The heated discussions led to a pact. They would become an entity to fight climate change. Let other organizations solicit donations and make political compromises; they would fight to save the planet. The battle had been joined; they would play their bloody part.

But history aside, Mia was annoyed at Zeke's rebuke. She just wanted to see the bridge while things were quiet, and was sure they had time. But discipline was essential to an efficient operation. She would not let her personal feelings interrupt the plan.

They synchronized watches and checked the two-way radios. The men from the bridge team applied face-blacking. Mia helped Kristof, and Daniel helped Guy. Ludd did his own. She glanced over at Ludd. The new man didn't speak but came across as capable and confident, quite imposing for someone whose day job was painting scenery.

Mia rechecked the climbing equipment while Daniel put the dummy West Virginia plates on both cars and tested the police scanner. Kristof went over again where on the map they should place the road signs and the ridge they would use for a lookout post. "You should have a wide view of the approach road from the valley and hear any chatter on the scanner. If we have any trouble, we'll reach you on the radio, and you can swing down to pick us up."

Then the moment was upon them. While the others exchanged good luck handshakes, she locked Kristof in a long hug, whispering her love. Then she and Daniel left in the two cars.

Daniel drove the Volvo and Verde the Camry to the rendezvous point, the dark edge of the empty parking lot behind a tourist "trading post." Daniel eyed the gaudy shop as they drove past the store, cheap tchotchkes filling its display windows. They would do the world a service by burning it to the ground, but that was just fantasy. They were engaged now—he was engaged—in something real, something to jar people out of the news cycle.

They left the Volvo and backtracked together in the Camry over the bridge toward the mountain. Half-way across Verde stopped on the empty roadway. "We have time," she said, "for one look at our target."

He shared her curiosity to see the view—if you could call it a view, illuminated only by dim moonlight. But after stepping into the cold and zipping his coat against the wind, he could not bring himself to look over the railing. The sound of rushing current below made him woozy, so he focused on how the jagged canyon edge cut a silhouette beneath the moon.

Verde dropped a stone over the edge, listening for a plop that was drowned out by rushing water. When she turned back to him, he could see she recognized his discomfort and recalled his aversion to water. Her sympathy embarrassed him, and he hurried back into the car.

They continued along the empty road. There would be no traffic from this direction, at least until the sun was up and the truckers started hauling trees. They stopped a mile on at a fork in the road. Together they hauled one of the large sheets of plywood from the hatchback and spray-painted "Danger! Bridge Closed for Repair" in fluorescent orange. They set it up leaning against a two-by-four on the shoulder of the road with an arrow pointing to the other fork. Eco had instructed them to double up these signs, one a mile out and another a half mile. They did not paint the signs before they set them up, so if they were stopped the police would not find incriminating signs.

This done, they recrossed the canyon, only slowing momentarily on the bridge near the bank, where ropes were attached to the railing and the men were presumably hanging over the side. They drove out the valley approach, again seeing no other vehicles, and set up the other two signs. They were on schedule when they drove up to the ridge.

Verde tuned the scanner to the police frequency while Daniel cleaned the hatchback of any remnant of plywood. They had tossed the spray paint cans off the road on the way back from the second sign, operational security outweighing their abhorrence of littering. Daniel put the back seat up—to avoid wasting time when they picked up the team—while Verde poured the rest of the coffee into two cups. They stood outside the car, stamping their feet to keep warm as they sipped the last of the coffee.

While Daniel used binoculars to watch the road, Verde called the bridge team on the two-way radio. "Beta in place. Alpha, are you there?" she repeated several times, but they heard only static.

"Damn this thing," she cursed. "We are no more than one-quarter mile from the bridge. What could be the problem?"

Daniel shrugged. It was concerning they would not know when the work was done so they could pick up the team. This felt like the fog of war rolling in.

But then the radio crackled and Eco said, "Beta, this is Alpha. Work slower than expected. Change meeting to rendezvous point. Repeat: do *not* return to staging area; meet at rendezvous."

"Understood," Verde said haltingly. "No pickup at staging area; meet at rendezvous."

"Confirmed, Beta. See you shortly."

The radio went silent. Verde turned to him with a concerned look. "We should have had better photographs of bridge structure. But why will we not pick them up?"

He had no answer. He was clearly out of his depth and knew only enough to follow orders. "Is the scanner reliable?" he said. "I mean, will we hear if the police are coming?"

"Unless the authorities are more cautious than usual and use different frequency."

"Is that something we can monitor?"

"That would take too much time; it is much more efficient to watch the road. If there is trouble, we will see it coming."

He looked at her, feeling sorry things were not going as she had hoped. But she seemed focused on the job. She reached for the binoculars to look at the valley approach. Then she turned toward the bridge, the arch of which was barely visible in vague outline above the trees.

"We need a better view," she said, "to gauge how the work is progressing."

Daniel tried not to be unnerved by the change of plans or let Verde see this troubled him. They had simply moved on to plan B. The team would finish their work and take the forest path to the rendezvous. That probably should have been the plan all along, rather than having Verde and Daniel drive back to the bridge.

Still, he did not have to say it out loud: the alternative meeting point was arranged in case of trouble, not because the painting took longer than expected. Why should that matter in the middle of the night? Was Eco sending Verde—and him—out of harm's way?

Then an explosion shook the air. Several moments later there was a second blast.

"What is happening?" Verde shouted.

They turned toward the bridge. Daniel could barely make out two trails of smoke rising above the trees.

"Alpha!" Verde shouted into the radio. "What has happened? What is explosion?"

The static belching from the radio broke with Eco's voice. "Change of plans, Beta. Hope you'll understand we have to do this. Meet at the rendezvous. Alpha over and out."

"What?" Verde shouted. "What have you done?"

Daniel reached for the binoculars, but she reflexively held on to them.

"Give them to me," he shouted, tugging them away. He raised

them to his eyes and looked toward the valley. "Oh, my God!" he said to himself.

From a considerable distance a line of vehicles was approaching, red lights flashing.

She looked toward the valley and didn't need binoculars to see they were in trouble. "The authorities...and those fools have nowhere to run."

Daniel grabbed the radio from her belt. "Eco, this is Al," he said urgently. "Abort mission. Police coming in force. Arrival in no more than fifteen minutes. Abort and disperse! Do you read?"

There was only static crackling over the distant sound of sirens.

Then intense white light through the trees illuminated features of the bridge arches. It looked as if the sun had come up where the approach road met the bridge. What could make such a bright light?

"I must warn him!" Verde shouted and took off running. She was into the woods leading to the road before he could react.

"No!" he shouted. "Wait!" He fumbled to untangle himself from the binoculars strap but then left them around his neck and ran, as if pulled after her by an unseen force.

Mia rushed down a dirt path and onto the road, nearly losing her footing on the gravel blacktop. She ran downhill and the sirens came closer.

She again lost her balance at the bridge when she stopped short. Light from two craters in the roadway lit the night into day. Broken concrete littered the road.

Kristof had tried to blow up a bridge, lying to her and betraying their sacred trust. But this was not the time for recrimination. She ran between the holes where liquid concrete bubbled onto the roadway, and stretched over the railing where the ropes were tied. Kristof and Zeke were hanging on the ropes supporting Ludd, who looked dazed.

"I'm here!" she shouted and started pulling Kristof's rope.

"Not me!" he yelled. "Pull Ludd up!"

She found Ludd's tie-off and tried to hoist him, but he was dead weight. "Too heavy!" she shouted down.

"Just take up the slack," Kristof grunted, pushing Ludd from beneath as Guy made Ludd's ascender take up the slack in his rope.

Moving the torpid man was painfully slow. By the time they got him to the handrail, Mia could see he was unconscious. And the sirens closed in.

"Go!" Kristof yelled at Mia. He was untangling the ropes and starting to pull himself up.

"I cannot leave!"

"You have to!"

She stopped for a moment. "But I must tell you."

He paused only long enough to look into her eyes and for understanding to fill his expression. "We're pregnant," he said with a world of warmth and joy and apology.

She nodded. "Just a little."

"Then fly for us all! Climb over the edge and hide. They'll take us away, but you and the new one must stay safe. We'll be together soon."

She hated how he always won the important arguments, but ran back toward the abutment. Flashing red lights reflected off the trees up the valley road. At a point where she could get a handhold, she climbed the railing and lowered over the side.

The metal bars were slick and cold through her gloves. She slipped, trying to stay clear of red-hot flowing metal and found solid footing on a crossbeam. Ducking her head under the edge of the roadway was hard in her bulky coat. She crammed herself into a space above the beams, and fought not to gag from the smell of molten metal.

From above came shouts and a faint sound of pounding feet.

Then there were shots. Why were they shooting? Where was Kristof? Surely he had surrendered.

"Give it up, son," a voice came over a bullhorn, "or follow your friend to an early grave."

After a pause, the same voice came back, now quite stern. "Listen, boy, we know all about you and your terrorist *comrades*. We've got one already on his way to the hospital and another dead in the road. It's time to give it up."

Her emotions tore at her just as sharp edges of the metal braces tore at her jacket. Kristof would surely be arrested...or worse. Their child would have a father in prison, lost to them both by his own duplicity. How could Kristof have lied? Where was the faith he had brought back into her life?

But she needed to think; she could not give birth in prison! She had to concentrate, move carefully, lean only on supports strong enough to hold her. She must keep out of sight and away from hot metal. How could she have landed in this mess?

She was livid that he had deceived her and followed Zeke into this mess. He deserved what he had created, but this reckless stunt was unfair when he was to be a father.

Another shot echoed through the canyon.

Chapter Twenty-Nine

Police sirens approached. Flashing lights lit the trees. Daniel jumped into undergrowth at the roadside. He tumbled to a stop, his face scratched, a root jabbing his ribs.

He laid still while the car passed. He couldn't see the bridge, but an ungodly white light came from that direction. It was daytime through the trees, nature flipped on its head.

What happened? What were they doing? Obviously *not* hanging banners. And whatever it was went horribly wrong. The only thing now was to find Verde and get away.

A police cruiser sped by followed by an ambulance, sirens wailing, covering the noise he made crashing through the bushes. He met a rough trail and ran downhill. But he quickly stumbled, landing face first, jamming his wrist and getting a taste of dirt and leaves.

He got up and picked his way more carefully. There wasn't far to go, and there was no sense bursting out of the woods just to be arrested. There still was a chance he might help.

He came to the bank two hundred feet downriver of the bridge. All that separated him from the water was a gravel road that skirted the bank. This dirt road and the river brought back torturous memories of the Guadalupe that made him nauseous. He backed into the trees and threw up.

When he recovered he moved to where he could stretch out on the ground in sight of the bridge. He piled up dirt and leaves to block his sight of the river. But the sound of rushing water still drove an ice pick through his head.

Two pillars of fire were pouring from or through the roadway; it wasn't clear. What looked like burning lava seeped into the braces and beams below. There was no way to guess how long the bridge would stand.

But where were the men? Where was Verde?

A dark shape climbed up the side of the bridge and vaulted the railing. A muffled voice growled through a bullhorn. Shots echoed off the mountains. Why were they shooting? Surely no one was getting away. It was all so confused.

The bullhorn barked again, but he couldn't make out the words over the sirens and the rush of the river. Did that voice say someone was dead...on the roadway? That must be the road over the bridge, where the emergency vehicles were parked. But how would anyone die? That couldn't be Eco! But who, then? And who were they yelling at? And where was Verde?

Beneath the bridge one of the red-hot streams running along a girder sputtered into a blinding light. For a split second it illuminated the underside of the roadway. Daniel pulled up the binoculars in time to see the color of Verde's coat.

She certainly didn't see *him*, and there was no way to signal her. But she looked secure and well hidden. Hopefully, they weren't looking for her. If he stayed concealed as well, he could try to reach her when things quieted down. What other choice was there?

The ground to his side was moist. He spread mud over his

face so it wouldn't reflect light from the bridge when he looked through the trees. But the spouts of pure light had died down. Activity on the bridge was illuminated only by headlights and a couple of spotlights.

At one point two men climbed over the railing. They trained flashlights on the supports. It looked like they were checking the damage, not looking for more terrorists to shoot.

When the climbers headed back up, Daniel realized he had stopped breathing. He gulped in air and laid his head on his hands. In time he caught his breath and took stock of the situation. They hadn't seen Verde. They would have to look up from river level to make her out, which they wouldn't do until the sun came up. She was surely miserable and cold, but they wouldn't find her, and she'd hold on; she was strong.

He checked his watch and calculated three hours until dawn. This was going to be a long, cold wait. Nothing to do but burrow into the ground, stay out of sight and watch the place where Verde was hiding.

The terrible prospect of losing Eco filled him with foreboding. This man had so quickly become like family to him. The way his eyes lit up made everyone feel like a community, or what he called "the movement." He was sure it was Eco who took the chance on him and talked the rest of them into trusting him. Daniel owed him this chance at redemption.

Blowing up the bridge was a moronic stunt, but wasn't Eco pushed to do it by people like Daniel? And Daniel was actually worse than most of them. He had personal impact on laws leading to the release of methane and pumping more oil.

With time to kill, Daniel played back all of the harm he'd done and all the responsibilities in which he had failed, with a nightmare soundtrack of the river and sirens fading into the distance.

It wasn't his parents' fault he ended up here. They raised him, fed him, kept him safe, sent him off to college. His mother must have been kind to him at first; she did give birth to him; maybe it was the heartbreak later on that obscured his vision of her. And then the accident at the mine wasn't his father's fault, although the company bosses made him their whipping boy. If his mother had been a stronger partner, what Verde would call a "comrade," his father might have held on to his self-esteem. But she turned on her husband like everyone else. Maybe that left him nowhere to turn in the end.

Losing his father was a shock, but it motivated him to push ahead. His mother could have helped there, too, but did not, and he had to stand on his own. That sunk him into despair and he considered quitting school; he couldn't study when all he could think about was losing his whole family. He really lucked out in meeting Bree. He recalled the first time he ever saw her. She seemed to float down the steps of the library like an angel. He was so distracted he spilled coffee on himself. She laughed and passed on with a smile. To think that together they would one day bring Annabelle into the world.

He could almost feel his daughter's little hand as she walked between Bree and him, begging them to swing her up as they walked down the sidewalk. Did all kids do that? Maybe just kids lucky enough to have two parents who would do anything to hear their joyful squeal.

Thinking of Annabelle reminded him again he deserved to be where he was, lying on the cold ground in the middle of nowhere, tortured by a river and hiding from the police. He actually deserved worse.

He imagined Annabelle's body sunk in the mud. Then, to stifle the scream inside his head, he forced himself to think of the last time he saw Bree and Annabelle. He was leaving for DC. Bree kissed him, wearing her brave face that was never very convincing. Annabelle wanted a hug but also wanted him to say goodbye to her alligator. He didn't pay enough attention and squandered a precious moment while his mind raced ahead to the work he would do on the flight. Did anyone ever recognize a last moment with someone they love?

Time dragged. The cold seeped through his clothes. There was no way to get warm, other than dig into the ground, cover himself with leaves, keep flexing his limbs.

He thought about how he first got mixed up with Pearce and the Oil Institute. He got into law school only because his father knew Jack Wolford. And then Pearce came along with his expensive cigars and pockets bulging with cash, the operatic villain in Daniel's life. Could he have resisted that devil, put his head down and worked hard like everyone else to build a life with his wife and daughter? It was nice to think so.

When he and Bree found the house on the river, they set out to make it into a palace for their grand life. She was ecstatic to have a beautiful home close by her parents and her brother, and in the midst of natural wonders and Hill Country dance halls. To him it was a perfect refuge from Washington. It was also an idyllic place for his daughter to grow up. But then the tab arrived, and it was more than he could pay.

So, here he was, finally fighting for what was right, and whatever he would have to sacrifice would be fair. But it was jarring, having made this move and embraced this new life, that he might have to live it without Eco, the man who had guided his moral awakening, and Verde, who would always be his vision of courage and beauty. "Please God," he prayed for the first time since he was a boy, "keep them safe."

They *had to be* all right. It could not be that everyone who came close to Daniel was doomed to die a horrible death.

His thoughts were lost in desolate spirals. He found himself craving a drink. But that was disgusting and showed once again how despicable he was.

"Not this time," he said out loud, startling something in the woods.

Feeling foolish for making noise, he focused again on the

bridge. Verde hadn't moved. He had to focus. She needed him. The goddamned planet needed him. He had to quit this self-pity and make a plan.

The bridge clearly didn't collapse. Whatever that explosion was, it just seemed to make a mess. When everyone was gone, he could pull Verde up and they could get back to the car through the woods. They just had to move before workmen and police started showing up. Still, the moon had set, and it was pitch black now. He'd wait until dawn so he could see what he was doing.

With luck Eco had been arrested and was okay. They'd defend him in court, whatever the charge. A trial would give him a pulpit, at least, and he was made for that.

As to Guy, who knew, or Ludd for that matter? And what this failure would do to the movement was hard to tell. After the pipeline defeat, it would hit hard. If they lost Eco and Guy, could Verde and Assisi keep things going? And without the four of them, where was he? Did he have to move forward on his own? Verde arrived in the country as an orphan and refugee and still fought for the planet; he could at least try to emulate her.

However the night might end, he was thankful for one thing: the intoxication of action. Though cold and in pain and scared to death, he felt more alive at that moment than he ever had before.

Dawn was just lighting the arches of the still-solid bridge when Daniel made his move.

He rose and brushed off leaves and dirt. His limbs ached. His clothes were wet. Through the binoculars he could now plainly see Verde. She was in the same place.

He hurried up the tree line and climbed to the road. There were no cars across the bridge or back toward the valley. The bridge was roped off with police tape. Beyond that the roadway was cleared except for a few piles of broken concrete. Cones stood on both sides where it looked like there were holes. Given this minimal damage, Eco and Guy might have had just as much impact by painting a crack.

There wasn't a sound, except the loathsome drone of the river. It rushed by no more than twenty feet below the near side of the bridge. Being this close to it made everything harder, but he had nothing left in his stomach and so after a dry heave he pushed on.

He ran cat-like onto the bridge, scampering from one covered post to the next, scanning both directions. At the spot where the ropes had hung, he looked over. Nothing.

He called softly, "Verde? Verde, it's Daniel."

"Here," came a weak voice from back toward the bank.

He scuttled back twenty feet and leaned over again. "Can you hear me?"

"Yes, thank God. Do you know what happened?"

"Not really, but it's all clear up here. Let's get you up."

"I am afraid…my legs are frozen; they won't move."

"Okay. Stretch out while I look for a rope or something."

He searched frantically but found nothing useful. He pulled off his moist jacket and his fleece and the dryer shirt beneath and twisted the shirt into a rope. Then he put the fleece and jacket back on and hung back over the edge.

"I'll climb down and you can grab this shirt," he said, watching intently for her to appear.

"Yes, I am coming."

He climbed over the railing, found a solid grip for one arm and stretched the other down, his reach extended by the knotted shirt. The wind chilled his hands. Hopefully, the shirt wouldn't rip.

Her head poked from under the roadway. Then she inched farther out, but something creaked and broke…and she fell.

Daniel saw her hit the water, her scream swallowed by the splash.

He froze.

Her arm popped up, bobbing downriver.

His body dry retched again at the sight of the water...and the sound. The river rose up to strangle him, but it also rushed Verde away, water again ripping life away from him.

His head spun, and he had to grab a brace to keep from falling. Everything was blurred.

His pulse raced. He struggled for breath. Could he run down-river? Could he catch up with her? Could she survive the fall and the cold? He tried to loosen his grip but his hand was welded to the bridge.

The river was a yawning chasm, a demon. There was no time. He wrenched his hand free and jumped.

Chapter Thirty

The river felt like concrete. Mia's boots broke the fall but then weighed her down. She struggled to stay on the surface and breathe but kept sinking beneath the froth. The current swept her along. She couldn't move her right arm.

But then her coat jerked her back and held. Was she caught on something? She could only think of gulping for air.

She was pulled toward the bank and soon her feet grazed the bottom, and then she could stand. She bent over and coughed up water.

When she caught her breath she looked up. Soaked and panting, hair across his face, Daniel held her upright.

"What...?" she said, trying to focus. "What happened?"

"You fell," Daniel said. "A beam broke and you fell."

"The bridge? Kristof!" she cried. "And oh...!" She looked at her arm.

The way the arm hung told Daniel it was broken. Hopefully,

there were no worse injuries. He helped her onto the bank where they sat huddled together, catching their breath.

He spat out river grit between questions: "Are you okay? Did you hit your head? What hurts besides the arm?"

She just shivered. She was in no shape to talk or walk, but he needed to get her away from this place and warm. He took a deep breath. "We need to go to the car...and find a doctor."

"Kristof?" she croaked, clearing her throat.

"You mean Eco?"

She nodded, squeezing her eyes closed.

"Don't know. It's a mess. But everyone's gone, and we have to get away from here, follow the plan, get to the cars."

Daniel zipped Verde's jacket part way up to support her injured arm while he helped her up the hill. They started walking on the road, as he was sure he'd see or hear any vehicles long before anyone saw them. Anyway, the main threat was not arrest, but hypothermia. The air was colder than the water, and even the slight breeze bit into his limbs, making it hard to walk. It had to be much worse for her, but she kept moving.

They twice hid behind trees at the roadside as cars approached. Both stopped at the bridge and then turned around and drove back.

They took the trail through the woods but it narrowed in spots, making it hard to support her by her good arm. She let out soft groans as they moved upward over uneven ground. She said nothing but stayed on her feet.

When they finally reached the Camry, Daniel helped Verde out of her sodden jacket and sat her in the front seat covered with a blanket. She couldn't do anything for herself, so he fastened her seat belt. He got in, started the car and checked the map for the safe house. As soon as warm air came through the vent, he cranked up the heat.

"Oh, that's good," he said out loud, feeling warmth reach his numb hands and feet. He looked at Verde; her eyes were closed.

"That's right," he went on, as if she had reminded him, "we have to call in."

He had lost his phone somewhere during the night, but there was a backup in the glove compartment. He stretched past her to retrieve it. Her head leaned against the door. Hopefully, she was just sleeping, but he was anxious. He touched her face, which was still cold, but her breathing was regular. She could be in shock; what should he do for that?

"It went bust," he told Assisi over the phone once they were on the road. "It wasn't what Guy and Eco told us. They were trying to blow up the bridge."

"We had a live feed," Assisi said. "But we couldn't see exactly what happened beyond the explosions and bright light."

"Whatever it was turned to shit. They made noise and could have gotten everyone killed but accomplished nothing. And the police showed up in a fucking convoy! Where did that come from?"

"Clearly, they were tipped off."

"How could they...?"

"We're tracking that down. We've still got eyes on the bridge, and it's quiet. That was you this morning, right? It was hard to see. What about Verde?"

"She hid under the bridge all night, but when I tried to help her back to the roadway, she fell into the river, a long way."

"That explains the video. But the camera wasn't aimed at the river, and we couldn't see what happened next."

"I fell in too."

His squishy shoes reminded him to focus on driving. "It's not important. We made it to the car. But there was shooting before that at the bridge."

"We don't know what happened with the police. We do know two ambulances returned from the site, and it looks like the bridge team is in custody."

"Oh, God!"

"Yes. It's bad. Where are you now?"

"We've got one of the cars. Verde is hurt and probably in shock. I'm headed to the safe house."

"I'll get a doctor to meet you. It shouldn't take more than twenty minutes, but don't speed. Don't draw attention. I'll send someone for the other car. You left the keys?"

"Of course, yeah. The Volvo is at the rendezvous, keys in the wheel well. It's still got the fake plates. But...how do we find out what happened at the bridge?"

"*We'll* sort that out. You just get to the house, watch over Verde and lie low. I'll gather information and analyze the video, but right now we're dismantling Alexandria. Keep to protocol; that's the best we can do."

It was annoying to keep hearing that word as if it were the answer to everything. Now, one of them might be dead, and two in jail, but protocol said stick to the escape plan. Eco and Guy would expect them to carry on. People got hurt or caught, but their best chance came through sticking to the plan.

The car was now warm. Hopefully Verde would sleep until they reached safety and medical help. He focused on keeping invisible and not getting lost.

The directions led off a country route onto a narrower road and then an unmarked dirt road that looked like a driveway. A hundred yards into the woods was a cabin, lit up as if they were expected. Two cars were parked against a small barn. As they pulled up, an elderly couple stepped out of the front door.

"Our visitors from Madrid," the man called out. He was in his mid-seventies, with a big belly pushing against suspenders and a broad face covered in gray stubble.

"This is no time for that, John," the woman at his side scolded, hurrying to the passenger door. She wore a hunting jacket over a long, paisley dress. Her thick gray hair was brushed into a bun. "We need to get these children inside."

Daniel circled the car to help the woman wake Verde, who looked up in panicked confusion that melted into relief when she saw the woman's face.

As Daniel and John helped Verde into the cabin, John said, "We got the call."

"Well, of course we got the call," the woman snapped. "Why else would we be up at this time of the morning? Now, you just concentrate on not dropping this poor young thing."

The woman stepped past them to hold open the cabin door. "Doc Patel is on his way," she said. "Meanwhile, we'll get you two warmed up."

Daniel was at a loss for words. But once Verde was seated, he turned to the woman. "I can't tell you how grateful we are," he said. "She has a broken arm, I think, and may be in shock."

The woman directed the men to bring Verde into a bedroom.

"You wait for the doc," she told John once they had laid her on the bed, "and put water on." John turned to follow orders before she added, "and close that door behind you."

The woman loosened Verde's clothes and gestured for Daniel to remove her shoes. "We've got to get her out of these wet things, but I'm afraid John's heart would stop if he saw a beautiful young woman with no clothes."

She smiled at his hesitation and paused. "I'm sure it's nothing *you* haven't seen before," she said playfully.

He smiled uncomfortably and found his reaction to seeing Verde undressed turned out to be less erotic than embarrassing. He focused on supporting the wounded arm and telling himself this was strictly a medical procedure.

He was not surprised by her lean figure, but he was captivated by her tattoo. It ran up her back between her shoulder blades, two intertwined flowers in jet black ink.

That image! It was the watermark Joe Coulder showed him, the one the FBI was using to track down the photographer.

After they got their charge into bed, the woman looked Daniel up and down. "You're all done in yourself, young man. You'll need dry clothes. My son has things here should fit—will have to fit Verde too, though she's mostly skin and bones. I'm certainly not her size."

"Wait, you know Verde?"

"Oh, dear me, yes. Verde and another young lady stayed with us; it must have been last April. Such brave young women."

Back in the kitchen John handed Daniel a cup of steaming tea. The warmth coursed down his insides while he took in the picture-postcard room, complete with heavy wooden table and fire in the hearth.

The woman watched with a kind smile. "We're not supposed to exchange names, of course," she said, "but drat it all, I'm Faye and this old anarchist is John."

"Al," he said, extending his hand.

"Well, Al," she said, "since we're not supposed to talk about what you two have been up to, seems the best we *can* do is clean up that nasty cut on your arm—so you stop bleeding on my floor— and get you into the bathtub."

He froze at the mention of a bath.

"You all right, son?" Faye said with concern.

"What? Yeah, I'm good." He realized he felt no panic. He had tensed, preparing for a jolt from his phobia, but his heartbeat remained normal. He wasn't dizzy or sweating. The thought of a bath only brought an intense eagerness to sink into it.

He finished his tea while Faye saw to his arm, and then he settled into the most luxurious bath of his life.

As he soaked in the incredible warmth and ran his fingers through the water, he wondered at how quickly his crippling fear had left him. Was it the shock of the cold water or the fear of jumping from that height? Doctor Haverly said a phobia could come in one instant and disappear in another. At least Daniel hoped that was what happened.

It made sense, he supposed. He jumped into a river, on purpose, and that leap broke water's hold on him. This all coming from saving Verde was incredible, but it was mostly a relief that this time he did his job, protected those who relied on him. He fought the river and his own tortured mind because someone else's life was worth more than his own.

When the water started to cool, he forced himself out of the bath, cleaner than he had felt in months. He put on the clothes Faye had laid out for him. When he returned to the kitchen, John told him the doctor was in with Verde and Faye. "He wants to take a look at you, too," he said.

The doctor wore jeans and a flannel shirt. He did a cursory exam of Daniel, checking his pulse and blood pressure and shining a light into his eyes, while Daniel marveled again at the diverse support Anthro attracted.

"The cut on your arm should be no problem," he said. "Just keep it clean and change the bandage once a day. Your companion's break was clean and easy to set. It should heal almost completely in six to eight weeks. She also suffered shock but should be fine after some rest. I gave her something to help her sleep."

Chapter
Thirty-One

Daniel was grateful for time to regroup while John walked the doctor to his car and Faye got to work in the kitchen. He had to find out what happened and what would come next. Fortunately, Assisi soon called. Daniel stepped out in the yard behind the house.

"More bad news," Assisi said. "Kristof—Eco—is dead. They shot him when they say he was trying to escape after igniting a bomb on the bridge. At least that's what they're saying."

Daniel gulped. There was no response for this. It was what he had most feared. Verde would be devastated. *He* was devastated.

"They also shot Guy in the leg. They say he was resisting arrest—which is believable—but he'll survive. He's in custody along with Ludd, who was badly hurt in the blast and is still in a coma."

"So, it stayed up?"

"The bridge? Afraid so. It's closed to traffic but there are repair vehicles there and structural work appears to be underway.

I don't imagine it will stay closed for long. They also aren't giving any play to a connection between this action and raping of the forest. They're spinning the whole incident as a domestic terror attack by bumbling anarchists. And—you should know—they are looking for accomplices."

"They saw someone else?"

"Not that they're saying—but when do they ever tell the public what they know?"

"And how did they arrive so fast?"

"We believe they had prior information. And all I can think of is Ludd."

"Damn! Are you kidding?"

"This is just for you and Verde, but yeah. Think about it. Ludd knew the target and the timing; who else knew?"

"I didn't know about the bomb at all, or much else until we prepped."

"You and me both, brother. Kristof laid this out for Verde and me as pure theater, a huge sleight of hand that would draw attention. So who knew what they were doing, where and how? Only Kristof, Guy and Ludd."

"Well, there's no telling what Verde knew; she can be inscrutable."

"I can assure you, without talking to her, that Verde didn't know about the bomb. She would have gone down and sat on the bridge if it would have stopped them."

Daniel paused. It was reassuring to think Verde was a victim of deception here, like him, and not one of the people who deceived him. "So," he said, "there's only Ludd...or me—and I swear it's not me."

"Yes, there's only Ludd. We're waiting for an update on his condition. We should have more by the time Verde's up and we can talk. Meanwhile, let her know I'm activating security measures."

"What does that mean?"

"Time to skedaddle, my good man. We closed this office and

dispersed the volunteers back to their quiet lives. We told them to cover their tracks and watch for instructions on *Monkey Wrench*."

Daniel had a sudden thought. "But Ludd knows about Verde and me...and the safe house!"

"No, not the names; Ludd wouldn't know real names. And he had a safe house address, but not the same as yours. Bottom line, he knows you two took part and what you look like, and I guess license plate numbers...and that other safe house address that can't really be connected to anything." He paused. "It could be worse, but it's pretty freaking bad."

"I don't think he saw the real plates on the Camry," Daniel said, "because I switched them out right away. But he drove in the Volvo so, yeah, he'd have that number. And, like you say, he'll recognize Verde and me. So we have a problem, but you said he's in a coma?"

"Right. We've got someone on the hospital staff; we'll know if he wakes up and our problem gets worse. For now, I'll see about burying the chain of title and swapping out the plates on the Volvo. Also, our source at the FBI thinks they suspect *you* were somehow involved, but they don't know how, and they are most interested in finding a woman known to associate with Eco."

"Oh, God!"

"Exactly. A pretty accurate picture. The good news is they don't seem to have any solid evidence Verde was at the site, and all they've released to the public is that one blurry photograph of her. The description is a tall white woman in her twenties or thirties with long brown hair and striking eyes either blue or green."

"This is all she needs," Daniel spat out, mostly to himself. Then he snapped out of it. "A doctor took care of her arm and gave her a sleeping pill, but she'll go back into shock when she hears about Kristof."

"You want *me* to tell her? We've known each other a long time."

"No, she should hear it in person, even if it has to come from me. I'll tell her when she's up and around."

"Okay, and then both of you call me. When she's fit to drive, Verde should drop you at a train into the city—with your cover story buttoned up. She'll know where to meet me."

"Not Alexandria?"

"Like I said, we're on to the next phase. But one other thing, make sure you dispose of the West Virginia tags, and get John to help you swap out the tires; we don't want big brother tracing tread patterns."

While so much was unsettled, Daniel felt secure for the moment. He slept like the dead and rose feeling sore but refreshed.

Faye said Verde was still sleeping. He poked his head into her room to see for himself and then borrowed a coat and wandered into the yard to take a walk in the forest surrounding the cabin.

When he returned a few minutes later, John joined him and waved an arm at the trees lining his field. "Birds love the berries from those mountain-ash," he said. "You should see the colors they turn in the fall."

Daniel was sufficiently impressed with the red berries and budding green leaves set off by the clear sky. The woods around the cabin looked almost like a screen saver, too perfect to be real.

"When you've had your fill, come on in for some breakfast," John said with a knowing smile and left him alone.

He tried to put aside what Assisi had told him and appreciate the setting, John's botany lesson and Faye's fabulous breakfast. But the crushing news about Kristof, the ache in his arm and the thought of Verde still recovering intruded. Dipping his toe into activism had turned out more like plunging into a violent sea. Just when he thought he had nothing left to lose, he had lost the man who in all his life felt most like a brother.

The long sleep did Mia good, despite her dreams of being squashed under a welcome mat. Waking up at Faye and John's house was such a balm, she had to assure herself this was not another dream.

It hurt to maneuver into the oversized sweatsuit Faye had laid out for her, but she was feeling stronger every minute. Even her arm was not too bad. She broke it...in a fall? Was that right? Did she fall into the river? She did! She could feel herself in turbulent water with something tugging at her. Then it was Daniel. But how could that be? He froze at a glass of water.

Voices seeped through the door. She got up to see who was there, her stomach growling with hunger. Her hosts sat at the big kitchen table with Daniel.

Faye got up and hugged her gingerly, avoiding the injured arm. "We've missed you these past months, child," she said. "And now," her voice turned maternal, "now you show up dripping wet with a broken wing."

"Faye," Verde responded, "you are a lifesaver once again." With a sincere smile, she then turned to John and added, "You and my boyfriend."

John got to his feet and held out his hand, but Verde pulled him into a hug. He looked delighted, while their hostess shook her head and frowned at him. Daniel had also risen to pull back Verde's chair.

She was content for the moment to be fed and fussed over by their hosts, who were clearly excited at having two desperadoes to entertain. But a feeling of disquiet hung in the air. What did Daniel know? Had he contacted the team?

It was a relief to see Verde dig into a pile of eggs and homemade bread. She looked revived though drawn. Her eyes told Daniel she wanted news about the action and Kristof, but she wouldn't ask about this in front of their hosts. Instead, she appeared to take strength from the food, the quiet stillness of the cabin and the couple's kindness. He even noticed an amused smile on her face at how Faye ordered her husband about while he rolled his eyes but did what he was told. It was astounding how the steely face she wore when they first met could express such gentle affection.

"The fire won't tend itself, you know," Faye barked at John, who was sitting comfortably, regaling their guests with stories of anti-nuke marches of his youth. "You let him go on, he'll pull out his scrapbook."

"I'll get the wood," Daniel volunteered, which drew a smirk from Faye but a grateful smile from John.

He made two trips to the wood pile, lingering along the way. The cabin nestled in this quiet country brought to mind a Currier and Ives print of burgeoning spring. But the job he had to do kept him from savoring the moment. He couldn't delay telling Verde about Kristof.

Faye finally rose to busy herself about the kitchen. "And you," she said to John, "better leave off your tall tales. Go check the barn for gasoline to fill their tank."

"Yes, dear," John grumbled, obviously reluctant to part company. But Verde had risen as well to carry her bowl to the sink, so he gave in and left through the back door.

"You two mosey along now," Faye said. "There are some coats hanging in the entryway, and it's nice enough for a walk in the sunshine. I imagine you have private matters to talk over."

Faye knew exactly what Mia needed: food and information. Daniel helped her get a heavy coat over her sling, and they ambled along the driveway.

"You have reached Assisi?" she asked.

He took a deep breath and then, as if forcing himself to speak, said, "The authorities are calling the action domestic terrorism, not even linking it with an environmental message. They knew it was planned...and Assisi thinks Ludd tipped them off."

"That snake." How did she not know? How could she let someone else vet that man when he was joining a serious action?

He nodded sadly.

"And the rest?" she said, girding herself for more bad news.

"Ludd was hurt in the blast, and as far as we know hasn't regained consciousness. Guy was shot, not too seriously, and is in a prison hospital...."

"And...?"

"And Eco...Kristof...was shot and killed."

"Oh, God!" she wailed. Her eyes burst forth in tears. Her thoughts spun in all directions. How could this be? Kristof, her love and her life...and what about the baby? What was she to do?

Her knees gave out, but Daniel helped her to the porch step. She had no sense of how long he stood by her side without speaking, but finally she did the only thing she could, hold to protocol.

"What else," she said numbly.

"Assisi says they're still after accomplices. They don't seem to know you were there, but they're looking for you because of your association with Kristof."

She turned to him in alarm.

"But all they have," he hurried to add, "unless Ludd wakes up, is a blurry photograph and a description of your long brown hair and the color of your eyes."

Verde kept to her room all afternoon, alone except for a brief visit from the doctor. Daniel left her to rest and grieve, although he wished he could do something to ease her pain.

At dinner Daniel set the table while John tended the fireplace and Faye prepared the meal.

"I don't understand it," Faye said. "She seemed much better this morning but then collapsed into herself. Was there news?"

"The worst kind," Daniel replied. "But please don't bring it up. She doesn't want to talk about it. We'll have to let her be. We'll stay another day to let her recover, and then we'll be off. We'll be fine, thanks to you."

"Oh, don't be silly. You are our champions; you are young and strong and give of yourselves to save us all. It is *we* who appreciate *your* service."

Faye turned back to her cooking, and Daniel stared at the fire. The range of people working with Anthro was amazing. It boggled his imagination how John and Faye got a call out of the blue and just opened their house and their hearts. Faye made him feel like a GI in the Normandy invasion, with her playing the part of a French resistance fighter. All the many others, who might drop off a package, forget to lock a door, report on a patient's condition...were united in a war effort unlike any other, for a cause universal and eternal. If they lost this one, there would be no rebuilding; they'd all lose everything.

Faye and John already knew Verde, but clearly they would have opened their home to him if he had shown up alone. They put themselves on the line to shelter someone they didn't know who was hiding for a reason no one would tell them. In one sense their lack of knowledge might minimize their risk, build a route to deniability. They weren't hanging off bridges, after all, or crawling around in the leaves; their actions might be explained away.

They also get to work from home, he thought, recognizing what Doctor Haverly would call an attempt to cope with grief through the distraction of humor. This time it didn't work.

Verde had asked them not to wait dinner for her. So Faye served up meatloaf and potatoes, and Daniel dug in with gusto. But they all stopped eating when they heard footsteps.

They glanced at each other in curiosity. Then the kitchen door swung open and Verde walked in.

They all stared. The transformation was simple but startling. Her long brown hair was cut short like a boy's and dyed jet black, which almost matched the new color of her eyes.

Chapter Thirty-Two

"You good to drive?" Daniel asked Verde.

"Why would I not be?" she snapped back.

He recoiled like she had slapped him. She realized she wasn't being fair. None of this was his fault. There was no cause to be angry with Daniel; it was Kristof who had betrayed her trust and brought on this catastrophe.

They sat in the Camry about to pull away from the house. "Please accept my apology," she said. "I...well, just that."

"No worries. I only thought your arm could use the rest."

They were both torn up about Kristof and on edge about Ludd and whether the authorities were looking for them. She reminded herself that this life was new to Daniel, and she should be understanding and help him adapt.

Assisi had said the doctors still didn't know if Ludd would come out of his coma. "We know Ludd was ex-military," he had said, "and trained in explosives, so whatever he planned for the bridge presumably was *not* to bring it down but just to make a show and set us up." He paused. "But he overdid the spectacle, it seems, which caused the explosion that might cost him his life—along with whatever blood money he had coming."

So, the feds had been on the inside of the bridge caper and had supplied the explosives and the technician, all to entrap Eco and her and all their people. It was frightening and disturbing but not surprising.

As they set out, she said, "I will drop you at the train station in Martinsburg. You will take the train to Washington and return to life as usual. Hopefully, your cover story will give no one reason to doubt you took just a long weekend vacation and have now returned to your work. If someone has questions, you must remain steadfast. The authorities may suspect your involvement but may have no evidence. You are attorney; you know to counsel a witness not to volunteer information?"

"Trust me. I won't incriminate myself or anyone else. But what will you do? When will I hear from you?"

"I will meet Assisi at a house in Pocono Mountains. He already has closed our office in Virginia."

"What does he think will happen?"

"At best, they have in custody two of our people. Guy will say nothing, but this Ludd—his real name is Paul Emerson—will be trouble when he wakes up."

"I guess we'll just have to deal with it. What will you do about Kristof?"

"We were married, so it is my role to be claiming body. But with the FBI watching, Assisi will assist me—with the documents that must be signed—and arrange for burial. We will release the date, and supporters will attend; we will see to that. I will slip in with the crowd."

"I'd like to attend, too."

"That would be foolish. You cannot compromise your position by attending the funeral for a leader of Anthro."

"Can I at least write a piece for *Monkey Wrench*?"

"This would be helpful, though anonymously, of course. But outwardly you must go quiet, concentrate on your work. Freeing yourself from suspicion is your only rational step, whether or not you will continue to work with us."

"You know I won't quit," he said testily, "not now. For Kristof, and for many other reasons, I have to keep at it."

She smiled, admiring his spirit and grateful for his esteem for her husband who, although he had deceived her in the end, was still a hero to the cause who would never gain the admiration he deserved from the world at large.

"So," he said, "how will we contact each other? Can't we use some kind of encrypted messaging, like Signal?"

This sounded personal, as if they were making a date, which was wrong before she had even buried her husband. She hoped Daniel did not think they could be more to each other than comrades in arms. She had just reached the point of trusting him not to betray Anthro.

He nodded and looked chastened. His expression had been affectionate, but only in a concerned way, and it was clear her coolness wounded him. Yet this man had leaped into his worst fears to save her. And he knew the anguish she was feeling; he had lost a wife *and* a child.

"We have begun to look at message applications," she said, trying to make the conversation less personal, "but have yet to test how secure they are. I suspect the authorities would find some way to monitor digital communications."

"Well, maybe I can help with this...once things settle down."

"Yes, that would be good. But for now let me please have the mobile phone; I will need to contact Assisi. When you are in the city, you should purchase a new one—and I do not need to remind you to pay with cash only?"

"Of course."

"So, then you can call to a store in Newark called 'Backcountry Trails.' Say you are planning a hike in Spain, perhaps on the

Santiago de Compostela. You should ask if someone knows this trail. You must reach a man called Eduardo. He will bring into conversation something about Madrid, and your response must be 'By way of Lisbon.' He will then know you have a message for me."

Daniel appeared to be satisfied, and she hoped he *would* call. She had lost so much so quickly; she could not afford to lose someone else.

"Also," she went on, "while no one should be watching for your return to Washington, you should wear a COVID mask and also the hat and eyeglasses John has given you. Remain invisible until you are back in place. Be aware of cameras and anyone paying too much attention."

"Especially men in suits," he said, smiling.

She grimaced.

"On the subject of disguises," he went on, "I see your eyes are now brown."

"Contact lenses, of course. I have sometimes been recognized because of the unusual color."

"I can appreciate that. And the hair couldn't be more different, though I'm sorry you had to cut it."

She shrugged. "They would cut it *for* me if I ended up in their prison."

He nodded. "I guess so. Anyway, it's very chic. But your eyes...I don't know. There's something more than the color that stands out —maybe the shape?"

His comments reminded her she still could be identified through facial recognition. At the funeral she would wear a wig and apply prosthetics to render useless the photographs the authorities would surely take.

"One more thing," he said. "I know you're crying inside, despite how tough you seem. I want you to know I came to see Kristof as a great man, a visionary. I'm honored to have known and followed him." He paused. "Actually, I feel the same about you, Verde."

"Mia," she said quietly, with a sad smile.

"Mia?"

"Yes, but please you must tell no one."

There were several messages from Jake on Daniel's answering machine at home asking him to call as soon as he could. His tone was so urgent Daniel thought he had better reply. He had purposely left his phone in the office to avoid bringing it on the mission so he used his laptop to text Jake he was back and ask what was so urgent.

A half-hour later someone buzzed Daniel's apartment from the lobby. He thought it was his food delivery but then frowned at hearing, "It's Jake, Daniel. Let me up."

This was unbelievable. After living what felt like months in the last four days, he needed a shower, a meal and some quiet, not a visitor, not even Jake. But something important must have driven the kid to show up like this.

Jake was almost out of breath when he came through the door. Daniel handed him a glass of water, saying, "Sorry I don't have anything else to drink."

The young man responded with a grateful smile. He downed half the water in one long swallow.

"Thanks," he said. "I needed that."

"What's mine is yours, man. But what's up? Why all the sweat and drama?"

"Oh, dude, I've got things to tell you, and you're not gonna like it."

For the next hour—stopping only for them to receive the food delivery and start eating—Jake told Daniel his story. Nell had apparently been blindsided at their last meeting and thought Daniel was betraying PJ&H and putting her job at risk. She tried to enlist Jake to help keep tabs on him for Pearce, but he refused.

"Then," he continued, "the more I thought about it, the more it pissed me off. She was supposed to be part of the team, the bitch, but she only cared about her job."

"Then I saw her meeting with Pearce. And on Thursday a guy from tech went into your office with Pearce and Nell, and they shut the door. Twenty minutes later they burst out. Nell bolted for her office, and Pearce marched down the hall shouting for someone to get Joe Coulder on the phone."

Jake gave Daniel a moment to digest that news and then said, "I thought I should find out more and so went back to Nell and pretended I'd had an epiphany; I didn't want to lose my job, yada yada. But after my first reaction, she didn't trust me, so she didn't say much. Still, she was into something because she kept meeting with Pearce.

"When I pressed her, she said you had gone rogue and would get nabbed. I looked at her like she was speaking another language, and she said, 'You didn't hear it from me, but Daniel went off with a bunch of eco-heads the FBI is about to bust. They're going to blow up a bridge. I just hope he isn't there when it goes bust.'"

"I didn't know what to say, or what it meant, but I could see Pearce and his law enforcement goons were coming after you. I also found out Pearce had called an emergency meeting of the partners for tomorrow morning. I think they're gonna kick you out.

"Coming on top of Pearce making such a big deal out of my screwing up in North Dakota and then dragging back up the weed thing, I was fed up. I figured: screw him. And, knowing Nell was feeding information to Pearce, I was ready to strangle her. I couldn't believe how sketchy they all were, but then I realized that's the kind of work we do, right? That brought back what you said about being on the wrong side."

Jake paused to catch his breath and lifted a forkful of food but held off putting it in his mouth to say, "With everything I had to pass on, I couldn't reach you. You didn't have your phone; they found it in your office and I think they broke into it. Nell wouldn't tell me where you'd gone, and I had no idea."

"I have to make this right," Daniel said, massaging with both hands next to his eyes. Then a thought popped into his head and he froze. A way to fight back! The forces of ignorance had won at the bridge but, like Kristof said, they could *not* win in the end.

Jake's expression said he saw Daniel was on to something, and with his mouth full he mumbled to ask how he could help.

Daniel checked his watch. It was seven-thirty. Was that store still open? "I need your phone," he said, realizing he had forgotten to pick up a new burner.

Jake keyed in his code and slid the phone across the table. Daniel found the number for the store in Newark. He called and told the woman who answered he needed help with a hike in Spain.

"We've got just the guy," she responded. "Hold on."

In another moment a man's voice said, "Eduardo here. How may we help you?"

"I'm taking a hike in Spain on that long trail that's like a pilgrimage?"

"*Santiago de Compostela.* Yes, sir. So you need equipment...a map...information?"

"Well, to start, how would I travel to the jumping off point?"

"To Santiago, yes, well from the US you would most likely fly into Madrid."

"I hear its best to go by way of Lisbon."

"I see," Edwardo said, in a quieter tone. "And the message?"

"Verde must call Al at this number. It's extremely urgent."

"Understood."

The phone clicked off, and he stared at it, as if a return call would come in seconds. That was nonsensical, of course; there was no telling how quickly Mia would get word. But they had to talk tonight. There was no time to wait.

He got up and paced. Jake watched him, continuing to devour

the food. Fortunately, the phone buzzed after just a few minutes. Daniel grabbed it.

"Madrid?" she said.

"By way of Lisbon," he replied.

"This phone is not traceable to you?"

"It belongs to a colleague...a friend who's helping."

"It is good to hear from you," she said with a hint of emotion.

"And you," he responded in as business-like a manner as he could muster.

"And so...the crisis?"

"I've got an idea, a way to go for the jugular without any more fireworks."

"I am listening."

Chapter
Thirty-Three

"It's the money trail," Daniel told Mia over the phone. "Senator Langston from Texas made a deal with the Oil Institute of America to use his influence to defeat a methane regulation bill in return for funding a super PAC for his campaign. We've got signed documents, tape recordings. It was a straight quid pro quo. They paid for his vote and those he controlled. This'll take those bastards down."

"The Oil Institute is your client?"

"The firm's biggest client. My job is to help them bend the law."

"Okay, and you have these things?"

"I can access these things. But it has to be tonight. The head of the firm is setting up a vote in the morning to throw me out of the partnership. By tomorrow afternoon I may not be able to get into the building."

"But tonight?"

"No one on night duty will stop me. I'm a partner; they'll do whatever I say. But once I have the materials, I'll need to pass them on fast. What should I do with them?"

"Let me think," she said and paused. "I have a contact, a reporter for *The New York Times*. He sympathizes but will not put his paper at risk without solid evidence. We will need originals. Copies will not do."

"That's the plan."

She didn't reply.

"We have to do this," he went on. "*I* have to do something for Kristof beyond posting an obituary. And I have to hope this will make a difference."

"So, we need some way to get this package quickly from your office to The Times Building in New York."

"Can't I just hand it to your friend?"

"That would be simplest, certainly. But no, we follow protocol. Assume the authorities will find out and stop you, or watch where you deliver the package to apprehend your contact."

"We could throw them off the trail."

"These people are professionals; you will not pass off even a smile without them seeing."

Daniel contemplated this. He had paid attention to his tradecraft lessons but doubted he could evade agents trained to follow him. But then...maybe they had a secret weapon!

"I've got this guy," he said, looking at Jake stuffing his face like a chipmunk. "He's a kid who works for me, and he's here right now. He grew up in New York and knows every backdoor and alleyway—yeah, and he's a runner. Hold a second."

He covered the phone with his hand and asked, "Could you lose someone trying to follow you on the street?"

"Where?"

"Manhattan...Midtown."

Jake chuckled. "No contest."

"Do you really want to help? There is some serious risk."

Jake stopped eating to consider this for a moment and then smiled eagerly. "If it's going to fuck them over, I'm your man."

Daniel spoke again into the phone. "He's in, and I trust him. If we get the package to him in New York, he can get it to *The Times*. But..."

"But what?"

"This is a young lawyer. He's got a whole career in front of him. We have to keep him clear of it all."

"All right. We will come up with a plan. Please put your colleague on speaker phone."

Life had generally come easy for Jake. In high school he was the smartest kid in the room and that got him into Middlebury, which got him into NYU Law School. He was good at sports and ran cross-country in college. He could usually get a date, although it was more fun to hang with friends from school, either in DC or home in New York. The job at PJ&H fell into his lap, and it had been quite an education seeing the seamy underside of politics from the perspective of a firm pulling the strings. The pay was really good, but that was never his main motivation. His parents had paid for school, so he had no debt. Sometimes he wondered if, rather than working at a law job, he should do something adventurous while he was still young enough to enjoy it. This mission for Daniel certainly qualified as an adventure, and maybe when it was over he'd travel or go work for the World Wildlife Fund or somewhere else he could believe in what he was doing.

He also felt deeply loyal to Daniel. The guy had been a real mentor, showing him the ropes; he was a master at the political game and had shared tips on how to get things done in Congress and in life. Daniel also had saved his job after that witch from HR caught him smoking on the fire stair and maybe even again when he messed up that court filing.

And now Nell and Pearce thought Daniel had "gone rogue." But what he had been saying all evening made sense, especially in light of what Jake had learned from the climate research. Daniel wasn't doing this for personal gain or because of a midlife crisis—though he had every reason to crack after his wife and daughter drowned.

Jake tended to look at things cynically, everything from his job of manipulating democracy to some girl trying to impress him. But it was hard to doubt where Daniel's head was at now. He was chucking his career because he believed in something, and what he believed was bottom-line for everyone. Jake's research had opened his eyes, but he needed to learn more, to really understand the science he had spent four years discrediting. But the truth of the climate crisis aside, he was genuinely in awe of Daniel's decision and trusted him to know what they were doing was right. And he was proud to know he was the guy they needed to see this through.

But when Daniel said he should alter his appearance in case he was photographed, things got real.

"I have dye that will color your hair but will wash out afterwards," Daniel said, opening a small briefcase. "Red, I think. Not bright enough to make you easy to spot in a crowd but unusual enough for your pursuers to remember."

"Does it have to be red?" Jake said with a grimace.

"It's just for a day, and it will distinguish your normal look from our courier, that and maybe slicking it down to contrast with your usual bush."

"Hey, thanks," Jake complained.

"Oh, I meant 'bush' in a good way. Also, I have a kit; I'll apply some prosthetics to your face."

"You know how to do that?"

"This will be my first time, but our makeup lady showed me."

"So, you're going to, like, give me a big nose?"

"That and maybe a more pronounced chin. It will be subtle, but hopefully enough to throw off facial recognition. And it's just plastic; it will peel off when we're done."

Jake was amazed at how different he looked when Daniel was through. The change didn't affect his appetite, though. While Daniel went to shower and dress, he finished the food, trying to recall hidden ways to get around New York City. There were out-of-the-way subway tunnels and stores with multiple exits. He realized it was a good thing he had forgotten to return the bikeshare fob his friend loaned him the prior weekend; that might prove useful.

Daniel came out to the living room cleaned up, looking like a high-powered lobbyist. He outlined the plan and asked if Jake had questions.

"I'm good to go," Jake said. "I'll pick up a few things and head for the airport. I'll crash at my parents' apartment and be in place outside Penn Station before you arrive at 8:40."

Daniel nodded. "Okay, but let's walk through this."

Jake waited with a smile, eager to get underway.

"Look," Daniel said, "this is serious. If someone comes after you, they won't be playing games."

"I get it," he said, wiping the smile from his face. Daniel was right. It was time to get real.

"Okay, the first overarching rule is to stay alert. Next, you will wear running shoes and the sweatshirt you're wearing now, which is reversible, right?"

He turned the hoodie inside out for Daniel to see.

"You will wear the blue side out at the station, and turn to the gray side after you lose the tail. It's supposed to be almost fifty degrees in New York tomorrow, and you may need to move fast. Also, there could be one or many people following you, on foot, in cars—there's no way to know. They may have local cops, so don't trust anyone. And the...wait here a minute."

Daniel ducked into his bedroom and returned counting out cash from an envelope. "Here," he said, handing Jake a wad of bills. "This should cover your expenses. Use cash for everything; don't leave a trail."

Jake chuckled to himself. Paying for *anything* with cash might be the hardest part of espionage to get used to.

"And you can't carry your phone. We're not sure how the FBI might be able to use it to locate you. Give it to me, and I'll return it when we meet." Then he paused to think. "So, you're all set?"

"Just one thing. How do I recognize the woman with the accent?"

"She'll be carrying this bag, although you might not see it." He held up a light gray string bag with a faded DC Athletic Club logo. "The package will be in the bag, but at the point you change your clothes, put the gray bag into this one." He handed Jake a red string bag.

"Got it. But why the go-between? I mean why don't I go with you on the train, or fly up and you can hand off to me directly?"

Daniel sighed with an appreciative smile. "This is dangerous business, Jake, and I already feel bad putting you at risk. If someone on the train is watching, or if the FBI gets a close look at you when you take the package, they'll be all over you now and going forward. No, we're grateful you're willing to help—we really need it—but we want to keep you off the radar as much as we can. With this plan, only Verde will get near me, and she'll be in disguise and has experience with this sort of thing. Hopefully, they won't even see you and, if they do, they'll only see your dust as you lose them on the city streets."

"You're the boss. Just tell me what to do."

"Right. Now, when Verde gets near, she'll give you a prompt about Madrid."

"Right, and I say, 'By way of Lisbon.' But how will I spot her?"

"She'll be in disguise, as I said, but the high cheekbones and almond-shaped eyes are hard to miss; just look for the best-looking woman coming out of the station, about five foot eight. Actually, she'll have her arm in a sling—from an accident a few days ago—so you should have no trouble spotting her. Still, she has this way of appearing out of nowhere, so you might not see her coming." He paused. "Don't worry; she'll find you."

"Sounds like someone we want on our team," Jake said with a suggestive smile.

It was the first time he had ever seen Daniel look embarrassed. His boss obviously hadn't realized how much he was revealing in describing Jake's contact. But that was cool. Even though Daniel operated at a different level from Jake, he was still a regular guy. And he obviously liked this woman with the accent, which was good to see after all he'd been through.

The ringing landline interrupted them. Daniel picked it up without thinking. That was a mistake.

"Are you hiding from the world or just from me?" Haley said in a tone somewhere between annoyance and amusement.

Daniel dreaded having to talk with her. He raised his eyebrows, gesturing at the phone. Jake gave him a shaka sign and left with the red bag.

"I've decided to give you one more chance," Haley said seductively. "But your cell phone seems to be dead, so I took the initiative to chase you down at home."

"Yeah, " he said, trying to think quickly. "My iPhone died for some reason. I need to pick up a new one."

"Well, fascinating technology issues aside, I wanted to remind you that I just gave you the pipeline bill," she paused, "and it's time to pay up."

"What do you mean?"

"I mean I want to stay friends, Daniel, and I want Senator Langston to keep playing ball, but you're making it difficult. You seem to have forgotten how this works."

He let out a deep breath. Haley's games seemed so trite after spending the night on the cold ground by the bridge. His jump into the Cheat River had done more than shock him out of his water phobia, it showed him his actions mattered more than just to himself. People like Kristof and Mia put themselves on the line. But back here, in the world of black humor, cynicism and corruption, Haley thought her wielding influence over a hack who wasn't qualified to sit in Congress justified her predatory appetite. The world should not work that way.

"I've done some thinking, Haley," he said. "The way you see things just won't work for me. I'm afraid you and the senator will have to get by without me going forward."

"You understand what you're saying?" she said sternly. "Does Pearce know about this?"

"Pearce will lose his mind when he hears I won't sleep with you to ensure Langston's loyalty, but there it is."

"You bastard. This will sink you."

"It was wrong to cheat on my wife—you knew that and encouraged it—and I'll suffer for that the rest of my life. And it's still wrong, even now, because it plays into your power games. I don't mean to hurt you, Haley, but I'm not down for it anymore."

The line went dead, which was a relief but set another time bomb ticking. There was no telling how she would torpedo him with Langston and Pearce, but did that matter if he moved quickly? By tomorrow he'd be through with this business, and they could all go to hell.

He almost had to laugh at how much better he was at burning bridges than Kristof and Guy. All they did was make a lot of smoke and noise; his bridge to ever working in DC again was down and would never go up again.

Daniel was anxious as he approached the PJ&H building. When he walked in the door Frank, the head of nighttime security, gave him an odd look. "Late night," Frank said, half in question.

Frank glanced at his computer screen rather than just waiving Daniel in. What was going on? Daniel was an important lawyer at the firm and it was not unusual for him to visit the office at all hours. Did Pearce bar him from the building? Could he even do that?

Daniel tried to pull Frank's attention from his screen. "Yeah," he said, trying to sound overworked but good-natured. "You know the old man; he's got us at it around the clock again."

Frank looked up and smiled sympathetically. "I guess we all have to answer to someone," he said as he buzzed the turnstile. "You have a good night, Mr. Lazaro."

Daniel let himself into the firm offices and stopped to take a long breath. He should have plenty of time.

He had seen Pearce check a day planner in his desk for the combination to his safe, and Daniel was able to jimmy open the flimsy lock on this drawer and find the combination scribbled on the last page. From the safe he retrieved photographs, signed checks and contracts. He then went into the secure server to which only a few partners had access and downloaded bank records showing money transfers from the Oil Institute to the firm and then to Langston's super PAC. He also pulled up the archive of recordings of phone calls among the conspirators. Pausing before he copied the calls onto a thumb drive, he decided not to copy recordings that included Haley. She was as culpable as anyone, and it was people like her—and Daniel—who brokered the deals between crooked politicians and the iniquitous industry types. But she had been straight with him—playing hardball and squeezing everything she could out of each deal but still being honest. In a way she had helped him learn to survive in a cutthroat world. And they had made love—or perhaps it was more accurate to say they had sex—and all cynicism aside, they had shared what felt like moments of tenderness. He didn't have many people in his life with whom he had shared *any* warmth or affection. He couldn't throw her into the pit with the truly evil actors. She might still end up entangled in the lies and dirty tricks, but he wouldn't disclose firm records to seal her fate.

He fit the evidence into one thick envelope, marveling at the explosive power of this small cache of materials. He placed the envelope into the string bag, put the bag into his briefcase, turned out the lights and left the building.

There was still an hour before his train to New York. He walked to Union Station, relishing the quiet dawn before the storm.

Chapter
Thirty-Four

It was not yet six-thirty—too early to get out of bed—but Joe Coulder hadn't slept well all night. There were still loose ends in the case. They caught up with Kristof Tyndall and identified him as "Eco," but there was no reason to shoot him; he had nowhere to run, and they should have brought him in instead of making him a martyr.

Their man inside Anthro turned out to be a loose cannon, blowing himself up, and he still hadn't regained consciousness so they could debrief him. Zeke Franklin, the other perpetrator at the scene, was hard core and would not give up any information.

They had expected to also find Eco's woman at the scene, the one called "Verde," but she mattered less than Eco.

There had been no sign of Dan Lazaro at the bridge, either, or any solid evidence he was involved. In a way, that was a relief. He had known Dan since college, played poker with him through the years and exchanged more information with him than was strictly legal, and so it was hard to believe he had gone over to the eco-terrorists. Branston Pearce must have been on drugs…or else the woman who said Dan was trying to recruit her was delusional.

They accessed the cell phone they found in Dan's office and his computer—which Pearce assured them was legitimate since they were both firm property. Dan had been searching timetables for shipments of timber from a site in West Virginia near the bridge. But without finding him at the scene or having testimony from the informant, they had nothing solid on him.

If Dan was involved—maybe in some support role—that would come out in time, and it would be easy to pull him in. He was a friend, at least he used to be, and Coulder would normally do what he could for him. But circumstances had pushed way past where Joe could, or even wanted to, protect him.

Then his phone rang.

"He came back!" Pearce roared so loudly Joe held the receiver away from his ear.

"Lazaro?"

"Yes, Lazaro, dammit! You were supposed to arrest him up at that bridge, but now he slipped into our office!"

"What do you mean? When did he go to the office?"

"Early today. He entered at 4:48 and left an hour later. We've got video, and the guards recognized him."

"They didn't stop him?"

"No, they didn't stop him! I told security in the building to watch out for him, but he's a goddamned partner of the firm—at least until later today, so all they did was save the videotape and call my office, where someone finally picked up and reached me."

"So, what did he do there? Wait, where are you?"

"I'm in my office, dammit! I got here ten minutes ago. He stole things from my safe, tapes and photos that *can't* fall into the wrong hands. This could be a bloodbath. We're talking major scandal—in Congress *and* at the Institute. I'm telling you so you can get your people on it, but I'll be talking to the director in an hour."

That brought Joe fully awake. The director was not an understanding man. There would be hell to pay if anyone found out how the Bureau shared classified information with PJ&H. "Do we know where he's headed or what he'll do?"

"So, you want me to do *your* job as well as my own?"

"No, Branston, I just want to hit the ground running."

"Well, that bastard isn't as smart as he thinks. He must have known we might search his laptop, but he made the mistake of using his secretary's computer to check trains to New York and then scribbled a time on a pad. We are almost sure he left Union Station," he paused, "twenty minutes ago. Our lobby cameras show him leaving the office with a black briefcase over his shoulder; he must be carrying the materials in that."

By this time Coulder had opened the laptop on his desk and pulled up a train schedule. "Okay, so he's on the 6:05, which gets him to Penn Station New York at 8:40. We can arrest him coming off the train, assuming we've got some basis."

"You grab him, and he's holding stolen goods; what more do you need?"

"That would be simple, but we also want to know where he's delivering the stuff."

Pearce hesitated. "You might be right; this is a chance to flush out Anthro supporters. With the botched bombing and the death of Tyndall, this would be its death knell."

"We won't lose him. Trust me. I can have a team in place in an hour. I'll hop a plane to take charge."

"If you lose that package, we're screwed," Pearce said, and then added, as if he had just changed his mind, "In fact, forget about waiting for a handoff. We can't take the chance. Just pick Lazaro up right off the train."

"With all due respect, Branston, this is now a Bureau operation, and it only makes sense to identify the contact in New York."

"Damn it, Coulder! I'm talking with your boss in, now, fifty-five minutes. He will agree this is too incendiary to risk a fuck-up. Just grab that bastard and get the package!"

Daniel found his reserved seat on the Acela. The package was in the gray string bag in his briefcase, which otherwise held only the *Post* and a second thick envelope full of old newspapers. He sat against the window clutching the briefcase with both arms. Pearce would definitely have heard by then that Daniel went into the office, but surely no one could be following him already. Still, he kept hearing Kristof say to assume at all times he was being followed.

He pulled the morning paper from the briefcase. First-class service provided digital newspapers, but he needed an actual paper. Prior to Baltimore, he went to the café car. He left his newspaper on the seat but wore his briefcase hung over his shoulder, one arm pressing it to his side. Short of handcuffing it to his wrist, he couldn't think of any other way to signal the briefcase was valuable. He bought a cup of coffee and, while he added milk, scanned the car. He saw nothing suspicious.

But when he returned to his seat, a man from the café car followed and took a seat across the aisle four rows back. He was sure that man wasn't there before Baltimore. He could be a commuter who just got on, but why go directly to the café car? The man must have been there to watch him.

A few passengers disembarked at Philadelphia. As they passed Daniel's row and blocked the Baltimore man's view, he slipped the string bag from his briefcase and pushed it into the corner of the seat, beneath his crumpled newspaper.

When the train pulled into New York, he rose, clutching the briefcase to his chest and not looking back at the newspaper and the bag hidden beneath it. He joined the short line of passengers to exit the train. He couldn't see Mia on the platform, but he did see in the window the reflection of the Baltimore man behind him in line. Daniel was sweating, which he realized was a good bit of unintentional tradecraft. If the man from Baltimore was watching, he'd think Daniel was anxious about what he was carrying and was not expecting a "surprise" greeting by the FBI. He had to trust Mia's plan and focus on his role.

The doors opened. Passengers filed out. As soon as Daniel stepped onto the platform, two stocky men in suits confronted him, one flashing a badge. He unconsciously took a half step backward into the person behind him, the Baltimore man who nudged him forward saying, "Just move across the platform, Mr. Lazaro."

The two goons took Daniel under each elbow and "helped him" to the center of the platform, where Joe Coulder stood shaking his head. The Baltimore man joined them, eyeing the people hurrying by.

"Hey, Joe, whaddaya know?" Daniel said without a smile.

"Hand over the briefcase, Dan," Coulder said.

One of the agents pulled the bag from his shoulder and handed it to Coulder, who opened it, pulled out the fat envelope and ripped it open.

"It's a bluff!" he shouted, holding up a handful of newspapers and shooting an urgent look at the Baltimore agent.

"What's this about, Joe?" Daniel said, innocently.

One of the agents shouted into his radio, "There's been a switch."

Coulder scanned the platform and peered at someone in the crowd of people on the stairs. "That woman!" he shouted, pointing.

Daniel saw a blonde woman turn away and hurry up the stairs. It must be Mia. He hoped she had enough of a lead to make it to the street.

Two of the agents ran after her but had to push through the crowd. The other agent spoke urgently into his radio. "There's been a handoff to a tall blonde woman, tan jacket. Cover the exits!"

Coulder turned back to Daniel. "What are you playing at, Dan?"

"No game, Joe. But fun fact: did you know this is the busiest station in North America? Nearly 600,000 passengers a day?"

They stood awkwardly on the platform for a few minutes, until a voice from Coulder's phone said, "Target exited to 7th Avenue. Small gray bag passed to white male, red hair, late twenties, blue hoodie, running shoes. He's headed up the east side of the avenue."

"Stay close," Coulder barked into the radio. "Don't lose that package!"

Coulder sneered at Daniel. "You think some kid is going to get away from us?"

"I wish I knew what you're talking about, Joe. But I am free to go, right?"

Mia had fitted herself with a platinum blonde wig that, she had to laugh, made her look like a US film star of the fifties, like Marilyn Monroe. She wore a loose overcoat draped around her shoulders to hide the sling supporting her broken arm.

If the organization had not been disrupted, she could have sent someone else to take the handoff, but the dispersal of the volunteers made that hard, and the betrayal by Ludd made her unwilling to trust anyone else. Besides, this action would make up for the failure at the bridge, and she needed to be involved.

She was in position on the platform when the doors opened. The suits waiting to greet Daniel could not have stood out more if they had worn "FBI" jackets. She saw him rise from his seat as the train came to a stop. When he moved toward the door, she entered through the door behind him. She hurried through the car and snatched up the discarded newspaper and the bag beneath it while she glanced through the window at two men escorting Daniel across the platform. She left the newspaper in the café car and exited the train just as the doors were closing. On the platform she hurried—though no more quickly than the commuters all around her—to the staircase, not looking back.

But then she inexplicably forgot protocol. With the package

in hand, she got stuck in the crowd crawling up the stairs and glanced back to make sure no one was chasing her. That was a mistake—and she knew better. Just then the agent on the platform spotted her and pointed. She hurried to the top of the stairs and through a reliably frenetic Penn Station.

The up escalator to 7th Avenue was blocked off for construction. This funneled everyone onto the staircase and slowed her down. She kept moving in the stream of commuters, cursing the delay.

At the top of the stairs, she spotted the blue hoodie. Daniel's friend was standing on the sidewalk looking around, as if he were waiting for someone. As she neared he nodded in recognition. She stopped two feet from him, turning back the way she had come and speaking the Madrid prompt as if talking into her phone. As soon as he gave the Lisbon rejoinder, she passed behind him and put the bag firmly into his hand. Then she quickly crossed the avenue with the crowd, knowing the agents would focus on the package.

She ducked into a clothes store, pulled a pair of jeans off a sales table and entered a dressing room. In an instant she had reversed her coat, shoved the blonde wig into her purse and returned to the sales floor no longer hiding her sling. Dropping the jeans back on the display table, she strolled out of the store and turned downtown on the busy sidewalk.

First thing Daniel had told Jake was to stay alert. Of course you had to be alert on these streets or else take your life in your hands. No one expected you to obey the traffic lights in Manhattan, but the tradeoff was you couldn't rely on them either. Jake had long had a fear of being run over by a delivery guy with one of those big aluminum boxes on his bike, and now with ebikes this fear was more real than ever.

On the sidewalk outside the station he scanned people

coming up the stairs, looking for short dark hair. Then he noticed a beautiful blonde he knew at a glance must be Verde. He nodded.

She moved toward him without acknowledging him. Then she turned back as if she were lost and said something into her phone about Madrid.

He smiled and spoke as if he were talking to himself. "You can get there by way of Lisbon."

She quickly passed behind him, and he found himself holding the string bag and the woman gone.

He waited until the light changed and four lanes of traffic started south on 7th Avenue. To the blare of car horns he bounded across the avenue and north across 33rd and 34th Streets. Backed against the corner of Macy's, he scanned the sensory overload of the corner for the anomaly: the person who stands out. In a crowd moving in all directions, he spotted one stationary brown jacket. The man appeared to be looking in a store window. He was fairly tall but otherwise undistinguished. Hadn't he seen a jacket like that at the station exit? That man had a Yankees cap, and this one didn't, but the stubbled face could be the same.

He would treat brown jacket as his tail and try shaking him. But Daniel said Jake must assume there would be more than one. He took some long, deep breaths to stay calm. First step was to confirm the tail.

He broke into a jog on the sidewalk, weaving in and out of pedestrians like a running back in the open field. When he crossed 42nd Street into Times Square he was slowed by the crowds, but any pursuer would be as well. It was crazy how close he came to The Times Building—his ultimate destination—but he first needed to dive into the city to lose his pursuit.

When he emerged from the chaos of Times Square, brown jacket was only a block behind him; baseball cap or not, that guy was following him. He entered 30 Rock and hurried around the hallway and out the side door back to 49th Street. At the next building in the complex he pushed through the revolving doors, and in the comparative darkness of the lobby hurried down the stairs to the underground concourse. At the windows opening onto the ice-skating rink, he took an unmarked tunnel west. After several twists and turns past shoe repair and sandwich shops, he emerged to street level west of 6th Avenue. No one appeared to notice when he hurried up the escalator to the atrium between two skyscrapers. Quickly, he moved around the corner of one of the buildings to where he could watch behind him.

Incredibly, a minute later brown jacket stepped off the escalator. How did he do that? Then a woman jogger ran up to meet him and gestured toward Jake, stupidly still looking around the corner. The two saw him.

He rushed toward 6th Avenue with his hand up. Luckily, a cab pulled over immediately, and he jumped in. There were at least two people following him! But he recalled Daniel's second rule—stay calm—and plotted his next move.

No way his pursuers would find a cab, so he could get lost in traffic. He had confirmed who was following him, and had lost them both. This espionage thing wasn't so hard.

But when he looked back, the jogger had taken off after him on the sidewalk and brown jacket was waving down another taxi.

When Jake's cab stopped for the light at 5th Avenue, the jogger came up beside them, not even breathing heavily and acting as if she didn't see him. Brown jacket was in a cab three cars back.

Jake's taxi started rolling across town, the jogger keeping him in sight. Jake fingered the bikeshare fob in his pocket—thinking the friend who loaned it to him was probably pissed off he hadn't returned it. He went to check his phone for the bike app that would show available bikes, but he had left the phone with Daniel!

"Damn it!" he shouted under his breath, eliciting a curious look from the driver. He closed his eyes to think. Where was there a docking station near the park?

"Turn up Columbus Avenue," he said.

He watched out the window. The bike station on 63rd Street

had four bikes, which was not ideal. There were two at 71st Street, and so he kept going. Brown jacket's taxi was still behind him, and it looked like it had picked up the jogger.

At 89th Street he saw what he wanted, a docking station with only one bike. "Okay, drop me here," he said and jammed a twenty-dollar bill through the plexiglass shield.

His cab had barely stopped at the light before he jumped out. He grabbed the one available bike and stood up to pedal through metal barricades blocking cars from entering Central Park. Once in the park, he'd be clear.

But at the short rise before the ring road, the jogger was almost on him and running fast. He peddled hard—as hard as possible on the tank of a bicycle—and a long downhill allowed him to leave her far enough behind to get out of sight. He jumped the curb below the reservoir and hid in a tunnel under the road.

He looked at the curved brick ceiling above him, calculating how long it would take for the runner to race by on the road above. She was probably moving fast to catch up after losing sight of him. She'd pass by before she realized she lost him.

But she was surely communicating with her team and others would join the chase. Anyway, he couldn't exit the park at Columbus Circle. They'd surely be waiting for him there.

The path out of the tunnel bent west and then south, hugging the edge of the park, mostly out of sight of the road. Where the path approached Tavern on the Green, a park ranger jumped out of his golf cart to yell for him to walk his bike on the trail. Little chance of that, though. He raced past and stuck to the sheltered path until he could push the bike up to the low wall separating the park from the sidewalk. Behind a cover of trees, he reversed his sweatshirt, stuffed the string bag into the red bag, pushed the bike behind a bush and jumped the wall to the sidewalk.

He hurried west. At Amsterdam Avenue he ducked into a clothes store. He bought a light jacket and stuffed his hair into a wool hat. He exited the store slowly, his sweatshirt and the string bag in his shopping bag. At a corner deli he bought a cup of coffee and poured half out, sipping the rest as he walked casually along the crowded sidewalk toward the subway.

He finished the coffee and reached the subway entrance, but at the bottom of the stairs he spotted a man wearing a Yankees cap.

Chapter Thirty-Five

Joe Coulder had no grounds to arrest him. Daniel had no stolen documents or tapes—at least not when they took him into custody. They knew he had accessed the firm safe, but they would have no evidence he had taken materials that, in any event, no one would want to admit existed. As to Stone Canyon Bridge, if Coulder had proof Daniel was involved, he would have arrested him at the train station.

Coulder had a bigger problem than Daniel; his attention was on the package. This was where the contest would play out—and Daniel had faith Mia and Jake would get this done.

He walked east a few blocks and up to 42nd Street. It was a brisk day. The air smelled surprisingly clean. At Grand Central Station he turned back west. After passing the library, he crossed the street midblock. No one followed him across the street, so he relaxed, bought a cup of coffee and sat on a chair in Bryant Park, with a wide view of the lawn. He would keep up his guard even though there was no reason for anyone to follow him; he didn't have the package, and they knew who he was and where to find him.

He sipped, enjoying the warmth coursing down his throat. It was surprising how peaceful this park was surrounded by skyscrapers and the hubbub on the streets all around. The London plane trees lining the perimeter of the park were bare of leaves now, but would soon fill the park with green. Businesspeople and mothers with strollers traversed gravel paths. Even with the chill in the air, a few chess games were underway at small tables.

His excitement was growing. They would pull this off if only Jake did his part. That was a concern, certainly, but it was time to have faith in something, or someone.

He had never really liked Joe Coulder; the guy was such a tool. He also bristled at how the FBI agent had wanted him to set up his brother-in-law. In Daniel's reordered world, he blamed himself for ever considering that. In the context of Anthro saving the world and Coulder shoveling shit for rich people, the thought now of turning on his own family was inconceivable.

But then someone else turned Pete in. It was sad, but his brother-in-law seemed to be a born victim.

He wondered if Pete was still active in the movement. The closing of Anthro's Alexandria headquarters would have disrupted communications but, as Kristof had described it, the cells were set up to propagate even if the feds cut off Anthro's head.

And word would get out. Daniel would write about Stone Canyon in *Monkey Wrench*—give the movement a martyr and Kristof his due. The planet was the worse for the death of a leader it could ill afford to lose.

Daniel recalled asking Mia what difference they were making. While he believed they would take down Pearce, Coggin and Bo Langston, what hope was there really of saving the planet? Weren't we all doomed, anyway? Wasn't this forlorn hope that this would change things like his clinging to the possibility Annabelle somehow survived the flood? Consoling to think it, but was it no more than fantasy?

He shook off this gloom and tried to focus on the matter at hand. He could only help by doing what he could do, and he took heart in knowing Anthro's supporters would need no newsletter to hear about the methane scandal. When it broke, there would be no place to hide from *that* story. And he'd make sure the celebration of this victory would honor Eco as the movement's inspirational leader.

Daniel was in this fight to stay but now had to figure out how that would work. He couldn't go back to lobbying, and who knew what would even be left of PJ&H after the dust settled? He would submit a formal withdrawal from the firm, consistent with the partnership agreement. Have to stick to protocol, he said to himself with a laugh. He might even be entitled to a payout— something maybe he should have considered before? Daniel had more than he needed, with what he had invested and the insurance payoff on River House, so maybe he should just give any payout to Anthro. He could make it an anonymous donation or, better yet, a gift in the name of Branston Pearce—and let him try to explain that away if it ever came to light.

The FBI would no doubt keep tabs on him once they located him. They surely would know he had exposed the methane deal, which indirectly connected him with the eco-activists, and his leaving his job would confirm their suspicions. The scandal also would put a target on his back for the Oil Institute, except it would be reeling from the scandal and focused on making money for its members going forward rather than seeking revenge for the past. He likely would end up testifying in court or before Congress; he was the one to expose the conspiracy, after all, and could connect all the pieces. If he could just navigate that mess, and hopefully trade his cooperation for immunity, he might be able to slip away and carry on the climate fight somewhere off in this big, beautiful country. Maybe he would visit what wilderness was left in North

America, see it before it disappeared. Then he might open a practice to defend activists and help them challenge the system.

Of more concern was Mia. Once *The Times* story broke and all hell broke loose, she'd have to find somewhere quiet to recuperate and eventually have her baby. Sadly, that hiatus would probably land her in the grief she had pushed aside while they completed this job. So little time had passed, really. Everyone needed time to mourn.

He would do anything he could to help. But he knew that was selfish. He wanted to stay with her, though her courage and dedication made him ashamed of being infatuated like a teenager. He could never be more than a pale reflection of Kristof Tyndall or nearly good enough for her. In the end, he would help her any way he could and only hope she would stay in touch one way or another.

Satisfied no one had cared to follow him, he tossed out his empty coffee cup, snaked his way through the chess tables, and continued across town.

In Times Square, he made a few erratic turns to see if anyone followed, laughing to think an FBI agent might be disguised as Mickey Mouse or Pikachu hitting on the tourists. Finally feeling confident he was in the clear, he walked south to The Times Building, checked the street once more and entered through the revolving doors. He felt like Deep Throat about to blow open the Watergate scandal.

Even though he thought he was in the clear, it was a relief that a sincere young woman rather than a pair of stoic agents greeted him when he got off the elevator. She showed him to an empty conference room and said Mr. Pullman would join him shortly.

He took in the expansive view to the south, which included the Freedom Tower on the site of the old World Trade Center. That sobering sight brought back the gravity of what he was about. This scandal would expose the putridity at the core of law making, how money corrupted all the members of Congress and high-powered lobbyists. He had to think his father would be proud of him for sticking it to the big shots.

But would Jake make it? The kid was smart and a competitive runner, and hopefully his knowledge of back alleys gave him an edge against those agents and all their technology. He reached to his breast pocket. Holding Jake's phone prevented anyone from tracking him—assuming Nell had informed on her friend as well—but it also kept Daniel from getting updates. Why hadn't Daniel given him a burner phone?

In a few minutes the door swung open and Mia walked in. The wig was gone. The edgy black haircut made her look beguiling but lethal—not an easy combination to pull off. He had to smile at how she had managed this action with her arm still in a sling, thinking how that would have been surprising in anyone other than Mia.

Her face lit up with a gleaming smile. He moved to hug her but stopped short when she gestured to the man at her side. "Daniel Lazaro, meet Gary Pullman."

He shook the outstretched hand of a man who looked the part of a reporter, with slightly unkempt hair and a loosened tie, which he was sure had a soup or mustard stain.

"Thank you for coming in, Mr. Lazaro," Pullman said.

"Daniel...please."

"Daniel, then. I have to say I am in awe of what you and Mia have been up to. We two are old friends; I don't know if she told you. I have published articles on the politics of climate change and am eager to hear about the methane payoff."

Daniel laid out the money trail. At each point he described supporting recordings and documents in their possession.

"When you say, 'in our possession,'" Gary said, "you mean in the package that will be delivered here today?"

"That's what we hope," Daniel agreed. "You have to understand, though, the Oil Institute of America and my soon-to-be former law firm will pull in all their favors to intercept it."

"Is your messenger safe?"

Daniel paused. He worried Jake might treat this as a game, a city-wide escape room challenge, while the danger was real. Daniel and Mia taking this risk was one thing; they knew what they were doing and had seen the possible consequences. But this kid went from wholly uninvolved two days ago to right in the thick of it. He could, at that moment, be running for his life just because he wanted to help Daniel. How could you put a value on that kind of loyalty, and was Daniel abusing it, a callous manipulator even when he was trying to do right? In the clear light of day it seemed there must have been a better way, a safer way. He could have delivered the package himself or sent it through the post office. If only they had had more time.

Any repercussions for Jake would add to the noxious mound of Daniel's well-deserved guilt. "I hope he's all right," he muttered, mostly to himself.

"It is too late to rethink the plan now," Mia said softly. "We must have faith in our young man."

Pullman looked apprehensive. "Well, I've got to be honest here. I believe your story, and you deserve all our respect for putting yourselves on the line. But it's not only the well-being of your delivery guy at stake. I've run through the general outline of the story—as you described it, Mia—with my editor, and there's no way legal will let us publish without hard evidence in our hands."

"We understand, Gary," she said. "Just please to give it a little time."

"And I could really use that drink now," Daniel said, "if you've got something stronger than water."

Gary grinned. Mia smiled sympathetically at Daniel, covering his hand on the table with hers. He thrilled at her touch but tried not to show it. She was probably just reassured he could maintain a sense of humor in the face of disaster—even if he wasn't very funny.

But then Daniel remembered he had sworn off liquor, when the fear of water had proven stronger than all the alcohol he had ever swilled. And it was the peril of the woman who didn't know the power of her touch that made him forget his phobia and plunge into that river. In a way he owed his cure to Mia.

"So let's run through how this will work," Pullman said. "Assuming we have the evidence, and it convinces my editor, I'll fill in the details of the story I've roughed out. Then we'll have fact-checkers chase down *every* loose end. We cannot have any aspect of this story blowing back at us. Then my editor—and the publisher on a story this big—will hopefully okay it. Finally, we will still have to run it by legal counsel because we will practically be inviting our targets to rush into court."

"But they'll be too late, right?" Daniel said.

"Too late to stop the firestorm. No way to take back an article once it goes out to our nine million subscribers around the world. Still, we'll be hauled in to defend our decision to publish, pressed to reveal sources, face efforts to enjoin further reporting: all the usual bullshit." He smiled. "This is *The New York Times*; it won't be our first dumpster fire."

Daniel smiled at Mia, who looked quietly pleased.

Then the phone on the cadenza buzzed and everyone tensed. "Mr. Pullman," a woman's voice said over the intercom, "a Mr. Jake Gambol is on his way up. He says he has a package for you from Portugal?"

Chapter Thirty-Six

Daniel was out early, walking with the dogs behind Daisy and Cal's farmhouse in the Poconos.

This farm was more than a safe house. Daisy and Cal participated in Anthro actions and Kristof and she had spent a month there working with them on a campaign to target private aircraft and superyachts. Daisy was about Mia's age, though to see Daisy in her beads and braids you'd think she was an ageless hippie child of the 1960s. Cal was a bit older but solid like a man who worked outdoors, whose rugged face was always on the verge of an easy smile. Along with offering aid and assistance to Anthro, they farmed their small plot of land and raised some animals, trying to live off the land as best they could.

Daniel wanted to see the stream at the bottom of the property. If he spotted any fish he'd come back in the afternoon with a pole. It had been a lifetime since he sat by a stream pretending to fish and he looked forward to enjoying the warm April sunshine. Maybe he could get Mia to join him.

By the time Jake had arrived at the newspaper offices, Daniel was more concerned about his young associate than about breaking open the methane scandal. He had sunk into deep gloom thinking this kid's loyalty to him might cost him his career or even his life. So, Jake's arrival with his familiar swaggering smile had been an incredible relief. Amid the excited hugs all around, Daniel was ecstatically thankful someone, for once, had helped him without meeting disaster.

Gary's eyes had lit up to see the assortment of notes, photographs and signed checks. Then Daniel plugged a thumb drive into Gary's laptop to play a recording. Bo Langston and Branston Pearce could be clearly identified cutting the deal that would sink them both. Another recording had Kent Coggin talking about what the Oil Institute demanded in return for funding Langston's PAC. The bank records on the table filled in the blanks. There was nothing left to do but put it all together and tell the world.

"This is decisive," Gary said, shaking hands again. "You folks have done a huge public service. Just wait here a minute while I get my editor."

He started from the room but stopped at the doorway to look back at Daniel. "And I'll see what I can do about that drink."

The laugh filling the room had less to do with what Gary said and more with relief and the triumph of the day. The three of them beamed at each other as only winning teammates can. Daniel was happier than at any time in the months since the flood. It finally felt like life would go on.

Mia stopped laughing to peer at Jake's face. "I do not know who has been doing your makeup," she said, looking over at Daniel, "but perhaps we can find a sink and give you back your face."

Jake laughed again. "I forgot about that stuff. And by the way, the red hair..."

"Yes, I can see you also might need a new hairdresser."

"Hey," Daniel said, "you get what you pay for."

When Jake looked back to normal—except for the hair—

Gary returned with his editor and proposed a toast with whiskey he had "just happened to find in my office." Daniel toasted but stopped with the glass at his lips.

"I guess I forgot," he said sheepishly. "I gave up drinking."

Gary nodded with a curious look. Mia smiled in encouragement.

"Well, it shouldn't go to waste," Jake said, downing his own drink and reaching for Daniel's glass.

He handed over the glass and joined in the laughter, trying to erase the memory of throwing up in the shower.

Jake walked them through his afternoon, ending with him realizing with relief that at least three men in his subway car were wearing Yankees caps—and they were *his* people, not FBI agents.

Gary sent an intern to find the bike in the park and return it to a docking station. Daniel said Jake should tell his friend he'd pay any penalties for losing it or keeping it out too long but shouldn't explain why. "We've got to remain anonymous, I'm afraid," he said, "for our own well-being."

"Like superheroes," Jake said, sipping the second whiskey.

"That's right, Jake, like superheroes."

While Gary walked his editor through the documentation and played the tape, Daniel nodded for Jake to join him at the far end of the table.

"You did it," Daniel said proudly, shaking his hand again.

"Oh, dude, you guys did it. I only took a couple of suits on the Circle Line Tour."

Daniel clapped him on the shoulder and laughed. "So what's next for you?"

"Now that I've got my phone back, I'm gonna meet up with some friends in Williamsburg."

Daniel laughed. "I meant long term, you knucklehead. What are your plans?"

"I guess I'll see what's left at PJ&H after they run Pearce out of town. I can't see working with Nell anymore; I couldn't stand even seeing her again. We were partners, and I was sure we'd both stick by you. But then she ran off the rails; it was all about her career and this manic need to come out on top. She essentially wanted to be you, well, you before you ducked into a phone booth and came out as Eco-Man."

Daniel laughed. He was going to miss this kid. "Don't be too hard on her," he said. "We never really know what pressures other people feel. I think Nell just got some wires crossed to where her need to succeed overwhelmed everything else."

"Well, that may be, but I'm done with her. And honestly, this whole thing has opened my eyes. PJ&H sucks, all those people clawing over each other to get ahead and not caring who it hurts. I hear what Anthro is saying, and I'm down for it. I can't keep working for the scumbags of the world, even if they do pay the best. Maybe I'll go on the trip I should have taken after law school or work somewhere like Doctors Without Borders."

"Let me know if you need a recommendation."

Jake laughed. "Right. 'Jake did some great work, although I can't actually talk about it.'"

"Hey, I spin facts much better than that."

Daniel was still out walking the day Stefan arrived. Mia looked up at the sound of the big Volvo coming up the driveway and hurried out to meet him. She hugged him as a greeting between old friends that turned into more like clutching Kristof and everything she had ever loved.

She knew Stefan would bring news, but it was mostly important he had come, that he was alive and free and still part of her world. Since her brother died, she had been close with so few people: Kristof, of course, and then Stefan and Zeke. Now Kristof was dead and Zeke was in jail.

"Have you recovered from your night at the bridge?" he said. "And how's the arm?"

She looked down at her sling. "The break is starting to heal. However, I think I have developed a fear of heights."

He laughed. "Well, that's understandable. I can tell you we had some anxious moments watching the video feed. I wish we could have convinced Kristof and Zeke that bombs were not the way."

She sighed, feeling she was finally able to hear Kristof's name without breaking down. "They were devoted to making a difference. Who can know if theirs is the only way to get the attention of the people?"

He pondered this in an awkward silence before saying, "So where's our intrepid attorney? I've got lots to download to you both."

"He will be back soon. Daniel has finally relaxed, I think. This life in the underground is new for him, and he has seen prying eyes in the forest. But there is something else; you will be only the third person to know."

He grinned. "Out with it, woman. The drama's killing me."

"It appears I am to have a child."

His mouth fell open. His eyes went wide. "Kristof?"

"Of course, you nincompoop."

He hugged her once again, more carefully this time. "My Lord, that trumps anything I've got to say. When? I mean, you're all right? The fall didn't hurt the baby?"

"I have seen a very nice doctor. He says everything looks hunky dory. Apparently, babies and women have resilience, especially in the early pregnancy."

He smirked. "Well, we always knew that about you."

After a pause, he added cautiously, "Did Kristof know?"

This time she could not stop a tear from escaping her eye. "Yes. At the end he knew. It is why he made me hide."

"Well, maybe the *best* but certainly not the *only* reason. You know he cared most about keeping you safe. But so, how do you feel about it...I mean, now that Kristof...?"

"I am just...thankful to have saved this small part of him. Despite the worst they could do to him, Kristof will live on."

"I'm happy for you, Mia, and relieved you both made it through your fall. You know I'll do everything I can for you and the baby, and you've got friends everywhere who'll do the same. You only have to tell us what you need."

"I never had doubt of that, Stefan. But...I smell hotcakes. Come inside kitchen. Daisy will be delirious to see you."

Stefan had spent time with Daisy and Cal the year before—when the authorities were looking for him in connection with the hazmat operation. Cal had been regaling Mia and Daniel with stories of how during his last visit their dogs and sheep followed Assisi everywhere he went, which convinced them he was indeed the reincarnation of St. Francis. Regardless of whether he was connected to a higher power, Mia felt a kind of spiritual comfort having him there. As they walked toward the house, she held tight to his arm and kept glancing over to assure herself he was real.

Daniel walked back from the stream throwing sticks for the dogs. When he neared the house, he saw the Volvo. The day was getting better and better.

He found Assisi sitting with Mia while Daisy fussed around the kitchen in her flowing skirt and tie-dyed shirt. Assisi jumped up and took hold of him. "You brought our Verde back to us," he said.

"Mia," she said quietly, so Daisy wouldn't hear, though she looked up with a knowing smile.

"I see," he said with raised eyebrows, and turned back to Daniel. "So welcome to the inner sanctum, young man."

Daniel smiled, wondering if he would next learn Assisi's real name.

As they dug into breakfast, Daisy said to Assisi, "Cal will be sorry he missed you. He wanted to ask your help with Sheila."

Daniel and Mia both looked up and said, "Sheila?"

Assisi laughed. "One of Cal's sheep," he said.

"One of Assisi's flock," Daisy countered matter-of-factly. "She has been nothing but trouble since her patron saint went away."

Daniel appreciated the humor in this but was more taken with the look of affection Mia gave Assisi. While there was still a trace of sadness behind her eyes, she seemed somehow to glow.

When breakfast was through, Daisy refused help cleaning up. "You three will have things to talk about," she said with a meaningful look. "I'll blast some music to give you privacy."

They retired to a porch filled with wicker furniture and sunshine, Grateful Dead music reverberating through the house. Assisi wasted no time getting down to business.

"The bad news," he said, "is the FBI and a pack of private security types are looking for Mia and Jake. The good news is the crappy descriptions they've circulated. Mia is 'a tall white woman in her thirties named Verde, possibly of foreign origin, who wears her blonde hair in a bob-cut and has distinctly blue eyes.'"

That made them all smile.

"Jake, for whom they have no name, is a tall, fit twenty-something white male with red hair whose facility with forensic countermeasures suggests he may have been trained by a foreign intelligence service."

Daniel laughed out loud. "Oh, he'll love that. So this was a Russian plot?"

"The story is one foreign government or another is sponsoring domestic terrorists."

"And what about Daniel?" Mia asked. "Does he earn no place on the most-wanted list?"

"They seem to be trying to keep the focus away from Pearce, Jones & Hurwitz, for obvious reasons. But I'd guess our Daniel is a person of interest."

"And Guy and Ludd?" Mia said.

"Well, Guy is still in FBI custody. We'll try to get him out on bail while we prepare a defense, but for now it's just as well he's in the prison hospital where the authorities have to nurse him back to health."

"What will they charge him with?" Daniel asked.

"You name it: conspiracy to destroy public property, unlawful transportation of explosives, resisting arrest...."

"Will he give us up?" Daniel said.

Assisi and Mia guffawed, and Assisi said, "Well, Guy—or I guess we should call him 'Zeke' now that his cover is blown—wouldn't crack if they pulled out his fingernails. What's more, we can be sure he'll raise a ruckus at his arraignment, which should energize the movement, not to mention putting Kristof in line for beatification."

"Who will handle the defense?" Daniel asked. "I'm not a criminal lawyer but I could find someone."

"Oh, we've got that covered. Ed Jasper at Morris & Jasper knows the drill and is already on it. And, as to Ludd, since we're almost certain he was an FBI plant, our only hope is he doesn't come out of his coma, or if he does he somehow loses his recent memory."

"I've heard a concussion can do that," Daniel said.

"I would like to give him one more concussion," Mia said, "to make sure."

Assisi paused and grinned at her. "In any event, Ludd only knows a few code names, and where Anthro was operating in Alexandria—and possibly that our blonde bombshell actually has long brown hair and eyes of blue *or* green, depending on the light."

Mia smiled self-consciously.

"What about Gary Pullman?" Daniel said. "I trust he's been busy?"

"Ah," Assisi said with a growing smile, "the best news. Get ready for fireworks; the front-page story goes to press today."

They all grinned. Daniel tried to imagine Branston Pearce's face as he lit his first cigar of the morning and opened the newspaper.

After they savored Assisi's news, Mia said to Daniel, "I too have news...on a less global scale."

From Assisi's knowing smile, Daniel could see she was about to let him in on another secret.

"I told Assisi this morning," she said, "and he is the only one to know besides Kristof and the doctor."

Daniel panicked. Had she suffered some added injury from her fall? But she looked strangely content.

"It seems the Lord works in mysterious ways," she continued. "A life passes and new life begins."

He couldn't keep the shock off his face. "You...you're...?"

"Going to have Kristof's baby."

Stefan could see Daniel's face revealed more than he intended. Saving a magnificent woman's life probably doomed the poor guy to fall for her. Stefan had been more than partly in love with Mia himself for ten years, and Daniel didn't have the long relationship with Kristof to temper his feelings.

They spent the sunny afternoon outside in the burgeoning spring colors. Stefan reconnected with his animal friends while Daniel and Mia walked down to the stream to fish. Dinner was another meal to make Stefan miss Daisy's home cooking. They sat long at the table trading stories.

In the morning he sat with Daniel and Mia in the sunroom sipping coffee and munching homemade scones. They were reading to each other snippets of news reports.

"Senator Langston's office has no comment," Stefan read from his laptop.

"I've got a contact there," Daniel responded, "but I'm not sure she's speaking to me."

"We knew about her," Stefan said. "Apparently, Haley Bourdain is taking a new job running the campaign committee for Senator Krinch from the great state of Alabama."

"Just can't keep a good woman down," Daniel said, looking embarrassed and drawing a curious look from Mia.

Then Mia looked at the new phone Assisi had brought for her. "Here is an interesting article: the House Intelligence Committee will open investigation of 'pay-for-vote' scandal. They will subpoena energy industry trade groups and their lobbying firms."

"Like the payments are news to them?" Daniel said sarcastically. "What town do *they* live in?"

"But it is gratifying to hear," she said.

"Of course," Assisi added, turning to Daniel, "they'll want *you* to testify."

He already knew this, but it was a sobering thought. He was witness to the whole scam, and his part would be unfinished until he helped the authorities pull it all together. Besides, the alternative would be to go underground for the rest of his life. "If that's what they want," he said. "But what about you, Assisi? What are your plans?"

He smiled. "First off, Daniel, maybe it's time you started calling me Stefan."

"But you must not tell anyone," Mia interposed with a serious look, "or we will have to snuff you out."

Daniel held up his hands as if defending himself but couldn't suppress a smile.

"Although," Stefan went on, "it may be time to adopt new names, especially you, Mia, with the FBI looking for someone called Verde."

She frowned. "I have grown accustomed to that name; it reminds me of my childhood."

"Yes, well," Stefan said, "I'm afraid we need to go back to the drawing board. Sort of like coming up with a new name for the band."

Mia shrugged. "This will give us something to occupy our days in this beautiful refuge."

"Ah," Stefan said, "that brings up an interesting thought.

What about asking Cal and Daisy if we can set up temporary headquarters here? We could help out around the farm at the same time as reconnecting with supporters. There is still so much to be done."

Mia looked doubtful. "That would mean giving up a reliable safe house and putting the farm at risk."

"I know," Assisi said, thoughtfully. "But we need someplace to operate until we set up a more permanent East Coast presence, maybe with Jill and Arnie running things out of Philadelphia."

"What about Cambridge? Charlie's got a solid base there."

"That's right," Assisi said. "Well, maybe we can impose on our hosts for the three of us, at least, while we get everything set. But we'll do nothing local to avoid bringing attention to the area."

"And I'm going to have to show my face," Daniel added. "I have to deal with pulling out of the firm and doing something with my apartment, but mostly I should try to cut a deal for my testimony."

"That's it, then," Assisi said. "We'll see if we can stay here for now, maybe set up a location nearby, and shift main operations to Boston or Phillie. Daniel will surface back in DC while Mia and I monitor Zeke's trial, put out *Monkey Wrench* and reestablish lines of communication."

They all nodded agreement.

"Once everything's in place," Assisi said, "I'd like to head out west, stop and see my wife, maybe catch the wildflower super-bloom after all their rain this year. Then I could join our cell in Marin County. I could also open a branch of the cover organization I ran in Dallas."

He hesitated to ask what Daniel intended to do if he didn't return to his law practice. Their new comrade's experience could be invaluable in defending supporters in their legal battles. But from the way his friend was acting, his plans could well depend upon Mia. It was not Stefan's place to rush them to decide their future.

Cal and Daisy were all in on providing a base of operations until things could be reorganized. Stefan suggested Mia and Daniel take a break while he went to gather the equipment they would need.

Mia spent the following week mostly by herself, within herself, and Daniel tried to give her space. At the same time he was anxious about her health. Bree had miscarried for no reason they ever understood; could Mia be okay after falling off a bridge into a cold river? Still, she seemed strong and untroubled by the life inside her or her broken arm.

She joined him a few times for walks in the woods. They didn't talk much, but she seemed revived by the fading chill of winter with the promise of spring. They both enjoyed returning to warm fires and evenings with Daisy and Cal and the dogs.

In April a big environmental protest was planned for London. Anthro had received an invitation to participate, but Stone Canyon put an end to that. The call to join "The Big One" came from a group called Extinction Rebellion. It was encouraging to see their English compatriots making some noise.

One day at sundown she led Daniel onto the front porch. "I have been in danger of losing my perspective," she said in a serious tone. "Now that I am responsible for a new life to come, I cannot let myself forget what we fight for." She waved her hand at the field leading into the trees, wind blowing the wild grass flat and the bright ball of the sun resting in a scarlet mantle of clouds.

The moment was transcendent. He longed to take her in his arms, but he caressed her only with his eyes. It was not fair to expect her to be ready to move on with her life, and he wouldn't risk disturbing this moment.

Everything now was wrapped up with Mia. Being with her would be such a departure from what he had known with Bree. He could share his innermost thoughts, rather than simply his bed and his household, in a way that might bring them even closer than by sharing a child. Bree had seen only what he chose to share with her, which excluded his work and ambitions, the things that most intrigued him. But he couldn't—wouldn't want to—hide anything from Mia.

He tried to keep from her how much she filled his thoughts. And one other thing he wouldn't share was how he helped Faye undress her when she was unconscious. That was something he could not unsee and, knowing it might be the only glimpse he'd ever get, it was an image he would not give up for anything. How had she looked so slender and strong when she was unconscious, in shock and pregnant?

At times when she wanted to talk, they discussed where climate policy would go with the Republicans in control of the House of Representatives. "Here we go again, right?" he said, realizing this was really the first time he had experienced a Republican Congress while he rooted for the other side.

"I am afraid you are correct. Most likely we will now have paralysis only. This administration will not be able to pass climate legislation. It is one more victory for a dystopian future."

Daniel wished he could think ahead, plan what the movement could still accomplish. Instead, he felt sorry for himself. These two weeks had been a dream, but it couldn't go on.

Stefan returned and they got to work. The elation of their methane victory faded quickly. The world was still riding the same roller coaster to destruction and there was much to do.

Daniel drove back to Washington and formalized his withdrawal from PJ&H, but decided to keep his apartment. It gave him a place to stay in town and an address the authorities could use to reach him, so they wouldn't go looking elsewhere. At the farm he penned a lengthy obituary of Kristof for *Monkey Wrench* titled "Environmental Champion Silenced" and introduced a regular column on methods for enforcing—or challenging—local laws.

The Big One came off in London. One hundred thousand people occupied streets and bridges. It attracted a broad cross-section, from families to pensioners, by assurances there would be no confrontation this time. Extinction Rebellion stated, however, that a failure of the government or industry to hear this call and act, would force it to conclude peaceful measures were ineffective.

Mia could almost script the debate about tactics among the leaders of this group, whom she knew. The similarity to the last debate on the roof of the Anthro building in Alexandria brought a lump to her throat. Kristof had seemed noble and resourceful in holding them together that day, giving them a way forward. Yet, now it felt like that was the moment he first decided to deceive her.

Mia forced herself to stop dwelling on the past. She was working to reestablish contact with volunteers when she said to Daniel, "Having this child grow inside me reminds me, our children have more to fear from climate change than we do, but they have no say in our failure to address the crisis. Is there no law that assures them protection against the burning of fossil fuels?"

Daniel looked up from his laptop. "I remember one case in Wyoming claiming that pollution and extreme weather threatened children's constitutional right to life."

"Is this a battle we could join?"

He smiled. Eco may be gone, but he sensed Anthro would not lack inspired leadership. He and Mia began to identify where they might assist in lawsuits brought by children, or encourage the filing of such lawsuits. He got the word out with his next *Monkey Wrench* column: "Children's Crusade Against Climate Change."

Over the next two months, Daniel visited Washington several times to assist the US Attorney's Office in building its case against Langston and Pearce. Kent Coggin lost his job at the Oil Institute and he and the Oil Institute were also named in the criminal case. Daniel hired a friend in town to represent him in this as well as to negotiate a trade of his testimony in Congress for immunity.

Daniel was tempted to take Jake out to dinner but by arrangement they had no contact. When things quieted down Daniel would do everything he could for his protégé—be his Uncle Jack, he thought with a smile. But unlike the young and rustic Daniel, this kid hardly needed help.

Daniel still was able to spend most of his time at the farm. The days there had fallen into a pattern of work for Anthro, chores around the property and big evening meals. Colleagues showed up for overnight visits and meetings, and the camaraderie helped everyone look toward the future. Daniel felt like he was finally doing useful work, and Mia seemed to have moved on from her grief to focus on the work and the life she carried inside her. Her pregnancy still didn't show physically but Daniel recognized the inner glow of a woman expecting a child.

The Poconos location was perfect for the work at hand and it was never meant to be permanent, but two months later they were jolted out of complacency. A supporter in a nearby town reported that two strangers had shown up asking questions and flashing the old photo of Verde.

"We must move," Assisi said to Mia and Daniel. "Those guys may not be FBI—maybe just investigators for the Oil Institute—but either way, they're too close."

They started closing down the operation, packing up the equipment and planning next steps. Assisi would take a train to Newark Airport and fly to San Francisco. Daniel figured he would just return to DC until he came up with a plan, but he wondered about Mia. She seemed unusually disturbed by this fire drill. It was understandable. She was likely a main target of any continuing effort to root out Anthro operatives, and she was more than three months pregnant and forced to abandon the nest. And where would she go?

While Daniel waited to hear about Mia's next step, he called to check in with Pete. He felt guilty that he had found little time or attention for him or Bree's parents, who seemed still shackled by grief over losing their daughter.

"Danny," Pete answered his call in an urgent voice, "I'm so glad you called. They found Annabelle's body!"

Chapter Thirty-Seven

The farm was alive with activity. Mia packed her few clothes and then sat on her bed listening to commotion all around the house, and taking stock of her situation.

"You need any help, hon?" Daisy said from the doorway.

"No," she said. "Just thinking." She had been thinking quite a lot but not of anything practical like where she should go from here. Instead, she was overcome with feeling the child grow inside her and the new kind of love that filled her. Here there was no room to distrust, no possibility of betrayal. There was only care and hope and responsibility. But thinking of responsibility brought her back to reality. She needed to leave the farm, but to go where?

Her ferocious need to protect her daughter gave her a window into Daniel's pain at losing Annabelle, now for a second time. How hard that must be for him.

She decided to offer him the Volvo to drive to the funeral in Texas. Assisi was leaving the car for her, since he was flying to

California. Daniel could fly too, she supposed, since he had no need to hide, but it still might make more sense for him to stay out of sight for now. Especially—she realized as the next logical step—if *she* went with him.

She needed somewhere to go. She had no home and no family besides Stefan and Zeke. She would need some place to stay when the baby arrived, but that was months away. By that time she could join Stefan out west.

Texas seemed like a good first step to get her moving. It would not be the first time impulse had altered her life path. Besides, Daniel had grown on her. He was considerate—and gallant. She laughed to herself that, excepting his leap into the river to save her life, he may have overcome his greatest challenge in putting up with her steely demeanor when they met, and for some considerable time thereafter.

Lately, in this Arcadian setting, he had brought sunshine into her days. Hopefully, the funeral would bring him some solace. He deserved it.

When Mia reached the porch, Daniel called out from the car. "Could you grab those water bottles I left in the kitchen?"

"Of course," she said and turned back toward the house, but then she paused. "What is that buzzing? It sounds like a swarm of bees."

He stopped to listen. "You're right; what is that?"

Then he saw it, a black drone coming in low over the trees. "Look out," he shouted, pointing. "Don't look up; it may be a camera."

She ran into the house. He ducked under the overhang of the barn roof.

The drone came lower, its hum filling the air. It hovered over the driveway fifteen feet from the ground, and seemed to turn toward Daniel. He didn't know if he should hide his face or find something to throw at it.

A shotgun blast solved his dilemma.

The drone crashed into the yard. Cal sauntered out of the barn with a smoking gun in his hands. "Can't have that noisy nuisance scaring the animals." he said, stomping the grounded machine to pieces. "Pretty sure it's illegal, as well."

Daniel and Mia were gone after quick goodbyes. But they had three days for the trip, and decided to take their time. They headed for the top of the Skyline Drive at Front Royal so they could trace its whole length and then continue south on the Blue Ridge Parkway.

The sight and smell of the unsullied mountains were invigorating. She and Kristof had long talked about taking this road trip, and she knew by this point he would have been waxing poetic about the virgin forest. She would always miss his way of painting the natural world with words. Possibly more than anything else, he was a poet. She still stung from his betrayal at the bridge. But he *was* the father of her child, and she hoped their daughter would inherit his gift for language and his determination to live— and die—for his beliefs.

"Let me know when you are tired," she said to Daniel, who seemed troubled, probably from thinking about Annabelle.

"How's the arm?" he said.

She stretched out her arm and flexed her fingers. "I am not ready to lift heavy weights, but driving is no problem."

"Okay, I'll pull in the next overlook and you can take over. This is what driving should be like."

Mia drove the rest of the winding road along the spine of the Blue Ridge Mountains. This allowed Daniel to gaze through sun-drenched trees at the sky. With his fear of water gone, nature again felt nurturing rather than threatening. He embraced the chance to experience the forest around them, which stood in his mind for the world they were fighting to preserve. Still, it was a sad journey to be taking through this wild, untouched place.

He thought about the afternoon he and Bree took Annabelle to Schumacher's Crossing. His daughter was amazed by the cascading series of dams and small waterfalls cut in rugged limestone and asked him later to build a waterfall in the river by their house. Bree had struggled not to laugh as she watched him respond to this earnest request.

There was something almost religious in his being granted one last chance to be a father to Annabelle. Was he entitled to come to peace with the memory of his little girl? There was so much more he could have done or should have done while she was alive, considering all she had taught him about what mattered, about joy and enthusiasm and wonder.

Maybe he didn't deserve closure about Annabelle's death, but he hoped seeing her one last time would stop the nightmares of her tiny body in the river. And he would try hard to hold onto the love, in spite of his regrets.

At the end of a long day they stopped at a roadside motel. Mia parked while Daniel went into the manager's office for a room.

She was surprised when he came out with two keys. Anthro operatives typically stayed together on the road, to preserve funds and for security. But it seemed he had the money and, whether this arrangement reflected gallantry or bashfulness, she was touched by the gesture.

Next day the road was not nearly as majestic. With less to appreciate outside the car, she turned inward. Then he prompted, "Are your parents still alive?"

She hesitated. She hardly ever thought about her parents and never spoke of them.

"I'm sorry," he said. "Didn't mean to pry."

She waved this off. "It is nothing. It is just that memories sometimes bring pain."

He gazed out the window, giving her time to think. But she

felt a long-buried need to share what she had kept bottled up for so long.

"My brother, Metica, was my hero. He brought me into environmental consciousness. But when I went to the forest to help him film illegal logging, we were attacked." She paused to collect herself.

"Metica died in hospital," she went on, "and of course there was no justice for him or the forest. My parents became frightened the police knew I was his sister and part of the film crew. And like many in Romania, they were conditioned to not question authority, no matter how bereft of legitimacy. They wished for me to forget climate change, to just live quiet life without trouble. But how could I do this while still honoring Metica's sacrifice? This would mean pretending there is no crisis facing the world."

"So what happened?"

"I moved out to live with family of a school friend. This would have been fine—except my parents would have no more to do with me, and this made me sad. And police started to watch the house where I stayed, as if *I* were criminal. It became hard for my friend's family, so I had to leave from there too."

She paused, sorting through images in her mind before she went on quietly. "After I reached England, they both passed away, my mother and then quickly my father. They never recovered from Metica's death and were doomed by the fragility of their minds and bodies. It left me in a lonesome place."

It felt freeing to unload the dark parts of her history to a sympathetic ear. But this also brought up the question of her future. Stefan would help, of course, as would many Anthro supporters, but she was going to need a place of safety for the child.

But that was months off. For the moment she would leave behind her sadness and resentment at Kristof's betrayal. She would hold onto only the good—which had been most of their time together—and the story she would someday share with their daughter.

Daniel responded with only a compassionate smile, which was precisely what she needed.

The third morning they woke up two hours from Foswell. When Mia joined Daniel for breakfast at the diner next door to their motel, he was almost speechless. She wore a black dress that, though conservatively cut, hugged a body showing no hint of pregnancy. The color of the dress matched the hair elegantly framing her face. Without the contacts her eyes had returned to luminous green, set off by a beaded necklace Daisy had made for her.

His dress shirt and dark sports jacket looked like they had been rolled up in a suitcase, which they had, but no one would be looking at him when he showed up with Mia. In confirmation of this, all eyes in the diner followed her to a seat across from him.

"So much for staying under the radar," he said, trying not to overdo his admiration.

She responded with an enigmatic smile, then focused on the menu and ordered a breakfast as if she were indeed eating for two.

They arrived at the church as the funeral began, sliding into a back pew. The service was somber in the way only a funeral for a child can be. There were remembrances from people who hadn't really known Annabelle, and lots of tears.

He didn't want to linger after the service, where neighbors would feel obliged to offer him sympathy. But Mia convinced him to go back to the house, where everyone was invited for lunch.

The first to greet them there was Pete. It was the first time Daniel had seen him in a suit, which drastically altered his bearing.

"Verde," Pete exclaimed, "I'm so happy you could come. And Dan, you know how sorry we all are. It means a lot to the folks that you made it."

"Well, Annabelle was my daughter...."

"Oh, for sure, and you know my mom only made the arrangements because we couldn't find you. I'm just glad you made it in time."

When they met Bree's parents, Julia looked curiously at Mia and said, "Come sit with me."

They huddled together at the corner of a sofa, as if they had discovered some instant bond. He left them and walked over to the flowers brought in from the church, glancing at the sympathy notes.

The card on a vase of yellow roses was from Uncle Jack. The congressman sent his apologies for missing the funeral because of duties in Washington. Daniel regretted not seeing his father's old friend, but it might have been awkward introducing him to Mia. With a congressional investigation underway into all aspects of the methane scandal, it was probably best that Jack have no contact with her—despite the irony that he would really like her.

He found Bree's father standing alone on the porch, looking old and broken. "She was my lifeblood," he said without turning. Daniel understood he meant Bree, not Annabelle.

"I'm so sorry, Ed. I promised I'd take care of her, but I let you down. I've lost a daughter, too. I know the feeling never goes away."

Ed turned to clasp Daniel's shoulder, wordlessly, and then returned to the house. Daniel followed him inside. Mia was speaking with a neighbor. She was so exotic looking and yet seemed totally at ease in this South Texas setting. When they met later at the cold cut table, he said, "You really fit in here. I expected to see you exchanging recipes."

"They are nice, honest people. They remind me of those from the countryside where I spent summers as a child."

It was encouraging she had become comfortable talking about her home country. "You especially hit it off with Julia," he said.

"She somehow guessed I was with child," she said with a curious look, "and she wanted to know the gender."

"Do you know?" he said, thinking he may have underestimated his mother-in-law.

"Yes, the doctor said I will have a daughter."

"Really? Well, that's great. Why didn't you tell me?"

She grimaced. "I know only since the last appointment, and I meant to tell you. But then you heard about Annabelle, and telling you of my own daughter would have been unfeeling."

That was remarkably considerate, though unnecessary. He marveled at how her grave sincerity masked her true generosity of spirit.

"Oh, one more thing," she said. "Julia insists we spend the night here...."

"We can't do that."

"I am afraid I already have accepted."

He looked at her impatiently.

"She was very gracious and also so very sad; I could not say we preferred to sleep in a motel. Besides this, we had no other plans. Did you think we would sleep in the car?"

He grinned, seeing he would have to go along. Maybe this would not be such a bad thing. It would give him some time with Bree's parents.

"You need not worry," she went on. "I told Julia we sleep in separate rooms—which pleased her, I think."

He was still processing this when Pete walked over to thank them again for making the trip. "So, out of curiosity," he added, "were you two involved with that big scandal in Congress?"

"Scandal?" Mia said with such an innocent expression she almost fooled Daniel.

"Oh, I get it," Pete said, nodding. "I guess I never was going to see things from the inside."

"Believe me," Daniel said, "it's for the best. But you should know law enforcement was tipped off by a guy calling himself 'Ranger,' and they were watching you. It would be smart to play it straight for a while—at least until they move on to other targets."

"Like you guys."

"Us?" Daniel said innocently. "Why would they trouble with us?"

They all laughed, and Pete said, "Okay, fair enough. In fact, as to moving on, I met a new lady. She's great. We're going to move in together...I hope. And, while I have to keep working at the factory, she is encouraging me to get back into photography."

"So where is this unfortunate woman?" Daniel said, genuinely pleased.

"She had to work...and, well, things are not completely settled, so I didn't want to push her to come to a funeral."

Daniel nodded. It was no surprise Pete had moved on to his next woman and his next passion. Daniel only hoped the romance would work out and the photography would keep him out of trouble and close to his parents.

"I picked up a lot from your photographs of Tanswego," Pete added, looking at Mia. "They convinced me I should focus on human subjects instead of just nature."

"We are all part of nature, yes?" she said with a knowing smile.

When the guests had gone and Pete left for Austin, Julia showed Mia her room. It was quite comfortable with a big bed, its own bathroom and windows looking into the yard. She wished every-one goodnight, soaked in the bathtub and spread out in sheets that smelled of sunshine.

Everyone must assume she was with Daniel—a legitimate conclusion from what they could see. This was not true, but it did no harm for them to think so. And the past few weeks, and especially this trip, had made her realize she was not ready to say goodbye to him. They traveled well together; could they move on from Foswell in some way that made sense?

After a big Texas breakfast and emotional goodbyes, Daniel

put the bags in the Volvo. Mia joined him wearing a flowered summer dress.

"This is a new style," he said approvingly.

She shrugged. "Julia would not let me leave without taking this dress." She looked down at herself. "It is quite bright, but it makes me cheerful. I may wear only floral prints from now on," she said, laughing with her eyes.

He had no words. The low back of the dress revealed the tattoo he hadn't seen since the night he pulled her from the river. The stark black design beneath the brightly colored straps made a stunning juxtaposition between Southern belle and revolutionary chic.

"I had forgotten that design," he said, lying.

"Forgotten?" she said, stretching to look over her shoulder. "You have seen my ink before?"

"Um...yeah."

She peered at him suspiciously. He felt stupid at putting his foot in his mouth. She could not have remembered when he helped Faye undress her in West Virginia.

"How have you seen this before?" she pried.

"Um...the FBI showed me the design; it was a watermark on photos from Tanswego; they were sure it would lead them to the photographer." He laughed to himself that Joe Coulder's "army of analysts" were still looking for the source of that logo and would never get to see how exquisite it was in the original.

"Yes, but this, I think, is not only time."

Her eyes looked right through him, while a hint of a smile crossed her lips.

"Uh..." he stuttered. "It was just in passing, when I helped Faye put you to bed."

Her penetrating look asked what else he saw that night, but with an amused smile, she turned to another subject. "So now you have said farewell to your Annabelle."

"Yes, I am...how would you put it?"

"In balance," she said. "Your yin and yang."

"My humors are neither wet nor dry, hot nor cold."

"But of course the world still races toward disaster." She frowned and raised her eyebrows.

"Well, there is that."

They paused on that fateful thought. The planet was going to hell, and still nobody seemed to care. They would just have to keep up the struggle, raise the alarm.

As he started the car, she turned to him. "Do we begin to head back now?"

"Back to what? Back to where?"

"You have the apartment in Washington."

"As long as I pay the rent, it can stand empty until I have to return to testify."

They sat immobile for a minute. Slowly he started to smile, wondering what might be possible. Then he turned to see the same inscrutable smile on *her* face. She bit her lower lip. "So, then," she said, "a new direction?"

He paused a beat. "Go west to meet Stefan in SF? We've got time for the trip, and I hear there's lots of big sky along the way."

Two hours along the road they stopped for supplies. While Daniel rearranged the bags in the back of the Volvo, Mia pulled a vinyl-bound *Rand McNally Road Atlas* from the pocket behind the driver's seat. "Will we have use for this while we have GPS?" she said.

"I had a notion about following the blue highways."

"I do not know this 'blue highways.' What is this?"

"A guy named Heat-Moon wrote a memoir about a road trip on out-of-the-way roads connecting rural America, roads shown in blue in *this* atlas."

"This sounds like immersive way to travel across the country. But will this not make travel quite slow?"

"What's the hurry? We've got no timetable other than for

your daughter's arrival. This is clearly a case of the journey being more important than the destination."

"So we enter the new exploratory phase?" she said with a grin.

When he took an exit off the interstate west of Sonora, everything changed. She started navigating from the atlas, pointing out amusing town names. The road was mostly two lanes, with wide-open ranges on both sides. There was little traffic—mostly pickup trucks whose drivers wore cowboy hats and waved as they passed.

Her serene smile made him feel like he should pinch himself to make sure this wasn't a dream. "This is much better," he said. "You can actually smell the land."

The afternoon became an adventure of looking for routes long closed. Given how big Texas was, these small roads likely went on forever.

On one stretch of desert highway, a billboard caught their attention. She looked over at him after they passed. "Did I imagine this," she said, "or did this garish sign advertise development of Madrid Industrial Properties?"

The way she exaggerated her accent perfectly matched her devious look. He slowed down. "You think maybe it should go by way of Lisbon?"

She nodded meaningfully.

Checking ahead and in his mirrors, he saw no other cars. He pulled the Volvo onto the shoulder, made a U-turn and flipped on four-wheel drive. He turned off the blacktop over scrubby underbrush to stop with his door up against the metal billboard supports.

They both jumped out the passenger side. Daniel climbed on top of the Volvo while Mia rummaged in back. She emerged with a spray paint can and tossed it up to him.

He did his work quickly and jumped back down. They both looked up in admiration.

"Next time will be my turn to create revolutionary artwork," she said with a laugh.

"A lady in your condition? There'd be a scandal."

A deep barking cry grabbed their attention. He pointed off to the north, where a big bird soared close to the ground.

"Magnificent," she said. "The orange beak and the black with white feathers. What kind of bird is it, do you know?"

"A hawk or even an eagle, I guess. But it's got to be lost; I've never seen a bird like that before."

They watched together, their hands unconsciously intertwining, as the bird rose on air currents while hardly moving its wings. It finally disappeared over a hillock.

The spell broken, he said, "We'd better get moving before someone comes by."

"Protocol requires this," she replied with a smile.

Mia took the wheel and pulled the car back onto the road. They left the smiling engineer on the billboard holding Daniel's rendition of Mia's tattoo flowers and speaking into a large speech bubble: "ECO LIVES!"

THE END

Acknowledgments

I relied on a number of published works in attempting to understand and address climate change. Starting with *Gaia: A New Look at Life on Earth*, which James E. Lovelock published in 1979 espousing the theory that the earth functions as a single, living organism, whose self-regulation is only threatened by the worst humankind might do. Judith Blau's *Crimes Against Humanity: Climate Change and Trump's Legacy of Planetary Destruction* provides extensive detail about the downward spiral of the planet and the kind of human-induced harm Lovelock could not imagine in the measures taken by the George W. Bush and Trump administrations. *The Ministry for the Future*, by Kim Stanley Robinson, melds science fiction with the reality of the climate crisis. In *Unsettled*, Steven E. Koonin lays out a statistics-heavy attack on how climate science is communicated to the public and the view that human activity has no clear effect on inevitable climate change, so we should focus instead on geoengineering and adaptation. Climate change reporting in *The New York Times* helped keep my references current, along with statements from the United Nations following COP27 in Sharm el-Sheikh, *State of the Global Climate in 2021: Extreme Events and Major Impacts* from the World Meteorological Organization, the United Nations Intergovernmental Panel (IPCC) Sixth Assessment Report (AR6) on Climate Change, released in February and April 2022, and the article "Changing Intensity of Hydroclimatic Extreme Events Revealed by GRACE and GRACE-FO," by Matthew Rodell and Bailing Li in the journal *Nature Water*. Also helpful in articulating industry arguments against restrictions on greenhouse gas production were a number of websites soliciting donations to fight government regulation of oil and gas production.

I have—with poetic license—incorporated anecdotes from the annals of environmental activism. *The Monkey Wrench Gang*, by Edward Abbey, describes actions taken by fictional eco-activists, which was especially helpful in its description of explosives. In *The Ecocentrists: A History of Radical Environmentalism*, Keith Makado Wodehouse critiques deep ecology and argues that radical environmentalists are out of step with widely held beliefs concerning economic growth and individual freedom, and they gloss over the impact of social differences, cultural complexity and economic inequality in the conflict between humanity and nature. Publishing *Climate Wars* in 2010, Gwynne Dyer laid out dire scenarios for the havoc likely to accompany climate change in the first half of the 21ˢᵗ century, but sadly his hypotheticals overestimated human efforts to slow global warming and underestimated the pace of warming. Additional resources were the February 12, 2002 testimony of James F. Jarboe, Domestic Terrorism Section Chief, FBI Counterterrorism Division, before the House Resources Committee, Subcommittee on Forests and Forest Health, published October 31, 2021; Matthew Wolfe's May 26, 2022 article "The Rise and Fall of America's Environmentalist Underground," in *The New York Times*; Vanessa Grigoriadis's August 10, 2006 article "The Rise & Fall of the Eco-Radical Underground," in *Rolling Stone*; Aileen Brown's March 23, 2019 article "The Green Scare: How a Movement that Never Killed Anyone Became the FBI's No. 1 Domestic Terrorism Threat," on The Intercept.com; and reporting on the website TheConversation.com. Enormously helpful in my description of the Guadalupe River and the (fictional) town of Tanswego was Eric W. Pohl's *Texas Hill Country: A Scenic Journey*. Additional help in depicting the terror of a flash flood came from *The Lynmouth Flood Disaster*, by Eric R. Delderfield, which collects first-hand accounts of the horrific 1952 flood on the River Lyn in the Exmoor in Devon, England.

I tried to paint a picture of the Texas Hill Country along the Guadalupe River but adjusted the topography to fit my story. The Two Valleys and the towns of Tanswego and Foswell are made up, as is the particular confluence of weather, wildfires and development underpinning the plot. Similarly, I created Stone Canyon and had to build my own bridge across the Cheat River in West Virginia. However, I'd like to think I, like Jake Gambol, know the streets of Manhattan well enough to make his evasive path around that island credible.

On the human side, I could not have published *Two Degrees* without the help of my editing team, starting with my wife, Megan, who helped me formulate the outline of the story. Two old friends, Drew Dawson and Richard Maki, read the early manuscript and offered encouragement and incisive criticism. Drew, who went from being the model for a major character in my first novel to my first reader of every book since, offered invaluable insight into characters and their inner voices. My college roommate Rich took me to task on smoothing out glitches in the plot. Mary Behan helped polish a later draft, and my daughter, Katie, whose voluminous comments showed me she is not only a great editor but she should be writing her own books. Finally, the professional in the room, Christine Keleny, of CKBooks Publishing, once again guided my editing efforts and handled publication. Assisting in the final stage were my proofreader, Alyce Kaye, and cover designer Nanne, through 99Designs, and my long-time collaborator Lorenzo Contessa created the elegant image of Mia's tattoo. I sincerely thank them all.

I dedicate this book to the people who struggle to sound the alarm about the environmental disaster fast upon us. Part of the impetus to spend countless hours writing and honing a story into a novel is the belief it will live forever. I only hope a world survives to make this possible.

New York, NY

October 16, 2023

About the Author

William Michael Ried was born on Long Island, graduated from the University of Michigan and Georgetown University Law Center and practices law in New York City. His first novel *Five Ferries* was a finalist in the 2019 American Fiction Awards for Best New Fiction. In 2021 his second novel *Backstory* won the New York City Big Book Award for Mystery and a Silver Medal from the Wishing Shelf Book Awards for Adult Fiction, was a semifinalist for the Kindle Book Award for Literary Fiction and was named a 2022 Eric Hoffer Award Category Finalist. His third novel *Pandion* was a 2022 Distinguished Favorite Mystery of the NYC Big Book Awards, a Red Ribbon winner of the 2022 Wishing Shelf Awards, was named to the 2023 Eric Hoffer Award Grand Prize Short List, and was awarded Honorable Mention in the category of Mystery/Crime for the 2023 Eric Hoffer Awards. Bill lives with his wife in Manhattan.

~

If you enjoyed this book, please post a review wherever you bought the book. For book club suggestions, the cover story, reviews and more information, see wmrauthor.com.

www.ingramcontent.com/pod-product-compliance
Lightning Source LLC
Chambersburg PA
CBHW060749190726
48285CB00002B/360